The
Genesis Factor:
Deception

~Book One~

A Christian Thriller by

DONNA R. WESTOVER

North Star Publishing

Donna R. Westover

Cover Art by Chris from KUDI-Design
http://www.kudi-design.com

Library of Congress Control Number: 2019901227

Westover, Donna R., 1958 –
The Genesis Factor: Deception / by Donna R. Westover
1.   Fiction. I. Title.

ISBN – 10: 0-578-44773-8
ISBN – 13: 978-0-578-44773-5

Printed in the United States of America

To my husband, Don.
The Love of my Life.

CONTENTS

PROLOGUE..6

CHAPTER ONE..11

CHAPTER TWO..19

CHAPTER THREE 24

CHAPTER FOUR...36

CHAPTER FIVE 43

CHAPTER SIX 57

CHAPTER SEVEN...69

CHAPTER EIGHT...77

CHAPTER NINE 94

CHAPTER TEN..104

CHAPTER ELEVEN 109

CHAPTER TWELVE..117

CHAPTER THIRTEEN 128

CHAPTER FOURTEEN 139

CHAPTER FIFTEEN..153

CHAPTER SIXTEEN 163

CHAPTER SEVENTEEN 189

CHAPTER EIGHTEEN..198

CHAPTER NINETEEN 206

CHAPTER TWENTY 211

CHAPTER TWENTY-ONE 215

CHAPTER TWENTY-TWO..220

CHAPTER TWENTY-THREE 233

CHAPTER TWENTY-FOUR 238

CHAPTER TWENTY-FIVE 244

CHAPTER TWENTY-SIX...256

CHAPTER TWENTY-SEVEN 275

CHAPTER TWENTY-EIGHT 282

CHAPTER TWENTY-NINE 284

CHAPTER THIRTY 287

CHAPTER THIRTY-ONE...297

CHAPTER THIRTY-TWO...305

CHAPTER THIRTY-THREE 319

CHAPTER THIRTY-FOUR 325

CHAPTER THIRTY-FIVE 336

CHAPTER THIRTY-SIX 343

CHAPTER THIRTY-SEVEN 348

CHAPTER THIRTY-EIGHT 351

CHAPTER THIRTY-NINE..360

CHAPTER FORTY 367

CHAPTER FORTY-ONE..375

CHAPTER FORTY-TWO..383

CHAPTER FORTY-THREE 388

CHAPTER FORTY-FOUR..394

CHAPTER FORTY-FIVE..402

EPILOGUE...408

COMING SOON:...412

OTHER BOOKS 413

ACKNOWLEDGMENTS 414

ABOUT THE AUTHOR..415

"More and more we are finding that mythology in general...very often has some historic base. And the interesting thing is that one myth which occurs over and over again in many parts of the world is that somewhere a long time ago, supernatural beings had sexual intercourse with natural women and produced a special breed of people."

~ Francis A. Schaeffer

PROLOGUE

April 12, 1884

I found them. After years of searching, I finally found them; thirty-three early, yet well preserved skeletons buried in an ancient burial mound. Uncovered, they look as if they had just been laid to rest a few short years ago; however, upon immediate observation, one can see these are not common human skeletons, but magnificent remains of giants. The smallest is 8' 4" while the tallest is close to 18 feet long. Upon careful examination I believe the former bones to be that of a child.

The skulls are elongated and much larger than the average human male; 25 percent larger and 60 percent heavier. They also have only one parietal plate, rather than two, but do not appear to be deformed. Each skull contains not one, but two rows of teeth. Long, flat foreheads end with a thick brow bone that hangs over the eye sockets. On each hand are six fingers, as well as six toes on each foot.

Thirty of these skeletal remains will be sent to the Smithsonian as ordered, but for the sake of preservation, and to conduct my own analysis, I will send three to my private facility. Should the controlling powers once again decide to hide these truths from the public, after careful research, I will make them known, regardless of the personal cost.

I make no mistake about who I am opposing by taking on such drastic measures, nor do I make an apology for the belief on which I make this decision. I believe this tribe to be related to the Biblical Nephilim. I trust my research will prove it.

Dr. Thomas Delano Arthur

Plum Creek, Virginia

1884

Detective TJ Arthur gingerly laid the weathered journal down on the desk and stared blindly at the bookshelf in front of him. "Three giant skeletons, gone. What could'a happened to them?"

Pulling the worn journal closer, he adjusted his glasses and tipped the green shade of his bankers' lamp so its light fell full onto the yellowed pages. He skimmed the words again, but nothing caught his attention. The mystery made him feel itchy. "I know it's in here. I know they're real and he left a clue to their whereabouts, I just gotta find it."

Pushing the journal aside, he took up several newspaper articles about the Smithsonian dig that his great-great grandfather had led in 1884 along with some written statements given by workers from the dig site. Still, after reading them several times, he found nothing; no clues to where his great-great grandfather had sent the remains of the three giant humanoids.

Those that had been sent to the Smithsonian were gone; deemed hoaxes or never to have existed at all, but the old man's journal confirmed that the skeletons were real and he'd hidden three of them so they wouldn't be destroyed; but where were they? Where was this 'private facility' he mentioned?

TJ re-read the articles. This time, slower, meticulously; he studied each line for a clue.

1848, Abraham Lincoln "The eyes of that species of extinct Giant, whose bones fill the Mounds of America, have gazed on Niagara, as ours do now."

1871, Toronto Daily Telegraph: Reverend Nathaniel Wardell, Messers Orin Wardell, and Daniel Fredenberg digging on Fredenberg's farm, found five or six feet below the surface, a pile of two hundred skeletons of nearly perfect stature. Some measured nine feet, very few less than seven feet.

1884, The Atlanta Banner, Smithsonian scientists found giant skeletons in an Indian burial mound. All the relics were carefully packed and sent to the Smithsonian Institution and are deemed to be the most interesting collection ever found in America.

The last entry read:

1910, The Boise Newport Miner, Prehistoric Bones Found. Unmoved, untouched, and unseen for hundreds of years, bones found hidden in the recesses of a deep cave 25 miles north of Shoshone, Lincoln County in southern Idaho. The giant was ten feet tall and of prehistoric origin. A rusty worn flintlock barrel of what appears to be an ancient gun weighing between twenty-five and thirty pounds was found lying beside the skeleton.

Frustrated, he pushed the papers aside and pulled the computer keyboard to him. Pounding "Finding Nephilim in America" into the search engine, several more articles popped up on the monitor:

1924, The New York Times: An eight-foot-tall skeleton, believed to be that of a woman, was discovered in Salmon River County by two members of the State Highway Department, who brought their find to the city. Physicians sent the bones to the Smithsonian for further study.

2014, AP Magazine: Instead of engaging the public, the Smithsonian Institution is alienating it by ignoring an aspect of their own findings that the public sees as intriguing. American archeology utilizes skeptics as sort of police force to silence critics and others.

2015, The Light Bearers and their Coordinators seek the fabled bones of the Smithsonian.

The last notation startled him. To the untrained eye it revealed nothing, but to him, it held a myriad of red flags blowing hard in an apocalyptic wind. It told him the bones of giants *had* resurfaced and the Light Bearers had released their dogs to find them. TJ didn't like it.

Time was running out. If a secret society made up of major world influences knew the bones were real and truly were remnants of an ancient Nephilim tribe as his great-great grandfather believed, the Light Bearers and their Coordinators would use whatever means necessary to find them then use them to strengthen their control over world affairs.

The detective sighed. "I can't even fathom what would happen if those bones fell into the wrong hands." As he pecked out the words *Light Bearers* on his keyboard, he mumbled, "The very DNA they contained could be used to destroy any semblance of the world as we know it."

Seconds later an article reflected off TJ's glasses. Its headline read, *Modern Nephilim*. To the common reader the article was about mystical creatures, giant bones, and farfetched ideas about crossbreeding, but to TJ it revealed an evil agenda. Staring at the monitor, he fought the fear that was worming its way up from his chest into his throat. He couldn't believe what he'd found, but there it was. The Coordinators were on the move. He wasn't sure what it would take to stop the world's most powerful people, but he was determined to find out.

CHAPTER ONE

The grey, pin-striped jacket had hung neatly on the teak valet all day; the last rays of the sun now teetering precariously on its left shoulder. He closed the last of thirteen files and studied it. To most, the jacket was just a piece of very expensive clothing, but to him it was a reminder. A reminder not only of how far he'd come, but from where he'd come.

He loosened his tie, picked up the crystal Matterhorn glass, and crossing his feet on top of his mahogany desk, inhaled deeply. It was time to celebrate the end of another successful day, and he knew of no better way to start than by raising a glass of sixty-four-year-old MacAllan scotch to the fading sunlight. Closing his eyes, he sipped the golden liquid. Slowly, and ever so slightly, the corners of his mouth turned upward.

He took a few more sips; relishing the deliciousness that caressed his tongue. Several long moments passed before the creaking of his leather chair broke the silence of the tranquil afternoon as he reached for a cigar that was resting on the edge of a glass ashtray. Its thin smoke swirled lazily upward until it disappeared in the same last rays of sun that had slipped off the shoulder of his jacket and were now sliding down the sleeve. Leaning back, he watched the vanishing sunlight pirouette across the tops of the multicolored trees as the flavors of the cigar and the scotch danced in his mouth.

His name was Henreich von Guten, born the fifth and last child of Ludwig and Marta von Guten in Munich, Germany forty-five years earlier. His father had been a factory worker; his mother a second-grade teacher and although they did the best they could for their children, he hated them for being poor. He hated his older brothers for getting everything first; he hated the hand-me down clothes, the miserable meals, and the meager celebrations without presents.

On his tenth birthday, void of cake or gifts, he determined to save every pfennig he found or scraped up. A few years later, at age seventeen, he stood on the chipped concrete stoop of the two-bedroom house that had been his only home; five 10-mark German banknotes crumpled deep in the pocket of his torn jeans.

A chilly mist pressed against rows of dilapidated houses and drifted across the dirty stream that wound through overgrown banks down to the factory where his father worked. Red light cracked the dark horizon; the clouds of black smoke from the factory growing darker than the morning sky. From somewhere, a baby's cry pierced the dawn. He stepped off the stoop and looked toward the horizon. It was then he swore he'd never be poor again. He'd do whatever he had to, but he'd not suffer as he did there. He was leaving this behind. He'd succeed on his own.

And for a few years, he did. As an apprentice at a small bank, he learned the business of numbers and the skill of embezzlement. That skill however, led him to a life sentence of hard labor in Stadelheim Prison; guilty of transferring $61 million dollars from the trusts of heirs whose accounts he managed to several accounts of his own.

At twenty-eight years old, the thunder of a judge's gavel gave him a ten by ten concrete cell to call home and stale bread for his meals. The lice embedded in his hair follicles were his only companions, and the repulsive odor of a stinking, urine stained jumpsuit his only cologne. These things were constant reminders that he once had dreams of being someone...something, anything, but poor.

Tapping the ashes of his cigar into the ashtray, von Guten thought it odd how he couldn't remember the year, but he could remember the month when all of that changed. He'd never forget the month. It was January, a freezing night in January.

He lay curled up in a tight ball, shivering on the tattered mattress of his cot; his clenched fists shaking between his knees; his cheek pressed against his shoulder. All hope of ever leaving the prison had finally faded, pulled down with the sun when it disappeared behind the glaze of ice that covered the small window above his head. His eyes raked the bare room, searching for something he could use to end his life. But even the hope of dying was stolen from him when the familiar 'clunk' reverberated off the prison walls and the cells went black.

Translucent, skeletal-like breaths seeped from between his chattering teeth. He tried to pull his knees tighter to his chest. In dark desperation, he whispered, "I'll trade my soul for just one more chance." It took an hour or so for sleep to show some mercy and carry him away, but only for a while.

Later, around midnight, a guard woke him and led him to the showers where he was given clean clothes and a bar of soap. Fifteen minutes later, his hair soaked, his feet still bare, his wrists shackled in irons, he was led down the dimly lit corridor to the warden's office.

The warden was a hard man, known to the prisoners as The Hammer. His only mission was to keep order within the walls of Stadelheim, even if it meant killing. But killing wasn't on the warden's agenda that dark morning. Instead, he looked calm, almost mesmerized by the handsome, well dressed stranger standing to his left.

The warden introduced the thin, pale inmate to the man who went only by the name of Samael. For several long minutes, von Guten stared petrified listening to the mumblings between the warden and the man Samael. He had no idea what they were saying, but he had no doubt they were negotiating his fate.

Was Samael a banker who was demanding a more permanent revenge on his losses? Or maybe the father, or worse, the husband of a woman that he'd seduced years before? The prisoner's knees shook more out of fear than cold. Around one in the morning, the warden looked at him and explained he was no longer the responsibility of Stadelheim, but was now the ward of the handsome stranger.

Samael quickly revealed to the emaciated von Guten that he had simply come to be the answer to the tortured man's prayers. He would serve Samael for the remainder of his life, and in return, von Guten would be given all his heart desired. In the backseat of a luxurious limousine, a contract was signed between the two men, and immediately von Guten's incarceration became a bad memory.

The small prison cell was swapped for a multi-million-dollar chalet in the magnificent Swiss Alps. Fifty-thousand-dollar Zegna suits replaced the stinking jump suit; ankle and wrist chains were exchanged for diamond watches; unscrupulous prison guards for voluptuous women; and a disgraced reputation for that of Kommandeur. It took a while for Henreich to fully appreciate who Samael was, but it didn't matter. The man was von Guten's savior and he would remain devoted to him until the day he died.

Now, nineteen years later, the Kommandeur rested his head against the back of his leather chair. The cigar wobbled between loose fingers. His breathing, slow and deep, kept time with the muffled ticking of the mantle clock. A soft snore escaped his mouth.

Watery sunlight; no longer teasing the Zegna jacket, lay sprawled on the floor, slowly crawling toward the western corner of a wall made completely of glass that framed the gorgeous Alps just beyond. The Kommandeur sat drowning in peaceful oblivion until the shrill blast of his desk intercom yanked him back to consciousness.

Reluctantly, he sat the Cuban on the ashtray and pulled his feet off the desk. Leaning forward, he flipped the small switch on the intercom.

His heavy German accent filled the room. "Yes, Antonia. What is it?"

"I have Captain Mora signaling to come on ze screen, Kommandeur. Are you ready or should I ask for a moment?"

He lowered his head and sighed. He hated Mora, but unfortunately, Mora was Samael's Captain of the Guard and he had no choice but to play nice. "Ach, no, I'm ready, my dear. Please bring him through."

"Yes, sir."

Von Guten grabbed the jacket from the valet and whipped it around his shoulders, slipping his arms into the sleeves just as wooden panels on the opposite wall began to slide apart. Casually leaning against the edge of his desk; he ran his fingers through his hair then straightened his tie. Arms coolly folded across his chest; one ankle crossed over the other, his body language said confident and relaxed, but his brain was sharp and his eyes focused.

The white screen turned grey. Seconds later, von Guten stared into a pair of large, black eyes; eyes deeply set under a thick fleshy brow that protruded above two dark nasal cavities from which slimy green threads of mucus dripped into a jutted jaw. The Kommandeur found Samael's monster repulsive, but looking directly into Mora's eyes, he faked a warm smile.

Mora chuckled. "I long for the day when I..."

Von Guten tapped his ear piece with a well-manicured finger. "I'm sorry, Mora, I didn't understand you."

Mora's thick grey lids covered his eyes and he sighed. "I said Samael has given the order for you to meet with your Coordinators immediately. He wants the way prepared for his heir."

The middle-aged man smiled broadly, showing perfect

white teeth. "We are to prepare for the Dark Heir?"

Mora smirked and mumbled under his breath, "Are you going deaf too you germ ridden piece of filth?"

Von Guten held his smile. "Say again, Mora."

"Yes, Kommandeur von Guten," growled the demon. "You are to prepare for his heir."

Unable to contain himself, the Kommandeur slapped the desk. "Vunderbar!" he exclaimed. "Please tell my lord that I will call a meeting to be held here in the Chalet within the month. We will deliberate until we have a plan that will please him."

Mora's eyes bore into the human face. "You fail, you die."

Von Guten leaned toward the screen. "We will not fail," he said soberly. "I am faithful to him too, Mora. He chose me because I am the brightest and most loyal of humans. He will be pleased."

The demon snorted. A string of mucus flew from his nose and slapped his monitor. Von Guten's stomach turned.

"Make sure he is or I'll send you to Uffern myself," snarled the demon.

"Pft," scoffed the Kommandeur. "Spending eternity in Uffern does not worry me, my friend." "Samael has promised me a special place there."

"I bet he has."

The two eyed each other. "If I didn't know better, I would think you were insinuating that Samael has lied to me, Mora."

"Think whatever you like human."

Their eyes stayed locked for several long seconds. Von Guten finally nodded. "Very well, I will call you at the end of September next year. I will have the final plan at that time. All preparations will have been made. All contacts, all players, everything will be in place. All Samael must do is approve the agenda."

"I'll let him know."

Von Guten smiled.

Mora hit the button on his control panel and the screen turned white.

The Kommandeur's smile faded. He stood stone faced, staring unbelievingly at the closing panels. It took a few moments for Mora's message to sink in, but there it was...he, Henreich von Guten had been directed to prepare for the Dark Heir. He turned quickly; his thoughts spinning wildly.

Rubbing his hands, he began to pace. "It is a good day. This event has been anticipated for such a very long time, and now it is here...and *I* have been chosen."

Breathing fast and labored, he grabbed the glass of whiskey and threw the remaining liquid against the back of his throat. Exhilarated, he slammed the glass down and dialed Antonia.

"You're needed here," he demanded. "We've a mission." Ending the call, he stood for a moment letting his conversation with Mora sink deeper.

The jacket landed across the arm of the chair. Excited fingers fumbled with the knot on his tie as he strolled up to the liquor cabinet. Watching his image in the large gilded mirror that hung behind it, he couldn't help but smile. "So, Samael has seen something in you, so unique, so rare, that he has chosen *you* to plan the arrival of the Dark Heir. And why not? You are so much smarter than those who served before you. With this mission a success, you are sure to become the High Priest of the Light Bearers."

He grabbed the crystal decanter of Blantons, popped off the stopper, and poured two glasses. Before he and Antonia got down to the business of detailing the upcoming meeting with the Coordinators, they would celebrate.

His mind raced while he waited for her to come into his office. Maybe they would pretend it was the two of them preparing the way for the Dark Heir. He closed his eyes and imagined his sperm holding the DNA of the Dark One and how she would be the Heir's mother.

Where was she? She was so beautiful. Long blonde hair, light blue eyes, and... He wiped a bead of sweat from his brow.

"What is taking her so long?"

Finally, the door opened. His eyes ran across her body and his excitement grew; pushing him to take her. He watched her walk toward him. A slight turn at the corner of her pink lips, the soft sway of her hips; her eyes bright and laughing. He could see she was ready too. Leading her to the sofa, he ripped the tie from around his neck. The drinks could wait.

CHAPTER TWO

Von Guten stood tall in front of the large screen in his office and stared into Samael's vivid green eyes.

"Well," Samael said impatiently. "Have you managed to pull yourself off that couch and meet with the Coordinators?"

The question took von Guten by surprise. He glanced nervously around his office. "How do you...? Is my office...?"

The handsome man folded his muscled arms across his chest. "Please Heinrich. Don't insult me. Haven't you realized yet that I have ways of seeing everything you do? I have ways of hearing everything you say? I don't need to bug your office with toys of technology."

The Kommandeur hung his head. "Forgive me."

"Up, Heinrich," demanded Samael. "I want to hear about the magnificent plan you and the Coordinators have come up with. Tell me how you are going to present the Dark Heir."

"But, my Lord, you must already know."

Samael's eyes flared red; crimson clouds exploded across his cheeks. "I do," he said evenly, "but I want *you* to tell me...now!"

The Kommandeur suddenly felt very small. Samael was not a forgiving man. He rewarded his faithful, but he was cruel too, especially when he was angry. Swallowing hard, the thought *please him or die right here in this leather chair* ran through his fevered mind. Clearing his throat, he stood up straight.

"We have been meeting at The Chalet over the last several months," he said with weak confidence. "All thirteen Coordinators have been present. It took us most of the past year to reach an agreement, but after much debate, this is what we have to present to you."

Mora, standing behind Samael, snickered.

Von Guten lowered his eyes. The last thing he needed right now was to be distracted by Mora and lose sight of who was standing before him.

"Yes, yes, go on," Samael said impatiently.

Von Guten's eyes flitted to Mora then to Samael. "There is a town in the United States, in Virginia, a town called Plum Creek. Like so many towns across that country, it is a small community. We chose it because it has a government laboratory that, despite its good work, has been forgotten. We believe because of this, it would be appropriate for your agenda."

Samael paced, his chin resting on the knuckles of his clasped hands. The wooden heels of his wingtip shoes tapped out the minutes against the stone floor of his library. Finally, he stopped and glanced at the Kommandeur. "Plum Creek? Is the house still there?"

"Yes. It has been preserved by the Coordinators over the years. One lives there now."

"Okay," Samael said, nodding approvingly. "The place is acceptable. Now tell me about the chosen one."

Von Guten pulled a silk handkerchief from his breast pocket and dabbed his brow. The corners of his mouth edged upward. *Almost over*, he thought. Smiling nervously, he continued with a little more confidence.

"There is a woman who lives in this small town. She is

searching for inner peace, and by doing so, is innocently becoming knowledgeable of your ways. She has been exposed to sadness, but not evil and we believe she can be easily persuaded to fall in love. She will make herself available to the right man, and once he impregnates her, she will carry the Heir to term."

"What makes you so sure she'll not abort the child? If she isn't evil, but merely an unsuspecting human, what would motivate her to assist me?"

The Kommandeur's brow furrowed. "Because one, she won't be privy to whom it is she will be giving birth to, and two, she doesn't believe in abortion. She will love the baby's father and be thrilled with the pregnancy."

Mora snickered again.

"Furthermore," von Guten said a little louder, ignoring his nemesis, "I will make sure she learns of our Genealogy Society. She will receive an invitation to attend the conference here in the spring. Naive to the truth behind the purpose of the conference, she will come expecting to participate in a special experiment, but instead, it will be then that I introduce myself to her and explain your plan and her role in it. She will not fully understand what we used her for until it is too late. By then, she will be at your disposal."

"And just what is the purpose of this conference?" Samael asked complacently.

"I beg your pardon?" replied the Kommandeur.

"I said, what do you plan to do at this genealogy conference?"

"Why, it is to show your Coordinator's, and our guests, their lineage. To further appreciate the advancement of your agenda, each must see that they are decedents of the Nephilim."

"And how will you make them 'see'?"

"I'm, I'm sorry my Lord. I thought you knew..."

Samael waved him off. "I do, Henreich. I like the plan. Go with it!"

Von Guten's chin fell to his chest. "Thank you, my Lord. It is such an honor to serve you."

Samael was already heading to the door. Before stepping over the threshold, he looked over his shoulder. "It is," he barked. "And don't either of you forget it."

When his footsteps faded, von Guten lifted his head. Mora was watching him. "For a minute, I thought I was going to have the pleasure of seeing you die," he said savagely.

"Ah, but you didn't, did you?" answered von Guten; a self-righteous smile spreading across his face.

Mora's hand moved toward the unseen control panel.

"Before you end this session by pushing that button, I believe I have something you will like to hear Mora," the Kommandeur said smugly.

"You've got five seconds, von Guten."

The Kommandeur's smile broadened. "My time is my own."

"Four seconds."

Von Guten shrugged his shoulders. "All right, my friend. If you do not wish to hear." He moved his hand toward his own control panel.

"Tell me," growled Mora.

Von Guten chuckled. Mora swore under his breath.

"It has come to my attention, by means of several of your, shall we say, colleagues, that besides the chosen one, this plan also involves a woman who is a direct descendent of someone in your distant past, back when Samael first came up with the diabolical plan to let his warriors come to Earth and degrade El's creation. I believe you wanted to kill a certain woman of Sargon, but a warrior of a different nature intervened and saved her from you."

Mora slowly lifted his finger away from the button. "You don't say."

"So, although you couldn't destroy *her* eons ago, perhaps you can have the revenge you so desperately crave *now*."

Mora stared into von Guten's face. "You better be sure of this old man. If you're wrong, I'll rip your..."

"Of course, I am sure," the Kommandeur said incredulously. "We humans may not be supernatural such as you are, but we can confirm our research. We have found the woman's descendant Mora, and although so many years have gone by, you can now destroy the ancient one via her descendant. Didn't you take on human form before? Can you not do it again?"

Mora's eyes glazed over. "I've done so with Samael's permission," he whispered more to himself than to von Guten. "But he doesn't need to know about this." Lifting his blood-colored eyes, he searched the Kommandeur's face. "Keep this to yourself von Guten," he snarled. "Do you hear me?"

The Kommandeur smiled. "Certainly, I do," he said jovially. With a wave of his hand, the screen went dark.

***

Mora typed a few letters on the keyboard and suddenly the screen filled with a map of Virginia. Glossy white light reflected off his dark eyes as he studied the picture. Stepping in, he ran a fat, crooked finger from the name Lynchburg to Roanoke and from Richmond to Virginia Beach.

With his face just inches from the board, his dark, round eyes scrutinized every square inch of the map. "Now," he muttered, "where in this god-forsaken place is Plum Creek?"

CHAPTER THREE

Rain splattered against the old concrete building; turning it from hard grey to liquid black, but it didn't matter what color the place was, it was an eyesore; looking more like an abandoned prison than an active laboratory. Chunks of the corners were gone, cracks splayed across the uneven sidewalk, and the lines in the parking lot had all but disappeared. It was the tall, dark windows; however, that told the truth. Dirty, but unbroken, they were proof that over time, it was nature and neglect that had marred the federal fortress, not vandals.

The inside was different. Upstairs, the chairs in the conference room had been pushed neatly under the large rectangular table, the burgundy blotters on its glass top lined up perfectly, and the cabinet in the far corner restocked with pens, tablets, and water glasses. In the basement mailroom the stamp machine had been replenished, fliers and junk mail swept up off the floor and thrown away, the counter straightened, and the door closed. On the ground floor, work labs up and down the hallway were dark and empty; their microscopes hooded and put to sleep over an hour ago; except for one; the one that belonged to a scientist by the name of Rachel Wall.

She often stayed late, preferring to work after hours because the solitude helped her think better. No small talk, no phone calls, no explanations; just her work... and her music; accompanied by the occasional dance move that only she could appreciate.

Tonight, the sounds of the Beach City Surfers jettisoned her from the coldness of a Virginia fall evening to the warm soft sand of California. Leaving the ladies room, she slid and shuffled down the hall, her long, dark ponytail swishing back and forth to music that bounced off the inside of her skull like a pinball gone wild.

I love the sounds of rockin'; I love the way she's walkin'...

Another shuffle... *I love the waves a rollin'...*

Her ponytail brushed against her white lab coat ...*the waves of music rollin' over me...*

Lost in the music, she barely glanced at the office door as she approached it...

*Ah eww, ah eww eww eww eww...*another quick look from the corner of her eye as she passed, followed by an obscure thought that managed to dig its way into her already crowded brain.

Hmm...light.

There wasn't anything unusual about a light shining from underneath Doctor Aberman's office door. Being the lead scientist, he often worked nights too.

I love the sounds... shuffle, shuffle, sssliide.

The ponytail stopped abruptly in mid-step. "Wait a minute!" she sputtered. "That's not right. There shouldn't be a light coming from Doctor Aberman's lab. He's gone. Not just gone out of the building gone, but out of town gone."

Pulling the buds out of her ears, she turned and glanced over her shoulder at the thin gold line beneath the door.

The music, seeping from the dangling earphones, sounded tinny and far away, and now, having lost its luster, failed to stave off the eerie feeling that was falling around her.

"Of course, he's gone," she said out loud. "After his

granddaughter's birthday party in Providence, he's scheduled to speak at some boring conference in Boston. There's no way he'd pass that up, so, no, he can't be here in Virginia hobbling between Bunsen burners and microscopes in his stuffy little lab."

A pale grayness rolled across the line of light for a brief second. If she hadn't been looking at the exact spot, she wouldn't have seen it. "But if he's not here, then who's in there?" she whispered.

She slid her hand into the pocket of her lab coat and turned off her phone. The ear buds slipped from her fingers and fell into a crumpled heap beside it. The sudden void left a deafening silence except for the drumming of her heart beating in her ears. Stepping up to the thick oak door, she tapped lightly. "Doctor Aberman, are you in there?"

No one answered.

She tapped again, this time a little harder.

Still no answer.

She grabbed the handle, but it didn't budge.

Taking a breath, she put her ear against the door and listened. Something rattled, like shuffling paper.

All five-knuckles rapped heavily on the door. "Doctor Aberman?"

The shuffling stopped.

She waited a few seconds, but when the footsteps of someone approaching from the other side of the door never came, she stepped back, slowly.

"That's weird," she muttered. "Maybe he just forgot to turn the light off. Maybe he left a fan on and it's hitting some papers. Maybe..."

Then just like that, the light went out; poof, gone.

The light disappearing caught her off guard and she almost fell backward.

"What in the world?"

Her throat tightened. Wiping her sweaty palms on her lab coat, she stepped up to the door and carefully placed her ear against the cold wood again.

"Doctor Aberman, its Rachel Wall. Is everything alright?"

Nothing came back to her.

Pushing her emotions down, she stepped back and threw her scientific mind into gear. Eyeing the door from top to bottom, she whispered, "There's got to be a reason, a credible explanation. He forgot to turn the light off and it just now went off because...?"

A few seconds later, her shoulders fell with relief. "Automatic shut off," she said half-smiling. "It was installed a couple years ago. Remember?"

She eyed the door again. "That explains it. Doctor Aberman accidentally left a light on and a fan running before leaving yesterday, so the system kicked in and turned everything off. That's all it was."

She chuckled lightly, but not for long. The smile that graced her lips slid downward forming a tight line.

That answer should have satisfied her. It should have made her shrug off the whole silly incident, take the ear buds out of her pocket, shove them back into her ears, and bop the rest of the way down the hall to her lab, but it didn't. It didn't calm her nerves or stop her palms from sweating. And it definitely didn't take away the feeling that something wasn't right. Staring at the door, the logic of her explanation melted; leaving her with a heavy, burrowing feeling in her chest.

She turned on her heels and hurried down the hall. "Everything's fine, Rachel; it was just a light."

But it was too late. The cold heaviness gripped her insides, pushing paranoia up into her brain until it felt like a hot poker searing her grey matter. She quickly glanced over her shoulder. The hallway was empty.

Her eyes darted franticly around her lab. This place wasn't just a small workspace. It was a haven. When life outside of these walls pressed in, broke her heart, or added more drama than she cared to handle, she came here to get lost in her research. But now, for some odd reason, she felt like her safety zone had been breached.

Was someone in here when I was in the restroom? Is someone following me?

With a few quick steps, she was at the storage shelves. "Five cylinders, ten disposable pipits, four pairs of goggles, a spot plate, a box of two, four...thirteen stirring rods; seven books, seven volumetric flasks, two forceps, one test tube rack with test tubes, one mortar with pestle, one hot plate, one balance, one Nikon's Eclipse Ti-E, and one Nikon Perfect Focus 3 System."

Satisfied everything was still in its place, she slumped into her chair, wiping a strand of hair from her face. But before she could relax, panic hit her like a baseball to the face. "But my research. Were my secret files ...?"

One good yank on the drawer by her left knee confirmed her secret files were still locked up tight. Everything she expected to find in the right drawer was there too, but since a couple minor files had ended up missing a few nights back, she did a quick count anyway.

"Purse, and inside purse is wallet, car keys, tissue, lip gloss, a couple pens, small tablet, and a comb." She pulled the earbuds out of the pocket of her lab coat and dropped them in the purse beside her wallet.

Nothing looked out of place on the top of her desk either. Not a pen had been moved, no uncovered cup ring, and no fingerprint left in a neglected pile of dust. Sinking back into her chair, she was pretty sure no one had been in her lab.

She rubbed her temples. "Come on, Wall," she whispered. "You saw a light under Doc's door and then it went out, so what? Stop being so paranoid. No one's out to sabotage your project because frankly, your project really has nothing to do with anything, so get over it. You're cloning blood for crying out loud. Who cares about cloned blood?"

Thunder rumbled in the far distance.

She turned to the only window in the room. "But you have to admit, other weird things have happened since the good doctor assigned this project to you? Like the missing files from your desk drawer."

She smirked. "Granted, they're not important files, just bits of research on old projects, but that's not the point. The point *is* someone has been in your desk without your knowledge." Her head fell back and she stared at the ceiling. "And let's not forget those hang up phone calls or those creepy shadows that only showed themselves in your peripheral vision. And, oh yeah, that big ugly guy on the motorcycle in the parking lot the other night. Who the heck is he?"

Drumming her fingers on the desk, she closed her eyes and dug through her 'brain files'. "Where...when...where...?" The realization took her breath away. "The coffee shop," she gasped. "He was there; the one who kept staring at me...but still, who is he?" She pulled her ponytail over her shoulder and twirled her hair through her fingers.

"So, look at this logically, Wall. Yes, we all borrow files from each other, people dial wrong numbers all the time, and what are shadows anyway? A light falling awkwardly across a tall tree; bushes waving in the breeze and catching the light of the moon; shadows aren't anything really." She hesitated a second. "But that doesn't answer the question about the guy on the motorcycle, does it?"

A flash of lightning lit up the window. Thunder followed, closer this time.

She got up and walked to the window. Laying her forehead against the cool glass; her eyes drank in the storm that was now pressing its dark face against the other side of the pane. The glass trembled against her skin.

Lightning flashed again. A searing pain cut across her brain. Pushing herself away from the window, she started to her desk, but something in her peripheral moved, and she froze. Something was just beyond the glass wall that separated her lab from one that had been deserted by a retired colleague.

So, someone has indeed been watching me.

She quickly rounded on the intruder and for a long while they stood and glared at each other; neither willing to be the first to move. Finally, Rachel gave in and raised her hand. Not surprisingly, the specter raised its hand too. It smirked at her just as she smirked at it. She sighed and it sighed with her. She pushed a lose strand of hair out of her face. It did the same. She and the bodiless figure across from her sighed heavily.

"You're not just my reflection," she said quietly. "You're the reflection of my existence; colorless, dull, and undeniably 'sap the happy right out of me' bleak." She cocked her head and looked curiously at the familiar apparition. "But tonight, for some reason, you look more translucent than usual; like you're fading; becoming more and more invisible."

She shoved her hands into her deep pockets. "And that's exactly why Doctor Aberman gave you this project, isn't it?" she said softly. "It makes sense. I mean, you hold a Ph.D. in Molecular Biology and Genetics as well as a Doctorate of Medicine from Harvard so cloning blood is not a great challenge for you. But you're invisible, a no body, so why? Everyone here is working on medicinal remedies, not cloning, so why is he asking you to clone? This blood thing can't be just busy work, so what is it? Will it raise you from your junior status here and put you in the medical journals?"

She and her apparition shrugged their shoulders. "I don't know either, that's to be seen, but what *will* give you a leg up is your secret project. Aberman knows what you're working on, but he doesn't know why. That should level the playing field except he doesn't care why, but when you discover how to keep a brain from going into a coma, he'll care because that's what will keep you from fading into the cold world of no name scientists."

Turning from her reflection, she squeezed the bridge of her nose. "You deserve more, Wall, and you're going to get it." The pain in her head pounded relentlessly against the back of her eyes.

She pulled the slide from under the microscope's clips, secured it in its protective case, put it on the small conveyor belt, and hit a button. She watched as it was carried off through a hole in the wall to some unknown storage location.

None of the scientists knew for sure where their slides came from or went to. They just typed in what they needed or what they were sending back, pushed a button on their computer keyboards, and the conveyor belt took care of the rest.

Her imagination quickly drew up a giant, half clad, fat man sitting somewhere in the basement spooning up hundreds upon thousands of glass slides from the belt to feed a ravenous appetite that was never satisfied. He always had room for one more slide.

"You're ridiculous, Rachel," she whispered.

Exchanging her lab coat for the light jacket she kept in the closet for nights like this, she gave the room one last glance. "Bring in a vase of flowers tomorrow," she mumbled. "Add some color to the place." Her fingertips brushed the light switch and the room went dark.

The hallway looked like a dull colorless tunnel. Doors were dark holes against ashen wall tiles. Exit signs glowed in neon green. She waited until the security lights flooded the long corridor with pools of yellow light before walking to the front doors. Glancing down the hall at Aberman's office, she was happy to see everything was as it should be. Dark and quiet. "Automatic shut off system, that's all it was."

After punching the security code into the alarm pad, she pushed through the front door and stepped out onto the stoop. She'd wait there, under the eaves, until she heard the loud thunk of the doors locking.

The giant oaks that surrounded the building swayed in the wind, their multicolored leaves raining fiercely to the soggy ground. Most hit the earth and laid still, some quaked fearfully as if not sure whether to run or die, while others scurried across the wet grass to find shelter among the skeletal remains of dying bushes.

Thoughts of the scientists who had worked at the lab long before she arrived suddenly filled her thoughts. At one time they were labeled as some of the most brilliant minds in the scientific world. They were the first to create life in a test tube, the first to clone animals, and the first to sequence the complete set of nucleic acid in the human genome. She'd even heard a rumor that the facility had once been a leader in cryonic science, but she'd never seen any proof of that. After all, that's old science. Why freeze and resurrect later when you can clone and live now?

How ironic that the public didn't mind rumors floating around about the Lab freezing organs to later resurrect the dead, but they certainly minded when rumors circulated that the scientists had moved beyond cloning horses to cloning humans. Cloned humans were still humans, but what are resurrected dead? Zombies? Wouldn't the public rather have the lesser of the two evils?

She sighed heavily. All of that was a long time ago. No one cared anymore. The tremendous pressure of civil protests, unending calls to state legislators, and personal threats rendered all the successes of those men and women forgotten.

One swipe of a presidential pen and Plum Creek Laboratory had become a silent partner of the Center for Disease Control. The laboratory's mission changed from finding cures for ravenous diseases to creating medicines that eased pain, masked causes, and numbed the human nervous system. Even though most of what they put on the market was more dangerous than the actual disease, the media inquiries into their work stopped and the winds of fear, especially those whipped up by the religious right, had been calmed.

The awaited 'thunk' sounded behind her. She clutched the front of her jacket and ran for her car. Just as she slid in behind the steering wheel, lightning cracked through the black clouds above her. The car windows rattled from the ferocious drumming of rolling thunder.

The storm had become a fierce beast, bending tree branches; ripping off twigs and ripping away leaves that had tried so desperately to hide. Rain and debris streamed down the windows of her car; tumbling to the wet ground below. The eerie feelings she'd felt earlier tumbled away with them.

"What if I can prevent the brain from shutting down and going comatose?" she said loudly over the pounding rain. "Wouldn't that be a great thing?"

The beams of the headlights cut through the torrent; hitting the front doors of the Laboratory. She smiled; her face illuminated by the lights on the dashboard. Like those trailblazers before her, she too was a scientist driven by a personal agenda.

"Yes, Rachel. That's what you focus on," she said aloud. "Not lights going off or papers shuffling in the wind. You stay focused on the science! And you'll reap the rewards for doing so."

She carefully turned the wheel and pulled out of the desolate parking lot and into a line of headlights; their attached vehicles unrecognizable through her blurred window.

The distorted traffic light above her car bobbed and bucked, pitching its red beam out into the rain until finally, in the throes of its awkward dance, the beam turned green. She gently pushed on the gas. Lights from cars around darted across the darkness and glanced off of the wet road. Beams from an oncoming car streaked across her face, temporarily blinding her.

Her right foot ground into the brake pedal, but it was too late. Between the swish of the wiper blades, she watched the car swerve then, in a weird sense of slow motion, come straight toward her. Closing her eyes from the oncoming light, the darkness was soon followed by the sickening sound of crushing metal.

Something heavy landed in her lap. Ribs snapped; her right side pressed hard against the console. Pinned, her body twisted violently. She couldn't feel her legs. Her face smashed into something hard. The back of her head smacked violently against the head rest. A shocking "thud" hammered her eardrums.

Nothing made sense. Through one good eye, she could see the world flipping over and over, but she couldn't make anything out. She never felt the impact of her car smashing into the tree, but she did hear something just before the light went out.

It surprised her, the sound a skull makes when it cracks.

***

Across town, the person sitting comfortably in Doctor Aberman's leather chair turned off his cell phone and smiled. The caller said the words he'd been waiting to hear; one dead, the other probably within hours. How lucky they had been that both met their fate at the same time, at the same place. "The devil is in the details," he mumbled.

The chair creaked as he turned to glance around the ransacked office. "I'll find the hard drive later," he muttered. "Right now, it's time for a drink."

Before getting up, he grabbed a file from the disheveled desk and slid it under his jacket. He picked his way through the papers that lay scattered across the floor; opened the office door, and peered out into the hall. Satisfied he was alone, he walked down the hallway under the yellow lights, but he didn't stop at the front door. Instead, he walked a little further. Just before reaching Rachel's lab, he turned into the break room and made his way to the back door. There, he reset the alarm, took one last look around then stepped out into the silver rain.

CHAPTER FOUR

The fogginess in her head eventually cleared. A beeping noise that had pounded in her ears earlier finally sounded distant; not gone, but distant. Opening one eye, she looked around. She opened the other eye. Nothing about where she was looked familiar. The walls had a weird green sheen to them. In the far corner, a small dark box hung from the ceiling, and underneath it she could only make out a huge brown bulk. She blinked hard and looked around again. Her eyes adjusted enough to see the dark box was a television set and the brown bulk was a recliner. She had no idea where she was, but she really didn't care. She was alive. That was her last thought before heavy lids closed over her eyes and once again, she slid into darkness.

That dang beeping noise again! What was it? Then a swooshing sound, like that of a door swinging open drowned it out for a few seconds. She didn't have the strength to open her eyes to see who had come into her room. Someone approached the side of her bed, imprinting the coolness of plastic hands on her arm. The words 'where am I' formed in her brain, but not on her lips.

She couldn't talk. But she could hear.

"Her brain's shutting down."

"Should we try this?"

A deafening silence filled the room. Then, "Yes. We have

her consent and right now, it's her only hope."

She felt a slight tug on her right arm, but then nothing. Darkness enveloped her like a soft cocoon. Even the beeping noise disappeared.

***

Rachel took a deep breath. Exhaling slowly, she opened her eyes. To her surprise, and somewhat relief, she wasn't in the green room anymore but was standing in her own living room. How she got there from that dismal place with the obnoxious beeping, she didn't know, nor did she care. She was home and that was all that mattered.

A tinny, small voice floated up to her. Surprised to find she was holding her phone, she put it to her ear.

A woman's voice kept going in and out; often disappearing into the scratchy sound of static. Rachel pushed the cell phone hard against her ear hoping to get the gist of what was being said. Finally, she recognized the voice. It was her best friend, Carmen.

"Really Carmen," she said calmly. "I'm fine. You sound like my mother. Stop being such a worry wart."

Carmen's voice turned shrill, almost hysterical. "But the accident, did you see it?"

"I didn't see anything. It must've happened after I went through that intersection."

Another bright flash lit up the window and their voices faded. Rachel pulled the phone from her ear and looked at it until the scrubby noise stopped. *Why is my phone doing this? It's never done this before.*

"Rachel, where are you?"

"I'm home, Carmen, safe and sound," she yelled into the speaker. "This storm is messing with my phone and I can barely hear you. Why don't you go fix yourself a cup of hot tea, or read a book, or just take some sleepy medicine and relax. We're not going to be able to talk until this thing passes."

There was a long pause. A few rounds of static filled the quiet spaces before Carmen said, "I will, Rachel, now that I know you're all right."

"You're a terrific friend, Carmen. Now relax, ok?"

"Ok, I will. I'll see you in the morning."

"In the morning? Wait! Why Carmen? Why will you see me in the morning?"

"Ugh! Don't tell me you forgot already! We're going to yard sales, remember?" Carmen said loudly.

"But, I..."

"You promised, Rachel and I'm not taking no for an answer this time. There's more to life than just work. I'm going to pick you up at shhhh, we're going to go snoop through people's old stuff, and we're shhhhhhh fun; whether you like it or not. So, be shah sav shhhh. Good night, Rach."

"Wait! What time? I didn't hear the time," shouted Rachel, but Carmen was gone.

Mikey, Rachel's orange tabby cat, was stretched out on a weathered, overstuffed chair; his large green eyes watching her face. She sensed his curiosity and looked over at him. "Seven, I think she said seven," she said to him, but once he had her attention, he lost interest and started cleaning his paws instead.

Rachel scooped him up and kissed the top of his head. He rumbled against her arms. "I know," she said softly. "She's right. I really do need to get a life." The cat butted her in the forehead and licked her nose with his sandpaper tongue. "And," she giggled, "find someone whose kisses are much softer than yours."

His round green eyes searched her face.

"I said softer," she whispered, "not sweeter."

His eyes searched her's a second longer before he jumped from her arms and scurrying to the kitchen, his tail stiffly pointing upward.

Rachel followed him. Grabbing a Best Ballard's Microwavable Chicken Pot Pie from the freezer, she tore it from the box and slid it the microwave then went to the living room and turned on the television. The black screen exploded with color. Images of the accident Carmen had called about earlier filled every crevasse of the room. Several fire trucks and police cars blocked off the intersection; their flashing red and blue lights bouncing off everything they touched.

Mikey appeared, twisting himself around her ankles. "Those were cars, Mikey," she mumbled, slowly sitting down on the couch. "I can see why Carmen was so freaked out. Those poor people."

A somber news anchor with watery, dark eyes looked into the camera.

"The accident that happened earlier this evening at the intersection of Chase Avenue and 4th Street has claimed one life. Allegedly, a man, reported to be in his mid-thirties and driving a Toyota 4Runner; ran a red light and struck a car coming through the intersection. He and the victim were airlifted to Plum Creek Memorial where he later died of injuries sustained in the accident. The driver of the car, a female, is in a coma and remains on life support. Investigators are concerned that alcohol may have been a factor in the accident. Their identities are being withheld until their families have been notified. More on this story on News at Nine."

Scenes of the accident reflected off of Rachel's wide eyes. "Wow," she whispered. Mikey jumped up onto the couch, planted himself against her thigh, and hummed softly. Her head fell back, her eyes floated across the ceiling. "So much we need to do to find a way to help people like that poor woman," she muttered. "What is the state of her brain while in coma? Will she remember? Can we recreate the brain cells? Can we bring her out of it? Will the body refuse? What will my new experiment tell me?"

She closed her eyes, trying to keep the images of the accident that took her parents several years earlier from flooding her thoughts. But she couldn't do it. Tears welled in her eyes and the memories flooded in.

Her parents hadn't died immediately. No, they endured the physical and mental anguish of waiting for their bodies to decide if they would cease to be or fight on. She'd stood beside their beds, numb and cold, quietly watching as the doctors removed the ventilators from their still bodies. Her mom, the first to die, took her last breath shortly after the vent was removed, never opening her eyes to see her daughter, never uttering a good-bye.

A few days later, her father was pronounced brain dead and he joined his wife in death. He too, never knew Rachel was standing beside his bed, praying for a miracle, only to watch him draw his last breath. From that moment on, finding a cure for coma, or at least the release from it, had been her personal quest and she knew she was close.

"But no more," Rachel said out loud. "Coma is over."

She thought seriously about calling Carmen and canceling their yard sale adventure, but after digging her phone out of her pocket she couldn't bring herself to do it. "She'd kill me," she said softly. "Work will have to wait until Monday. But in the meantime, we've got to find something a little less depressing to watch," she said, softly scratching behind Mikey's ear.

Somewhere between *Aliens through the Ages* and *Gator Haters*, she ran across *Planet Z*. "Pft," she sputtered. "Zombies, now there's a scientific dilemma; dead people walking around, eating brains, but not getting any smarter. How boring! Are people really watching this stuff, Mikey?"

The cat didn't bother to lift his head.

She turned the channel back to *Aliens through the Ages*. She'd heard something earlier that had piqued her interest and wanted to catch some of it.

The blue light from the television bounced scenes of primeval altars, colossal carvings, and perfectly cut boulders made by ancient man off Rachel's fixed eyes. The narrator was insinuating aliens, or perhaps alien gods, lived on Earth thousands of years ago and our own DNA proved they mated with humans to breed a new race that may still be among us today. Transfixed, she slowly laid her spoon down on the TV tray and took in everything she saw, everything she heard, until the last credit rolled across the screen.

When she turned the volume down, Mikey's heavy breathing filled the dark room. His warm body lay against her leg where he'd fallen asleep, not even waiting for a morsel of chicken from the cold pot pie.

"Good grief," she whispered. "Aliens mating with humans...a new race...still among us. I can't believe I sat there and watched that stuff. I'm a geneticist for crying out loud. Nothing like that could ever happen without people like me knowing about it."

She turned the volume back up and flipped through the channels until she found an old Sherlock Holmes movie. "This is more like it," she mumbled through a yawn. "This is real. Well, he's not real, but his methods are...logic, deductive reasoning, and analytics. *That's* how you solve mysteries, Mikey, not by creating some ridiculous plot about alien gods or a superhuman race."

On the television, Sherlock looked up from studying whatever he was holding and smiled wickedly at a man across from him, presumably, Doctor Watson. From under the rim of his deerstalker, the detective's eyes flickered, then with great enthusiasm, he said something about the game and a foot. That was the last thing Rachel heard. Her heavy eyelids slammed shut.

A close clap of thunder forced her to swim back up to

consciousness. Bleary eyed, her fingers fumbled around until she found the remote wedged between the couch cushion and Mikey's warm body. Somehow, she managed to hit the 'off" button.

Half asleep, she pushed herself off the couch, gathered her dinner things, and shuffled to the kitchen. A soft 'plunk' behind her told her Mikey had jumped off the couch to go hide in the folds of her pillow.

From the window above the sink she watched dark clouds cover the face of the moon like the mittened hands of a shy child. Rumbling thunder echoed across the valley.

"God," she said quietly. "I don't know if you can hear me, but if you can, be with her...the woman that was in that terrible car crash tonight. Please help her."

She wanted to say more, but the words wouldn't come. She and God hadn't talked in a long time and she wasn't sure if he'd want to hear from her now. Why would he? Is it normal to ignore someone for so long and then expect them to answer you when you ask for something?

What was left of the moon's light was quickly swallowed up, leaving Rachel feeling quite alone. Her eyes searched the sky for a brief moment, but all she saw was darkness. She quietly turned and left her prayer, the storm, and God, at the kitchen sink.

CHAPTER FIVE

A trace of sunlight squeezed through the small gap that ran between in the bedroom curtains and quietly slid across Rachel's face; its warm fingers softly caressing her cheek. A muscle in her jaw twitched ever so slightly. Soft, warm...thunder? Mickey unraveled himself and stuck his head out from underneath the comforter just as Rachel bolted upright, frantically slapping strands of matted hair out of her face. Her wide eyes scoured the room. Her clothes were strewn over the arm of the chair, right where she'd thrown them the night before.

His tail swishing back and forth, Mikey slowly ambled up to her. Noticing the unoccupied pillow, he quickly made use of it and curled into a tight ball.

"Whaz it, Mikey?" she whispered.

Swiping at a piece of hair that had dried to her bottom lip, her glassy eyes found the alarm clock. The bright green numbers blared 7:09.

Tilting her head, she listened, but heard nothing above the ordinary moans and creaks of an old house stretching in the morning sun. "Mussa been dreamin'," she mumbled. Grabbing the comforter, she fell over and covered her head.

Bam, bam, bam! "You better be in there, Rachel Wall."

Rachel's eyes sprang open just before her feet hit the floor.

"Oh my god," she shrieked. "Carmen! *I'm definitely not dreaming!*" Her dark eyes darted back to the clock. "Seven o...Seven ten!"

Stumbling toward the bedroom door, she yelled a hoarse, "Coming."

Rounding the corner into the living room, she saw Carmen's short, stout silhouette just beyond the lace curtain that hung across the small window on the front door. She knew Carmen could see her too, but that didn't keep her friend from banging on the door again.

"Hold your horses!" she fussed. "I'm coming." She scurried to the door, ramming her toes into the foot of the sofa as she went. Trying to keep her face from contorting into something that resembled a screaming banshee, she yanked the door open. Carmen's knuckles flew forward; rapping her in the forehead.

She lost the fight with her face. "Owwww," she groaned, rubbing her head. "If I didn't know better, I'd think you did that on purpose."

Even under dark sunglasses, Rachel could see Carmen's eyes penetrating the lenses. "Serves you right," she quipped. "I said 7:00 sharp. I was a little late...and you still couldn't be ready!"

"I'm sorry," moaned Rachel, still rubbing her head as she limped to the bathroom. "I didn't hear you say the time last night, my phone cut out on me."

Carmen stepped over the threshold; pushing the door closed with her foot. "You knew the time, Rach," she protested. "We talked about this before last night. Now we're gonna miss all the good stuff."

The bathroom door closed a little too hard.

After a quick shower, Rachel threw on a pair of old jeans and a flannel shirt, pulled her hair up into a pony tail, and grabbed her tennis shoes. She put them on in the living room under Carmen's impatient glare. "Ok," she finally said. "I'm ready; just let me grab a jacket."

"I fed Mikey," Carmen said coolly.

Rachel sighed heavily and rounded on her friend. "Look Carmen, I'm sorry. Ok? Last night I almost called you and canceled, but I didn't. I've got tons of work to do for Doctor Aberman, not to mention a new experiment I have under the scope, but you said I promised, so I'm here, ready to walk out that door to go pick through heaven knows what with you; unless you're so upset, you'd rather go alone. If so, I'll go to the lab."

Carmen swiped the toe of her shoe across the carpet. "Ok," she said sheepishly. "I forgive you."

Rachel sighed. "Good, now before we leave, I need to..."

Carmen took Rachel by the shoulders and gently nudged her toward the door. "Uh, I don't think so," she said warningly. "Don't press your luck, let's go."

Before long, Carmen's little red Subaru was heading into the rolling hills of Virginia. "Thought we'd start in Quail Hallow," she said way too cheerfully for Rachel's mood. "It's a nice neighborhood. Lots of money so the pickings should be good."

Rachel pulled herself away from her thoughts. "Are you looking for anything in particular?"

"Books," chirped Carmen. "The school is having its annual book fair in a few weeks and I'd like to find some good classics to donate to the cause. Oh, and anything to do with genealogy."

"Genealogy? But you teach World History, not Science."

"Well, World History *is* related to genealogy, Rach. I'm trying to get my tenth graders to think about their lineage. If I can help them understand who their ancestors were, then maybe they'll take a real interest in the history of the world and how they, through their ancestors, shaped it."

"Interesting," mumbled Rachel. "What gave you the idea?"

"Strange thing," admitted Carmen. "I got this letter the other day, well, an invitation really, to attend a genealogy seminar this coming spring. I looked it up online and after reading up on it, it hit me. Wow, genealogy. What a fantastic way to get the kids to connect to world history!"

Rachel nodded.

"I mean, I'm not sure why I got the invitation. I've never filled out anything for a genealogy event before, or at least I don't think I have, because as you so clearly pointed out, I teach History, not Science, but for some reason I got this one." Carmen pondered a thought for a second. "Maybe it's because some other genius came up with the same conclusion I did, that genealogy makes history more personal and sent invitations to scientists AND teachers."

Rachel turned her attention back to the window. Colors of fall raced in the opposite direction.

"But anyway, I got the invitation, filled out the registration form online and then boom, in a matter of minutes I got an email back confirming my reservation. It was almost like they were expecting me."

Rachel threw her an awkward glance.

Behind the glasses, Carmen's brown eyes danced in the morning light. "I know, impossible, right."

"Virtually," agreed Rachel.

"What really caught my attention though was the part on their website that said they're going to introduce some cutting-edge technology that really connects people to their past. The seminar's in Europe, Switzerland to be exact...at a place called The Chalet. Ever hear of it?"

"No."

"Well, it sounds like history in the making, no pun intended...and fun. Wanna go with, since genetics is your bailiwick and all?"

"What's the name of the company sponsoring the

seminar?"

Carmen hesitated a second. "Um, Gen...Core? I think."

"GenTrak?"

"Yes! GenTrak. That's it."

"I didn't think for a second that you'd be interested in genetics or I would've signed you up when I did a few weeks ago."

"So, you're going?"

"I am. Got my invitation last month. This technology you mentioned intrigued me too, so I went ahead and signed up. Got my plane ticket and everything."

"That's great!" bubbled Carmen. "Then I'm definitely going. After the lectures or whatever they do, you can tell me what everything means. I won't understand half of what's going on, but you can explain it to me."

Rachel chuckled. "I'm sure you'll do fine. I'll keep my eye out for genealogy books today too. I might even have a few things at the lab you can use to help the kids...,"

"Uh uh," Carmen said firmly. "Your job is to look for pots and pans, silverware, glasses, art work, pieces of furniture, bedro..."

Rachel rolled her eyes. "I get it," she interrupted and turned back to the window. "I need to make my house a home. You've told me that a million times."

"Yes, you do my friend, and do you know why?"

Rachel didn't like the excitement she heard bouncing in Carmen's voice. It always meant Carmen had something planned. "I'm going to hate myself for asking, I know I am, but no, why?"

"Because you're going to start dating," Carmen said giddily.

"What?"

Carmen's eyes peered over the rim of her sunglasses. "Yep. I volunteered to chaperon the high school's Halloween dance this coming Friday night, and you, and the date of your choice, are going to go with me."

"But I don't know, well, wait, no!" snapped Rachel. "I don't want to go on a date this Friday night."

"Well, if it's not a date of your choice, it will be a date of my choice."

"Come on Carmen, I..."

"I know," Carmen said in mocking husky voice. "I've got work to do. I'm doing some great experiment that will change the world. I'm getting older by the minute and have no idea what life is about, but that doesn't matter. I'm going to change the world. Bwahahahaha."

Rachel snickered.

"Come on, Rachel. Lighten' up. Life, my friend, is too short."

"But you're not dating. You're not..."

Thin lines of red streaked up Carmen's neck and boiled into crimson across her face. Rachel did a double-take. "Who? What? When?" she demanded.

The little Subaru zipped between two brick pillars, the name Quail Hallow stamped into concrete plagues on each one. Slowing down, she glanced from house to house. "Ok, be on the lookout for our first yard sale. Get ready to find some treasures."

Rachel kept her eyes locked on her friend's pretty, round face. "You're not getting out of this, Carmen O'Leary."

After a few twists and turns, Carmen pulled the car over and cut the engine. Before getting out, she pulled her glasses down and glanced at Rachel. "And neither are you, Rachel Wall," she said matter-of fact. "We'll talk more about this later, but right now, there's a coffee pot out there with your name on it, and by golly, we're gonna find it. If it takes all day!"

Rachel scowled. She knew just how stubborn Carmen could be. Reluctantly, she let the subject go.

Several hours later, Rachel lay face-planted against the hood of the car realizing just how serious Carmen had been.

"Carmen, this is the tenth yard sale," she whined. Lifting her head just inches off the hood, she glanced over each shoulder. "Actually, we've been here before, but I'm still gonna count this one," she muttered. Louder she said, "This is the eleventh yard sale. Can we go home now?"

Carmen didn't reply, but stayed planted in the middle of the yard with her face buried in an old book. Rachel's head fell back down onto the warm car.

"Carmen!" she said loudly.

"What?"

"Are we done yet?"

Carmen waved her off and turned the page. "Just a minute," she murmured. "This is so cool."

Rachel pushed up and drug herself over to see what had Carmen so enthralled. "What can be *that* cool?" she groaned.

Carmen flipped the page. "It's a book of spells."

Rachel stiffened. "A what?"

"A book of spells. You know, eye of newt, hair of toad."

Rachel's jaw clenched. Exhaling slowly, she said, "Oh, well, that's different. For a minute there I thought you said it was a book of spells; like you don't already have one, or seventy."

Carmen stuck out her tongue.

"Oh, that's mature," snapped Rachel.

Carmen slapped the book shut and glared at her.

Rachel took her stance; one foot out, hands on her hips, and looking at Carmen through squinted eyes.

"Don't go there," muttered Carmen.

"Go where?"

Carmen giggled. "In your scary ninja with the evil eye stance."

Rachel's chin fell with her shoulders. "Listen, Car, I'm tired and have a headache. You have a trunk full of old books, so many in fact there was barely enough room for my new, er...old coffee pot. Do you really need a spell book, and if so, do we have to stand here and read it until you learn how to pull a rabbit out of a hat?"

Carmen ignored her. Instead, she looked around until she saw the old lady who was hosting the yard sale. "How much for this book?" she shouted.

The old one's sharp eyes found the one who had shouted. Watching Carmen approach from over the rim of her cat-eye glasses, she looked amused until she saw the book in Carmen's hand. "Oh dear," she mumbled. "Won't do, won't do."

She shuffled toward Carmen as fast as she could, her thin crooked fingers nervously pushing strands of her long gray hair back up into what looked like a bird's nest sitting on the top of her head.

"That wasn't supposed to be put out on the table. I've had that since my sixteenth birthday," she said in a wobbly voice.

Carmen whistled. "Wow, that long?"

Rachel's mouth fell open. "Carmen!"

The old lady smiled a toothless grin. Her hunched shoulders shook when she chuckled. "It's alright, dearie," she said warmly. "I *have* been around a long time." Extending a translucent hand, she cooed, "May I hold it?"

"Certainly," replied Carmen.

The old woman gently took the book from Carmen. Sliding a weathered hand across the worn leather cover, she closed her eyes, pulled it to her sagging breasts, and whispered words that neither Rachel nor Carmen understood. When she opened her eyes, they were filled with tears. Holding the book out to Carmen, she smiled. "It likes you," she said softly. "It's yours now."

This amused Carmen. "But how does a book..."

Rachel rubbed her arms. "Man, I just got a chill. Did anyone else feel that?"

Carmen and the old lady didn't seem to hear her. They were huddled over the book in deep conversation.

Shaking her head, Rachel muttered under her breath and left them.

A few minutes later, Carmen opened the car door and climbed behind the wheel. "What a bargain!" she said breathlessly.

Rachel forced a smile. "How much?"

"Free. The old crone gave it to me. She said it was meant to be."

"Good," Rachel said wearily. "You now have enough to buy dinner since we missed lunch."

"Drive through ok?"

"Chinese," mumbled Rachel

"Sounds great. We'll grab it then I'll take you straight home. I want to dive into this as soon as we get to your place."

"Why the rush?"

Carmen looked at Rachel like she'd never seen her before. "Because it's so interesting. Why else?"

"Well, don't be doing any hocus pocus around me," Rachel said firmly. "I want no part of that."

"But you like hocus pocus, Rach."

"Um, sometimes. I did...do I?"

Carmen giggled. "You have to be my assistant or at least

my volunteer from the audience."

"Not tonight," rumbled Rachel.

Carmen smiled. "Close your eyes. I'll wake you up when we get to your place."

"My head hurts too much to try to sleep now. I'll be ok."

"Well then, tell me. Are you happy with what you bought today?"

"Yeah. I need to pick the big stuff up tomorrow, I guess. Know anyone with a truck?"

"Eric has a truck."

"Mmm," Rachel responded softly.

A few quiet moments passed between them.

"That book is phenomenal," Carmen whispered.

Rachel kept her eyes closed. "Which one?"

"The last one; the spell book. It's really old and it has some creepy stuff in it."

"Like what?"

"Well, when that old lady and I were thumbing through it, we came across a spell about raising the dead, or something like that."

Rachel's head came up fast. Eyes wild and round she turned to her friend. "No way," she said firmly. "There's no spell that reverses the curse of death, Carmen. You know that. Only God has that power and if that book says anything different, it's a hoax. You just wasted our time."

"Hey, calm down little sister," Carmen said jovially. "I'll get a better look at it once we get to your house. I'm sure it's referring to raising a cat or a dog from some hypnotic state, or, um...from a coma, nothing to do with really being dead, I'm sure."

Rachel relaxed. "You leave Mikey alone," she mumbled.

Carmen smiled then broke out into a high-pitched cackle.

"Maybe he'll be my assistant," she screeched. "Mikey, come here. Come here my little pretty."

Rachel didn't laugh. "Stop," she said somberly.

"Oh, come on," Carmen scoffed. "Witches don't fly around on brooms at night or huddle around boiling cauldrons. That's Hollywood. You know that! We're merely herbalists. Back in the day, folks used herbs to cure diseases, warts, and headaches. They were the scientists of their time. No different than what you're doing now, only they didn't have the luxury of modern technology."

Rachel looked at Carmen like she was nuts. "Are you serious?"

"Think about it, Rach," Carmen argued. "Natural witches of old didn't do magic like we think of magic today. Oh yeah, there were sorcerers, masters of dark magic, but the naturalist just mixed plants and things to concoct cures that people weren't used to or didn't understand. Back then people feared what they didn't understand, so they called them witches. Today, we call them scientists. And just so you know, I prefer to be referred to as a caster, not a witch."

"Yeah, okay!"

"But anyway," continued Carmen, "we've come to realize how simple, but fundamental their concoctions really were. Their findings are the foundation of modern medicine. Now, not only can we pop two aspirin to get rid of a headache within minutes, but we can use lasers to remove malignant tumors with such precision no other organs are damaged. Now, that's real magic."

Rachel grunted. "I could use about 500 milligrams of modern magic right about now."

"And you know what else is amazing," Carmen went on, "even today, in this modern age of technology, people still fear what they don't understand."

"Like what we do at the lab? Instead of cutting edge, some consider it over the edge."

"Well, yeah, but I was thinking more along the lines of everyday things that aren't fully appreciated or understood, and when talked about can scare the bigeebees out of people."

Rachel yawned. "Like witchcraft?"

"Really, Rach? You've got some nerve..."

"Go on, Car. What were you going to say?"

Carmen slowly shook her head. "Love, Rachel."

Rachel tried to suppress the moan that crept up her throat, but she couldn't stop it. "Buh. Wake me up when we get to my house." She turned her face toward the window.

Coolness glanced off the glass and touched her face. Rachel loved this time of year, but this particular fall had a melancholy feel to it, like an old lullaby...or a sad memory.

She had hoped to be married right about now. He'd asked her just a few months ago and, although they had what some call a whirlwind relationship, she had never been happier in her life. He was tall, very handsome, not rich, but financially comfortable, sensitive to her feelings, and had a marvelous sense of humor.

They met at the coffee shop on a rainy and an unusually chilly July morning. She rarely left the lab, but that morning, she needed a break, so she drove to the coffee shop to listen to the chatter and read the newspaper.

She didn't see him at first, but heard him place his order, and after paying for it, he casually walked over to her and asked if he could share her table. Her first instinct was to say no. Men scared her. She'd given her heart to a couple of them over the years, neither of which appreciated the gift. After them, she decided not to give it to anyone. It wasn't worth the hassle or the pain, but he hadn't asked for her heart, just a seat. As he talked and cajoled, she watched his eyes and they told her he was different.

Carmen hummed to the radio while Rachel tried to push away the haunting memories, but she had never been good at turning off her brain. The memory of the night he took her out to a fine restaurant in Lynchburg kept creeping in and forcing her to remember. Not just a thought, but the whole memory, in living color. No matter what she tried, her mind simply wouldn't listen to her heart. It was determined to relive the anguish, just because Carmen mentioned the dreaded "L" word.

She squeezed her eyes, but that didn't work either. She could see their table against the blackness of her eyelids. She could smell the sweet aroma of the beautiful pink roses that graced the center of the intricate lace tablecloth. She could hear the soft music they slowly danced to in front of the large bay window, lulled by the pastel colors in the evening sky.

Tears pushed hard against her closed eyelids and the intimate scene dissolved like water thrown on a chalk drawing. *Stop it, Rachel,* she scolded silently. But the voice in her head sounded too late. One tear escaped and slid down her cheek. She quickly brushed it away.

Trees, rolling hills, barns, and farmhouses rushed past. Surely there was something in the serene landscape that could distract her, something that would block the memory of their first night together, but her eyes couldn't focus. They saw nothing; nothing but him.

Simon, pulling a small black velvet box from his jacket pocket and leaning over the table toward her. Simon, opening it to reveal the most beautiful diamond ring she'd ever seen. Then, despite the glances and whispers from the other patrons, Simon getting down on one knee, telling her he loved her, and asking very sincerely, if she would honor him by being his wife. What they had together just felt so right. She couldn't help but say yes. Then Simon, grabbing her and kissing her passionately amid the roar of applause that erupted from the diners around them.

The rest of the night was heaven. His soft caresses and strong embrace as he held her close; each deep kiss tearing down the doubts, the inhibitions, and the thick impassable wall of mistrust. There, in her tiny house, as the man in the moon smiled above them, she surrendered.

He was everything she ever wanted in a man, tall, handsome, smart, kind, sincere. Even his small tattoo, the one above his heart, made her feel safe. She didn't understand what it symbolized, it was a knife of some sort, or a sword, but it made her feel as if no harm would come to her as long as he was watching over her.

Rachel sat up and ran her hands over her face. How would she ever be able to erase the memories of their time together; the feeling of his warm lips as he kissed her neck, the slow dances, the songs that spoke of love? She fell hopelessly in love and believed he had too. She was certain, with her whole heart that the passionate love they shared was real. She never dreamed after all they said, all they had planned together, he'd just walk away. That was months ago. After all this time, she didn't know if he was alive or dead, but one thing was sure, he was gone.

Carmen, glanced over at her. "Are you ok, girlfriend? You're awfully fidgety."

Rachel's head pounded unmercifully. Feeling nauseated, she rolled the window down a little and breathed in the cool air. Purposely keeping her head turned away from Carmen's incriminating glances, her eyes darted across the rolling hills beyond the window. "I'm fine," she mumbled. "Just hungry."

"Ok," Carmen said quietly. "We're almost there."

Rachel grit her teeth. What she really wanted to do was yell, to spit, to tell Carmen never to bring up her love life, or the lack of it, again. Carmen would never understand that what Simon had done to her was enough to scare her into solitude. He not only broke her heart, he crushed it. Totally crushed it and lying in the dust and debris were shards of broken trust. No, she wouldn't trust again. And she wouldn't love again. She would rather live alone in a bare, empty house than to live with suspicion and doubt. Some men were cruel liars. Not even Carmen's spell book could change that.

CHAPTER SIX

Flakes of crusted chicken splattered with sesame seed and kernels of rice trailed from half-empty takeout cartons to two paper plates. Rachel and Carmen ate in silence, but Rachel didn't mind. Carmen, although quiet, was still entertaining.

Carmen's sparkling, brown eyes, darted across the pages of her new book. That, and the piece of rice clinging to the corner of her mouth, kept Rachel biting her lip to keep from laughing.

Finally, Carmen lowered the book. "Wachel, wisten to dis. It's a shummons fo a zombie!"

Rachel winced. "A summons for a zombie? Why on earth would you want to summon a zombie?"

Carmen stopped chewing and swallowed. She turned her face toward the dining room window; her eyes looking past the glass as if searching for something. Several quiet seconds later, she inhaled deeply and gazed pitifully over at her friend. "Because then," she said softly, "I'd finally have a man who will want me, not only for this drop-dead gorgeous body, but for my brain too." On cue, the rice tumbled from the corner of her mouth.

Rachel burst into laughter.

Carmen snickered. "When you're finished, we'll proceed."

"Heem, Mmmm, um," Rachel stifled another laugh. "Proceed with what?"

Carmen tilted her head and looked at Rachel with one opened eye. "Don't argue with me. We're just going to have a bit of fun."

"Fun? With your book of spells?"

"Yep."

"I don't know, Car..."

"Just finish your dinner, Rach," Carmen said as she tore the wrapper off a fortune cookie. Breaking it in two, she popped one piece into her mouth and tossed the other into an empty carton. She unraveled the rolled-up paper and read the prophetic fortune to herself.

"So, are you going to win the lottery?" Rachel asked, picking up the cellophane wrappers.

Carmen raised her eyes to meet Rachel's and smiled. "Better," she chortled. "Listen to this. 'Be on the lookout for coming events; they cast their shadows beforehand.'"

Rachel slowly sat the cartons down on the table. "What do you think it means?" she whispered. "It uses the word cast. You're a caster, so tell me o' great one. What does it mean?"

Carmen's eyes darted around the room like she was trying to make sure no one else was listening.

"Oh, stop it," fussed Rachel. "What does it mean?"

"I've no idea," Carmen answered, rolling the paper between her fingers. "Maybe it's a warning that Christmas is coming. That's an event that's foreshadowed to come, and is cast by something from something, right?"

"Some witch you are."

Grabbing a carton, Carmen shoved the paper and other pieces of trash into it then went to the kitchen. "A caster, Rachel. I'm a caster. And yes, let's have fun with the spell book. You and me."

"But I'm a scientist," Rachel called after her. "I don't believe in such nonsense."

Carmen stuck her head around the corner. "I know you're a scientist, Rach. A scientist who believes in God. Like that's not weird."

She retreated back into the kitchen and yelled, "You already told me there's no spell to reverse death, so zombies can't be real, can they? And if zombies aren't real, then there isn't a problem, is there? Now, help me get ready. I'll finish clearing the table, you grab some candles."

Rachel brushed the crumbs onto a plate, picked up the cups and chopsticks, and dumped them in the trashcan. "If I can't argue with you, then tell me again why we're doing this?"

"Because it's fun," said Carmen. "Remember fun, Rachel?"

Rachel decided it was best to be quiet and just go along with whatever Carmen had in mind. A few minutes later, while Carmen scurried around the house gathering odds and ends, she sat down at the table and lit a candle.

Carmen finally slid into the chair across from her friend. "Oh no," she said shaking her head while unloading her arms. "One candle won't do, we need five."

"Five? I don't know if I have five."

"Got any birthday candles?"

"Oh, bother," groaned Rachel. "I think I can scrounge some up from somewhere. Give me a second."

"And I forgot the garlic, Rach. Will you grab some while you're in the kitchen?"

"Garlic? Why do you need garlic? I thought that was for warding off vampires, not summoning a zombie?"

Busy making sure she had everything else she needed, Carmen didn't answer.

Rachel pulled out several drawers before she found a half-burnt candle that she used during a thunderstorm, and two old, but unused birthday candles. Before leaving the kitchen, she grabbed a bulb of garlic from the veggie basket.

"Can't be too careful," Carmen said as Rachel laid the three candles and the garlic on the table.

"When did you become so superstitious, Carmen?" she asked in passing.

Carmen smirked. "Really? My first name is Carmen. My last name is O'Leary. I'm half-Spanish, half-Irish. You don't get more superstitious than that!" Carmen eased back into her chair. "Yep, my family is a real blast around Halloween. Half of them celebrate the dead and the other half curses them."

Rachel had disappeared into the dark abyss of her bedroom closet. "What side are you on?" she yelled.

"Neither," Carmen said loudly. "I celebrate life. Now get back in here and sit for a spell."

Carmen's laughter filled the small house. "Get it? Sit for a spell." She laughed again. "Geez, I crack myself up."

Rachel was still digging through some boxes in her closet.

Carmen sighed impatiently. "Come on, Rach. Time to get this zombie party started."

A few minutes later, Rachel plopped into her chair and set the fifth candle on the table. Carmen picked it up and eyed it curiously. "What is *this*?" she asked.

"It's a candle," retorted Rachel.

"I can see that, but what does it have on it?"

"Horses," Rachel replied sharply. "And cowboy hats. I believe you can even find a pair of boots if you look hard enough."

Carmen raised her eyebrows. She looked at the candle then over at Rachel.

"I'm sorry," Rachel said cynically. "I bought it years ago

when my cousin and I visited the Grand Canyon. It's all I've got. If I'd have known we were going to have a zombie party, I would've gone to the store and bought more candles, along with some cake and ice cream."

"It's ok," Carmen said. "But you really do need..."

"I know," Rachel huffed. "Get a life. I got it."

"Right! Now that's settled, would you please light all the candles?"

"Why do we need five anyway?"

Carmen's brow furrowed a little as she eyed her friend. "I was hoping you'd remember, but since you don't, I'm glad you asked. In Wicca, there are five elements; one candle for each element."

"Let's see," said Rachel, "earth, wind, and fire..."

Carmen chuckled. "Not to be confused with the rock band, but, you're close. The five elements are Earth, Fire, Water, Air, and Spirit. These candles will represent the five elements." Carmen placed the candles at specific points, creating an invisible five-pointed star. Beside certain candles, she put one of the objects she'd collected earlier.

Rachel studied what was on the table. "The flames on the candles are the fire, the glass with water is obvious, but what is the bowl of cat litter for?"

Carmen blushed. "It was the closest thing to earth I could find without going outside. It would'a helped if you had a plant hanging around, but ..."

Rachel, sitting back in her chair, giggled. "Ok, kitty litter will do. Air is around us, and Spirit?"

Carmen pointed to the candle that was closest to her. "Spirit is always at the top of the pentagram," she explained. "Spirit is not only within us, but also around us. This candle represents the Sacred."

She pulled the spell book closer to her. "Now, would you mind grabbing the lights?"

Rachel stared at the pentagram. "This makes me a little uncomfortable," she said softly. "Aren't pentagrams used in devil worship?"

Carmen cleared her throat and relaxed. "Good question," she said stoically. "The two stars are similar, but in Wicca the top of the pentagram, which is only one point of the star, is our acknowledgement of the Divine. It's a respected place that nothing else can fill. However," she quickly added, "with Satanists, the pentagram is different."

She quickly rearranged the candles so Rachel could see the difference. "See here," she said pointing to the candles at the top of the star, "now the pentagram has two points on the top. The two points represent the horns of a ram, or the Great Goat, by which Satan is often referred."

Rachel stared at the configuration. "Wow".

"We don't worship Satan," Carmen said ardently. "We worship nature through two deities we refer to as God and Goddess. ENORMOUS difference, even in our pentagrams."

Rachel fell silent.

Carmen stopped talking and looked over at her. "What is it, Rachel? You don't look well."

Rachel was staring at the pentagram. Swallowing hard, her face paled. "I've seen this before."

Carmen leaned in close. "Where, Rachel? Where would you have seen a pentagram like this?"

Not taking her eyes from the candles, Rachel shook her head. "I'm not sure, but I have."

"Probably in a book," Carmen replied casually while setting up the Wiccan pentagram again. "We looked at a gazillion of them today."

Rachel glanced over at Carmen; the color still drained from her face. Nodding slowly, she said, "Maybe. Yeah, I guess it was, or maybe on *Aliens through the Ages*. Or maybe..."

Carmen sniggered. "Whaaat?"

Rachel blushed. "Oh, hush up."

"But you actually watch that stuff?"

"I watch all kinds of stuff." Looking back at the candles, Rachel's countenance changed again. "But, no, I didn't see the Devil's pentagram on TV." Her smile faded, and her eyes grew dark when the memory hit her. Her voice softened as she spoke, almost trance-like. "I saw it on someone, a tattoo, not too long ago; on his arm." Rachel's eyes widened, "The guy on the motorcycle. He was a big..."

Carmen clapped her hands, startling Rachel so badly she almost came out of her chair.

"Okay, great," Carmen said loudly. "So, now that your question about our star has been answered, let's roll. We're burnin' candlelight."

Rachel relaxed, but smiled nervously. "This is just for play, right?"

Carmen smiled back. "No such thing as a real zombie Rach, right? It's just for fun."

Rachel leaned back in her chair and brushed the light switch with her fingertips. The room went dark, lit only by the five odd candles flickering on the dining room table.

"We gotta be quick," said Carmen. "The birthday candles aren't going to burn long."

"I'm ready when you are," replied Rachel.

"Ok. Whenever I perform a ritual, I always cast a protective circle, which isn't to be taken lightly. Unlike this spell, a circle is very serious, so may I ask that we remain respectful, at least for the first part."

Rachel nodded.

Carmen stood and moved around the little table, stopping a quarter of the way to acknowledge someone, or something she referred to as a Guardian. She did so four times, until she'd completed a full circle and had acknowledged the Guardians of the North, South, East, and West.

When Carmen finished, she took her seat again, reached across the table, and grabbed Rachel's hands. A strange intenseness filled the room. The only sound was their breathing. Carmen looked down at the book before her. Ready to read the spell that lay on the open page, she took a deep breath then.... nothing.

"What's wrong, Carmen," whispered Rachel.

"Um, I can't see the words," she whispered back. "It's too dark in here."

Rachel giggled. "Oh, good grief. Pull one of the candles closer."

Carmen grabbed the cowboy candle and pulled it closer to the book. "That's better," she said quietly. She took Rachel's hands again and began to read:

"Life of man, which is gone,

Find for him, another home.

Make him tall, make him wise,

Make him youthful, in disguise.

Come to us, in human form,

Come in peace and bring no harm.

The time is now, through Spirit's power,

Be made known, this witching hour.

And zombie haste, please don't be late,

Halloween is nigh, be Rachel's date."

Rachel struggled to keep from laughing. She dared not look at Carmen, but it was Carmen's laughter that broke the silence.

"Thought I'd throw that last part in for free," she quipped, her eyes bright with candlelight.

"Won't that dampen the spell?"

"No, the spell instructions specifically say the caster can add anything that might enhance the spell. I thought a date for Halloween was appropriate."

A cold draft slithered across the table and tugged at the flame on the cowboy candle. Rachel shivered.

"Whoa," whispered Carmen. Her round eyes scanned the room. "Did you feel that?"

Rachel sat motionless. "I did," she whispered back.

"Do you think it was the spell working its magic?"

Rachel shook her head, "No, I think it was the window. It's cracked just a bit. I forgot to close it when we got here."

Carmen smirked. "Party pooper! Be still till I reverse the protective circle."

When Carmen finished the ritual, Rachel got up, flipped on the lights and closed the window. "Not a party pooper," she said over her shoulder. "I'm a scientist; a realist."

"Scientist and realist," muttered Carmen. "Sounds like loads of fun."

As she was walking back to the table, a yellow streak of fur dashed in front of Rachel, almost tripping her. Making an abrupt stop in the middle of the living room, the cat hunched down on all fours, looked up at the living room light and hissed. It then backed up slowly, turned, and darted into Rachel's bedroom.

"What in the world?" she muttered.

Carmen didn't notice. She was into the book again. "Hey," she said loudly, her face buried in the pages. "There's a real easy love spell in here. Wanna do that one?"

Rachel blew out the candles and began clearing the table. "No, I do not," she said sternly. "I think we've had enough supernatural excitement for one night. Besides, I think we spooked Mikey."

"Mikey?"

Rachel stopped and looked at her friend. "Yeah, Mikey. You know, my cat."

Carmen rolled her eyes. "I know who Mikey is, but how do you know he got spooked?"

"Because he just hissed at the living room light."

Carmen shook her head. "He couldn't have."

"Why not?"

"Because unless you let him in, Mikey isn't in the house. I let him outside first thing after we got here."

Rachel looked towards her bedroom. "But he's under my bed."

"Did you let him in?"

Rachel, staring at her bedroom door, shook her head slowly.

Just then a cat called from outside. Rachel went to the kitchen and looked out at the stoop where Mikey was staring up at her, his eyes pleading to be let in. When she opened the door, he zipped past her straight to Carmen.

"My goodness," whispered Carmen. "What's gotten into you?"

Rachel stopped at the bedroom door. "Carmen, I saw him; or a cat just like him, run into my room. Come help me get this stray out of my house."

She walked around to the far side of the bed and got on her knees, lowering her head until her cheek rested on the floor. Carmen did the same on the other side. Together, they lifted the bed skirt and peered underneath. The only thing they saw was each other's face.

"I think your sweet and sour chicken must've been more

sour than sweet," Carmen said from across the dark underneath of the bed. "Not a thing under here." She looked around a little closer. "Good grief, Rachel. Not even a dust bunny. You really do need to get a life girlfriend."

Rachel stood up. "Thank you, Inspector Cousteau," she said, tugging at her shirt.

Carmen struggled a little but made it to her feet. "The only cat in this house is Mikey. You must've imagined something," she said breathing hard. "Now, we've got a big day tomorrow, so I suggest you get some shut eye. Eric is going to pick me up around eight o'clock in the morning. We'll be here around eight-fifteen."

Rachel, glancing around the room muttered "For what?"

Carmen sighed heavily. "Stop looking. There's nothing here."

Rachel yanked her closet door open and dropped to her knees again.

"Unless this ghost cat has opposable thumbs, he couldn't have gotten into your closet, Rach."

"Oh! You're right." Getting to her feet, she pulled the rubber band from her hair. "Now, why are you going to be here so early in the morning?"

"Do you not remember buying all that stuff today?"

"Oh, yeah. My yard sale stuff."

"There you go," said Carmen, patting Rachel on the shoulder. "It isn't going to get here by magic, I can guarantee that, so, I'm gonna go home and go to bed. I suggest you get some sleep too. Moving furniture is never easy."

Rachel didn't answer. She was watching Mikey. He'd started to run toward her but stopped suddenly. Picking him up was out of the question. He made that clear by taking off down the hall toward the kitchen. Confused, Rachel ran after him.

"No, really, don't bother, I'll let myself out," Carmen called over her shoulder.

No answer came from the back of the house.

"Stop worrying about that cat and get to bed! We'll be here bright and early."

"Come here, Mikey," pleaded Rachel. Carmen rolled her eyes and left.

As Carmen's Subaru zipped around curves and under bridges and Rachel frantically chased Mikey through the house, a tiny, crumpled white piece of paper, soiled with cookie grease, fluttered out from under the kitchen trashcan and slowly began to unfold.

At the same time, in that shadowy, sinister place that resides beneath all beds, an animal with large, bright yellow eyes, lay still and scared.

CHAPTER SEVEN

"Is your heater heating, your filter filtering, your pistons...well, if your car needs a tune up, bring it on down to Royal T. Car Maintenance. We'll make sure your car is running smoothly before the winter snow flies. We promise we'll treat you like Royal T. This is..."

Yawning deeply, Rachel reached over and slapped at the radio alarm. After several attempts, her fingers grazed the button and the room fell silent. Peeking at the time with one eye, she fell back onto her pillow.

Neon green numbers burned against her closed eyelids. "Oh, for Pete's sake. If I have to stay home on the weekend, can't I sleep in?" Mikey jumped onto the bed and nudged her with his cold nose. "Guess not," she muttered. Throwing the comforter back, she slid her feet off the side of the bed.

Mickey paced, rubbing his face against her arm. "I know," she said tenderly, scratching behind his ears. "I'd like nothing better than to snuggle with you, but if I'm not ready when she gets here, I'll never hear the end of it."

He licked her thumb then hopped over to her pillow. Before she pushed herself off the bed, he'd curled up into a tiny ball. In the kitchen, she flipped on her yard sale coffee pot and watched it gurgle to life then shuffled to the bathroom.

Looking at herself in the mirror, she shook her head. "Why

do you do that? Why do you let Carmen talk you into doing things like buying stuff you don't want and participating in spells you don't understand?" Three beeps from the kitchen told her the coffee was done. "Well, at least *that* really works," she mumbled, grabbing the toothpaste.

While brushing her teeth, she heard something over the running water. Listening, she made out the pleasant chimes of church bells. She even recognized the song. Everyone knew the song. It was a southern spiritual; a bagpipe wonder. *Amazing Grace.* It was coming from the old Presbyterian Church in the valley. She finished brushing and turned off the water, but before dropping her toothbrush into the holder, she lifted a slat of the window blind and peered out. A white wooden triangle with a thin cross balanced on the point could be seen just above the multicolored tree tops.

"Been awhile since you've darkened the door of a church, ol' girl. Maybe God wouldn't mind if you visited."

The song ended, but the last note reverberated through the trees, leaving her feeling empty and alone.

"Naw. He wouldn't want a hag like you darkening the door of his house." The hymn stirred up feelings she thought she'd managed to bury deep within her. "But that church...in the valley. You *have* darkened its doors," she said to her reflection. "But when?"

She could see it; a little white church surrounded by blazing fall colors, a wrought iron fence with a squeaky gate separating it from an old graveyard. Inside, rows of high back pews with worn red seat cushions; a pulpit in the center front, and everywhere the aroma of old wood and new hymnals. But she hadn't gone to church since before she went to college, and never since she moved to Plum Creek. Why would she have memories of this one?

"Probably because your memory is a description of every country church in America," she said, dropping her brush into the drawer. "You were raised in a similar church outside of Charlottesville, so yes, you'd remember those details." She was pretty sure she'd never seen the inside of this church, but something still made her feel a little unsettled.

Church had been a big part of her past. Father spent hours in his home office studying passages for his Sunday School class. She'd spent hours doing homework in a pew while both of her parents attended choir practice on Thursday nights. Pot lucks, sick calls, and Wednesday night prayer meetings; priorities all, yet, no matter how faithful her parents were, they never knew the joy of watching her give her life to God.

Frankly, it wasn't because she didn't believe in God, but simply because she never saw the need to surrender to a God she knew very little about. She heard the sermons, she knew the songs, but God remained elusive; living somewhere up in the big, wide universe, not in the small, crowded hearts of men.

After her parents' deaths, God started to disappear from her life. As a student at UV, he drifted even further, but after Simon left, he disappeared altogether. He hadn't shown himself since.

But for some reason, her heart still moved her to pray sometimes. Perhaps out of habit or maybe because she hoped if her words got above the ceiling, they'd float out into space and he'd hear her. She doubted she'd ever know.

That's why she loved her work. It was confirmation that miracles happen, even if they were the outcome of human work and not by an unseen God. But then again, whenever she got to the point of almost becoming a true-blue atheist, something would tug at her heart and pull her back to the things she was taught as a child.

She gathered her hair up and wrapped a rubber band around it. Taking one last look in the mirror, she turned her head from side to side. "Maybe one day, I will go to church," she whispered. "If God shows me he's real."

Carmen, on the other hand is a devout believer, in two deities to boot, she thought.

She and Carmen had known each other their entire adult lives, but she couldn't recall a time when Carmen mentioned ever going to church, but she believed in something, someone. She said once that she often worshipped in the comfort of her garden and if she ever got married, she'd want to marry there, among the scents of rosemary, sage, mint, angelica, and all the other wonderful herbs she had so carefully nurtured.

Rachel gave herself one last look-over. "It must be nice to believe in something," she whispered.

A knock sounded at the door. She glanced at her watch. Seemed Carmen and Eric were a little early. Turning, she stepped away from the mirror and left her reflection to disappear.

"Coming," she hollered. Quickly pulling the bow on her shoe, she hopped out into the living room, but stopped cold when she saw the silhouette of the person just beyond the lace curtain. *That isn't Carmen.*

Slowly, she pulled the curtain back and looked up into the face of a very attractive man. As subtly as she could, she gave him a quick once over. The face underneath the cowboy hat was slightly tanned, which mercilessly highlighted his chestnut brown hair and piercing blue eyes. She also thought he had the nicest smile she'd ever seen. She lowered the curtain. "I don't trust men and if this isn't the devil himself, I don't know who it is," she muttered.

Almost as if he'd heard her, he said, "Miss Wall, I'm sorry if I startled you. My name is Trace Ardor. You probably don't remember me. I worked at Plum Creek Laboratory with you a few years back. Anyway, your friend Carmen O'Leary asked if I'd help move furniture today, so I thought I'd come over and introduce myself before she and Eric got here."

She thought about calling Carmen but didn't because the name Trace Ardor did sound familiar. *And besides knowing what they were doing today, he knows Carmen's full name. Only she could've told him all that. And he mentioned Eric too.*

With some reservation, she opened the door. "Good morning, Trace," she said, trying not to sound leery. "When did you see Carmen?"

The cowboy tipped his hat. "Good morning, Miss Wall." He smiled his gorgeous smile again. "I saw her last night, after she left here. I was walking back from Memorial Park and we ran into each other just outside her house."

"Memorial Park?"

"Yeah. The company I work for had their Oktoberfest celebration down there. Some kind of shindig it was too."

"Ah," nodded Rachel. "Well, please, come in. Carmen and Eric should be here soon. Would you like a cup of coffee?"

"That sounds great!"

Rachel led the way to the kitchen. "Have a seat," she said, pointing to the two stools under the counter. Trace put his hat on the counter and pulled out a stool.

"How do you take your coffee?" she asked without turning to face him. *I cannot look at him. I'll gawk like a school girl.*

"Black," he said. "Nice place you have here."

"Thanks. It needs some work, but I like it."

After handing him his cup, she quickly turned back to the coffee pot. She felt uneasy with her back to him, but she needed a few seconds to talk herself into maturity. *It should be against the law for any man to be that good looking.... but you can't trust men, Rachel. Don't let your guard down...ever.* Taking a deep breath, she grabbed her cup and turned around to face her unexpected guest.

Blowing on her coffee, she watched him from over the rim of the cup. "So, you live over by Carmen?"

Before he could answer, Mikey bolted into the kitchen. "Why, hey there," Rachel said cheerfully. But instead of running to her and wrapping himself around her ankles as he did every morning, he jumped up onto Trace's lap, leaned against his chest, and purred loudly.

"Mikey, get down."

"Oh, it's alright," Trace said, softly stroking the cat's head. "I had a tabby just like him once. His name was Tigger. Just up and disappeared one day, though."

"Oh, I'm so sorry."

"Yeah, I think he was hit by a car or something. I never did find out."

The cat gently pawed at his face.

"He's never been so, so..."

"Assertive? Tabby's can be that way. Calm, cool, collected one minute, then bam, they're all whacked out the next."

"Well, he's never taken to anyone like this before, but he needs to get down and eat so I can let him out before we go."

The whole time she fixed Mikey's breakfast, the cat leaned against Trace and purred, but when Rachel set the bowl on the floor, he didn't hesitate to jump from Trace's lap and run to it.

"I've never," whispered Rachel.

After he'd licked up every morsel, Rachel picked him up and carried him outside. "You be a good boy today, Mikey. I won't be gone long."

Stepping back into the kitchen, she heard Carmen's jovial laugh. She and Eric were coming through the front door and chatting with Trace. All three of them were laughing like they'd known each other all their lives.

"Well, I can see I don't need to make introductions," she said as she joined them. "Did you two have coffee yet?"

"We're good," answered Carmen. "In fact, we figured we're going to have to make a couple trips, so we better get goin'. We're burning daylight."

"Let me grab my jacket." Rachel turned to go into her bedroom, but stopped, her gasp filling the small living room.

Carmen came up beside her and glanced down the hall. "What?"

"Mikey," she whispered.

Carmen could see him sitting beside the empty bowl in the kitchen. "Yeah, so? He looks hungry."

"I, I just fed him," Rachel stammered, not taking her eyes from the cat. "He ate, and then I put him outside. He should be outside."

"Well, apparently he found a way back inside, just like he did last night," Carmen said in her 'matter of fact' voice. "Go get your jacket. I'll tend to Mikey."

Rachel looked helplessly at her friend.

"Go on. I can handle a cat."

"But why, how?"

Carmen leaned toward her friend and whispered, "Its ok, Rach. Go get your jacket."

Reluctantly, Rachel walked into her bedroom.

Carmen went to the kitchen, picked up the cat, and gently pulled his face up towards hers. His pale green eyes darted away from her gaze. He was scared.

Kissing the top of his head, she scratched lightly under his collar. "It's ok, Mikey," she said. "Everything's alright. A little messed up right now, but alright."

With Mikey in her arms, she walked to the kitchen door and peered out the window. Below, looking up at her with golden, forlorn eyes, sat another yellow tabby. "Just as I thought. Looks like our zombie party has started."

She glanced at Mikey again. "At least I know how to tell the two of you apart." Setting Mikey back down on the floor, she opened another can of food. He wrapped himself around her ankles and purred heavily.

She paused to scratch his head. "I bet you are hungry."

Carmen put the bowl in front of the hungry cat and stroked his bobbing head. "You're not use to sharing, are you? Surprises me that phantom cat would eat at all, but at least we now know to feed two of you."

CHAPTER EIGHT

Carmen blotted her face with the back of her sleeve. "Man, whose stupid idea was it to go to yard sales anyway. And why did you buy so much stuff, Rach?"

Rachel threw a mean look at her but didn't say anything.

Eric pushed the tailgate shut, turned Carmen by the shoulders, and guided her to the front of the truck. "That's it. Let's get these things back to Rachel's, then it's pizza time. I'm buyin'."

Rachel slid onto the backseat beside Trace and poked Carmen on the shoulder. "Now *we*, meaning you and me, get to put all this away since it was your stupid idea to go to yards sales and insist I buy stuff to, how'd you put it, make my house a home."

"I'll be happy to help," offered Trace.

Rachel glanced over her shoulder to check traffic. "Oh, no, Carmen's not getting out of this. She and I will take care of it all next week. Right now, we're just going to unload the truck one last time and then eat. We all need to enjoy what's left of the weekend."

The two rode in silence for a while, listening to Eric and Carmen trade barbs. Finally, Trace asked, "Do you still work at the lab?"

Rachel nodded. "Yeah, I'm still there. Haven't climbed the

ladder, but I love what I do so I'll probably be there till I die."

Trace grinned. "One of the lucky ones."

Rachel looked surprised. "What do you mean by that?"

"Just that once in a while, some lucky stiff actually gets to do what he loves for the rest of his life, or at least until he retires."

"Do you feel that way about your job?"

"No. I'm not one of the lucky ones."

"What do you do?"

"I work the midnight shift over at the dog food plant." He glanced at Rachel and caught her shriveling her nose. "I know; pretty disgusting. But at least they don't make dog food out of horse meat anymore."

"Oh, I'm sorry. I didn't mean to..."

"It's ok."

"Earlier you mentioned you use to work at the lab. What did you do there?"

"I worked in the cryogenics department."

Rachel's eyes widened. "Really? I heard rumors we had one, but I've never seen it."

"Oh, it's there. I don't know if they use it anymore, but a long time ago, those tombcicles were used for everything from freezing sperm to storing decapitated heads."

Rachel's mouth dropped open. "You're kidding me. I don't think they do any freezing now, especially heads. There's no talk of it, and surely if that was going on, there'd be talk."

Trace shrugged. "Don't know. I've not been in that line of work for a long time."

"What did you do, specifically, at the lab?"

He looked over at her, his eyebrows raised. "Are you sure you really want to know?"

"Well, unless you killed people, how bad could it be?"

"No, I didn't kill people, but I retrieved parts from the morgue and took them to the lab for freezing. Saw lots of stuff."

"Heads?"

Trace nodded. "Heads, brains, hearts."

Rachel covered her face with her hands and looked at Trace between her fingers. "And they really thought parts could be used in the future?"

Trace snickered. "Well, say some rich guy believes time and technology will bring him back to life so, upon his death, he bequeaths his head to science. The lab freezes it and works on coming up with that special technology. In the meantime, the deceased's family pays out the ying-yang to keep Daddy's head on ice, but regardless of cost, everyone sees it as a win-win-win situation. If that special technology arrives, the responsible company makes a mint; Daddy gets resurrected, family gets daddy back, as well as fame, I mean, imagine the publicity, and the government makes a ton."

"That's terrible," cried Rachel. "It's more about money than science."

"Now you're getting the picture."

"Is that why you left?"

"It was becoming a dangerous job," he said quietly. "I saw and knew too much. I had to, um, disappear."

"Wow," whispered Rachel. "I never would've thought..."

Eric pulled the truck into the driveway; giving instructions to Carmen, but from where Rachel was sitting, it looked like Carmen wasn't listening to him. She was looking down, her ear turned toward Trace.

"That was when the lab was involved with a bunch of crazy stuff and the government came in and, well, restructured it," Trace said a little lower.

"The cloning? That was before I was hired."

"Well, that was then, and this is now," he said, opening the door. "And if you don't mind, I like the now much better and would like to stay in it as long as I can."

"I hope you do," Rachel replied softly.

Trace threw her his drop-dead smile and without realizing it, Rachel smiled back.

An hour later, four adults and two cats were sitting in four matching chairs around Rachel's new dining table enjoying pizza and beer. Mikey was on Rachel's lap. Not laying comfortably and purring like he normally did, but rigid, eyeing the other cat that was curled up on Trace's lap.

"Where'd that cat come from?" Rachel asked. "He looks identical to Mikey, except for his eyes."

She caught the glance Carmen threw at Trace and the nod he gave back to her. Her eyes met Carmen's and held them captive. "What's going on, Car?" she asked nervously.

Playing with her napkin, Carmen cleared her throat. After doing this several times, Rachel finally grew impatient. "Are you going to answer me or give me an origami lesson?"

Finally, Carmen raised her eyes and looked at Rachel. "Remember the spell we did last night?"

Rachel looked at her like she'd lost her mind. "Yes. I remember. I mean, it was just last night."

"Well, Mr. Cat here is part of that spell."

Rachel's brow furrowed. "What?"

"Um, if you recall, I also asked for garlic."

"Oh please," Rachel said sarcastically. "Tell me yellow eyes here isn't a vampire! And didn't you specifically say, 'in human form'?"

Carmen continued to nervously play with the napkin. "Yes, Rachel. Yes, I did specifically say 'in human form'. And no, this cat isn't a vampire; however, as I said, sometimes spells have a tendency to, well, to bring the unexpected; especially if the caster hasn't ever cast the spell before."

"You said that? I don't remember you saying that!"

"Well, if I didn't, I meant to," Carmen answered sheepishly.

Rachel watched the other cat intently. It stared back at her without flinching. "Ok, so if he isn't a vampire, then he must be a ...." She looked over at Carmen. "Do you mean to tell me he's my date for Halloween?"

Carmen burst out laughing. "No, not unless you want him to be, but then you might have some explaining to do to Mikey."

"But if this cat is the 'zombie' you summoned last night, then..."

Carmen cleared her throat. "He isn't," she admitted. "Although he is a remnant of the past."

Rachel turned to her friend. "Then nothing happened?"

"Something did happen," interrupted Eric.

All eyes turned to him.

"How would you know? You weren't here when the spell was cast," said Rachel.

Eric stared dreamily at the table. "No, but I was with Carmen when it came about though. It was the weirdest, but coolest thing I've ever seen."

"What? What happened?" Rachel said eagerly. Pulling Mikey closer to her chest, she looked at Carmen and gasped. "Oh my god, the graveyard; the one by your house. Did you actually see him...?"

Carmen placed her hand on Rachel's arm. "No," she said soothingly. "Nothing like that. Eric and I were sitting on the front steps enjoying the beautiful evening, when yes, a mysterious fog rolled in, a couple of street lights flickered and then, well, Trace here just kind of strolled out of the mist and walked right up to us and told me he'd been summoned."

Trace shifted uncomfortably in his seat. "Well, it *is* October," he muttered. "Sometimes we have fog in October here in the valley. Nothing mysterious really."

Eric snickered. "Like I said, it was the coolest thing. Right out of Nightmare on 34th Street."

Carmen rolled her eyes and shook her head. "It's Nightmare on *Elm Street* and *Miracle* on 34th Street, Eric."

"Excuse me, professor! It could've been Nightmare on Sesame Street for all I care. It was still cool."

Rachel couldn't believe how nonchalant her friends were acting. "Wait a minute," she said angrily. "I don't know how you can joke around at a time like this. He told me earlier he met you guys after leaving Memorial Park, that his company's Oktoberfest was held there and...and. I mean, he lied to me, so for all we know, this guy could be a serial killer. Did you ever think of that? I mean, that spell wasn't real, Carmen. You said so. Zombies aren't real, and the spell was just in fun."

Trace took a hanky from the back pocket of his jeans. "Here," he said grimly. "I couldn't tell you the truth this morning, Rachel, but Carmen summoned me last night and I'll prove it." He wiped his forehead with the dew rag and Rachel saw, for the first time, the real color of his skin. She suddenly felt sick.

Carmen stood up. "He was dressed in what he's wearing right now when he showed up at my house last night."

She went to the kitchen and quickly grabbed another beer then fell back down into her chair. "Seems that candle, the one with the horses, cowboy hats, and boots determined how our um, summoned would be dressed, which is cool, but he definitely needed a touch of my foundation to bring some color to his face."

She sat back and closed her eyes. "Good thing I didn't pull one of the birthday candles closer, huh? We could've ended up with a clown or something and from what I've read, clowns can be worse than zombies." She couldn't help but chuckle. Rachel's glare was frozen.

Mikey fell to the floor with a thud as Rachel slowly stood to her feet, grabbing the back of her chair to steady herself. "You mean to tell me that this, this…"

"Man," Trace said softly, looking up at her.

Rachel was almost in tears. "This *man* is a zombie?"

Carmen sat quiet for a long minute. When she opened her eyes, she looked into Rachel's somber face. "Yes," she confessed. "The spell was real."

"No," Trace rebuffed sharply. He glanced at Carmen. "Not the zombie part. I'm not a zombie! I'm a, well, I'm a shadow. A shadow of consciousness, a fleeting collection of memories and experiences, an assortment of choices past, who just happened to get summoned back to this realm because of the spell you cast last night."

Carmen looked at the person sitting next to her, fully enthralled by what he was saying. "Please, explain," she coaxed. "A fleeting collection of memories and experiences? It seems you have more personalities than Sybil." Everyone thought that was funny except Rachel.

Trace noticed and turned back to her. "Would you mind having a seat while I explain this?" he asked, motioning to her empty chair.

"No thank you. I'd rather stand if you don't mind."

"Ok," he said, looking up into Rachel's eyes. "Remember today, when we were talking about my job at the lab all those years ago."

Rachel nodded.

"Well, I didn't tell you all of what happened back then."

Rachel slid into the chair.

"You're as pale as he is," whispered Carmen.

"Shh," scolded Rachel. "Go on, Trace."

"I did work as a courier, and as I said, I learned too much. I found out what was really happening at the lab, but before I could say anything to the authorities, I was..."

Carmen threw a hand to her throat. "Murdered," she blurted.

Trace smiled. "Fired. I couldn't find work until I landed the job at the dog food plant."

Carmen let out a long sigh.

"But I found out more there than I did at the lab."

Eric sat his beer on the table. Rachel could see by the look in his eyes that the jokester had been deflated. "Like what?" he asked gravely.

"I found out that human parts are bought and sold there. The plant is a front for selling organs on the black market." He hesitated for just a second. "Along with stem cells and DNA." He paused and studied each face. Rachel locked eyes with Carmen; each watching the other as their eyes grew large with revelation.

"Here, in little ol' Plum Creek?" belted Carmen. "No way."

"Yes way," nodded Trace. "In fact, places like Plum Creek are perfect for these kinds of operations because the small, unassuming community has no clue, no idea of what's going on right under their noses. Unfortunately, because of this false sense of security, they fall into the 'it won't ever happen here' mentality."

Rachel abruptly turned and faced him. "What you're saying implies that some of what was being sold on the black market starts at the lab. Like someone at the lab knows about this, and therefore, is guilty of this."

Trace lowered his eyes. "That is correct," he said quietly.

"Who?" the three asked in unison.

"I don't know," he muttered. "I never got the chance to

find out before I died."

Eric placed his elbows on the table and rested his chin on his fists. "You must've been getting *very* close."

Trace nodded. "Apparently."

Rachel's expression softened. "How did you die, Trace?"

"Car accident. This past Friday night."

Eric's ears perked up. "You mean the one that happened around six-fifteen? The one that was on the news?"

"Yep. That'd be the one. That's why I referred to myself as a shadow. I've not been dead long enough to be classified as a zombie."

"But I'd read, or heard, that man was coming back from his daughter's bah-mitzvah. Are you Jewish?" asked Carmen.

Trace smiled. He couldn't help it. "Why, is there no such thing as a Jewish zombie?"

Carmen's face turned crimson. "I'm sorry, I wasn't implying anything. You just don't look Jewish. You know, your features, your, your hat. I mean, it's clearly a cowboy hat, not a beanie."

"Kippah," Trace corrected her.

"Carmen," whispered Eric. "It's time to be quiet."

Carmen sat back into her chair and took a healthy gulp of beer.

"Are you married? I mean, were you married?" asked Rachel.

"Divorced. She filed when I lost my job at the lab. Once she was rid of me, she married a rich Jewish guy. They're raising my daughter in his faith."

"Ah," whispered Carmen.

"Getting back to the accident," interjected Eric, "were you drunk? The news said alcohol may have been to blame."

"I wasn't drunk," Trace answered sharply. "I swerved to

keep from hitting a man who was standing in the middle of the road. I didn't see him at first, it being dark and raining."

"Was *he* drunk?" asked Carmen.

"Definitely not," answered Trace.

"How can you be so sure?" asked Rachel.

"Because he was aiming a gun at me."

The word "gun" reverberated through the room.

Carmen pulled herself up to the edge of her chair. "You mean you were shot and that's what caused the accident?"

"I think so," Trace said somberly. "Like I said, I knew too much. They were out to kill me, no matter who else died. The lady was probably collateral damage."

"Whoa," Eric said holding up a hand. "Now you're talking murder."

Trace nodded in agreement. "I am," he said decisively.

"The woman," muttered Rachel, "she's in coma." Looking at Trace, her eyes searched his face. "Where are you, Trace? I mean, if you were murdered, where did the ambulance take your body?"

He shifted in his seat. "Ironically enough, they dumped me in one of the tombcicles at the lab."

"Are you kidding me?" roared Eric.

Trace smirked. "No, no joke. Whoever wanted me dead apparently thinks he can sell my body parts, so they put me on ice. If you go to the morgue, you won't find me there. Nope, I was dumped into a freezer at the lab."

"And then hopefully forgotten about?" whispered Rachel.

"I don't know. I've only been gone for a couple days, but it seems like the plan would be for them to sell what they can and forget about the rest."

"Did you recognize the man who shot you?" asked Eric.

"No. He was wearing a ski mask. That's another thing that

startled me. I saw him standing in that grassy part of the median, just after you go through the intersection, then the flash from the gun. I swerved and, well, it happened so fast."

"Do you think the woman knows anything?" asked Rachel.

"I don't know. I doubt it."

"Well, I've got my work cut out for me," she exclaimed.

Carmen's brow furrowed. "What do you mean by that?"

"Well, for the woman's sake, I've not only got to find this cure for coma that I've been working on, but I've got to find out who at the lab is participating in this illegal, not to mention immoral and unethical business."

Carmen shook her head vigorously. "Oh no you don't," she said with conviction. "You leave all of that to the police. Your job is medicine my dear friend. Remember that! Medicine."

Eric slid another beer over to Trace. "It sounds like *you and I* have a murder to solve," he said.

Carmen looked at him in disbelief. "Didn't you hear what I just said?" she said angrily. "All of this is up to the police. It's a local crime, not your league, and besides, an investigation could take years, and frankly, Trace doesn't have years."

"How long?" asked Rachel.

"Maybe a couple weeks. The only date I specified in the spell was Halloween, this Friday. I don't know what the spell allowed when it summoned him."

"But if the report has been doctored and concludes that alcohol was involved, the media will just chalk this up to another guzzler killing himself and possibly an innocent woman. No one will investigate his death," Eric argued.

Carmen rounded on him. "That's not your job, Rodriguez," she said sternly. "I know who you work for, but that could actually play against us. You can't get involved in this, Eric. If what Trace claims is true, there is a murderer out there, but you've gotta let the local police handle it. Until there's proof of external influence, you have to lay low or you could be killed too."

"But what if...."

"Not until," Carmen said vehemently, her face darkening. "As you said, alcohol will probably be noted as the leading cause of the accident, so for now, we leave well enough alone."

Eric threw his arms up in frustration. "So, I'm just supposed to sit around and eat pizza and drink beer while all this illegal stuff is going on, right here in Plum Creek?"

"That," Carmen said stoically, "should be investigated, but right now, there's no proof that Trace was murdered, and if he was, that his murder is tied to the illegal stuff at the lab."

"Of course, they're tied together," Eric answered heatedly. "And who died and made you head of the..."

"Whoa," Trace cut in, "Let's take a timeout and cool off."

Before Carmen could answer, Rachel's giggle lightened the heaviness in the room. "Trace ate pizza and drank beer!"

Eric and Carmen stopped fussing. The look of confusion on their faces made Rachel laugh harder.

Trace chuckled too. "Yes, I did."

A smile danced at the corners of Rachel's mouth. Looking at Carmen she asked, "Does that mean he can digest food?"

"Well, it does mean one thing for sure," Trace said. "I prefer pizza over brains."

She smiled back. "So, you died, came back to life, but you're not a zombie?"

Trace chuckled. "Dead is dead," he said quietly. "But no, I'm not a walking stiff that eats brains. I'm not your typical zombie. I'm just a shadow, a conscience, remember?"

"Way cool," said Eric, before taking a big swig of beer. "But, how do you, um, how do you use the bath...?"

"He doesn't," interrupted Carmen. "He has no bodily

fluids, he has no digestive system. When he eats or drinks, it all dissolves within him. It doesn't pass through him, it just, well, it just goes away."

"Awesome," said Eric.

"Good to know. I've only been zombiefied for a few hours, so I wasn't quite sure how to answer that question. Kind of wondered about it myself."

Rachel studied her friend. "How did you come to know so much about all of this," she asked curiously.

Carmen tossed her hair back. "You're not the only one who does their research, Rach. I know more than you think I do, especially when it comes to the underworld."

Eric got up; kissed the top of Carmen's head. "You never cease to amaze me," he whispered.

Carmen looked up at him. "You can't tell a soul about this," she said pleadingly. "I know it's unbelievable, way cool, bizarre and freaky, but you have to keep quiet about *all* of this."

Eric gawked at her, his eyes wide and bright. "Aw, come on," he jeered. "You mean I can't go around saying things like, 'Hey guys, guess what! My girlfriend's a witch, and you wanna know what that crazy crone did the other night? She summoned a zombie. Yeah, no kidding. She just opened a book, whispered the magic words all mystic like, and poof, this zombie came out of the fog. Wanna meet 'im?"

Eric smirked. "If I went around talking like that, I'd be locked up in the loony bin." Looking over at Trace, he sniggered. "No offense, man."

"None taken, but that does raise the question. Why am I here, besides this Halloween thing?"

Rachel held a finger up to Trace. "Hold that question for one second, please." She turned her gaze to Carmen. "First things first. Did he just call you girlfriend?"

"Oops," laughed Eric.

Carmen blushed and nudged Eric's arm with her elbow. "See, you can't keep anything quiet."

She turned to Rachel. "And you. You don't miss a beat, do you? You're the only person I know who has the living-dead sitting at their dining room table and you want to know about my love life."

"Just answer the question," insisted Rachel.

"Yes," Carmen said firmly. "We're officially dating."

"And when were you going to tell me?"

"We thought you'd figure it out."

"Uh, no," Rachel said defiantly. "We don't hold secrets, Carmen, remember?"

Carmen looked away. "You're right. No secrets."

"Good. Well, then, um, great. I'm glad you finally came to your senses and saw what a great guy Eric is. So yes, you have my blessing. The two of you may date."

Eric shook his head. "Girls!" he mumbled. "Well, now that our love life has been officially blessed by the great Doctor Wall, I've got to go to the little boy's room. Unfortunately, beer doesn't just evaporate in me. While I'm gone, maybe you two can answer Trace's question? What *is* he doing here?"

The women looked at each other.

"I don't know," said Rachel. "You summoned him."

"I didn't think it would work," mumbled Carmen.

"But it did," Eric yelled as the bathroom door closed. "And now we have to figure out what he's going to do until Friday night."

Trace answered for them. "I was thinking about doing some serious sleuthing. Bum around town for a while."

"You'll need some serious makeup," Carmen added.

While Carmen was explaining how she would take care of that issue, Rachel's cell phone buzzed. The phone number on the face was Doctor Aberman's, from the Lab.

Doctor Aberman? The Lab?

She jumped up and walked to the kitchen, a little apprehensive, but when she heard the voice on the other end, the apprehension was quickly replaced by fear. She stood frozen at the kitchen sink. The laughter of her three friends filled her tiny house, but Doctor Aberman's hysteria deafened her to everything.

"Calm down, Doctor Aberman. I'm sure it's not…"

"No sir, only me. I was the last one to leave Friday night."

"Yes, sir, I set the alarm. I made sure of it."

"I don't understand. How could that be?"

"Did you call the police?"

"Yes, I understand. I'll come right down."

"Yes, sir, I understand. I'll see you in a few minutes."

Rachel turned her phone off and plopped down onto a stool. She was so numb she didn't realize she had started to cry. Carmen suddenly appeared across from her; Eric and Trace came up behind her.

Carmen caressed Rachel's face, wiping away the tears. "You're as pale as a ghost, girl," she said, pushing a strand of loose hair out of Rachel's face. "What was that about?"

Rachel's red eyes searched Carmen's face. "That was Doctor Aberman," she whispered. "He wants me to come down to the lab right away."

"I got that Rach," she said calmly, "but why do you have to meet with Doctor Aberman now?"

The answer came in a very hushed voice. "Robbery."

"Robbery? The lab?"

Rachel nodded. "His office. Someone broke into his office."

"Ok, I'm sorry to hear that, but what does that have to do

with you?"

"He said the police," Rachel's face fell into her hands. "The police suspect me," she cried.

"That's ludicrous! How would you, no, better question, why would you rob the lab? I mean, what in the world?"

Eric squeezed Carmen's shoulders. "Calm down, babe," he whispered.

Carmen looked up at him. "I know," she said excitedly, "but come on. Rachel? Apparently, Doctor Aberman doesn't know her very well."

"That could be true," Eric said evenly, "but the best thing to do is take Rachel down to the lab so she can find out what this is all about. You being upset isn't going to help her."

"Ugh!" groaned Carmen. "I hate it when you're right!"

Eric leaned down and kissed her cheek. "I know."

Trace put a hand on Rachel's shoulder. "I'll go with you, Rachel."

She wiped her face with the back of her sleeve and looked up at him. "But what if someone recognizes you?"

"Not likely," he said. "I didn't see Doc Aberman much when I worked there. I'm pretty sure he wouldn't know me from Adam. But there's another reason I have to go with you."

Rachel's eyebrows arched.

"I have to slip back into the tombcicle."

"Why?"

"Because I need the freezing temperatures to continue to, to..." He looked helplessly over at Carmen.

"Um, survive?" she answered.

Rachel's eyes lit up. "Oh, the freezer preserves your current state."

"Yes," Trace said, exhaling deeply. "Leave it up to a

scientist to word it perfectly. If I don't refreeze, so to speak, I'll fall apart."

"Fall apart?" asked Eric.

"Yeah. Literally. I'll fall to pieces if my core goes above 58.6 degrees."

Carmen grimaced. "Really? Well, that's disgusting. Do all zombies do that?"

"Carmen. Enough!" Eric said sternly. "We've got more important things to worry about right now."

"Ok," Carmen said, somewhat distracted. "Let's go find out what's going on down at the lab and Trace, you jump back into the freezer."

Carmen took Rachel's face in her hands and gazed into her eyes. "Don't worry my friend. If it takes all the herbs in my garden, all the rituals in my books, all the spells from the four corners, we will find out who did this."

"Thank you," Rachel whispered. "I appreciate that, but I'm going to use my own magic too."

"What do you mean?" asked Carmen. "Are you coming back to..."

"Prayer," Rachel interrupted, nervously rubbing her hands together. "It's been such a long time, but I think it's time I practice the kind of 'magic' I was taught as a child. Somewhere deep down, I believe there is still some faith in my cynical heart."

Carmen helped Rachel up from the stool, wiped the tears from her face and walked arm in arm with her toward the door. "It may take all of what we both have then," she said softly. "Miracles and magic; it may take it all."

CHAPTER NINE

The large oaks that lined the lane down to the lab and around the building had been dressed in bright colored leaves just a few days ago, but now they were stark and bare, their branches draped only with pulsing flashes of blue and red lights. Rachel's heart beat hard against her chest. "I've never seen so many police in my life," she said nervously. "There's gotta be at least twenty black and whites here."

Eric sat on the edge of the back seat to look over Rachel's shoulder. "This looks really serious," he said low. Something in his voice made Rachel's heart pound harder.

She swung the car into an empty parking spot on the back row of the lot and turned off the engine. Quickly, she glanced at her friends then back at the army of deputies. "You three stay in the car," she said firmly. "I need to find Doctor Aberman and get to the bottom of this. I'll be back as soon as I can."

"You can't leave us here, Rach," yelped Carmen. "The wait will kill me."

"You'll just be in the way, Car. Police don't like people who get in the way. Besides, you wouldn't be able to touch or say anything, so just sit tight. I'll be back as soon as I can."

"She's right," said Trace. "You're safer in here."

Rachel turned to him. "You too. For now, anyway." She glanced around the car again. "All of you stay here."

Sliding out from behind the wheel, she steadied her feet on the asphalt. Watching the chaotic scene below, she slowly stood to her feet. Squeaky voices crackled from radios; others, more pronounced, floated from small huddles. Orders cracked the brisk night air; the sound of boots scraping against the pavement as officers ran to where they were commanded to go. Yellow crime tape crisscrossed the front doors of the lab. Rachel's knees trembled, and she slumped against the car.

Closing her eyes, she searched her soul for confidence. "You're Rachel Wall," she whispered. "You've nothing to be afraid of here. This is your haven, and no one can take that from you. Stay calm, and before long everyone will believe in your innocence."

She held onto the car until she knew she could stand on her own. Squaring her shoulders, she walked toward the lab. The penetrating eyes of policemen followed her; their mumbles and whispers fading in her wake. Getting closer to the building, a deputy stepped in front of her, one hand wrapped around the butt of his AR-15, the other holding the barrel. He did a quick visual then firmly said, "I'm sorry Miss, but you can't go in there."

He doesn't understand, she thought. *I don't want to be here; I've been called here. All I want to do is find Doctor Aberman.*

"But I was told to come down here."

"Who told you to come here?" he growled.

A searing pain ripped through her temples. She cringed and threw a hand up to her head, but the quick move almost cost her. When she opened her eyes, she was looking down the barrel of his rifle.

"Whoa," she groaned. "What are you doing?"

"No Miss," he said curtly. "What are *you* doing?"

"I, uh, my head hurts. I'm getting a headache. I was just rubbing my forehead."

The deputy lowered his weapon. "Don't make any more sudden moves," he warned.

"Listen, Deputy, um," she leaned in slightly to read his badge.

"Jackson," he said.

"Yes, well, Deputy Jackson. Believe me; I don't want to be here anymore than you do. I normally spend my Sunday evenings curled up on the couch with my cat; watching some boring show on television, so please, stop getting all ninja on me and just tell me where I can find my boss. He called and told me to meet him here."

"Who's your boss?"

"Doctor Aberman. Bruce Aberman."

"Who are you?"

"Rachel Wall. Doctor Rachel Wall."

The deputy stepped aside and took Rachel by the elbow. "In that case, you need to come with me."

Rachel pulled her elbow from his grip. "I can walk on my own, thank you." The man's face turned to stone. He gripped his AR-15 tighter.

Stopping in her tracks, Rachel looked up into his face; shades of blue and red bouncing off everything around them. "Are you really going to shoot me with that?" she asked wearily. "Because if you are, just do it. Right now, I don't care. My head is killing me, and I don't care. But if not, lower that gun and tell me where I can find Doctor Aberman."

The deputy's facial features softened a little and he pointed to a car parked closest to the front doors. "He's over there, in that squad car."

She glanced in the direction he was pointing and nodded. "Thank you, Deputy Jackson. I can find the way from here."

He let her go, but she could feel his eyes on her as she made her way through the sea of black and whites.

Squinting against the blinding lights, she finally made it to the car and tapped on the dark passenger-side window. "Doctor Aberman?"

A tall, middle aged black man stepped out of the car from the driver's side. The insignia on his collar told her he was the man in charge. "Can I help you?" he asked.

"My name is Doctor Rachel Wall. I'm a colleague of Doctor Aberman. Is he with you?"

The Sheriff walked around the car and opened the back-passenger door. He stood at least a foot taller than she and the look in his eyes told her he was no one to tangle with. "Please get in," he said gruffly.

She peered inside. Doctor Aberman was sitting in the front seat. Without much thought, she ducked her head and slid in behind him. It wasn't until the Sheriff shut the door, she realized she was sitting in 'the cage'. A lump swelled in her throat, making it hard to breathe, until she looked at the back of Doctor Aberman's head. If anyone could clear her of this, it was him. He knew her projects. For Pete's sake, he assigned her projects. All he had to do was vouch for her and everything would be fine.

"Doctor Aberman, what happened?" she whispered, leaning toward his ear.

The doctor turned slightly in his seat. "I've been robbed Rachel."

"Yes, sir, I know that. You told me that over the phone, but of what? Why all the cops? What really happened here?"

The driver's door swung open with a fierce jolt; Sheriff Jones climbed into the car. He laid his hat on the seat then adjusted the review mirror until he could see Rachel's face. She looked up into the reflection of his large, brown eyes.

"Don't say anything more, Doctor," he said with a not-so-subtle firmness. "I'll ask the questions or pass out need to know information from here on out." The doctor's eyes searched Rachel's face for a quick second before he nodded and slowly turned away from her.

The Sheriff's eyes locked with Rachel's in the mirror. "Miss Wall, are you aware of what was taken from Doctor Aberman's office?"

Rachel shook her head. "No. How would I? I just got here."

The eyebrows in the mirror raised. The sheriff apparently hadn't missed the hint of sarcasm in her voice.

"Are you aware that your fingerprints are all over the Doctor's office?"

Rachel hesitated.

"Did you not understand my question, Miss Wall?"

Rachel slid back onto the seat. "I understood it perfectly, Sheriff. Of course, I'm aware my fingerprints are all over his office. Doctor Aberman is the lead scientist of this Laboratory. All of us are in and out of his office all the time, asking questions, retrieving files. I'm in there for a myriad of reasons. Sometimes I go in just to shoot the breeze. Is that a crime?"

Doctor Aberman glanced over his shoulder at her. His face stern, but he stopped short of scolding her sarcasm.

The Sheriff sighed. "Miss Wall, are you aware you're one word, one gesture, one blink away from being arrested?"

Rachel bolted up and wrapped her fingers around the steel fencing. "Oh no you don't," she said coldly. "Just because I was the last to leave on Friday, just because I go into Doctor Aberman's office, just because you have no one else to blame this on and you need to close this as soon as possible for whatever political reasons, you're not going to pin this on me! You've nothing to charge me with, Sheriff. I'll cooperate and answer your questions, but you're not going to sit there and threaten me."

This time Doctor Aberman turned until he could see

Rachel's face. "Be careful," he warned. "No one is accusing you of anything...yet, but right now, it doesn't look good. Don't make matters worse by copping an attitude."

Rachel turned to her boss. "Doctor Aberman, I was here Friday night until around six o'clock, but I was in my lab. I only left once to use the..." Right then, she remembered the light. "Oh my god!"

The Sheriff and the Doctor turned and looked at her. "What?" they said in unison.

Rachel looked at the Sheriff. "Friday night. I left my lab to use the restroom, and when I came out; I noticed a light underneath Doctor Aberman's office door."

"Did you go in?" asked Aberman.

Rachel fell back into the seat and laid her head against the headrest. Closing her eyes, she sighed heavily. "No, I couldn't. I knocked a couple times. I even tried the handle, but the door was locked. Then..."

"Go on."

Rachel sat up to find the sheriff's cold eyes searching her face. "When I turned to leave, I noticed the light had been turned off. At first, I thought my eyes were playing tricks on me. I'd been working with the microscope all day and my eyes were tired, so I thought maybe I had just imagined seeing a light. I mean, I wasn't sure I had really seen anything. Then I remembered the automatic turn off system and figured that it had kicked in and the system turned the light off in his office."

"Did you hear anything?" asked Doctor Aberman.

Rachel looked over at him. "Yes," she said nodding. "Yes, I did. I heard what sounded like papers being shuffled. Very faintly, but when I knocked and called your name, they stopped. I listened a bit longer, but I heard nothing, so again, I chalked it up to the automatic system and being tired."

Doctor Aberman squeezed the bridge of his nose.

"Did you think to call the police?" asked the Sheriff, turning in his seat to watch Rachel through the mirror.

"Well, no. Why bother the police over an automatic light system?" She hesitated a second then added, "But I guess if I had, I wouldn't be sitting here now, would I?"

The Sheriff nodded. "Got that right. Now, instead of explaining the situation, you're explaining yourself."

Rachel ignored his comment and turned to the Doctor. "I thought you were in New England for a few days?"

Doctor Aberman stared ahead; his face clouded with concern. "We were," he said, nodding slowly. "Edith took ill, so we came home early. I thought I'd drive over here to check emails, sort things out before flying back tomorrow to speak at the conference. But when I opened the door...files everywhere...chairs overturned...my office ransacked..."

"I'm so sorry," Rachel whispered. That's all she knew to say.

Sheriff Jones' stark voice broke the silence. "Miss Wall, are you aware of what Doctor Aberman has been researching?"

"Not particularly," she answered. "Although he helps with our research, he doesn't share much about his projects since they're usually classified."

The Sheriff looked at Aberman. "Would you like to tell her, Doctor?"

Doctor Aberman sighed heavily. Long seconds passed before he finally said, "Cloning."

Rachel couldn't believe what she'd just heard. "Cloning? Cloning what?"

"That isn't anything you need to know," answered the Sheriff. "As you said, his research is classified; however, it seems someone is interested in what he's doing."

"Why? Who? I mean, why do you think that?"

"Because those are the files that were taken," answered the

Doctor. "And not just the paper files, but my computer hard drive as well."

Rachel's mind raced. Finally, she mumbled, "But you know what happened years ago. Why would you be researching that again?"

"Classified," snapped the Sheriff.

"And you think I took his files?"

"We're not sure at this moment, but we're considering it."

"And why would you think that of me?" she asked indifferently.

The Sheriff was still watching her through the mirror. She felt like an organism under the microscope. "Well, let's see," he said with a smirk. "Attention, ego, spite, resentment, fame, fortune, the list goes on Doctor Wall. You've made it known that you detest being classified as a junior scientist, so you could have done this to make a name for yourself."

Rachel scowled at his reflection. "That's preposterous," she said heatedly.

"Is it? You steal the doctor's work and claim it as your own. I don't think that's too preposterous."

Red heat burst up Rachel's neck and across her face. "You can search my house, my lab, my desk, everything 'til the cows come home," she said angrily, "but you won't find anything that belongs to Doctor Aberman, especially files regarding cloning."

"Oh, we intend to Miss Wall. Once we get that warrant, we intend to."

Rachel opened the door.

"Where do you think you're going?" the Sheriff asked irritably.

"Back to my car," she answered coldly.

"No, I'm afraid you're not. You'll be staying with me for a while."

"But I've got family waiting for me in my car. Can I at least give them my keys, so they can go home?"

"Who are they?"

"Well, a very close friend, who's like my sister, her boyfriend, and..." Rachel thought for a second. *Would it be wise to mention Trace?*

"And who?"

Rachel cast her eyes downward. "No one, that's all."

The Sheriff rolled his window down and waved a deputy over to the car. "Please walk Doctor Wall to her car so she can give her friend the keys. When she's done, escort her back here. Got it?"

"Yes, sir," said the young man. He opened the door for Rachel; hesitating only a second when the Sheriff said, "Oh, and son, find out exactly who is in that vehicle."

The deputy nodded and took Rachel's elbow. This time, she didn't resist. When they got closer to the car, Carmen rolled down the window. "What's going on?" she said quietly, noting Rachel's escort.

"I'm not at liberty to say," Rachel answered. "But here, take my keys, go get Eric's truck and go home. I may be here awhile. I'll call you as soon as I can."

Carmen's face fell; her eyes wild and her breathing labored. "I can't leave you here alone, Rachel. I need to..."

"Go home, Carmen. You've got classes tomorrow and I'll be fine."

Carmen's liquid eyes searched Rachel's face. "Are you sure?"

Rachel nodded, slightly smiling. "I'm sure." She glanced inside the car, her eyes scanning the dark interior. She finally looked questioningly at Carmen. Carmen didn't say a word; she just glanced at the lab. Rachel understood.

"So, see you soon."

The young deputy walked around the car, peering in the windows. "Who's that man in the back seat?" he asked loudly.

Carmen glanced over at Eric. He sat up so the deputy could see him better. "The name's Eric Rodriguez," he said without hesitating. "I'm a friend of Miss O'Leary here and Doctor Wall."

"Just the two of you?" asked the deputy, looking through the car again.

"Yes, sir," said Eric. "Just us two, sitting here, waiting for the keys so we can go home. Had a long day moving furniture and stuff that Doctor Wall bought at yard sales yesterday. I know that doesn't sound very exciting, but that's what we did today, just the two of us, or, Er, the three of us actually, counting the good doctor here."

The deputy snickered and knocked on the hood of the car with a knuckle. "Go on," he said.

Carmen slid over to the driver's side and after getting settled, looked up at Rachel. "Don't worry. We'll see you soon."

Walking back to the Sheriff's car, the sound of an engine roaring to life, rays of headlights cutting across the parking lot, and tires grinding against the asphalt sent a feeling of loneliness through Rachel like she'd never felt before.

She got back into the patrol car behind the Doctor and laid her head against the headrest. The deputy mumbled phrases like 'Rodriguez,' 'talks too much,' and 'good to go' to the Sheriff. She closed her eyes, took a deep breath, and tried to relax, but the red and blue explosions that battered the back of her eyelids made it impossible.

CHAPTER TEN

S he didn't realize she'd dozed off until the car turned and her head slid to the side of the headrest. Her mouth and eyes were dry. Trying to sit up, she felt sluggish, like her insides were made of cotton. She fell back, squinting at the line of white lights that zipped past them. "Where are we going?" she mumbled.

"To the station," answered Jones. "The warrant's ready and I want to review it before I send my detectives out to start their search. Plus, I need your written statement."

Rachel glanced at her watch. "Will this take long? I've got important work to do in the morning."

He looked at her through the mirror. "It will take as long as it takes, Miss Wall. Your important work will have to wait."

"But it could be a matter of life and death," she said firmly, making herself sit up this time.

"Well, our investigation means about the same for you, figuratively anyway. Now, make things easier on yourself and let us do our job. Hopefully, when we're done with ours, you can go back to yours."

It was then Rachel realized she and the Sheriff were the only two people in the car. "Where's Doctor Aberman?"

"Don't worry about the doctor. He's safe."

"You let him go, but not me?"

"We're not investigating him, Miss Wall."

Rachel closed her eyes and rubbed her temples. "Oh, good lord," she grumbled. "I didn't do anything Sheriff, except work Friday night."

"Well then, once we're done with the search, I'll let you go home. We'll consider you a non-person of interest; albeit I strongly recommend you don't leave town. So why don't you look at all this inconvenience as a good thing, from the perspective of process of elimination."

An image of Sherlock Holmes popped into her head, "Ok," she muttered. "Whatever you say." She closed her eyes again until they got to the station.

Inside, the Sheriff pointed to a desk on the far side of the room. "Have a seat over there. Sergeant Finley will be here momentarily to take your statement." He left her, and she made her way across the noisy pit. She plopped into a cold metal folding-chair as her eyes wandered across the desk beside her. A few folders sporting coffee cup rings; the cup itself sitting on a pad of paper on the opposite corner; a half-eaten doughnut teetering on the edge of the desk, saved from the fall by a pen that had been stuck through it. A paper clip snake slithered around the base of the desk lamp.

Pens were strewn everywhere, some looking as if they had just been burped up from the slightly ajar tummy drawer. Rachel pushed away some of the papers to clear a spot on the desk for her elbow. She rested her chin in the palm of her hand and looked around again.

A manila folder, victim of the leaky coffee cup, caught her eye. Cocking her head to the side to read what had been scribbled across the tab; it took a minute before the name registered.

Her jaw muscles flexed; her eyes darted around the room. The desk in front of her was occupied by an officer who was processing a hooker who was either stoned or drunk, it didn't matter to Rachel. She took advantage of the opportunity.

With her chin still resting in the palm of her hand, she nonchalantly took in the room, searching casually for surveillance cameras. From where she sat, she didn't see any. She was after all in Plum Creek, but taking precautionary measures anyway, she covered her fingertips with a tissue and carefully moved the coffee cup from the writing pad, then, just in case, blew her nose. She stood, calmly looking for the trashcan. Seeing it, she edged over to it and while dropping the tissue, covertly covered the file with the tablet, picked them up together and sat back down. One fluid, smooth move. Without hesitating, she grabbed a pen from the desk with one hand and with the other, slid the file into her purse. A quick glance to make sure the file was hidden, she leaned over the pad and began to write.

An hour later a heavyset officer came through the pit, angrily shoving chairs out of the aisle as he walked toward the desk. Rachel signed her name to the paper and looked up at the clock. It was a few minutes past mid-night. She noted the time under her signature.

The officer grabbed the back of the desk chair and fell into it; squirming around a few seconds to adjust his large bottom.

"You Rachel Wall?" he asked coarsely. His flabby jaws jiggled as he spoke.

Not having to fake a yawn, she said, "I am."

He grabbed the cup of cold coffee and slurped down a mouthful of the thick, inky drink while his other hand rummaged through the mess on the desk. "What the...? Where's that blasted pad?"

Rachel held up the tablet. "Looking for this?"

The officer's face turned molten red; he grabbed it out of her hands. "You always take stuff that isn't yours?" he barked.

Rachel's back stiffened. "I did not *take* your tablet, nor did

I take anything from Doctor Aberman, if that's what you're implying."

The man grunted and slapped the tablet down onto the desk. "Whatever," he mumbled. He shoved a pen and the pad back over to Rachel. "Give me your statement and make it quick."

Rachel pushed them back to him. "I already did," she said coolly.

The big man's beady eyes moved across the pad. Rachel, try as she might, couldn't help but sneer as she watched the crimson thread flow up his neck again. "Well... I... you," he stammered.

Rachel grabbed her purse and stood up. "It's all there," she said, letting the aggravation seep into her voice. "I even listed everything I bought at the ten thousand-yard sales I was drug to on Saturday. Now, while you read it, process it, shove it, I really don't care what you do with it, I'm gonna go home. I need to get some sleep before I go back to work sometime today."

"Sit down, Miss Wall," he growled.

"Do you have reason to charge me?"

"It doesn't matter what I have or do not have." His heavy face turned darker with every word. "Sit down!"

Rachel shifted feet. She leaned over the desk until she was almost nose-to-nose with the man. "Reason or not Thomas?"

The officer stood up so fast the desk slid into Rachel's thighs, but before she could complain about it, he was in her face. "Look Wall," he roared. "I'm tired too. I've been running through town following leads, trying to solve cases since four o'clock *yesterday* morning, and then I get a call to work a search warrant on *your* house. I should've been home hours ago, but no, little Miss Witch Bit..."

"That's enough Thomas," sounded a tired, but gruff voice.

Rachel looked past the cop and into the Sheriff's face. She

was never so happy to see someone she really didn't want to see.

Thomas' shoulders dropped, but he didn't take his small, snake-like eyes off Rachel's face. She didn't move her eyes either but accepted the stand off without flinching. Slowly, he turned, grabbed his chair, and sat down.

"Does he have your statement?" asked the Sheriff.

Rachel continued to glare at the cop. "Yes, he does," she hissed.

"Then you are free to go."

Her eyes jumped to the Sheriff's face. "Are you done with whatever it was you needed to do?"

"Yes, we are Miss Wall, but as I said before, don't leave town."

"I'll be here, Sheriff. I don't mind cooperating with the police, but I refuse to work with this deputy," she said, pointing at Thomas.

"Corporal," he snarled.

"Whatever," snapped Rachel, "I'll see Finley, or whoever, but not him!"

"Understood," said the Sheriff. "If we need anything else, I'll be in touch."

"Thank you."

At the doors of the station, she stopped to call a taxi. Glancing back, the corners of her mouth curled upward ever so slightly as Corporal Thomas followed the Sheriff into his office. Finally, in the middle of this whole mess, she had something to smile about.

CHAPTER ELEVEN

The wheels of her chair skated across the tile floor as she rolled back and forth, sorting the clutter on her desk. It seemed like ages since she sat in front of her microscope, wrote in her notebooks, or ordered a slide from the basement fat man. She picked her coffee cup up and looked at the dark crust of dried coffee. Her life hadn't been boring, it had been peaceful. "I'll never take things for granted again," she whispered.

She sat the cup down and carefully studied the room. It was just as she'd left it; undisturbed, almost tranquil. A hint of happiness fluttered in her chest. It was so good to be back in her space, to work, and she was glad she had plenty to keep her busy.

Stepping quietly out of her lab, she made her way down the hall to a small room marked the freezer. Before going in, she shot a glance at Aberman's office. Yellow police tape crisscrossed the door. To think she had stood so close to that door with an intruder sitting just a few feet away made her shudder.

Tearing her eyes away from the crime scene, she turned back to the freezer and palmed the doorknob. Once inside, she grabbed some goggles and a pair of gloves and quickly put them on before walking through the wintry blast of air and over to the metal shelves. Without much fuss, she found the Petri dish she'd put there a few nights before and slid it into the pocket of her lab coat. Turning to leave, she heard a voice.

"Rachel, is that you?"

She glanced around the room. "Trace?"

A dark figure stepped out from behind a metal rack.

"Hey, beautiful. Come here often?"

She giggled. "Actually, I do."

"How'd things go down at the station?"

"Fine. You know, same old same old. Write down your statement, sign this confession."

"Sorry you had a bad night."

"I can't stay in here too long," she said rubbing her arms.

"I know. I think I can go out for a bit, but I want to make sure no one sees me."

"Are you afraid of someone seeing you here, at the Lab?"

"Yeah. It's been awhile since I've wandered the halls during work hours."

Rachel shivered. "It'll be alright. Aberman's not here and the others won't take the time to notice. Now, come on before I freeze." She walked briskly to the door and waved him to follow.

A few minutes later, Trace was sitting across from Rachel in her work lab. "So, this is where the great Doctor Wall makes world changing discoveries?"

Rachel grabbed a visitor's badge from the middle drawer of her desk and tossed it to him. "Just in case," she said grinning. "And, yes, it is." She pulled the Petri dish out of her pocket and held it up. "And this little dish here may be my greatest discovery of all."

Eager to check out her experiment, she quickly twisted the lid off and looked inside, her eyes wide with excitement. But the smile immediately disappeared; her brows furrowed deeply across her forehead. She couldn't believe what she was looking at, or what she wasn't looking at. Finally, she raised her head. A flame of anger crossed her eyes, but her face was blank of emotion.

"What Rachel? What is it?" asked Trace.

"It's, it's..."

Trace stepped around the desk and peered into the dish. "What Rachel, I don't see anything?"

"That's just it. It's gone. This dish has been scraped clean. My experiment is gone."

"Are you sure it's your dish?"

Her hands were shaking so badly she had a tough time tipping the cover over to look at the tape. "My initials are on the tape, just where I put them."

"Maybe someone switched the tape."

"Who? Who would do that?"

Trace put his hand on her shoulder. "I think you know who, Rachel. Someone you trust or did at one time."

She sunk into her chair and covered her face with her hands. "Trace, do you think this is related to the robbery?"

"Yes, Rachel," he said quietly. "But you need to keep this to yourself."

Her liquid eyes searched his face. "Not report this to the Sheriff?"

"No," he answered.

Rachel closed her eyes and swallowed hard. "Why?" she gasped. "It would prove that I am actually a victim too, not the perpetrator."

"No, actually, if you report this now, the police could use it against you, saying this proves you were trying to go above Aberman's head and work on unknown and unapproved projects, then you destroyed your own experiment to make it look like you were a victim of the robbery and not the robber. This dish could actually incriminate you."

Rachel fought back the tears. "My lord," she whispered.

"What was this experiment for, Rachel?"

"Coma," she said quietly, picking up the dish and turning it in her hands. "I concocted a formula from an old equation I found, mixed in some newer ingredients, and hoped, after some research and tests, to end up with a drug that will pull people out of coma within a matter of hours verses a matter of days, months, or years."

"Really? That's incredible!"

Rachel shook her head. "No, the most incredible thing about it is it leaves the patient with little or no brain damage." She looked at the empty dish again. "This truly could've been a world changing discovery."

"Are you focused on coma because of your parents?"

She quickly brushed her hand across her cheek. "It's such an ugly way to die. No closure for anyone."

Trace took her hands, pulled her up from her chair, and held her close to him. "You can try again, Rachel," he said softly in her ear. "You still have the formula. Do it again, but this time, let me put it away. There's a room downstairs, another refrigerated room that looks forgotten, like no one uses it anymore. It's full of old pieces of equipment, including Petri dishes. I'll hide it there."

Rachel stepped back and looked up into his face. "You really think we could?" she asked softly, a tinge of hope edging her voice.

He shrugged his shoulders. "I don't see why not. I'll take care of the dish once you've worked your magic."

Rachel wrapped her arms around his waist. His body was hard and cold, but she didn't care. It felt nice to her. "Thank you," she whispered. "Thank you so much."

Trace gently tightened his arms around her. "You're

welcome," he answered tenderly. "I'll help you through this if you let me."

Trace's words suddenly pulled Rachel into an old memory, of something or someone she'd tried so hard to forget. It was a vague memory of losing someone who had wanted to comfort her, telling her he'd help her through it if she'd let him, but the memory couldn't gel in her brain and it frustrated her.

Rachel quickly snapped back into reality and out of Trace's embrace. "I'm sorry Trace. I didn't mean to..."

"Did I do something wrong?"

She stiffened with anger, this time at herself. "Thank you for helping me," she said callously. "I need to get on this. Will you be alright while I work?"

Trace grabbed his hat. "Certainly. I'm sure I can manage to find something to do while I'm waiting for you."

"Good. Would you mind meeting me back here around five o'clock? I promise I'll lock up at five o'clock sharp. No overtime. After we hide the dish, we'll go see Carmen and Eric. I know she's dying to ask about my visit to the station."

"Sure," he said, walking to the door. "I'll be around. Holler if you need me."

Rachel smiled and mouthed the words, "Thank you."

Trace turned before stepping into the hall, nervously tapping his hat against his knee. "I didn't mean while I'm waiting for you to get off work," he added. "I meant while I'm waiting for you to make up your mind."

Rachel did a double-take. Right then, she didn't find him as attractive. "Make up my mind? I know I'm going to hate myself for asking, but make up my mind about what?"

Slowly turning his hat in his hand, Trace shifted his weight from one foot to the other. "About men."

Rachel sneered. "Men? You're going to wait until I make up my mind about men? Do you mean whether I like them or whether I trust them?"

Trace's head fell. "Both, maybe," he sighed.

Seeing his uneasiness, Rachel took a deep breath and swallowed her anger. "Listen, Trace. I like you. I really do. And I can't say that about most guys. Maybe it's because I really do believe you have my best interest at heart, and I *never* say that about any guy. Or maybe it's because I feel a connection to you, like we were cut from the same cloth. I don't know, but there is one thing I do know all of you men have in common."

"Not true," whispered Trace.

Rachel stepped up closer to him and gazed into his eyes. "Really?" she said softly. "Then you look me in the eyes right now and tell me you won't leave me."

His gaze fell to the floor. "You know I can't..."

"Exactly," she whispered. "None of you can."

Trace looked defeated. He put his hat on his head and turned around. "Not fair, Miss Wall," he muttered. "Not fair to blame all of us for something he couldn't control."

That last comment struck Rachel as odd, but she was too tired to ask him to explain it. And she didn't want to talk. She wanted to work, so she brushed it aside. Turning to her desk, she saw the file she'd confiscated from Corporal Thomas' desk.

"Trace, wait a minute," she called. "I need to give you something."

He stuck his head back through the doorway. "What?" he said coldly.

She handed him the file.

He flipped the folder over showing no interest in it whatsoever. "What's this?"

"Something that I believe rightfully belongs to you. It's a police file."

Even under makeup, she saw Trace's face turn white. "You took this from the police station?" he asked angrily.

Rachel lowered her head. When she lifted it, she met Trace's eyes. "I got a bad taste of how good folks can be treated by our local police; how the system blames before they try to find the truth, so I had no second thoughts about taking this from Corporal Thomas' desk."

"But..."

Rachel held up a hand. "Don't Trace. I don't need the lecture. Just take it and do with it as you will, I don't care, but when I saw it, I thought you had the right to know what the cops had on file. I've not had the chance to read it, but it's yours to read first anyway." Trace looked at the name that was scrawled across the tab.

"You took this because it has my name on it?"

"Yes," she said quietly.

"You should've taken it because it has..."

"It's yours, Trace," she said boldly. "I promise I won't mention it again unless you do." He stared at the file for a second longer then turned and left the room without saying a word. A pang of guilt hit Rachel, like she had done something wrong by taking the file, but it only lasted a second. "Not my problem anymore," she whispered. "I've got work to do and we've wasted enough time."

Unlocking her desk drawer, she pulled a second Petri dish from a false panel hidden behind hanging file folders. Turning the plastic dish in her hands, she marveled at how the cells were dividing so nicely. She went down the hall to the sequencing lab and after putting on the proper gear, pulled a sample of the stem cells out of the dish with a syringe; injecting small portions of it into eight PCR tubes. Taking an eye dropper, she filled each tube with a dye solution. The tray secured in the sequence machine, she flipped the switch. The machine hummed, slowly spinning and rolling the small tubes to properly mix the ingredients.

While the machine mixed, she went back to her lab and grabbed three clean Petri dishes, a tourniquet, a couple of needles, and a few other items. Slides were ordered from the basement fat man, tablets were crushed in mortars, and concoctions boiled on Bunsen burners. She watched results form through the lenses of her microscope. At four forty-five, she put two Petri dishes of the 'blood cloning' formula in the false compartment of her desk drawer and made sure it was locked up nice and tight. Then at five o'clock she slid a fresh Petri dish into Trace's hand. "I'm hoping these little stem cells grow and divide, Trace. If I stop coma, I've made it, so guard this with your life."

He smiled at the pun.

"Oh my gosh, I'm so sorry."

"It's ok, Rachel," he said warmly. "I can handle it."

She quickly slipped into her coat and grabbed her purse from the desk drawer. "Show me where you're going to put it," she said excitedly. "I've never taken the time to go down to the basement."

Trace watched her face; his blue eyes radiating with warmth. There was nothing dead about him. His heart didn't beat, but he was as alive as she was.

Placing a hand on her arm, he softly said, "Another time, Rachel. Right now, you need to go on to Carmen's house. I'll take care of this and meet you over there."

His touch left her breathless, her face drained of blood. The feeling made her angry, and somewhat sad. Angry at herself, because despite the freezing temperatures this man had to endure to survive, he was melting the icy wall she'd built around her own heart. Sad because, well, because he felt like an old friend who had good intentions, but really messed up and ruined things. Something about him tugged at her heart.

CHAPTER TWELVE

She stood beside her car and studied the little house; wondering just how far she should go. Carmen was like a sister to her; the only family she had left, and although she wanted to share her deepest secrets with her, something held her back; something uncertain, perhaps even sinister. *How well do you really know a person, even if you love them? Heck, how well do you know yourself?*

Before she could answer her own questions, the door of the house flew open and Carmen's arms were enveloping her. "When I saw you pull up, I couldn't decide whether to hug you or hit you, but when I saw you get out of the car, I decided on the hug." She squeezed Rachel tightly.

Rachel struggled to catch her breath. "I'm glad you didn't decide to hit me."

Carmen stepped back. "I just might if you ever go so long without calling me again. I was worried sick."

"You know I would've called if something went down worth reporting, but really, Carmen, it was a very dull and tiring night. And I did have to go into work today."

Carmen cringed. "I don't care if all you did was sit in lockup and teach genetics to any poor soul who had the misfortune of being stuck in there with you. I want to hear about it, so please, don't leave me alone with my own imagination again. It does nothing to help calm my nerves."

Rachel sighed. "Let's hope the opportunity never rises again."

"I agree," said Eric, stepping around Carmen and giving Rachel a bear hug. "Now let's get in the house before we all freeze to death."

From somewhere behind them, Trace laughed. Eric turned. Seeing him, he walked over and grabbed his hand. "Hey there. I'm always saying stuff like that aren't I?" he said apologetically.

Trace shook his head. "Hey man, no worries. It's all good." He threw a half-smile at Rachel.

The crew piled into the house where a small fire welcomed them. Rachel walked over to it with outstretched arms. Its warmth felt good against her hands and face. The sound of Carmen's laugh made her chuckle. She was in a safe place again.

The wonderful aroma of Carmen's fabulous chili made her mouth water. Her stomach growled, reminding her that she hadn't eaten anything since the night before. "Dinner's ready," Carmen called from the kitchen. "Chili and corn bread. It's a 'help yourself and find a seat' kinda night."

Rachel stifled a yawn. "Sounds wonderful."

After filling her bowl, she sat down at the counter with Carmen. Trace and Eric found seats far away from the fireplace. No one said a word until Eric, who was diving into his second bowl, managed to come up for air. Crumbs of cornbread dusted his mustache. "How'd you do your first day back in the rat race, Trace?"

Trace pushed back in his chair; cradled his head in his hands and propped his feet up on the chair across from him. "It was very interesting. I did a room by room investigation of the Plum Creek Lab and now I probably know things about that building the builders don't know."

The sound of spoons clinking against ceramic bowls stopped.

"Really? Like what?" asked Eric.

"Like all the air ducts on the upper floor merge into one solitaire duct that empties into a hidden, small, insignificant room in the basement, and if one listens, one can hear different conversations going on throughout the building." His eyes rested on Rachel, "And, that your phone number is written on the men's bathroom wall down there too." He glanced at Carmen and winked.

"Wow. That explains a lot," chuckled Carmen. "No one uses the bathrooms down there, so no one sees her number. Would you do her a favor and move it up to a wall in the first-floor bathroom so this poor girl can get a date?"

Rachel glared at her friend, a flash of anger burning in her eyes. "Enough," she warned. Carmen threw her a Cheshire cat grin before taking another bite of corn bread.

"Wha' el?" asked Eric, chomping on a spoonful of chili. Carmen slapped his arm. "Sorry," he said sheepishly. "Still haven't learned not to talk with my mouth full."

Trace pulled his feet off the chair and put his elbows on his knees. "After poking around town, listening and watching, I think I know who wanted me dead."

Eric choked, Carmen stopped chewing, and Rachel gasped.

"Who?" they asked together.

Trace shook his head. "I'm not ready to say. There are a few pieces of the puzzle I still need to put together before I can understand exactly *why* they wanted me dead. Once I know why, I'll know for sure who."

Rachel looked worried. "There are so many unanswered questions. Why would someone want to kill you, and why would someone want to frame me for trying to steal Doctor Aberman's files?"

Carmen sat up, her mouth open as if to say something, but her breath caught in her throat and she slid back in her chair.

Eric put his bowl on the coffee table and looked over at

Trace. "Do you think the two are related somehow?"

Trace nodded. "I do. Rachel's path crossed mine a long time ago and although we really didn't know each other, the one thing we have in common is the lab. It's going to take some time to determine how my past job and the recent robbery are linked."

Carmen squirmed in her chair. "That's just it, Trace. You don't have time. Like I said before, I think we need to let the police handle all of this."

Rachel cleared her throat. Trace threw her a quick look. "Isn't gonna happen," he said. "I've been given some vital information directly from the police station and believe me; they want to pin something on me. And I can say with confidence that sentiment goes the same for Rachel. I may not be able to finish investigating my murder, but I'm going to make sure she's cleared before I return to the tombcicle for good."

Eric leaned in. "What exactly and how did you get information from the police station? That is, if you don't mind telling me."

Trace smiled. "All in due time, my friend, all in due time."

Carmen's lips were a hard, straight line, her eyes grew dark. "Well, I hate to end this discussion," she said not reserving the annoyance in her voice, "but I've got to grade some tests and get ready for another day of classes."

"I need to get going too," chimed Eric. "Got a busy day tomorrow."

"Let me help clean up before I go," said Rachel.

Carmen laid a hand on her arm. "I think you need to go home and get some rest," she said quietly. "Maybe find something on the computer about knowing your rights."

Rachel stared wide-eyed at her friend.

"I'm not a Seer, Rachel, but I do have a strong sixth sense, and that little voice is telling me this situation is going to get worse before it gets better."

Carmen's warning hit Rachel so hard she grabbed the counter to balance herself. Wha...why, Carmen?" she stuttered. "What could go..."

Carmen looked over Rachel's shoulder at Trace. "Please see her safely home."

Trace nodded and gently took Rachel by the elbow. "It's Ok, Rach," he whispered. "I'm right here. I'll help you through this." His words resounded in her head again, but this time, she pushed them away. Whoever it was, that memory was a long time ago.

***

She and Trace rode in silence for a while, but finally, Rachel looked over at him. "Were you referring to the file I gave you when you said you had vital information straight from the police?" she asked softly.

Trace stared straight ahead. "Yep."

"May I ask what information it contained? I mean, you mentioned the information in that file included me. I'd like to know what that is."

"Nothing I don't think you already know, Rachel," he said briskly. "They suspect you of breaking and entering, robbery, stealing government files, etc."

Rachel turned her head so fast she almost wrenched her neck. "Stealing government files! That's a felony," she cried.

"It is," he said, grabbing the steering wheel and veering the car back into their lane, "but I don't want you worrying about all of this. You keep your mind on your work. It may prove more vital than anything else."

Rachel smirked. "Right! That's easier said than done."

"I know, but we're working on getting you cleared, so you

just focus on your experiment."

Rachel's eyes flew to Trace. "*We're* working on getting me cleared? Who's 'we're'?"

He hesitated just a second and then smiled. "You know, we, you and me, Rachel. We're working together, albeit, taking different approaches, but we're both working on the same result; getting your name cleared of this whole mess."

Rachel suspected he was lying, but she didn't want to argue about it. "Where's the file?" she asked firmly.

Trace glanced over at her. "I have it," he said assuredly. "In a safe place."

"Like at the bottom of your tombcicle?"

"Maybe! Would be a perfect place, don't you think? I mean, who's going to think of looking there? And if they do think about it, would they really want to?"

"Good point, but I really think I need to return it, don't you? Sooner or later, someone will notice it's gone missing."

The glow of the overhead stop light blushed their faces. "I'll take care of it."

Rachel threw him a quizzical look.

"I don't need eight hours of beauty sleep, Rach. In fact, I don't sleep at all, so, once I know it's safe, I venture out. Matter of fact, I've done a lot of exploring the last few nights."

"Really? Have you discovered anything interesting?"

Trace snickered. "Lots."

Rachel swerved to keep from driving off the side of the road. "About the robbery?"

"Hey," snapped Trace. "Keep it between the lines, girlfriend. I'll fill you in when I've..."

"I know," Rachel interrupted. "When you have more of the pieces put together."

Trace chuckled and turned on the radio. They listened to a toe tapper, but the holiday mood was abruptly interrupted by a somber, no nonsense voice. Trace turned up the volume.

"We interrupt this hour of holiday music to bring you a special report. WKRZ has just learned that there has been a fire at the home of Doctor Bruce Aberman, lead scientist at Plum Creek Laboratory. Fire Chief James McCoy confirms that the fire has been contained, but Aberman's historical Antebellum-style home has suffered damage. Just prior to the call to the fire department, Doctor Aberman had called police, reporting a possible intruder."

Rachel slammed on the brakes, leaving skid marks across the black asphalt.

"Doctor Aberman suffered a minor concussion from being struck on the head. He also suffered smoke inhalation. He was flown to Memorial Hospital in Roanoke for observation. Police stated no one else in the Aberman home suffered injury. Investigators believe the fire was set to cover up a botched robbery, and although we have not yet confirmed this, it is believed police are investigating a lab tech employed at Plum Creek Laboratory as a possible connection with the Aberman fire."

They didn't hear the rest of the report. Trace had turned the radio off.

"Doctor Aberman in the hospital? Joshua being investigated?" Rachel started to turn the car around, but Trace grabbed the wheel.

"No Rachel," he said firmly. "You can't go to that house, to the hospital, anywhere. You *cannot* connect yourself to this."

"I won't be connected if I just go to check on the family," she protested. "Doctor Aberman is my boss and I..."

"No," Trace said defiantly. "I understand your concern, but the police won't. Keep driving...straight to your house."

Rachel shook her head hysterically. "But I don't understand, Trace. I don't understand any of this."

Trace's voice was low and slow. "You have an alibi, Rachel," he said calmly. "The time you left Carmen's to the time you reach your house. I guarantee the cops know how long that takes. They won't be able to argue when you tell them the truth. Stick to it."

"How will they know that I was at Carmen's? How will they know what time I got home? Geez, Trace. Do I have to have an alibi for every move I make?"

"You might! They'll know you were at Carmen's because they'll visit Carmen. She'll say 'yes' and Eric will vouch for you too. Then they'll come see you and ask what time you got home. You'll tell them and what you say will be very close to what Carmen told them, so you'll be ok."

"And who will vouch that I got home when I say I did?"

Trace cleared his throat. "They'll know," he said delicately.

Rachel turned. "What are you telling me, Trace? That I'm being watched?"

"Remember what I said about the file containing things about you too?"

"Yes."

"Well, that was part of it. And didn't Jones tell you not to leave town when you left the station?"

"Well, yes, but how did you know..."

"Just trust me, Rachel."

Rachel waited until her breathing returned to normal before starting home. Her mind was buzzing, but she couldn't utter a word. The rest of the ride home was in silence. Finally, the beams of the headlights scraped across the bushes of her front yard and the car drifted into her driveway.

Turning the engine off, she looked over at Trace. "What's happening, Trace? I've tried to sort this out, but I can't get anywhere? The more I try to understand, the more confused I get. First, Doctor Aberman's office is robbed then this fire at his home, and now he's lying in a hospital room with a concussion...and poor Josh. I can't believe he's guilty of anything."

"Is Josh the lab tech they mentioned in the newscast?"

"Yeah, his name is Joshua Connor. He seems like such a nice kid. I can't imagine him doing anything like this."

"How well do you know him?"

"I don't know too much, but what I know doesn't match the kind of person who would set fire to someone's home and rob his office."

"Interesting," muttered Trace.

"He isn't actually a lab tech," continued Rachel. "He's an intern, a senior at the Community College. He oversees the mailroom and does mediocre jobs, but he seems to be a happy sort, always smiling. We've talked briefly in the break room a couple of times. Just recently I asked him to copy some files for me."

Rachel lowered her head.

"He seems so nice. He mentioned he hoped to be accepted into the University of Virginia to major in Biology when he finished his Associates degree at the College. He even has a steady girl; has a picture of her on his desk down in the mailroom. I just don't understand what would've driven him to try to rob and then set fire to the man's house."

"This may sound cold and callous, Rachel, but don't do or say anything about any of this to anyone, even Carmen. Don't talk about the office robbery, the fire, Joshua, anything to anyone. Go on as if nothing has happened. You go into work tomorrow, you do your job, you go home; you take care of Mikey...life goes on."

"But..."

"Trust me, Rachel. Just do your job and let me do mine. The more you stick your nose into all of this the more you raise the risk of incriminating yourself."

"And just what is your job?"

Trace opened his car door and got out. "Come on. I'll walk you in, and then I've got to go."

Rachel pushed her car door closed and walked up beside him. "Are you thawing out?"

"Not yet, but I want to check out a few things before I go back to the lab."

He followed Rachel into the house and did a quick walk through; checking out all the closets, corners, and cubbies. Facing Rachel at the front door he assured her she was safe. "And don't be upset if you don't see me for a couple of days," he said, turning the knob.

Rachel grabbed his hand. "Wait! What does that mean?"

Trace pulled the door open and stepped out onto the front porch. "I'm investigating. I'll be around, but don't think I've gone back to, to, wherever just because you may not see me for a while." He took Rachel's chin in his fingertips and lifted her face up to his. "Besides, we've got a date in a couple nights, don't we?"

"We do, and you better not stand me up. After all, it's Halloween and I know a witch who'll turn you into a pumpkin if you're not here by six-thirty."

Trace kissed her on the forehead. "No worries," he whispered. "I wouldn't miss this date with you for all the heartbeats in Plum Creek."

"That's not funny, Trace."

"Good," he said warmly. "It wasn't meant to be. Now, lock the doors. Make sure the windows are locked too."

"Ok," she whispered.

She pulled the lace panel back and watched him walk down the street; his dark silhouette visible under the shower of light pouring from an overhead streetlight then slipping into darkness only to reappear under the next shower of light. When he rounded the corner, his dark form disappeared completely; melding into the shadows of the night.

Mikey wrapped himself around her ankle and rumbled deeply as she turned the dead bolt. Phantom cat, who Carmen decided was really Trace's Tigger, dove under the bed; a nighttime ritual. She walked to the kitchen to get a bowl of milk for Mikey.

CHAPTER THIRTEEN

The next day at the lab no one spoke about the robbery, the break-in at Doctor Aberman's home, or Joshua being taken into custody. In fact, no one spoke much about anything. Heads stayed bent over microscopes, fixed eyes stared at blue computer screens, and muddled brains threw out dull words to stiff fingers as they tapped out monotonous reports. Someone, sometime during the day, stopped in the middle of their mundane routine and sorted the mail.

Rachel found a couple lab updates on her desk, but she tossed them aside, not interested in whatever government regulations the feds were pushing that week. What she really wanted to do was work on her 'coma' experiment, but she couldn't because she wasn't exactly sure where Trace had taken it. Besides *that* little irritant, today wasn't the day to go search for it. Too many voices in the breakroom, too many nervous laughs in the hallway. People were on edge.

So, she did nothing. Oh, she made it look like she was working diligently on some mind-boggling project, but her notes were mere doodles of Mikey and other ridiculous creatures. Computer work consisted of web searches for cookie recipes, and her microscope research involved one slide which had absolutely nothing to do with cloning blood or anything else of minute interest. She must've looked at it a million times throughout the day and after each peek, doodled a little more on her tablet.

At four forty-five, she traded her lab coat for her winter coat and left with most of the other employees, something she hadn't done in a long time.

Waiting for her car to warm up, she pulled her phone from her purse and checked for messages. Not surprised, there was only one, and it was from Carmen. She hit the return call button. Carmen answered after the first ring. Rachel put the call on speaker phone, dropped the phone in the console, and pulled out of the parking lot.

"Hi Rachel."

"Hey there. Whatcha doing?"

"I couldn't believe the news last night. What in the world is going on?"

Rachel hesitated. "I don't know."

"Would you mind coming over for a little while? I'd like to, well, can you come over?"

The light at the end of the lane turned green and Rachel pushed on the gas. "I'll be there in five." She turned onto a side road instead of going onto the highway.

"Thanks," sighed Carmen. "I'll see you in a bit."

A few minutes later, Rachel pulled up to the curb in front of Carmen's house. It was twilight, but the house looked completely dark except for a faint light ebbing from the dining room window. If she hadn't just talked to her, Rachel would've thought Carmen wasn't home.

She knocked on the door and waited, but Carmen didn't answer. She tried the knob and to her relief, the door wasn't locked, moaning slightly as it swung open. She stepped inside; stopping to let her eyes adjust to the dimness.

Several cabinets stuffed with books, world globes of different sizes huddled on shelves, and flourishing potted plants filled Carmen's tiny living room. Square pillows, round pillows, a lot of pillows, covered her sofa, lay strewn in front of the fireplace, and piled in a couple corners of the room. Candles of different colors, sizes, and shapes covered a small table in front of the couch. Some of the candles had never been lit, others had been burnt down almost to the holder, while most were burnt mid-way, the wax frozen to their sides like strings of beads. None were lit now, but the house smelled of incense; its thin wisp of smoke snaking its way from the dining room.

"Car?"

"In here, Rach," answered Carmen. "In the dining room."

"What's with the lights? Did you forget to pay your electric bill?"

Carefully stepping through the living room, she thought it odd that Carmen didn't respond with a sarcastic remark. When she reached the dining room, she understood why. Carmen wasn't alone.

Two strangers were sitting at her table; two women, whose pale features, in blatant contrast to the dark room, almost looked transparent. On the ceiling, shadows cast by a single candle, danced to a mystic rhythm.

She felt like she'd walked in on something very personal and stepped back, but Carmen eased up beside her; gently taking her arm and sliding it through her own. With their heads almost touching, she said, "Rachel, I'd like you to meet a couple of, um, colleagues of mine." She pointed to the woman closest to them. "This is my Wiccan sister, Kaida." Despite the lack of light, Rachel could see the woman was old. Not like eighties old, but ancient old.

Light bounced off what looked like a disheveled bird's nest sitting on the top of the old woman's head and it took Rachel a few seconds to realize it was tousled, gray hair, held loosely in a bun by too few hairpins. Runaway strands of long grey hair brushed against the tops of the ancient one's bent shoulders. The woman's face held eons of hard years, proven by the deep lines etched around her eyes and mouth. Old waves of time lay motionless across her boney cheeks; but her eyes, glistening in the candlelight, were dark and clear.

A glint of green led Rachel's eyes down the old woman's banded neck to the flickering emerald eyes of a dragon pendant that lay flat against her chest. The backdrop of the woman's black dress brought out every scaly detail of the gold reptilian body right down to the coiled tail. It held a spectacular diamond pentagram firmly in its long, smooth talons. The whole pendent glistened as brightly as the woman's eyes.

Rachel looked back up to the old woman's face and when their eyes met, the primitive wrinkled lips curved upward into a familiar smile. Rachel smiled back.

"And this is my Wiccan sister, Carollan Bryn," continued Carmen.

It wasn't hard to see, even in the dim light, that Carollan Bryn was much younger than Kaida, but her youth was camouflaged by a high forehead, sharp cheekbones, and a thin pointed chin. Her mouth was a straight, hard line. Only her brown eyes looked remotely friendly.

She too wore a dragon medallion around her neck, but it wasn't like Kaida's, in design or significance. Rachel wasn't sure how she knew Kaida's pendant was something of importance, after all, she knew nothing about these women, but for some reason, she was sure of it.

Carollan Bryn didn't smile. She nodded, slowly, and only once; her eyes never leaving Rachel's face.

Rachel returned Carollan Bryn's acknowledgement then turned to Carmen. "What's up, Carmen? What's going on?" It was then she noticed Carmen was wearing a dragon necklace too. "And what's with all the dragons?"

"Later," Carmen whispered back. She took Rachel's purse and set it on a nearby chair. "Keep your coat on," she said quietly. "We're going outside."

Just then, as if on cue, Kaida and Carollan Bryn pushed away from the table and pulled long black cloaks from the backs of their chairs, carefully draping them over their shoulders. To Rachel's surprise, Carmen did the same.

When she had finished fastening her cape, Carmen whispered, "Come with us."

Carollan Bryn picked up the incense smudge as Kaida took the candle from the middle of the table. Old and bent, it looked as if Kaida's nose would bob through the candle's flame when she walked. Her dragon necklace clicked against the button of her cloak, and the hem of her cape trailed across the wooden floor. Carollan Bryn, brushing the wisp of smoke with her hand, walked tall and straight, her cape swaying gracefully behind her. Carmen's stride was heavy, full of determination. Her arms swung with every step. The dark shadows cast from the flame of the candle drew a scene on the wall that looked as if all of them had just stepped out of a Grimm fairytale.

The three women stepped off the back stairs and walked out into the yard, but when Rachel reached the stoop, she stopped; suddenly overwhelmed by a sense of déjà vu. Had she been here before? Or was this a place she'd seen in a book, or on television? If so, it was more beautiful in real life.

From where she stood, she watched hundreds of small featherlike flames bend and flicker from the caresses of the cool night air. Luminaires dangled from bare tree branches over small pools of light; each puddle flowing into the next, transforming Carmen's sleeping garden into a mystical wonderland.

A large circle, made from river rock, had been set up in the middle of the yard and inside the circle were five large candles. They formed the Wiccan pentagram. Inside the pentagram, four large white stones marked each point of a large compass. A white candle had been placed on top of a white stone to mark both the Spirit point of the pentagram and the Northern point of the compass. Her eyes followed the hidden line from the candle up into the dark velvet sky; stopping at the North Star.

"Wow," she whispered.

Carmen, who had stopped at the bottom of the stairs, turned around and looked up at her. "Rachel, would you mind sitting in the middle of the compass, next to the small altar?" she asked quietly.

Rachel tried to hide her apprehension, but she knew her face had given her away when Carmen offered her hand. "It's alright, Rachel."

Carmen's hand felt warm in hers. They walked together into the circle and when they reached the middle, Carmen took both of Rachel's hands and faced her. "I fear something bad is going to go down, Rachel," she said quietly. "In fact, I know it is. So, to help in the situation, my sisters and I would like to cast a protection spell over you. Would that be alright?"

Rachel's grip on Carmen's hands tightened. "What's going down, Car?"

Carmen's jaw muscles flexed. Her eyes were hard, but her voice was soft. "I've always feared this situation with the police could get worse before it gets better, you know that."

Rachel nodded.

"Well, if that is the path that has been placed before you, I want to do what I can to protect you, Rachel."

Rachel's eyes searched Carmen's face. "How is it going to get worse, Carmen?"

Carmen smiled. "Everything is going to be alright, Rachel. You believe in prayer, don't you?"

"You know I do," she said anxiously.

"And so do I," Carmen replied calmly. "That's why I've asked you to join us here."

Rachel's eyes searched out the other two women. "You know you can trust me, Rachel," Carmen said softly. "Just as I trust you when you pray for me."

Their eyes searched each other for what seemed like a long time. Finally, Rachel took a deep breath and exhaled slowly. Nodding, she pulled her coat tight around her body and slowly sank to the ground, crossing her legs under her.

The ground was hard and cold. She shifted her weight a few times before finding a position that was somewhat comfortable. When she finally settled, she browsed the contents of the small altar beside her. A small statue of a woman stood beside a large white candle. The candle had symbols on it. It surprised her that she knew they were runes, and even more so by knowing what a few of them stood for. *Wow,* she thought. *You really have been paying attention. Carmen will be impressed.* The candle reminded her of her cowboy candle and she smiled.

A beautiful dragon figurine was on the other side of the candle and from its murky silver color, she guessed it was pewter. Candlelight bounced across it, adding an orange hue to its ruby eyes. Beside the dragon was a dagger, about six inches long; pointing north. The small smudge pot carried out by Carollan Bryn was behind the dragon figurine. Rachel was lost in studying the altar when Carmen's subtle whisper startled her. "This won't take long, Rach. I promise."

Rachel turned her attention to the three women as they took their places outside the circle. Each stood beside a candle, but left the top point, the place for the spirit, empty. They remained motionless for several seconds then in one graceful motion, they simultaneously lifted the hood of their cloak and pulled it over their head.

The hoods hid their faces and completely enveloped the women in darkness. Rachel couldn't tell one from the other. All she could make out were black silhouettes standing against the backdrop of a murky night. Even the gleam that Rachel had often seen in Carmen's eyes had disappeared.

Rachel knew she was going to witness something bigger than the casting of some small spell found in a ragged old book purchased at a yard sale. "If there are levels of seriousness in Wicca, this ritual must be held in a place of high seriousness," she whispered.

Suddenly, it dawned on Rachel where she had seen Kaida. She was the old lady who gave the book of spells to Carmen at the yard sale. It seemed Carmen had formed a circle of friends of whom Rachel knew nothing, except that they were witches.

She smiled at the pun, but for some reason, the thought of Carmen deciding to move from merely working with herbs to delve further into the occult without talking to her about it stung her. Carmen had never mentioned these other women; that they had struck up a friendship; or that she had joined a coven...or whatever it was. Rachel stopped smiling. "I thought we agreed no secrets," she mumbled.

She looked around the beautiful garden and dug deep into her memory. If that were the case, if Carmen had kept such a thing like being a part of a coven from her, then why did she have a sense of familiarity to all of this? Had Carmen told her? Was she just too busy with her own work, her own discoveries to care?

The three witches stood in silence for several minutes, then, like someone had counted to three, they started to walk around the circle, singing something in soft cadence. The first one in line, Rachel didn't know who it was; they all looked the same in their hooded robes, kept time by tapping a small drum that was apparently hidden in the long sleeves of her robe. The last of them dropped pinches of a white substance behind her as they walked. Rachel knew enough to know it was salt.

Witches believe salt has protective powers, so it would make sense that it would be used to outline the circle. Each time they passed a point of the pentagram, the chanting and the drum beat got louder.

On the third walk around the circle, they stopped at each of the candles and called upon the Guardian of the represented cardinal point. When they finished, they were standing beside the very candle from where they started.

Once again, all fell quiet; no chanting, no drum, nothing. In fact, Rachel didn't hear the usual sounds of night either, not even the wind brushing against the limbs of the barren trees.

The three witches stood still and silent for several minutes; their arms hanging freely at their sides and their covered heads bowed to the earth.

Rachel couldn't help but wonder if they were waiting for something to happen. She found herself looking up into the sky, over her shoulder, and behind her, almost expecting something, or someone to appear. But nothing happened.

The lead witch then whispered something. Soon, the middle witch joined in, and shortly thereafter, all three were whispering, chanting, and swaying back and forth. It looked as if they were being gently rocked by an invisible wave. Rachel watched; fascinated by what she was witnessing.

Slowly, the middle witch stepped away from her compass candle and toward Rachel. She wasn't sure, but she thought it was Carmen. The other two fell silent but continued to sway back and forth as the witch prepared to cast her spell. Raising her arms toward the star lit sky, the lone enchantress chanted her request.

When the chant concluded, just as the three had walked the circled before, they did so again in reverse. A steely feeling gnawed at Rachel deep in the pit of her stomach. She couldn't put her finger on it, but something felt wrong, out of sync, but she quickly pushed the feeling aside to let a warmth wash over her as she watched the ritual come to an end.

This warmth wasn't conjured from the witches' ritual or the mystery it held, or because of the wonderland created by all the candles, or the beautiful dragons, the strange incantations, or the mystical spell that was cast over her.

No, none of those stirred the warmth she was feeling within her. That kind of warmth could only be created by the love of a true and dedicated friend. The only reason Carmen had invited her here was to perform this ritual. Not to talk, not to 'catch up', but to present her to whatever god she believed in and to pray a prayer of protection for her.

This whole ceremony was a tribute to what Carmen thought of Rachel and their friendship. Carmen was her dearest friend. It seemed they had always been close, but Rachel now knew that what Carmen had shared with her that night was a bond stronger than blood, stronger than religion, stronger than anything that made them different. Rachel knew that Carmen loved her; loved her more than any sister could ever love her.

Ironically, it was Carmen's ritual that convicted Rachel about her own lack of faith. She felt a tug, heard a small voice from deep within that what her parents had taught her, but had never accepted, was real.

The realization was overwhelming. She wasn't sure how to go about accepting anything from God. She had pushed him aside long ago, blaming him for the death of her parents and over time, for the hurt that had been caused by Simon. But there, strange at it might be, she knew he had never left her. He was with her, watching after her, calling to her right there.

The three women went back into the house, leaving Rachel alone in the middle of the circle. She lay back onto the hard ground and searched the diamond studded sky. "If only those stars could talk, what stories they would tell."

Picking out a bright one, she said, "You." It twinkled quickly. "Yes you. Who have you looked down upon through history? Did you shine on some small village along ancient hills thousands of years ago?" Looking at another, she said, "And you? What secrets do you hold? Shining in the night since the beginning of time, I'm sure you've witnessed so much."

Her eyes darted across the sky until she found the North Star. "And you. You are said to be close to his throne." She inhaled deeply. "Just beyond those beautiful gemstone stars is Heaven where God, angels, and...and my parents live." She tried to soak in the vastness of what hovered above her; the unseen planets, millions of galaxies, and all that had yet to be discovered in the vague mystery called the Universe, but what she found most mysterious of all was that amid all of this splendor; God loved her the most.

"I'm not worthy of any of this," she murmured. "For my life, even though it's such a tangled mess right now, but especially for your love. Please God, show yourself to me so I can believe. I so want to believe. I'm a scientist. I know how to research and find answers, but with you, I don't know what I'm looking for, I don't know where to begin, so please, show yourself to me. Your greatness is evident in what I'm looking at now. You are so...big." She swallowed hard. "But I need something personal, God. Something, well, something to let me know you see me, that I'm not invisible."

She sniffled, lifted her arm, and with the sleeve of her coat, wiped away the second tear that had slipped from the corner of her eye. It had tried to flow down the path set by the first one; the one she missed; the one that was dripping off her jaw onto the frozen ground.

CHAPTER FOURTEEN

Mikey sat on the edge of the chair, his head following Rachel as she paced in front of the fireplace. She was mumbling something about not having seen Trace for several days and now, it being Friday night, he was still nowhere to be found. His green eyes followed her to the mantle where she watched the long hand on the clock move to the half-hour mark and "thunk". It was six-thirty. Trace was a half-hour late. Disappointed, she plopped down on the chair beside her cat.

"Well, looks like another night with you and a pot pie dinner," she said sighing.

Her phone startled her. She pulled it from her pocket with hope, but it was only Carmen.

"Hi Car."

"Where are you?"

"Um, I'm at home, waiting yet again for a man to come pick me up."

"Well, I can't answer for him, Rach, but you need to get to the high school. We need you to help chaperon this dance."

"I don't want to be a third wheel, Carmen. Can't you and Eric manage without me?"

"Nope. You promised, and I expect to see you walk

through these gym doors in fifteen minutes. By the way, what are you?"

"I'm a scientist."

"I know, but what's your costume?"

"That *is* my costume, Car. I'm a scientist."

It got so quiet Rachel could hear the faint sound of electricity buzzing through her phone. Finally, Carmen sighed. "Really, Rach? A scientist? That's like me dressing up as a witch."

"Hey, I don't have to come at all. I could just stay here and..."

"Oh, come on. You'll get a kick out of some of these costumes. These kids came up with some really cool stuff."

Rachel sighed heavily. "I don't know Carmen. I think I'd rather..."

"Oh no you don't, Rachel. Just get here!"

Before Rachel could say, 'empty boxes' a loud click ended the call. She pulled the phone from her ear and scowled. "You're doing that way too often, Carmen. Don't make it a habit."

She thought of the daunting task of unpacking and moaned. "Oh, bother. I really don't want to sit here alone tonight...and I really don't want to mess with all of this...and I did promise I'd go." Mikey leaned against her leg. She scratched his head. "And a promise is a promise, isn't it Mikey?" Rubbing his whiskers against her leg, he flicked his tail a couple of times. "I know," she muttered, "I'm a loser."

She pushed herself up from the chair, turned on a table lamp, looked around the room one last time then stepped out into the crisp October night. Memories of late dates, missed dates, and no dates of long ago flooded her head, but she squared her shoulders and walked to her car anyway. It was time to go to the high school Halloween dance, and she would go alone, again.

The gym was dark, lit only by a few dimmed lights and a large mirrored ball hanging from the middle of the ceiling. Spinning slowly, it threw a kaleidoscope of colors around the room. Orange and black paper chains hung in lazy loops across the walls, plastic skeletons dangled from the two basketball nets on opposite ends of the floor, and up in the dark corners of the room, hundreds of black and orange balloons huddled close together, periodically nudging and pushing until they'd changed places. But the best decorations were the kids.

Carmen was right. Some of them had come up with genius costumes. Not the typical devil, cat, or pirate. Oh, there were those, but one kid was an iPod, another a giant Lego piece, his costume made from a box and a few solo cups. She even thought she saw twin sisters dressed as ear buds. Another kid was a car. Well, he was a car when he was folded up and sitting on the floor. When he stood up, he unfolded into a Transformer.

Four or five kids on stage were belting out a rock tune. Of course, they were dressed as mummies and skeletons, except the drummer. He was a scarecrow. They weren't good, but they weren't bad either. They were typical high school. Rachel chuckled. "Welcome back," she whispered to herself.

She scanned the room; eventually making eye contact with a short, stout older woman who was making her way over to her. She wasn't in costume and Rachel immediately recognized her pleasant, smiling face.

"Hello Rachel," said Mrs. Aberman. "It's so good to see you here. Are you with someone?" She crooked her neck over Rachel's shoulders looking for whoever might be lurking behind.

Rachel fought the urge to say something about her missing date but smiled warmly instead. "It's good to see you too, Mrs. Aberman. It's been awhile. And no, I didn't come with anyone. I'm here alone."

"Please dear, call me Edith. And I'm sorry to hear you've

come alone. You're such a lovely girl and I'd like to see you find someone. Someone better than, well, you know."

Rachel grimaced; hoping the dark gym hid her red face. Mrs. Aberman never liked Simon for some reason. She often made the comment that he wasn't good enough for her, yet she barely knew him.

But it wouldn't behoove her to anger Edith Aberman. Not only was the woman's husband her boss, but Mrs. Aberman had her own little fiefdom among the socialites in Plum Creek. She was somebody in this small town. She wasn't the mayor, but she was a powerful force and Rachel wanted to keep that power on her side. *For your sake, Rachel, just keep things on an even keel, no matter what she says.*

Laying a hand on the older woman's arm, Rachel said, "I'm fine, Mrs. Aberman, um, Edith, but more importantly, how are you? How is Doctor Aberman?"

Mrs. Aberman patted Rachel's hand. "We're fine sweetie. The news made it sound like our house was almost burnt to the ground, but the main part of the house wasn't damaged at all. Just some smoke and water damage in the Doctor's study, but nothing insurance can't handle. And he's fine too, the old goat."

Rachel bit her lip to keep from laughing.

"Some of the ash from his cigar fell onto the carpet, so he tried to stomp it out, but fell and bumped his head on the corner of his desk. Of course, I called 911 and had him rushed to the hospital, but he's fine. Resting, if that's what you want to call it. He always has to be doing something, so he's supervising the renovation of his home office right now."

Rachel's relief must've shown on her face because Mrs. Aberman patted her hand again and leaned in toward her ear. "And don't you worry about that office robbery stuff at the lab either. It'll all be taken care of and then we can lay all of this to rest."

"But what about Josh?"

Mrs. Aberman bit the inside of her cheek. "Josh who?"

"Oh, I can't say for certain it was Josh, but the news said the police suspected a tech from the lab."

Mrs. Aberman waved her off. "Oh, that. Bad reporting, that was. I'm so glad they didn't mention that poor boy's name on the air or he'd be blackballed from here to Timbuktu."

"But why would the news say anything at all about a tech if..."

"Now, don't you worry your pretty, little scientific head about this," said the older woman. "I'm sure your Josh is fine. Doctor Aberman is fine, and soon, you will be too."

"Thank you," replied Rachel. "That means so much to me, Mrs. Aberman."

"Once this is over, Bruce and I are going back up to New England to visit family again. Our first visit was interrupted, you know, with him having to leave for a few days to attend that medical conference. We want to go back and spend some quiet time up there. We had a wonderful time at our youngest granddaughter's birthday. It helped us realize he needs to consider retirement and maybe a move. Our kids are getting older, well, for that matter, we're getting older, and the grandchildren, well; they're all young adults now. I'd like to be a little closer to them. Besides, I'd like to travel a bit too, go back to Switzerland. I love Switzerland, and of course the United Kingdom and so forth. Maybe even a visit to Australia. That's one place I've not been."

Rachel smiled. "Sounds wonderful." She liked the thought of all of this being over and life getting back to normal for everyone. "So, you're feeling better?"

Mrs. Aberman cocked her head. "What do you mean, dear?"

"Well, I'd heard you weren't well while you were visiting your family and that..."

Mrs. Aberman frowned for a second then smiled. "I'm

right as rain, sweetheart. I haven't been sick in years. Just had a physical a few months ago and my doctor is quite pleased with my state of wellbeing. I'm much too busy to be sick, don't you know."

"Yes, ma'am, I imagine you are...have to be."

Mrs. Aberman patted her arm again. "Well, I've got a few more 'hellos' to say and then I'll be off. Looks like there are plenty of chaperons here. The kids are in good hands."

Rachel bent down and gave Mrs. Aberman a hug. "Take care," she whispered.

Mrs. Aberman looked up into Rachel's eyes. "If you need me for anything, anything at all, you call me, you hear?"

"Thank you. I will."

She watched Mrs. Aberman walk away before strolling deeper into the dark gym. Off to her left, she heard Carmen laugh. Following the familiar giggles, she was led right to them; Wilma and Fred Flintstone. She got a little closer and took their picture.

Carmen finally stopped yelling in a ghost's ear and saw her. Rachel thought she would've skipped to her if she weren't wearing boots that looked like bear cubs had swallowed her feet.

"I'm so glad you're here," Carmen yelled over the music. "I was afraid you wouldn't come." She gave Rachel the once over and yelled again. "And you do make a good scientist."

Rachel smirked. "Thanks," she yelled back. "Good to know."

Just then, Carmen looked past Rachel. "Oh, my stars," she said loudly. "You've got to be kidding me."

Rachel muttered "what now," and turned to see what had distracted her friend. Although the sight of him made her angry, she had to laugh. He was a bloody, irresistible mess. Tattered clothes, rumpled hair, a death-colored face, and dark liquid eyes that looked as lifeless as stagnant pools of oil. One arm was stretched outward, like he was reaching for a victim while one leg slid lifeless across the gym floor. He moaned and growled at those who stopped dancing to look at him and gently pushed between those who didn't. He was a typical zombie.

Upon reaching the small group of friends, he gave himself up with his killer smile. "Hi there," he moaned pitifully.

"Let me guess," said Carmen. "You're a zombie."

Trace looked disappointed. "How'd you guess?"

Carmen threw her head back and laughed.

"No, really," he persisted. "What gave it away?"

Carmen pointed to Rachel. "You're as innovative as our scientist here."

He glanced at Rachel and winked. Twisting his lips to look revolting, he let a little drool slide out of the corner of his mouth. "I think we make a great pair; mad scientist and her sidekick Igor."

Carmen reached over and wiped her thumb across his forehead.

"Nope," he said, shaking his head. "No makeup. All natural. I mean, why should someone who has to wear makeup to look normal, just put on more make up to look abnormal, when I can do that normally? Tonight, I can just be, well, normal."

Rachel giggled.

Carmen stepped back and pushed Rachel toward him. "Well, I think you two should..."

Eric, who was standing behind Carmen, leaned over her shoulder. "Listen," he interrupted. "They're playing our song. How 'bout it Wilma? Wanna cut a rug with this caveman?"

Carmen looked up into his face. "Sure, but I didn't know we had a song."

Taking her hand, he yelled, "We do now. Follow me."

"I'll follow you anywhere, Mr. Flintstone," she yelled back and off they went to the dance floor.

Trace's gaze followed them. "I wonder who we really need to chaperone tonight, the kids or them." He snickered, but Rachel, who was watching her friends too, didn't say anything. She just shrugged her shoulders. Turning to her, Trace's eyes flowed across her face. "Hey, can I buy you a drink? I hear the punch is to die for."

Rachel rolled her eyes.

"I'll take that as a yes." He took her hand and led her to the refreshment table.

Ladling up a cup of orange sherbet punch, he quietly said, "I'm sorry I wasn't there to pick you up, Rachel. I lost track of time. In fact, I've not been back to the lab in several hours, so I'm not sure how long I can stay here." He put his finger in the punch bowl and gave the punch a quick stir.

Rachel's eyes widened with alarm. "Get your finger out of the punch," she demanded.

"Oh, it's ok. I washed..."

Rachel almost panicked. She grabbed Trace's jacket and pulled him closer. "No," she said wildly. "Really, get your finger out of the punch!"

Trace looked, and sure enough, floating on top, slightly covered in orange sherbet was his finger. He plucked it from the bowl and squished it back onto his hand. "See there," he said awkwardly. "Don't know how long I'll be able to..."

"Well, hello Miss Wall."

Rachel jerked around quickly while Trace lingered with his back to whoever it was that had greeted her.

"Um, hello Mr. Rockwell, Mrs. Rockwell. How are you two this evening?" She nervously wiped her palms on the front of her lab coat before shaking their hands.

Mr. Rockwell was the high school principal and a friend of her deceased father. He was tall and lanky while his wife was short and plump. Standing there, he in coveralls and her in calico, kind of reminded her of the picture of the old farm couple; him holding the pitch fork and her holding a chicken or something. The thought almost made her laugh out loud, but she bit her lip and kept it together.

"We're fine," replied Mr. Rockwell. "Getting ready to retire in a year or two but doing alright. The real question is, how are you? We've heard of the goings on around the lab and were wondering about you. Are things ok?"

"Oh, I'm fine," Rachel said, trying to sound confident.

"Splendid," said Mrs. Rockwell. "You call us if you need anything."

Trace had turned around, apparently feeling confident his finger wouldn't fall off. Mr. Rockwell turned his attention to him. "I'm sorry young man; I don't believe we've met."

"Oh, I'm sorry," Rachel said. "Mr. and Mrs. Rockwell, this is John. John Doe...ter...y."

"John Dougherty?" asked Mr. Rockwell.

"Yes, sir," answered Trace. "I'd extend my hand, but I'm covered with makeup and don't want to get it on those fine-looking coveralls."

"Thank you," said Mrs. Rockwell. "That stuff is so hard to get out of clothes."

Rachel smiled, hoping Mr. Rockwell wouldn't insist. It would be hard to explain if he ended up shaking a bodiless hand.

To her relief, he didn't, but he didn't seem as anxious to move on as his wife. "Have you two known each other long?"

"Well," started Rachel.

"Not really," said Trace. "She actually just caught me with my finger in the punch bowl." Rachel suddenly felt warm. A bead of sweat rolled down the side of her face.

"Oh, is that all," said the principal. "For a second there, I thought we'd walked up and caught you spiking the punch."

"Oh, no sir," Trace said, holding up his orange finger. "You might catch me red handed at something, but I wouldn't do that."

Rachel couldn't help but wonder if that mirrored ball hanging from the ceiling had started to spin faster or if it was the room that was moving.

Mrs. Rockwell laughed. "Well, you two young people enjoy the evening. We've got a few more folks to greet and then we're going home. There are enough chaperons here to do the job." She looked over at Trace and smiled. "And keep your fingers out of the punch bowl young man."

Trace flashed his smile. "Yes, ma'am," he said, tipping an imaginary hat.

He and Rachel watched the older couple walk away and when she knew they were out of ear shot, she turned abruptly to him. "What in the world?" she said edgily. "I caught you with your finger in the punch bowl?"

"Well, you did."

"I know, but what if they felt like playing 100 questions, then what?"

Trace ignored her question and tilted his head. "Do you hear that?"

Rachel looked around the room. "What?"

"Listen," Trace said softly. "I think they're playing our song."

"We don't have a song."

He smiled and grabbed her hand. "We do now. Follow me."

She pulled her hand back. "I don't know how to dance," she protested. "I haven't danced since my own high school days and that was a very long time ago, and even then, it wasn't very often. Dancing with me now would be like dancing with an ironing board."

Trace stepped in close and gently took her hand again. "It's okay," he said softly. "I'll guide you." His imploring eyes were too hard to resist.

Rachel sighed, her shoulders fell, and she surrendered. "Ok. But just one song."

He led her onto the dance floor and found a spot between a zombie couple and Batman and Cat Woman. Trace couldn't resist and leaned closer to the zombie couple. They were just young high school kids; both dressed in ratty clothes and bad makeup. The boy looked over at Trace and smiled through false rotting teeth. "Nice costume, Mister," he said carefully, sounding like he had a mouthful of marbles. "Best zombie costume I've ever seen, even on TV. I mean, you really look dead!"

Trace snickered. "Well, thank you, young man. Not half bad yourself; goes for your girl too. A bit of advice though, ease up on the brains. They can leave you bloated and feeling kinda gassy." Trace left the kids laughing.

Rachel's eyes sparkled. "You're something else Mr. Ardor."

Trace squeezed her hand and pulled her closer to him. Looking deep into her brown eyes, he whispered, "So are you Miss Wall."

The lights in the gym dimmed and the lead singer of the band stepped up to the microphone. "This one's for all the sweethearts out there," he said, pointing to the crowd. "Hold each other tight, keep each other warm, and...don't let the magic die."

The band went into the introduction of the song and Rachel thought they sounded decent. Trace pulled her into his arms and led her through the tune. There were times she stepped on his foot or didn't turn as far as he did. Her insecurities about being a lousy dancer rushed to the surface. She really was as stiff as an ironing board, but Trace didn't seem to notice. He held on to her and kissed her hair. Soon, she lost herself in the feeling of his closeness, and the words of the song.

The night is drawing close
So, hold the one you love
It's been a lonely road
You've waited long enough

Believe that this is it
Don't let this magic die
Don't be afraid to love
Just look into her eyes

The answer's right in front of you
She longs to hear you say
That she's the one you long to love
Don't let her slip away

Release the hurt and pain
Feel free as your souls' dance
Don't be scared to let it go
This is your final chance

No, no, don't let the magic die,
Don't let the magic die

Release the hurt and pain
Feel free as your souls' dance

Don't be scared to let it go

This is your final chance.

The words touched Rachel and she was disappointed when the song ended. Reluctantly, she pushed herself away from Trace, but not out of his embrace. "Thank you," she whispered.

Trace didn't reply but turned his eyes from hers to someone behind her. She watched his eyes darken then slowly turned to see who had caused his look of consternation.

Behind her stood three people; two men and one woman. They were dressed in black and cautiously moving their jackets aside to reveal the gold FBI shields that hung from their belts. No one else seemed to notice them, probably thinking they were in costume if they did, but Rachel knew they weren't there to chaperone high school kids.

The tallest of the men cleared his throat. "Miss Wall? Miss Rachel Wall?"

Rachel left Trace's arms and turned to face them. "Yes, my name is Rachel Wall."

"Miss Wall, we need you to come with us?"

"Why?" she asked boldly.

The female agent stepped forward and put her mouth close to Rachel's ear. "Miss Wall, we don't want to cause a scene. We have a warrant to hold and question you. We'd prefer you just come with us quietly."

Trace stepped in front of Rachel. "If you didn't want to cause a scene, then why here, why now?" he asked firmly.

The woman stepped around Trace and placed a hand on Rachel's sleeve. "Miss Wall, we just want to ask you some routine questions. Please come with us quietly. You'll be in my care and I promise nothing will happen to you. We just need answers to some simple questions."

Rachel's mind raced. *Government files, felony. Is this why they're here?* She frantically looked around the gym. The kids, the chaperones, no one was paying any attention to them. She couldn't even see Carmen and Eric. The sense that she was invisible to them, to everyone, fell over her like a wet, cold blanket.

Everyone was having a fun time. No one wanted their night to be ruined; certainly not because of her. If she refused to go, no telling what these agents would do. Causing a scene would surely make the whole community angry with her; probably convince them that she was guilty of everything they'd heard. And an upset community meant a disappointed Mrs. Aberman. She looked at the woman agent and nodded. "Okay," she whispered.

"I'm coming with her." Trace's voice was firm.

Rachel turned to him. "No, you can't. You've got to, you need the..." She stood quiet until the stammering stopped. Fighting tears, she said, "Take care of yourself. I'll be okay."

The three agents circled Rachel and together they walked across the gym and out through the large metal doors.

CHAPTER FIFTEEN

Rachel sat in the back seat of the black Lincoln with the female agent while the two men sat up front. Other than their mumbling back and forth to each other, the ride was quiet. She was scared and couldn't relax; afraid to say anything for fear of incriminating herself. She had no idea the investigation into the robbery had taken this direction. She'd heard nothing from the Sheriff; nothing until this.

The further they got away from Plum Creek, the faster her confidence resurfaced. Surely, she would be back home before the night was over, exonerated and worry free. All she had to do was answer their questions. *But if they think you're innocent, why are you in this car, heading to the Poff Federal Building in downtown Roanoke?* She quickly pushed the question aside. Now was not the time to let thoughts like that creep in.

No one said anything about pressing charges, being guilty, or even being a person of interest. The agent beside her said she was only going to be asked some simple questions. In fact, if they searched her record, and she was sure they would if they hadn't already, they'd see that her only offense was a parking ticket back in 2005. And then she'd only missed putting more money in the meter by a few seconds.

The FBI was barking up the wrong tree if they thought they could pin anything on Rachel Wall. No siree. Her life was as exciting as watching grass grow. They'd learn that soon enough. But she did have to admit she was a bit confused as to why the FBI wanted to talk to her. She half expected to be asked to pay another visit to the Plum Creek Police Department, especially if they've discovered a file was missing, but the FBI?

That was a puzzle, but maybe they wanted to ask her about someone else. Maybe she was going to be asked to be a lead witness or something. Whatever their reason, she would learn it soon enough. Taking a deep breath, she finally sat back and relaxed into the plush leather seat. After a few twists and turns, they were soon in the midst of the city where she watched the urban scene pass before her through the glass of her window.

The reflection of green neon lights from local bars slid across her face, sporadically replaced by the white lights that penetrated plate glass storefronts. Passersby's stopped to peer into the windows at the dresses and suits displayed on life-like mannequins. Older buildings sported the year they were built high above carved keystones while newer structures proudly modeled glass walls and revolving doors. Rachel was mesmerized by the dance, the rhythm by which the city moved.

The car pulled into a brightly lit three-story parking garage, but instead of winding upward, it headed underground. Within minutes, Rachel was led to the elevator and up into the heart of the building. When the elevator doors slid open, the two male agents disappeared into a world of cubicles while the female agent led her down a hall then up a couple flights of stairs.

They finally stopped at a door and when the agent opened it, they stepped into a room that resembled a small living room complete with a couch, two high winged back chairs, a coffee table, end tables, lamps, a few pieces of decent artwork, and the wonderful aroma of a freshly brewed pot of coffee. Off to the right was a kitchenette and to the left a small restroom.

The agent walked over to the large picture window and closed the blinds while Rachel timidly walked over to one of the chairs and sat down; looking around the room to take in her surroundings. She glanced up at the clock. It said eight forty-five. *How long am I going to be here?* she wondered. *Hope this doesn't take long. I've got to feed Mikey. And by the way, who in the devil is going to drive me home?*

The door to the 'living room' opened and a middle-aged man in a dark grey well-fitting suit walked in. Every step shouted authority, smooth and perfected. Rachel noted he wasn't exactly handsome, but not bad looking either. His black hair was sprinkled with flecks of grey. His hazel eyes, behind silver rimmed glasses, were alive and alert. She thought they looked friendly enough, as did his smile. He definitely commanded attention, but it wasn't the man that interested her. It was the thick file he was carrying.

He and the agent didn't speak, but they made eye-contact, and once the door closed behind her, the man said, "Hello, Miss Wall."

Rachel started to get up, but he waved a hand. "Please, stay seated. No need to get up. Are you comfortable?"

"Yes, I am. Thank you."

He extended a hand. "My name is Zachary Osborn. I'm the Unit Director here in the Roanoke Office."

"Nice to meet you, Mr. Osborn," Rachel said politely, shaking his hand. "I am a bit confused as to why I'm here, so I hope..."

"I've no doubt you are," he interrupted, "but I hope we can clear things up pretty quickly. I'm sure my agents assured you I only want to ask a few questions. Once I've received satisfactory answers, I'll make sure you get home safe and sound. But before I get started, would you care for a cup of coffee?"

"No, no thank you. I'd really like to start and finish, so I can go home."

"I understand. Mind if I get one?"

Rachel shook her head. "No, please."

"While I do that, why don't you make yourself more comfortable? Take your coat off and sit back."

It was then Rachel thanked her good senses that she had gone to the Halloween dance as a scientist and not some monster, goblin, or worse, a clown. Sitting in the FBI office dressed in black pants, black turtle neck sweater, a white lab coat, dark rimmed glasses, and tussled hair, with a few pencils stuck here and there for effect didn't look nearly as funny as she would've if she were dressed in a rainbow-colored jumpsuit, a purple afro, a stark white face, and a big red nose. The thought made her chuckle softly.

Mr. Osborn plopped the file onto the coffee table and went to the kitchenette. Rachel turned her nose up and took a deep breath. The aroma of the coffee made her mouth water, but she fought the urge to ask for a cup. She wasn't going to give the impression she wouldn't mind if they kicked their feet up, sipped coffee, and chatted the night away. She wanted to go home, and the sooner the better.

Mr. Osborn carefully placed his cup on the table and took a seat in the wing-backed chair beside Rachel. She thought it rather strange that he decided to sit beside her, not across from her, but then again, maybe he didn't like the couch. She was pretty sure this wasn't the first time he'd been in this room.

He sat back, folded his hands across his stomach, and crossed his legs. He laid his head against the back of the chair and closed his eyes. The room was so quiet she could hear him breathing through his nose and for a second, she thought he'd fallen asleep.

Listening to the clock in the kitchenette pounding out the seconds, she started to feel uncomfortable.

He stirred at her heavy sigh. "Miss Wall, do you know where you are?"

That's a strange question. Of course, I do.

"Yes, I do," she answered.

"Would you mind telling me?"

She sighed again. "Are these the simple questions you wanted to ask me, Mr. Osborn?"

If he caught the annoyance in her voice, he didn't acknowledge it. "No ma'am. Please, tell me where you are."

"I'm in the Poff Federal Building, Roanoke, Virginia."

"What does the word 'federal' bring to mind?"

"Government," she answered quickly.

"Ok, good. So, you know we're not your local police?"

Rachel sat back in her chair, folded her hands across her lap, and closed her eyes too. It was that or scream. She decided to save the scream for later, especially if these types of questions continued. "Yes, I do know the difference," she said, trying not to sound impatient.

"Do you know what the FBI does?"

"Yes."

"What?"

"Well." She did have to stop and think for a second. "They protect the country from terrorism, white collar crimes, fraud, things like that." She opened one eye and peered over at Mr. Osborn. He didn't stir.

"Yes, very good, that is some of what we do. There is one responsibility you mentioned that I'd like to elaborate on. That we investigate white collar crimes. Do you know what a white-collar crime is, Miss Wall?"

Rachel opened her eyes and sat up. "Mr. Osborn, I'm a scientist. I have a PhD *and* a Doctorate in Osteopathic Medicine. I am not an unintelligent person, so please, would you stop with the elementary questions and let's get down to why I'm here."

At this, Mr. Osborn opened his eyes and looked over at her. "Ok, Miss Wall," he said firmly; the muscles in his jaw flexing and his eyes stern. "Yes, let's do get down to business."

He reached over and picked up the file. Handing it to Rachel, he said, "I apologize that you mistook my questions as demeaning or insinuating a lack of intelligence. My intent was quite the contrary. You see, Miss Wall, I know how intelligent you are. In fact, I think you down play your intelligence to keep yourself under the radar."

Rachel rounded on him. "What in the world are you talking about? You know nothing about me."

Osborn leaned over and picked up his cup. He took a couple gulps of the black liquid before setting it back down. "Boy, there's nothing like a good cup of coffee to calm the nerves." He smiled at Rachel before easing back into his chair and closing his eyes again.

"Let's see, where were we? Oh, yes, your statement about me not knowing anything about you. Well, I do know this; you were born in Strafford Memorial Hospital, Strafford, Virginia, November 17th, 1977, at 11:07 in the morning. Your parents were Jennifer and Stephen Wall, who, after spending several months in coma, died of injuries they'd sustained in a car accident the night of June 10th, 1998. They were on their way to the movies. If I'm not mistaken, to see *Armageddon*. That was the summer of your sophomore year at Princeton University, where you eventually earned your post-graduate MS, and your two doctorate degrees, holding a 4.1 GPA every term you attended. After your parents died, you threw yourself into your schooling and are now doing the same with your work. But all of that is public record, isn't it? I mean, I could find all of that just by searching the internet, couldn't I?" He shrugged his shoulders. "Well, most of it anyway."

Rachel blinked. She'd never thought of the internet as a place where one could learn so much about others, but Mr. Osborn was right. Most of this could be brought up with any search engine.

"What would impress you more is if I knew secret things, or little things that no one else would know, like your blood type is A-, your fourth-grade crush was Billy King, you have a mole on your left breast, just up and to the left of the nipple."

Rachel came straight up out of her chair.

Osborn didn't miss a beat. He opened his eyes and continued, "It wouldn't take much to learn your credit card numbers, but to know your pin numbers...5958, which is way too simple, and 1976, which is worse. You must change those." Mr. Osborn took a deep breath. "But what is even more impressive is I know the pin numbers to your grandparent's credit cards too, including the one that your Grandmother Ingram kept hidden from your grandfather." Rachel sat back down, very slowly.

"Should I go on, Miss Wall?"

"No," she whispered. "You know enough."

Osborn snickered. "You still don't get it do you, Miss Wall. I don't know enough, I know everything."

Rachel felt sick to her stomach. "Why am I here, Mr. Osborn?"

"The file that you are now holding on your lap contains the pending charges against you, Miss Wall. They are, but not limited to public corruption, grand larceny, espionage, and counter-terrorism."

Rachel laughed out loud. Mr. Osborn didn't.

"I'm not kidding, Miss Wall. An allegation has been filed against you by your employer, Plum Creek Laboratories; more specifically, Doctor Bruce Aberman."

Rachel couldn't believe what she'd just heard. "Doctor Aberman. But why? I've done nothing..."

"Miss Wall, if questions arise that even insinuate a federal violation has occurred, then it's the duty of the executive of that federal organization to report it to the FBI, and as the director of this unit, it is my duty, the FBI's duty, to consult with the US Attorney's office in the district where the alleged offense, or offenses took place. In your case, Doctor Aberman has brought forth such federal allegations and that is why you are in my building here in Roanoke."

She felt a migraine quickly forming behind her eyes. "What does that mean for me?" she asked quietly.

Osborn sighed. "In short, I'm going to have to detain you for a while as we investigate these alleged violations. I need a bit more evidence before submitting all of this to the federal prosecutor."

Rachel mouthed the word "prosecutor." This couldn't be happening to her. She only had a parking ticket in 2005. Why would Doctor Aberman do this?

She cleared her throat and swallowed back the fear that was creeping steadily up through her abdomen toward her chest. "I don't understand why I'm here, nor do I understand why Doctor Aberman would've brought these allegations against me. I couldn't even tell you how I'm involved in anything that would vaguely resemble counter-terrorism or any of those other crimes you mentioned. I'm being framed, simple as that, but I can't prove that, Mr. Osborn. I trust, through your investigation you will."

Mr. Osborn stood up, walked his coffee cup over to the small sink then turned and looked at her. "Miss Wall, my investigation isn't to try to prove or disprove your guilt or innocence. My investigation is to gather data. The federal prosecutor will review it, sort it, and then decide if there is enough evidence to charge you. If it were up to me, what's in that file is enough to put you away for years. Nothing in it smells of you being framed. In fact, it points to guilt, through and through."

"But..."

Mr. Osborn held up a hand. "But thank whatever god you believe in, I'm not the US attorney. I don't make those calls. I just provide data, evidence to the federal prosecutor. Once we're done, she'll decide where to go from there."

Osborn walked to the door. He placed his hand on the knob, but before leaving, turned to Rachel once more. "We can only hold you for seventy-two hours without charging you, Miss Wall. Believe me; agents will be working around the clock to ensure that no rock has been left unturned these next few days. We believe it's better to have too much information than not enough. In the meantime, Special Agent Montgomery, she's the female agent that escorted you up here, will take you to the detention center. She'll be with you at all times. In fact, she'll be the one taking care of your cat, Mikey, too. You'll not want or need for anything while you're in detention, unless at some time you feel you need to retain a defense attorney. That is one thing we can't provide for you. The court, however, can." With that, he turned and left, the door closing behind him with a loud click.

Rachel was alone.

The shaking started at her knees then worked its way up into her arms and down to her fingertips. The first tear fell off her chin without her feeling it, but then the numbness wore off and her face fell into her hands. "Dear God," she whispered, but the rest of her prayer couldn't get past her lips. Her skull felt like it was splitting in two. "Angel's wings," she muttered. "If there are such things as angels, please take what I cannot say to God on angel's wings."

With every pulsating thump, the muscles in her face convulsed, sending searing pain down the middle of her brain. She ran to the small restroom and threw up in the toilet. Carefully lowering herself to the floor, she stretched her arm over the rim of the bowl and rested her head on her elbow.

"Never mind, sweet angels," she whispered. "Please God, let me die." Kneeling in front of the toilet, the invisible ax came down hard and split her skull again. That was the last thing she remembered.

Moments later, or maybe it was days later, she didn't know which, her eyelids fluttered. With tremendous effort, she managed to open them to narrow slits. Bad idea. Spears of light slipped through the thin openings and pierced her eyes. Slamming them shut, she whispered a prayer for relief.

"Rachel." Her name was spoken softly.

She wanted to say something, but she couldn't think of a word that she could easily push between her lips. A moan floated up from somewhere, but even it got caught in the fat, dry walls of her throat.

The hot shards of pain stabbing her brain found a new rhythm that came from a mechanical beeping noise. *Beep, stab, beep, stab, beep, stab...*

Make it stop, she cried.

It did.

CHAPTER SIXTEEN

W hen the soft hand of consciousness gently shook her awake, she eased her eyes open again. No bright lights. Her head felt like it was full of cotton, but there wasn't any pain. For that, she was grateful.

Without lifting her head, she looked around the room. Thick heavy draperies covered the windows. They looked brown, but it was hard to tell. The room was dark. Everything looked brown.

"Where am I?" she muttered.

Taking her time, she sat up and slowly slid her feet off the bed. Perusing the room, she saw a business card perched against the base of the lamp on the night stand. Picking it up, it took a second for her eyes to focus, but she was able to make out "Federal Bureau of Investigation, Detention Center, Special Agent Sarah Montgomery". The phone number started with a 202-area code. "Humph," she groaned, tossing the card back onto the table. "A DC area code. Definitely not her direct number."

As if signaled, the phone on the night table rang. Resting her head in her fingertips, she shook her head. *Good lord. Who would be calling me here?*

She picked up the receiver with a shaky hand and put it to her ear. "Hello."

"Good morning, Miss Wall. This is Agent Montgomery. I hope I didn't wake you."

Rachel pushed hair from her face. "Um, uh, good morning Agent. No, you didn't wake me. I'm awake. Well, almost anyway."

"Good. Have you found your belongings in order?"

Her eyes darted around the dark room. "I've not had a chance to look yet but thank you for getting my stuff for me."

"You're welcome, Miss Wall."

"And thank you for taking me to the hospital too. I don't remember being taken but thank you. My head was killing me, almost literally."

There was a long string of silence on the other end.

"Agent Montgomery?"

"I'm here, Miss Wall, but I'm not sure what you mean. You were never taken to the hospital last night."

"But I remember hearing my name and a beeping noise, like from a heart machine or something."

"Fascinating," replied the Agent. "I'm not sure who you heard calling your name or what machine you're referring to, but I assure you, once I delivered you to your room at the detention center, you never left it."

Rachel rubbed her head. "Well, I must've dreamt it," she muttered.

Montgomery hesitated. "Yes, you must have. You were pretty much out of it. I hope you slept well."

Rachel sighed. "I did, thanks."

"And I hope you're hungry. I've ordered breakfast for you. It should be there in about twenty minutes."

"Migraines don't leave me very hungry, but I can nibble on something, I guess," Rachel answered sullenly. "Thank you for thinking of me."

"Right now, Miss Wall, it's my job to think of nothing or no one else but you. Eat what you can and then rest. I'll be by later to check on you."

"Thanks again, Agent Montgomery."

Rachel listened to the dull hum of a disconnected call before setting the receiver back down on the cradle. She turned her head, careful not to make sudden moves, and took in her surroundings. Someone had changed her into her favorite red plaid comfy pants and a long-sleeved t-shirt with a picture of The Eagles on the front. Her tennis shoes were on the floor beside a chair and her Halloween clothes were slung over the back. A pair of jeans and a pullover sweater hung on a wooden valet. She got up and walked over to the dresser. Every drawer she pulled out had her clothes in it. A few pieces were hanging in the closet and on the shelf above them was the smallest suitcase in her set.

In the bathroom, she found her toiletries in the same places she kept them at home. *Osborn does know everything, doesn't he?* She closed the medicine cabinet and looked at her reflection in the mirror. "Well, no," she whispered. "If he did, you wouldn't be here." She grabbed the jeans and the pullover sweater from the valet and made her way to the shower.

Hot water pummeled her tense body. She inhaled the steamy air and stretched her aching ribcage. *What was the song? Hurt so good?* Yeah, that's how it felt to breathe.

The migraine had taken the last of her energy, but the shower was like pouring water on a wilting flower. She turned her back to the shower head and let the pulsating stream beat against her shoulders. Standing there, she tried to piece together what she remembered about being taken to the hospital. Who took her? Who signed for her? How long was she there? What did they do? The migraine must have been the severest yet because her mind kept coming up empty, or half empty.

How strange that Agent Montgomery insisted she was

never taken to the hospital, that she hadn't left the detention center since she was delivered there last night. But that couldn't be true. Someone had called her name and there was a beeping noise from a machine. It was some sort of monitor. She'd heard it a million times at the lab.

They didn't leave a trace. Man, these people are good.

***

One monotonous day turned into the next while she waited in FBI detention. She read anything she could get her hands on, watched television, slept, but had no contact with anyone on the outside other than Agent Montgomery. Often, she'd sit and stare out of the large picture window; blindly staring at the barren trees, worrying about Carmen and wondering about Trace. Was he even still around? Did he have to return to, to, wherever it was he'd come from?

On the morning of the third day, just hours before Osborn had to release her or charge her, one question was answered. Trace came to visit her. She threw her arms around him and held him close for several minutes.

"I missed you too," he said softly.

She pressed her face to his chest. "How'd you get in here?"

"Very carefully," he chuckled.

She stepped away from him and he apparently caught the look in her eye. Before she could give him the "what if you get caught" lecture, he took her by the hand and led her toward the couch. Before sitting, he looked around.

"Pretty nice place for a detention center."

Rachel's eyes followed his around the room. "I guess the FBI puts a little more money into their facilities, so they don't look so, so prison like."

Trace smiled and gave her a look of approval. "Well, while

you've been staying here at the Ritz Carlton, I've been really busy following some leads, and, well, putting some of those pieces together so the puzzle is a bit more complete."

Rachel forgot about the "what if you get caught" lecture. "What'd you find out?"

"Let's sit down, Rachel. This could take some time."

He kept her hand in his. "First things first, how are you?"

"Oh, I'm fine," she lied, forcing a smile. "You know, just another day in FBI detention."

"I'm sorry," he said quietly. He leaned over and kissed her forehead. "I've been working hard to make sure your name is cleared in all of this. What I couldn't do, I've left in the hands of my partner. You're going to be alright."

"Partner? You have a partner?"

Trace lowered his eyes for a minute. When he looked back up at Rachel, her eyes were searching for an answer.

"I guess I do owe you the truth."

"You *owe* me nothing," she replied.

"Yeah, I do, Rachel. I only told you half of what I did at the lab when I worked there a few years ago. I did work with the morgues and body parts, all of that, but I was an undercover agent. I was part of the very organization who is detaining you now."

Rachel's eyes widened. "You worked for the FBI?"

Trace nodded. "I did," he confessed. "That's why the Plum Creek police have a file on me; not a very thorough one, but one nonetheless." He looked away in the distance. "I really thought my file would be much thicker. Oh well, guess we all can't be James Bond."

He chuckled and continued. "Anyway, we knew something was amiss at Plum Creek, but we couldn't find the evidence. Someone was moving body parts, working on cloning humans. They were going down a dark path, but just as soon as we thought we had something, we'd lose the lead. The District thought I was getting too close. Certain people at the lab were suspecting and the agency was afraid my cover might be blown, so they moved me from the lab to the dog food plant. We knew things were going on there too, but we weren't sure what."

"What did you eventually find?"

"It all has to do with cloning."

"Doctor Aberman said he was working on a cloning project," she said cautiously. "He mentioned it in the police car the night his office was robbed."

"Yeah, we know. We knew he had been working on those kinds of projects a long time ago. Since he was an expert in the field, we asked him to help us find the perpetrators. He drops that line occasionally; just to see if he can hook a lead. We figured once the right person heard he was back in business they'd contact him. Nothing of the sort happened until the night his office was robbed. Someone definitely wanted to see his files.

And right now, all fingers point to you, Rachel. You were in the lab that night. In fact, you were the only person in the lab that night. Right at the same time the robbery was being committed. That's why Aberman brought accusations against you."

"But, I was..."

"I know. And fortunately, the evidence against you is all circumstantial, but strong cases have been built on circumstances, Rachel. I'm just hoping what I've been able to learn will clear you."

"What's the worst of it?" Rachel asked bravely.

Trace pressed his lips together and sat quietly for a minute, slowly drumming his fingers on his knees. Finally, he looked up at her and said, "Well, I guess you have the right to know that too." Resting his elbows on his knees, he stared at the floor. "Have you ever heard of the Genesis Factor?"

Rachel blinked. "The what?"

"Guess that answers that." Sitting up, he studied Rachel's face. "The Genesis Factor," he repeated.

Rachel's brows arched. "I saw that name in the file Mr. Osborn showed me the other night, other than that, no. I don't know what the Genesis Factor is. I know what Genesis is," she said emphatically. "It's the first book in the Christian Bible and the Hebrew Torah. It tells of the creation of all things, the fall of Adam and Eve, and so forth. Why would that be of importance to Plum Creek Laboratories?"

Running the palms of his hands across his knees, he sat back and sighed. "Usually, when one hears the word Genesis, they immediately think of creation, but this, The Genesis Factor, goes a little beyond the creation theory. It specifically deals with Genesis chapter six, verses one through six."

"I'm, I'm sorry. I don't know what those verses specifically pertain to."

Trace rested his elbows on his knees again and rubbed his hands together. "I'm not sure if I should tell you now," he said quietly.

Rachel stiffened. "If I'm going to be charged with federal crimes, Trace, I'd like to know what I'm up against. Especially if they have to do with the very book on which I was raised."

Trace shook his head. "I only hesitate because it sounds so unreal, Rachel. It's like something right out of some science fiction novel, not what some consider the holiest of books. And I don't just mean the Bible. I mean most ancient religious texts."

"Well, I've often heard that truth can be stranger than fiction," she muttered.

"It certainly can be." Taking a deep breath, he went on. "Okay, as you said, you should know what you're up against." He cleared his throat, sat back, and stared at the ceiling.

"Before we go into the Biblical scenario, there is something

I'd like clarity on. I am, after all, just an FBI agent, not a scientist, so maybe you can help me understand a thing or two."

"Sure," said Rachel.

"I know what cloning is, but how is it done? The cliff note version, if you will."

This time Rachel cleared her throat and sat back in her seat. "Cloning of human cells has been researched for therapeutic reasons," she started. "So many diseases can be cured through stem cell cloning. The long name is Somatic Cell Nuclear Transfer, or SCNT. For short, it's referred to as Therapeutic Cloning, as I mentioned."

"Go on," said Trace.

"Scientists in this line of work use the same process used when Dolly was cloned. You know, the sheep. Do you remember Dolly?" Trace didn't open his eyes, he just nodded.

"The process consists of taking body tissue from a donor cell. The tissue is then fused with an unfertilized egg from which the nucleus has been removed. The egg 'reprograms' the DNA in the donor tissue. This forms the embryonic state. It divides until it reaches the early blastocyst stage. The cells are then harvested and cultured to create a stable DNA line that genetically matches the donor. The cells can become any type in the human body; hence, therapeutic cloning."

Trace opened one eye. "Is that it?"

"That's the elementary version of it, yes," Rachel replied. "Or the cliff note version, as you put it."

Trace closed his eyes and sat in silence; occasionally pursing his lips and muttering something. Leaning forward, he rested his elbows on his knees again. Rachel couldn't help but wonder why he was so fidgety.

"This is actually bigger than I realized," he finally said. "I can see why the feds are concerned about this."

"Cloning?" asked Rachel. "It's not really new. It's been

around for..."

"Not just cloning alone," he interjected. "But cloning as it pertains to the Genesis Factor."

"And you were just about to explain that to me," she said impatiently.

Trace nervously rubbed his hands together and took another deep breath. "Okay," he said exhaling. "As I said, The Genesis Factor is related to Genesis six. Now, please understand Rachel, I'm not a religious man, but because I was assigned to this case, I had to study these verses as thoroughly as possible, which meant reading and researching until I'd looked at this particular event from every possible angle."

Rachel nodded. "It's ok, Trace. Just explain the best you can."

"Ok, here goes. I've read and re-read these verses so many times, they're embedded into my brain, but I still have to paraphrase, okay?"

Rachel nodded eagerly.

"Well, according to ancient texts, of which there are several, sometime after creation, after Adam and Eve were dismissed from the Garden of Eden, the population on earth began to increase. Among having a lot of sons, couples were also having daughters. And these girls were so fine, so beautiful; they caught the attention of some, well, some really bad guys. The ancient texts refer to them as sons of God. After considerable research, I've concluded that these guys weren't humans, but demons, or fallen angels."

"But I thought Jesus was the only son of God," replied Rachel.

Trace didn't look up. "Different meaning," he said quickly. "We can talk about that later if you want, but regarding these demons, they're lust for human women became so strong, they decided to come to Earth and take these beautiful women."

"I didn't think angels could marry," interrupted Rachel. "They're not sexual beings, or that's what I was taught anyway."

Trace glanced at her. "That is actually a misnomer. Ancient texts don't say angels *can't* have sex, they say they *don't* have sex, meaning, they're so focused on their spiritual missions, worshipping God, that they don't consider having sex. They don't need it like humans do, but again, that's a different topic for a different discussion," he said edgily.

"I'm sorry. Go on."

"Well, after these fallen angels came to Earth and started having sex with human women, God decided he would limit the years man would live. In other words, he wasn't going to give the offspring of this evilness the opportunity to live on Earth as long as man had done prior.

"However, that didn't seem to bother them or their human counterparts. In fact, humans apparently started considering these offspring, or Nephilim as they're referred to in the texts, heroes, a race to be respected, even worshipped. More out of fear than adoration, but they became their gods nonetheless. But because these offspring were evil, mankind, who in their worship of them and desired to not offend them, became very wicked. So wicked that God regretted he even created humans." Trace rubbed his palms on his legs. "And well, I think you know the rest of the story."

Rachel nodded. "I do," she said softly. "It's the story of Noah and the ark. So, the Genesis Factor is why God destroyed the earth with a great flood?"

Trace smiled. "Yep. In short." The smile quickly faded. "But it's the long reason that concerns us."

"Please Trace, I'm confused. What does all of this have to do with me?"

Trace sighed heavily. "Think therapeutic cloning..."

"Okay," said Rachel.

"So, take DNA from humans who also have DNA from evil

beings."

"I still don't understand."

"Let me start from a different perspective. The ancient texts I mentioned use the term 'sons of God' when referring to the beings who lusted after human women and came to earth to have sex with them. In Hebrew, the original words are "Bennai Elohim" and Bennai Elohim is always a reference to angels. Apparently, God considers his creation, whether man or angel, his sons. And regardless if the angel decided to go rogue, once a son, always a son.

"Theologians, or some of them, confirm that these 'sons of God' were not good angels, but fallen angels, or part of the legion of angels that were kicked out of Heaven because of their rebellion against God. You are familiar with that part of Genesis, aren't' you?"

"Yes," said Rachel. "So, what you're saying is after Lucifer rose up and rebelled against God, and he and his legion were kicked out of Heaven, these fallen angels, or demons, were somewhere in the heavens looking down on the earth, and one day they noticed the daughters of men, who were absolutely gorgeous. They lusted after them then they called a meeting and agreed to come to earth and marry them."

"In essence, yes," agreed Trace. "However; in actuality, they came to Earth to rape them."

"What?" cried Rachel.

"The texts say, 'marrying who they chose', but the act of marriage then wasn't the same as we define it today. It literally meant 'to have intercourse with'." Trace grew very somber. "They didn't court these women, Rachel. They didn't fall in love with them then go ask their dads if they could have their hand in marriage.

"No, being evil incarnate, they forced themselves on them. That's rape. And the worst part, some women got pregnant and had children by them; giant, evil children. Half human, half demon giants walking among humans as if they belonged here. These offspring of demons and humans were called the Nephilim. I referred to them earlier, and, if you read the verses, the Bible refers to them by name too."

"Ok, if these, Net, Nem.."

"Nephilim."

"Ok, if these Nephilim were giants, why are there no giants on the earth anymore? Did they just die out? Get killed by an asteroid? Survival of the fittest? What?"

"Whether there are giants still here or not can be argued. There are archeological sites, and even current sites that differ from the opinions of the naysayers; however, the point isn't about the existence or non-existence of giants, the point is about their DNA."

Rachel stood up. Lost in thought, she paced the floor. "You mean..." She stopped pacing, her eyes resting on Trace. "You mean, if this factor is true, there were beings on this earth that, apart from their height, looked like us, but had different DNA; a more powerful, evil DNA?"

"Yep."

"And because of the Nephilim and the evilness they brought to Earth, God destroyed them and everyone else, except Noah and his family in the flood?"

Trace shook his head. "Nope."

No?" she said defiantly. "The scriptures say everything, and everyone was destroyed in the flood except Noah, his family, and the animals in the ark."

Trace rubbed his forehead. "There are various theories on that too," he sighed, "but the Nephilim made it through the flood, or at least their DNA did. We're not sure how, could've been by either going back into spiritual form, leaving their earthly bodies for a time, as demons have been known to do and therefore not being killed in the flood, or by going underground. Some even believe that although Noah was of Adam's pure lineage, maybe one of his three daughters-in-law wasn't. If even one of those women was from Nephilim lineage, they would've started the process again when they had children, thus putting the Nephilim DNA back into human lineage."

"Just so I understand, these Nephilim, or offspring of human women and evil celestial beings were half human, half demon giant beings that lived here on earth before the flood?"

"Yes."

"And then after the flood, they were still here, and then they mated and had children?"

"Yes."

"And the children of the Nephilim were known as...what?"

"Rephaim."

"Were they giants too?"

"Some of them, but not all."

"And so, if one of Noah's daughters-in-law was of Nephilim lineage, as you just mentioned, then she would have been a Rephaim."

"Yes, if she was of Nephilim lineage."

Rachel spun on her heels. Her defiant stare drilled into Trace's eyes. "Wait a minute," she scowled. "What you're telling me is that the Nephilim had children. So then, did their children have children, and their children have children, and so forth until we end up here, with our modern population?"

Trace dropped his eyes. "Now, you're getting the picture."

Rachel folded her arms across her chest and stared out the window, the morning sun shining off her face. "Just how evil were these Nephilim, these hybrids?" she asked quietly.

"They were master herbalists and..."

"That doesn't sound so bad," she interrupted. "Carmen's a master herbalist and I don't think she's evil."

"They weren't just experts on how to grow herbs, Rachel, but they mastered cross sectioning DNA, and not just with plants, but with animals alike."

"Go on," encouraged Rachel.

"Well, knowing how to clone an animal, what if you crossed DNA of two varied species, say a human and a horse. What could you get?"

Rachel thought for a minute and then snickered. "No, uh uh, Trace. That's ludicrous. Centaurs are mythical creatures. They weren't and never have been real."

"So, you know what kind of animals, or types of animals walked the earth before it was destroyed by the flood?"

"Well, no, but..."

"They cross sectioned DNA, Rachel. You're a geneticist. Think about it!"

Rachel's face paled. Speechless, she turned to the window. A few seconds passed before she swallowed hard and words came to mind. "So, the mythical creatures we read about could have been real at one time, like unicorns, and flying horses, women with snakes for hair, and mermaids, and Cyclops, and sea monsters, and so forth all due to these experiments done by Nephilim?"

"Satan commissioned his demons to destroy the beauty of God's creation, Rachel. Mankind especially, but not only mankind. God didn't bring all species of animals to the ark, Rachel."

Rachel grew very somber. "What else," she mumbled, lowering her head.

"Astronomy, astrology, war science, weaponry, drugs, piercing the body, painting the body ..."

Rachel held up a hand, but Trace didn't stop. "And it's also believed that Nephilim and their children were cannibals."

"Cannibals?"

"Yep. Imagine their ravenous hunger. They were giants with giant appetites. Once they decimated the animal population, including their own creations, what would they have turned to?"

"My lord," whispered Rachel. "Sounds like a horror movie."

"Yep," said Trace.

Rachel started pacing again, staring intently at the floor.

When she stopped, she looked over at Trace. "Goliath," she said resolutely. "Goliath was a giant. Was he a Rephaim?"

Trace, grinned. "Yeah, ol' Jack didn't have anything on David."

Rachel's eyes darkened. "What? Who? Jack who?"

Trace chuckled. "You know, Jack. Jack the giant killer. He didn't have anything on David. David was the original giant killer."

Rachel stopped pacing and stared at him like he'd lost his mind.

"I just thought I'd throw that in for free," he said sheepishly.

Rachel still didn't smile.

"Again, Rachel, truth woven into a Grimm fairytale."

Rachel threw her arms up in frustration.

Trace cleared his throat. "Okay then. Getting back to the ancient texts...Og, King of Bashan was another giant mentioned in the Bible. It's recorded that his bed was made of iron and was eighteen feet long by eight feet wide in our measurements."

Trace sat back in his chair and sighed. "But even before the time of David and Goliath, do you remember the story of Joshua, going into the Promised Land for the first time?"

Rachel nodded. "Yes," she said quietly.

"Well, the first um, people, I guess, they ran into were the Anakites. Anakites were Rephaim. Again, the Biblical record states that Joshua and the twelve spies that went with him into the Promised Land brought grape clusters back to camp that were so large they had to be carried by two men."

He sat quiet for a second. "Grape clusters, Rachel. Not some animal they'd killed while hunting, but grape clusters so big it took two men to carry them."

Rachel looked at Trace with wide eyes. "And when God told them to go into the Promised Land and claim it, he told them to kill every living thing. That really bothered me when I was a kid. Why would God demand that people kill people, but that's why! Because the inhabitants were Rephaim."

Trace nodded again. "Yes," he said slowly. "And he didn't order them to just kill the humans, but *every living thing.*"

Rachel lowered her head. "Animals, perverted I'll admit, but plants? That's a bit absurd."

Trace leaned forward and did what he always did when he put his elbows on his knees; he rubbed his hands together.

"You do that a lot, don't you?" she asked, watching him from the corner of her eye.

"What?"

"Lean forward and rub your hands together. It's a dead giveaway that you're nervous."

Trace picked at the palm of his hand. "This isn't easy to talk about, Rachel. I mean, we're talking evil here. Not just mean or perverted as you put it. Not promiscuous or people experimenting with their sexuality. These, um, things were pure evil. An evil we can't really get our heads around. Their agenda was to defile EVERYTHING that had anything to do with God's creation. Just like the first demons that came from the heavens and had sex with human women, those after them were hell-bent on destroying all that was good and holy."

"Speaking of 'the first place,' I'd like to go back to the

Nephilim for a minute."

"Ok, shoot."

"Didn't you say the Bible called the Nephilim heroes of the day, men of renown?"

"Yeah."

"So why were they considered heroes if they were so evil?"

"It's believed the people became so afraid of them, they started to bow to them. Remember, besides being able to speak of heavenly places, and show them things humans had little or no knowledge of, they were cannibals, so the people were in awe of them. There was plenty of reason to fall and worship them. Nephilim were super intelligent, herculean strong, probably good looking too. After all, they were part celestial. And that's why many believe they became the gods of old, Rach. Gods known to us as Zeus, Hercules, Thor, Ra, Poseidon, some of the Pharaohs, the whole lot of them."

"Roman, Greek, and Egyptian gods?"

"Yes, those guys...and gals."

Rachel rubbed her head. It had started to ache again. "But they're just myths," she said wearily. "I've watched enough of *Aliens through the Ages* on television to know that some suspect them of being from outer space, but they weren't real, they're just mythological gods drummed up by ancient cultures."

"Were they? Almost every culture on earth has a story in their 'religion' about spiritual beings coming to earth, impregnating human women, and living as gods. Not just the Hebrews, but the Egyptians, Hindus, Native Americans, Islamist, the list goes on. In Christianity, theologians believe these beings to be the Nephilim. Real beings who, because of their intricate knowledge of God and Heaven, but pure evil, struck fear into the hearts of men and made themselves gods in their eyes.

"Power, Rachel! Immeasurable power, and with that power, they taught men the sciences of physics, geometry, and engineering by helping them build great structures like the Egyptian Sphinx and Pyramids, the Moai of Easter Island, Stonehenge, even the Biblical Tower of Babel. They taught men how to fight, how to make weapons, how to hate, and cheat, and lie; how to steal, rape, and make war."

Rachel's heart grew heavy. "And because men had turned their backs on their Creator, worshipping the Nephilim instead, God was sorry he had made humans, and set out to destroy his own creation to rid the universe of this evilness?"

Trace nodded slowly. "Yes, that, and because his creation had been so utterly defiled. The verses I referred to earlier also say that man's every word, every deed, and every thought of his heart was evil, and therefore, God was sorry he had created them."

Rachel went back to the window. A few minutes later, she turned to Trace. "And that's why Noah and his family were spared, as well as two of every animal; male and female of undefiled animals. Humans and animals that were still pure; still made of the DNA that God had created in them."

Rachel sat back down on the couch beside Trace. "Unless one of his daughters-in-law was of..."

"Yes," interrupted Trace, "but that can't be proven. "What can be proven, or at least confirmed via all the ancient texts throughout the world, is that the Nephilim were here before the flood and their children, the Rephaim, were here after the flood."

The two sat quiet for a long time. Trace watched Rachel's face. The big picture began to take form in Rachel's mind. "Wow," she whispered. "This is a lot to take in. I mean, I was brought up in a Christian home, I know the story of Noah and the ark like the back of my hand." She hesitated a moment. "Or at least I thought I did...until now."

Trace was going to say something, but she held up a hand and went back to the window. She stood there watching the birds fly from tree to tree, cars going up and down the street, people walking up and down the sidewalks, crossing the streets. "What does all of this have to do with us today, Trace?" she asked quietly.

He glanced at her from the corner of his eye. "The more specific question is what does all of this have to do with Doctor Rachel Wall?"

He folded his arms against his chest, and watched her face, especially her eyes. Her scientific mind whirled from all that she'd just been told until his last question hit home.

She slowly raised her head and stared into his face. Fear shone blatant in her eyes. "Someone wants to recreate the Nephilim," she said softly. "By extracting their DNA from human blood. There are no recorded skeletal remains, but if Rephaim reproduced generation to generation, their DNA is in our blood. We, geneticists, could extract their DNA from blood, fuse it with a donor cell, and ...the possibilities would be endless; armies, world power, terrorism, all the crimes listed in that file."

Her hands began to shake. A sharp spear of pain slid down the middle of her brain. At the same time, an intense, excruciating light pierced her eyes. "Oh my god!" she screeched as she grabbed her head. "The project...my project at the lab. To clone human blood..."

Trace took her in his arms and held her as she buried her face in his chest and cried. "Someone suspects me of doing this?" she mumbled.

"Shh," Trace said soothingly. "Shh..." He held her close for a long time, until her sobs eventually turned to sniffles.

She finally wiped her wet, swollen face with her hands.

"No," he whispered. "Not recreate, Rachel. Just, well, reactivate. We believe they're already here. They've always been here."

Rachel looked up at him in disbelief.

"Evil incarnate," repeated Trace. "Men like Hitler, Stalin, Vlad Dracula, Napoleon, and Ted Bundy to name a few. We label them serial killers and psychopaths; people who can kill without blinking. Do you know studies have been done on the brains of serial killers and they all have one thing in common?"

"I know about it," murmured Rachel. "They have the MAOA gene and, and sometimes a variant of Cadherin 13. The MAOA gene codes for the enzyme Monoamine Oxidase A, which is important for controlling the amount of dopamine and serotonin in the brain and CDH13 has previously been associated with substance abuse and ADHD."

"Yeah," said Trace, softly kissing Rachel's hair. "Amazing isn't it? Wonder why their DNA is different than mainstreams?"

Rachel buried her face deeper into Trace's chest. "This can't be?" she moaned. "My god, this can't be."

"Pretty heavy stuff, I know." He pushed her back a little, so he could look into her eyes. "And there's something else, Rachel," he said, wiping the hair from her face.

"More?" she asked, her breath coming in gulps.

"The reason I was killed. I know why now."

Rachel sat up; her liquid eyes staring blankly into his.

"Although the public will never be told this, over a hundred years ago, giant skeletons were found at a Georgia excavation site. A government operative at the time sent three to a private lab; a private lab in the basement of his house. Keeping his work secret, especially from the prying eyes of the government, he was able to extract DNA from them and what he concluded was that type of DNA had never been seen or recorded before. Those beings were not from this world."

"Oh my god," she whispered. "What does that...?"

"A few months ago, those same skeletons resurfaced and, well, I don't know all the particulars, we're still looking into those, but we do know DNA samples from those giant skeletons were sent to various labs throughout the world."

Rachel's breathing became labored. "Not?"

Trace averted her eyes and looked at the floor. "Yes," he said, finally lifting his face up to hers. "Including Plum Creek."

"No," Rachel said loudly. "You don't know this. You don't..."

"But I do," Trace said calmly. He faced her and boldly said, "I was the one who delivered the DNA to them."

Rachel covered her mouth with her hands and fell back into the couch. "I can't believe this," she moaned.

"Remember I told you that the dog food plant was a front for selling human organs on the black market; well, when we dug deeper, we also discovered they were in the business of selling alien DNA.

This DNA came in through the food plant with final orders to be taken to Plum Creek Laboratory and I was the stooge who was assigned the task. Because of it, I knew who it went to, who signed for it. I knew too much. I had to be eliminated."

"Doctor Aberman?"

"We believe he knows about the significance of the DNA and that's why his office was broken into, but we're not sure. One thing we are certain of though, *he* didn't sign for it."

"Then who?" she pleaded.

"In time," Trace whispered. "All in due time, my dear Rachel."

"You said DNA samples were sent to other laboratories as well."

"We figured about three others here in the states; one in each time zone. DNA was also sent overseas to a few labs in Europe, Asia, and Australia, basically to our allies."

"Why to our allies?"

"Think world dominance, Rachel. Think of the possibilities

if our Allies were able to create a super army with super-soldiers. Strong, undefeatable men with iron clad skin like armadillos, soldiers who can sniff out their enemies from a mile away, literally like dogs, and soldiers who wouldn't blink at killing. They'd have no remorse in constantly killing and mutilating their enemy. These beings wouldn't only be part human and part Rephaim, but they'd have characteristics of various animals and certain plants.

"Back in the time described in Genesis, to defile creation, the evil ones had to imbed their DNA into everything, even plants, and if they were as intelligent as we give them credit for, they probably did it in a similar fashion as we do today. Easily mixed in a bowl or something then injected into seeds, planted in the earth, and then up springs various plants like Waterwheels, Pitchers, Flypaper traps, and the infamous Venus flytrap. Now, granted, those are small examples, but who knows what existed before the flood and what's taking place in our laboratories today."

"Surely nothing like that is going on at Plum Creek," Rachel said thoughtfully. "Mixing human DNA with animals and plants, making weird Manimals like those on the syfy channel."

"I don't know, Rachel, but someone wants that DNA. And they'll kill to get it. I'm proof of that."

"And this is why I'm being detained here?" she said slowly, tears welling in her eyes again.

"One of the Petri dishes you asked me to hide for you is related to all of this, Rachel." She looked at him incredulously.

"Are you accusing me of..."

"No, not in full, but being a geneticist, you know about the Rhesus monkey and how some of us have the same gene in our blood as those monkeys; hence the name."

"Yes, it's the Rhesus factor or better known as the Rh factor. Blood is typed as A, B, or O. All of these can be classified as either positive or negative, depending on the presence of the Rh factor, or the lack thereof. For example, if someone has A positive blood, it means that their blood type is A with the presence of the Rhesus gene. If one has A negative blood, their blood type is A, but there is no presence of the Rhesus gene."

"Why would humans have a gene from a monkey in their blood, Rachel?"

"Evolution."

"That's exactly why secularism has accepted evolution as 'the norm.' To do so provides an easy out, but don't look at this from the secular view point; look at it from the view of the Genesis Factor."

Rachel went pale. "Nephilim cross sectioning human DNA and monkey DNA."

"And why would some people have this gene while others don't?"

"Preservation," she whispered. "Through Noah."

Trace nodded. "It is said that those who are positive for the gene are normal, and those whose blood is negative of the gene are of Rephaim decent...but I beg to differ."

Rachel stared at him curiously.

"You just said it yourself, doctor. Only cross sectioning human DNA, human DNA that had already been defiled by demons, with monkey DNA would cause some humans to share that gene today. Doesn't that lead you to logically determine that the positive blood line is the corrupt bloodline?"

Nodding her head slowly, Rachel agreed. "Yes," she said, "logically it would." Her dark, round eyes darted up to meet his, "but, but that would also mean..."

Trace nodded. "Yes, it would. That's why I said no one is trying to recreate the Nephilim; they're just trying to reactivate it. Taking what they have in human genetics today and interjecting it with old DNA to reestablish the unique strength, height, skills, knowledge, and even evilness of the Nephilim."

"I'm not involved in that Trace. I don't know why I'm being accused of it, but I..."

"But you heard of it, and that's why there are two other Petri dishes. You wanted to find out for yourself if a scientific rumor is true."

She searched his eyes intently. "How did you know about the other two dishes? They're locked in my desk drawer."

One corner of his mouth curled up and he snickered. "I know you, Rachel. I know you better than you know yourself."

She turned her back to him and walked back to the window. He followed her, placed his hands on her shoulders, and kissed her head. "It's ok," he said tenderly.

"I know you had to see it for yourself, to the point you even used your own blood. You are after all, a scientist."

Rachel glanced around the room. "And all of this has brought me here."

"You're a deterrent, Rachel. You're being used to throw the FBI off track."

"The FBI doesn't seem to think so," she said quietly, letting her head fall against his chest. "I've got to go take some migraine medicine, Trace. Wait here, I'll be right back."

She walked slowly to the bathroom where she washed her face and gulped down a couple of pills. When she came back out, Trace was standing by the door.

"I've got to go back, Rachel," he said softly.

"I understand," she said, tugging at his shirt sleeve. "You've been out of the freezer too long."

Trace's eyes searched her face. "No Rachel. I've got to go back to, well, to sleep, to wherever I was before Carmen summoned me. My time is up."

His beautiful eyes searched her face and he smiled. Her heart skipped a beat. "Trace," she whispered, "don't leave me, not now."

"We knew this would eventually happen, Rachel," he said affectionately. "I've wondered what it would've been like to have had the chance to get to know you before the so-called accident. I would like to see all of this to the end, live out this fantasy with you, but you and I both know that's not possible. No one ever promised I'd be able to stay. In fact, we knew the opposite to be true, even if we didn't want to admit it."

Rachel bit her lip and fought the tears. Leaning in, she closed her eyes as her lips softly brushed against his mouth. Suddenly, she felt a rush she hadn't felt in a very long time. She pressed her lips against his as her hands slid up around his neck. Pushing herself against him, she kissed him harder, but he didn't kiss her back. Instead, his cold hands gripped her wrists and brought her arms down to her side.

"No, Rachel," he said, taking a step back. "Even if I could stay, this wouldn't work."

"Why?"

His look penetrated her heart. "Rachel, I'm cold. I have no blood running through these veins. I mean, I have no heartbeat. In fact, I think I left my heart in San Francisco." He chuckled at his small attempt at humor, but she didn't appreciate it at all.

"Rachel," he whispered. "Look at me. I mean, really look at me. I have no color, no spirit, and no emotions. I'm dead."

Tears rolled down her face. "You don't understand Trace. I'm the one who's dead. I breathe air through my lungs, I'm warm to the touch, my heart beats in my chest, but there hasn't been life in me for years. You've brought more, given me more life than I've felt in a very long time. No Trace, you're more alive than I am. I'm the walking dead!"

Trace wrapped his arms around her. "Don't say that,

Rachel. You're alive. One day, and one day soon, someone will walk into your life and boom, he'll sweep you off your feet and you and your knight will ride off into the sunset on his fearless steed."

Rachel backed away and turned her head. "Please don't patronize me."

Trace leaned over and kissed the top of her head. "I love you, Rachel," he whispered, 'but you don't need me anymore. There's someone else now who will help you through this."

She closed her eyes and sighed. "Love is an emotion, Trace."

There was no response. Opening her eyes, the room was empty.

Trace was gone.

CHAPTER SEVENTEEN

R achel fell into the chair. Her conversation with Trace plowed through her mind; making her nauseous. Alien DNA, super soldiers, world dominance, all of it, as it pertained to Plum Creek fell on her shoulders. Every thought made it harder to breathe. Sweat poured down her face. She grabbed her purse, slid onto the floor, and dumped everything out.

She didn't care that her choices were unusual, she used what she had; lipstick, pens, tablets, old pieces of candy, tissue, paperclips, anything and everything. When she finished, she sat in the middle of a makeshift circle, shrouded in total silence. Raising her arms, she closed her eyes and chanted a prayer. She invited God to come into her circle of protection, to be her Guardian.

A bead of sweat rolled down the back of her neck and under her collar. Her breathing quickened. She was scared. She had no idea what to expect, where all of this would lead, what the outcome would be, but she did know she didn't want to face it alone.

When she lowered her arms and opened her eyes, she heard nothing. There was no clap of thunder, no voice telling her all was well, no angels singing songs of celebration of her return to the fold...nothing. She looked around, not even knowing if her prayer had reached the ceiling, but she had reached out to him. Now, if God had been listening, he'd have to come to her.

No sooner had she finished tossing her belongings back into her purse, she heard a key turning in the lock. The door opened slowly, and she found herself face to face with Director Osborn; behind him stood Special Agent Montgomery. She glanced at the Director, at the agent, then back to him.

"Well, Miss Wall," Osborn said matter-of-factly. "We can't hold you any longer. The evidence against you is circumstantial and because she doesn't have solid proof, the prosecutor will not bring charges against you right now."

Rachel's hand flew to her throat. She fought back the urge to yell, "I told you so."

"But bear in mind, Rachel, this isn't over," continued the Director. "We're still investigating this matter. We will find something, it's just a matter of time."

Time is our most precious commodity, Mr. Osborn. She looked up into his face and smiled. "That's all I need, just a little bit of time."

"Special Agent Montgomery will take you wherever you want to go, your house, your family's house, it doesn't matter, as long as it's in Plum Creek."

Rachel didn't wait for him to finish. She ran to the closet and pulled down the suitcase. It was time to get back home, and even though she wasn't sure how, it was time to put an end to this nightmare.

Director Osborn stuck his head around the door, "Don't leave Plum Creek Miss Wall," he said loudly.

***

The tires of the Lincoln Towncar were crunching against the stone driveway as Rachel slipped into Carmen's house. The living room was empty when she collapsed onto the couch, but before she could get out one good yawn, Carmen was all over her, shooting out questions as fast as her mouth could form the words. Too tired to listen, Rachel closed her eyes and summoned a calming darkness to fill her head. Finally, out of steam, Carmen fell into a chair.

"I'm sorry, Rach. I know you're wiped out. In fact, I'm surprised you're here. Why aren't you at home?"

Rachel fell over, her head sinking into a cushion. "I just needed to be with family right now, Carmen. I've been alone for days, and I just needed to be around you. Is that alright?"

Carmen pulled a blanket from the back of the couch. "Of course, it is," she said softly. "Would you like a cup of tea?" Rachel's heavy breathing answered her.

The smell of freshly brewed coffee tickled her nose. The living room was dark and quiet, although she could see light coming from the back of the house. Sipping the drool from the corner of her mouth, she sat up, catching what she'd missed with the sleeve of her sweater.

It took a second to remember where she was and that it was Carmen's Columbian coffee that had flirted with her nose. She glanced at her watch. *5:30.* She drug herself to the bathroom before shuffling to the kitchen in search of a coffee cup.

"A cup of coffee and breakfast burritos too." Pulling her hair over her shoulder, she slid into a chair. "Everything smells delicious."

"Enough for all, and then some," said Carmen.

"I love having breakfast for supper."

Glancing over at Eric she gave a sleepy smile. "I didn't see you come in, Eric."

Eric looked at her over the rim of his cup and smiled back. "That's because you were sound asleep my dear. And this isn't supper. It's breakfast. It's five-thirty in the morning."

Rachel wrinkled her nose. "No way," she mumbled,

"Yes way," said Eric, taking a gulp of coffee.

"Five thirty in the morning? But how can that be? Agent Montgomery dropped me off around five. I looked at my watch before I fell asleep. I thought I'd only been asleep for thirty minutes."

Carmen raised her fork to her mouth. "You've been asleep for twelve hours, Rachel. You were worn out, so I just let you sleep."

Eric laughed. "Yep, you were one tired puppy."

"No wonder I'm hungry." Rachel dug into her breakfast.

"I'll take you home later," said Eric. "Mikey misses you."

"I know. I miss him too."

"Mikey's been taken care of by some woman, but when Eric and I went over to your house yesterday, we didn't see Tigger," said Carmen. "He's not been around lately."

Rachel's heart rose in her throat. She didn't want to get into a long diatribe about it, but she had to tell them. "I guess when Trace left, Tigger left too."

Carmen's eyes grew round. "Trace is gone? Are you sure?"

Rachel's face grew hot. She nodded and took another bite of her burrito. "Dis is gwait."

"Thanks. When did you see Trace last?"

Rachel sighed, but didn't stop eating. She was too hungry. "Yesterday afternoon," she said between bites. "He came to the Detention Center to see me, helped me sort some things out and say good-bye."

"Mmm," muttered Carmen.

Eric cleared his throat. "Well, I'm gonna miss the guy. He was kinda cool."

Carmen looked at him and smirked. "No pun intended, I'm sure."

Eric chuckled and shoveled another fork full of food into

his mouth.

"I do have a bit of investigative work to do on my own," Rachel said vaguely. "I entrusted him with an experiment of mine and I've no idea where he put it."

Carmen looked alarmed. "But Rachel, you can't go back to the lab. Not yet."

Eyebrows raised, both Rachel and Eric threw her a questioning look.

"What I mean is you just left the FBI. They're watching you. Don't you think going to the lab will look suspicious or something?"

Rachel suddenly lost her appetite. "No, I don't. Quite the contrary. Everyone knows I'm a workaholic, so it would be more suspicious if I don't go to the lab. And like I said, I've got to find that petri dish. It's probably been exposed and of no use, but I've got to see."

Carmen looked over at Eric and then back at Rachel. "How do you propose to get into the facility? Walk through the front doors?"

Furrows stretched deep across Rachel's forehead as she looked at her friend. "What are you not telling me, Carmen? Why can't I just walk through the front doors? Mr. Osborn didn't say I couldn't. In fact, he said nothing about the lab at all, other than acknowledging they are my employer. Do you know something I don't?"

"No, she doesn't," said Eric. "You know Carmen, Rachel. She's just being a mother hen. Plan on going over tomorrow?"

Rachel thought for a second. "I don't know, what's tomorrow?"

"Wednesday," said Eric. "If you'd like, I can go with."

Rachel shook her head. "Thanks Eric, but no. I'm sure the lab will be in full mode tomorrow, so there'll be plenty of people who'll see me and, if necessary, can testify that I didn't try to do anything sinister. I just want to find my experiment and get back to work."

The three friends finished eating their meal in silence; everyone in deep thought about whatever topics concerned them. Rachel glanced around the table. She was sure Carmen was mentally grading papers, Eric wondering about whatever Eric wondered about, probably Carmen, and she, well, she had to admit, she just couldn't get Nephilim out of her head. The more she thought about the whole ordeal, the more it worried her.

This situation was huge; bigger than she initially imagined. The 'simple' project that Doctor Aberman assigned to her, although he might not have realized it, had everything to with it. Cloning blood for blood banks? Really? What she was supposed to do was figure out how to clone blood so whoever was leading this deplorable project would be able to clone soldiers and if necessary, have extra on hand to keep them alive. She was sure of it.

There's no way I can explain this to Carmen. She'd think I've lost my mind. One has to consider ancient texts somewhat factual in order to even start to believe in this Nephilim, and I don't know what Carmen thinks of the Bible. She made a mental note that one day she needed to ask.

Chewing on a bite of bacon, she thought of going to the lab the next day. How was she ever to look at life the same way? Now, after what she's learned about the darkness that fills everything, nothing will be the same. Nothing will hold beauty or joy. How she longed for the quiet, boring ignorance she had before. Snowflakes, sunrises, sunsets, ocean waves, the awesomeness of an airplane taking off, hearing the wind in the trees, lightning, the four seasons; children laughing, heck, her own laughter; how will life maintain its beauty if in the background there is the threat of dark, wicked people who live only to subject humans to their evil agenda?

Why is someone always trying to devise a plan to take over the world, to end life as we know it? There are so many unknowns out there. *God, how can this be?* A sinking feeling came over her and she didn't feel like being around anyone anymore. She just wanted to go home.

Eric drove her home, but they didn't talk. She planned to pretend to be half asleep, but she didn't have to pretend too much. The warmth of the car soon lulled her into semi-consciousness until Eric gently touched her arm and told her she was home.

Once inside the house, she dropped her suitcase and soaked in every detail of every item she owned. Even with boxes piled in the corners and the neglected pictures that were leaning against the walls waiting to be hung up, her small house had never looked as good to her as it did at that moment. Compared to Carmen's house, it was empty, stark and well, not much, but it was home, her real haven.

Mikey ran to her. Weaving between her feet, he purred louder with every twist. She picked him up and buried her face in his neck. "Hey sweet boy," she whispered. He rubbed his whiskers across her cheek and rumbled.

"I know, and I'm sorry. I didn't mean to be gone so long. It'll never happen again, I promise." His green eyes searched her face before he brushed the tip of her nose with his sandpaper tongue. "Thank you," she giggled. "Guess I should feed you, huh?" The cat whirred his approval and they headed to the kitchen.

Reaching up into the cupboard for a can of Royal Cat Chunky Chicken, her eyes slid over to the kitchen window. For some reason, what she saw surprised her. The trees were totally bare. A few dried leaves lay stretched out across the pale grass, surrendered to their winter deaths, while others raced hopelessly across the yard to hide under withered bushes. Gray clouds rolled listlessly across a murky sky; threatening snow. She set the can on the counter and took in the view of her backyard. "Good heavens, Mikey," she said quietly. "It's November."

Mikey whirled around her feet, purring louder. "Ok," she

muttered. "I'm getting it. I just didn't realize so much had changed since last Friday."

Something flickered in the corner of her yard. It shocked her to see a fleeting shadow. Was it a person's shadow or the swaying of a bare branch that caught a fleeting ray of sun in its gnarly limbs?

She ran to the door, yanked it open, and fell out onto the stoop. Stopped by a spear of frigid air, she pulled her sweater tighter around her shoulders and yelled, "Who's out there? What do you want?" The only sound that came back to her was the whistling of a freezing wind as it whipped in and out of the naked branches above her.

Winter's icy fingers slipped around her and gripped her whole body, but she wouldn't relinquish. She stood there, shaking uncontrollably and examined every inch of the yard until she was satisfied no one was there. Slowly, she turned and walked back into the house, making sure the dead bolt clicked into place.

Mikey was loudly protesting the delay, eyeing the unopened can that she'd left on the counter. She grabbed the can opener and stood at the window, keeping one eye on the can and the other on the back yard.

As Mikey ate, she walked room to room, pulling a sliver of curtain back, or raising a blind to peek out into the yard. Each time, she saw nothing. Satisfied, she went to her bedroom and pulled down the bedcovers. *There might be someone out there,* she thought, *but I'm too tired to care anymore.*

Crawling under the comforter, the Genesis Factor seemed like a bad dream. *There can't be any truth to it, can there? But the verses, the other ancient religions that acknowledge the same event, it can't be all myth can it?*

She yawned deeply and closed her eyes. *Whatever the future holds, Rachel, you must leave it alone. You, after all, are mere human. You can't stop the progression of evil. There are other 'warriors' out there who are better equipped to fight that battle. You just have to clear your name from this mess.*

She rolled over onto her side. Mikey plopped down in the curve of her stomach and curled up into a tiny ball. Scratching the top of his head, she closed her eyes and whispered, "The Lord is my shepherd." The last thing she heard before falling into a peaceful sleep was the soft, rhythmic purring of her sleeping cat.

But when evil is present, peace is an illusion. It's a deception, a mirage that fills a heart, a room, a space in time, for just awhile. Then it slips away, leaving behind darkness and a bitter rage, just like the torturous memories left by an untrue lover.

CHAPTER EIGHTEEN

Rachel's ponytail swayed back and forth from the loop in the back of her McArthur High School baseball cap; not to music, but to a silent rhythm she kept in her head. Earlier, a few people had stared and murmured when she walked by, but refusing to acknowledge their curiosity, they soon lost interest.

Most of the morning was spent piddling, giving people time to forget, until after feeling she'd waited long enough, she pushed away from the microscope and sent her slides back to the basement fat man. Making her way down the hall, she stole glimpses of those who stayed to eat lunch at their desks. The green light from their monitors reflected off their faces as they munched on food that had been stashed in crumpled paper bags that now laid across laps or teetered on the edges of work stations. No one looked up as she walked by.

Down the hall, past the restrooms, she pushed through the metal door and stepped into the stairwell. Grabbing the railing, she peered upward the dark abyss that filled the void between staircases. A conference room and a large area known as the living room were on the second floor above her. She'd only been up there a couple times. Once for procedure updates and then more recently for Doctor Burwell's retirement gathering. Turning, she leaned over and studied the dark well below. A story down was the basement; a place she thought she'd never have to go.

Each step was calculated. One misstep and the clang from a heel hitting a metal stair would cause more than just an awkward glance or an accusing whisper. She had no intention of trying to explain to Doctor Aberman or Director Osborn why she was going to the basement.

When she opened the basement door, she was greeted by dull yellow bulbs hanging single file from a high concrete ceiling. Thick, grey metal doors, standing like ironclad sentinels, lined each side of the hallway. Rachel knew many of the rooms probably hid secrets that some might think she had no business discovering, but with all that was at stake, everything in this lab was now her business.

She took a few steps, stopped to read the brass plate on the door; took a few more steps then stopped again. Cargo Elevator, Mail Room, Ladies Restroom, Mens restroom...Office equipment, File Room, Cold Storage, and Dry Storage.

"Just a second." She walked back to the door of the Mens Room. "I wonder." She stepped in and tip toed across the room, trying not to look at the urinals that were lined up on the opposite wall. Giving the wall around the sinks a quick once over, she didn't see her name or number, but she did see plenty of other things that made her blush. "Men! It doesn't matter if they're degreed scientists or not, they can be such boys."

With a quick spin, she was back in the hall, reading brass plates. Half-way down, a loud clunk came from somewhere behind her. She spun around; struggling to hear past the beating of her own heart.

But the hall was just as dull and empty as when she walked through the basement door a little earlier. A few seconds later, the familiar hum of a conveyor belt came from one of the rooms she'd just passed. Someone up above was replacing or recalling a slide from the fat man. She found her breath again and relaxed.

"Ok," she said softly. "Everything's good. Keep going."

A few doors down, she stopped; her eyes transfixed on the brass plate: Cryonics. "The Tombcicles," she whispered. This door was different than the others. It wasn't solid metal, but had a small window, about head high.

Cupping her hands around her eyes, she pressed her face against the glass and searched the darkness beyond. The yellow lights from the hallway didn't help much, but she could make out a small room with counters and cabinets. To her right, the arch of a small faucet caught the light. Straight across from her was another door with another small window with a pitch-black face. "That's where the freezers are. It has to be," she muttered. "That has to be where Trace...where he..."

The yellow bulb above her head flickered just before the bell to the cargo elevator dinged. Muted laughter and loud talking came from behind its steel doors.

Mail room. People are coming down to get their mail.

With Josh gone, it was every man for himself. Without thinking, she grabbed the handle to the Cryonics room and turned it. To her relief, it opened, and she slipped into the small, dark room.

She crouched behind the door, pressing hard against it in case someone's curiosity got the better of them and they too looked through the window. She knelt there for several minutes, waiting for the small group to get back on the elevator. Her knees ached against the concrete floor, but she stayed there until she heard the elevator doors close and the muted chatter of its occupants corralled behind them. Slowly, she stood up and stretched her legs.

After searching a couple drawers, she found a flashlight, and then the cabinet of protective suits. "Might as well see what there is to see while I'm here," she whispered.

Twenty minutes later, she pressed the last snap on her suit. With her gloved hand resting on the door knob that led into the freezer room, she grimaced. "Great work Sherlock," she murmured. "Should've checked to see if it was unlocked before you crawled into this get up. And heaven forbid you have to use the bathroom." To her relief, the knob turned, and the door opened.

The beam of her flashlight cut through the darkness; catching the small green lights from control panels that filled the darkness like fire flies on a warm summer night. "My Lord," she whispered. "So, it's true We really are cloning."

She walked around the room, shining the light on each panel. Some canisters were marked with names of body parts, but one read 'DNA: A~~ta~'. The second word was illegible; parts of the panel no longer lit. She bent closer, but still couldn't make it out.

As she walked through the darkness, Rachel counted ten storage units that looked like they could hold the body of a fully-grown adult. *One of these must've been where Trace...*The thought stopped her. She couldn't help but wonder if his body was still in one of these mini freezers. But if so, which one? There was no way she was going to start prying them open to see. The thought of seeing his dead body didn't appeal to her, even her scientific curiosity.

She rolled the flashlight beam around the entire room, giving it a solid sweep. In the far corner a long metal tube sat in the dark by itself. No green lights glimmered from its control panel. Curiosity got the best of her. After a closer look, she saw the tube had been broken and not used in several years.

Still, she pushed the "OPEN" button. A loud sound that resembled air brakes filled the room and the lid slowly opened. Cautious, she pointed the flashlight down into the cylinder and flooded the tube with light. It didn't surprise her to find it empty of a body, but it did surprise her to find a file folder lying at the bottom. "I thought Trace was going to return that," she mumbled.

She bent low into the cylinder and picked up the folder.

When she read the name on the tab, she stepped back. It wasn't Trace Ardor's name scribbled across the top. It was hers. It clearly read Rachel E. Wall, Ph.D. She flipped it open, ready to find performance evaluations, personal notes, project assignments, but there was none of that. What she did find were articles about recovered giant remains, large skeletons found in Michigan, as recent as 2015 and pictures pulled from the Internet of various mounds and ancient locations. "How in the world did this get in there?" she whispered. Puzzled, she glanced around the dark room. She folded the file and slipped it into her boot. She'd worry about it later.

Before leaving, she scanned the room one last time. To her left, something metallic bounced off the beam. Getting closer, she was surprised to see a small door, almost hidden from view by a large vertical cylinder. When she read the plate above it, the words brought a fear so deep, so dreaded she had to grab the doorframe to keep her knees from buckling. In bold black letters were the words "Genesis Factor: Avatar Project."

Her brain buzzed, searching its cranial files for a definition. *Avatar, a movie, about giant blue people. Giants! Dig deep, Rach. What does it mean literally?* "Hindu, I believe," she said quietly. What she wouldn't give to be able to reach her cell phone right then and search the Internet, but it was buried in the pocket of her pants, which in turn were buried under a jump suit.

She really didn't want to, but she tried the knob. To her dismay, it was unlocked, and she knew as a scientist she had no choice but to go in and see what was there.

The handle stopped in mid-turn. "No, Rachel. Not right now. You need to look for that Petri dish. That's why you came down here. That's the mystery you need to solve today."

She looked at the plate above the door again. "But it's the Genesis Factor: Avatar Project. It's got to be directly related to the Genesis Factor here, at this laboratory?" An overwhelming feeling of dread came over her. "Stop arguing with yourself, Wall. Get a grip and get this over with," she said too loudly. She pushed the door open.

Her flashlight landed on a large, square machine sitting on an old wooden table. She carefully walked over to it to read the logo on the front. "Genesis 2000. It's an old sequencer," she whispered. "This is what they must've used when they were cloning back in the day."

She turned slowly; studying every object in the room. An old four-drawer filing cabinet was in one corner. It's top drawer slightly open. To the left of it were three large wooden crates, stacked on top of each other. The letters TDA had been spray painted on the end of each one. The lid to the top box was ajar; long strings of straw hanging precariously down its sides. Some had fallen to the floor, lying in clumps.

To the right of the cabinet was another table, smaller than the one holding the Genesis 2000. On it was a single burner stove that was still plugged into the wall. A well-used coffee pot lay on its side beside it; a teaspoon lay on a paper towel, browned by coffee stains, and beside it, a Plum Creek Laboratory porcelain coffee cup. A jar of instant coffee stood off to the side. A metal folding chair had been pushed neatly under the table. Next to the small table was an old desk.

She went to reach for the contents that lay strewn across the desk but stopped. Something was wrong. Something was out of sort. She walked back to the Genesis 2000 machine, shone the light across it and then walked over to the table with the coffee pot. From there she went back to the desk.

Files on cloning with hand written notes, a file folder with several pages of test results including DNA and blood types, various slides, and a petri dish lay scattered across the top of the desk. Part of a small piece of hardware; something from a computer, peered out from underneath a folder. A phalanx, albeit a very large phalanx lay close to the edge of the desk. She supposed it was what had been dug out of the wooden box over in the corner.

But none of what she saw bothered her, including the

giant jaw bone, that alone should have rocked her, but instead, she felt as if she knew it was here. Didn't Trace tell her three boxes of giant bones found years ago by some archeologist were here?

It was what she didn't see that worried her; the fact that nothing in this room was covered in dust. This room wasn't where they cloned years ago, it was being used now. Someone came here regularly and worked on whatever all these files contained.

Picking up a tablet, she read the notes that had been scribbled across the front page.

DNA from bones active. Type: O Positive. Cloning attainable.

Negative blood, of any type, cannot be cloned.

It can only be concluded it is the preserved and protected line of Adam.

Immediately recognizing the handwriting, she threw the tablet back onto the table like it was a poisonous snake. Her own voice bounced back into her face within the protection helmet. "Get out, Rachel." Sweat stung her eyes as she scrambled to the door. "Get out, and don't come back in here!"

She ran from the room, managing to close the small door behind her before darting across the cryonics area. Stumbling around the small entrance room, she threw the flashlight into a drawer, pulled the helmet off, and wiped her face on the back of her sleeve. Falling to the floor, she pulled her knees up under her chin; trying to control the short dagger-like gulps that pierced her lungs. The thought of the dark, ugly monster she'd just escaped filled her head. *I know who is responsible for all of this. I know who is working to reactivate the Nephilim, who signed for alien DNA. I know now. If I keep it locked in that dark room behind me it can't hurt anyone anymore, can it?*

So many things were running through her head. Nothing

was real anymore. Were people even who they said they were? All she knew for sure was that the dark side of Genesis had just stared her in the face. Her life would never be the same.

CHAPTER NINETEEN

B ut the monster wasn't behind her in the small room. It was in front of her. She had to stop trying to convince herself that dreadful things weren't happening in Plum Creek. Events, people, reasons were coming into focus, but what she was starting to see were things she still had to face.

"It's time to find that Petri dish and get back to the lab," she said with determination.

She crept back down the hall, glancing at the plates on the doors as she passed them. At "Cold Storage" she flipped on the light and took a quick mental inventory. Walk-in refrigerator units were on both sides of the room. In front of her was the fat man. "You're not so bad," she said breathlessly. "I thought you'd be a bit more intimidating."

The 'fat man' comprised of a giant, square metal box, the small conveyor belt, and robotic arms that sent out and retrieved glass slides. The face of the box was a computer monitor on which Rachel found some very interesting information.

Lime green letters spelled out the names of the scientist who were working above her along with what slides were ordered, the time they were sent out, and when they were retrieved. The list was immense. She scanned the screen for a minute, careful to figure out how to scroll and retrieve information without pushing the wrong button. The last thing she needed to do was mess up a giant computer, but to her relief, she found getting what she wanted from the fat man was simple enough.

Scrolling down, she found her information; when she had sent her last slide back down to the big refrigerator. It was the night Doctor Aberman's office had been robbed and her life had changed so dramatically. She looked at some of the other names on the list and noted the slides they'd taken from the 'fat man's belly.'

One name continued to stand out. "Really?" she whispered. "And why would you need those slides?" She pulled her phone out of her pocket and took a picture of the screen. In fact, she ended up taking several pictures. She paid close attention to the date-time stamps. She hoped she wouldn't need the photos, but if she did, they'd be good to have to confirm an alibi.

Satisfied she had what she needed; she left the fat man and walked into one of the large refrigerators. It was dark, dingy, and hot. It hadn't been used in years. Hundreds of yellowed Petri dishes covered in thick robes of dust lay scattered on the shelves. Some were empty; some still held old, discarded remnants of science past.

Since scientists constantly experiment, old dishes weren't scrapped. That would be dangerous. They were kept and eventually sterilized, but these had been forgotten. Several dishes still had pieces of crumbling masking tape barely stuck to the lids; the corners curled up and the writing faded or blurred. Others were cracked and dull.

"Hmmm, interesting. 1989." Tossing the dish back onto the shelf; she picked up another forgotten experiment. It rattled too. "This has got to be the place Trace told me about, land of the forgotten lab stuff."

She diligently searched through everything, every shelf until she found the one dish she'd hoped to find. The name R. Wall and the date she'd handed it over to Trace was printed in her handwriting on the lid. *Hidden in plain sight,* she thought. *Clever!* She wiped the thin film of dust off the cover and carefully slipped it into her pocket.

Before leaving, she gave the room a quick once over. An odd shaped door caught her eye in the far dark corner. At first glance, she wrote it off as a broom closet, but why would there be a broom closet in cold storage. On closer inspection, she read: OFF LIMITS: IT Personnel Only. "And why off limits in cold storage?" she whispered.

The door was locked, but she didn't leave. Instead, she inspected the door frame until she found what she'd been looking for. Just above her head, a faint set of fingerprints ran along the dusty edge.

Instinctively, she stood on her tip toes and... *Bingo!* She pinched the key and carefully brought it down. "So, what does this secret room contain that only IT personnel are permitted to see," she whispered, sliding the key into the lock.

The door groaned open. Her fingers slid along the inside wall until they found the switch and she turned on the light. The room held another surprise.... nothing. No computer servers, no wires, no cables, nothing but one lone air vent on the far wall.

She walked over to it and stood on her tip toes. Initially, she heard nothing, but after a brief time, she heard voices; voices coming from the various rooms above her.

She couldn't understand what was being said, it all sounded like gibberish at first, but the more she listened, the more she was able to understand parts of conversations. Some of what she heard made her giggle.

Then one voice grabbed her. It was a man's voice, and although she couldn't place where she'd heard it before, she knew it. A second man spoke. She knew that one too, and there was no mistaking who it belonged to. She listened as best she could as the two men made small talk, chatting about the latest articles in the Medical Journals then saying something about DNA. Their voices hushed, she strained to listen until anger took them both.

"No, I will not allow it," yelled one man.

"But you've no choice in the matter," yelled the other. "And you forget, the Coordinator gave me the lead. I'm running this show, not you."

What Rachel heard next made her slip off her toes and slam against the wall. It was a third voice, but this one belonged to a woman, and she recognized it immediately.

"What are you doing up there?" she muttered.

She scurried back up onto her toes and focused on the female's voice.

"Good lord," the woman scoffed. "Stop acting like children." The men fell silent. She continued to lecture them, in angry emphasis, but in a language Rachel couldn't place. She thought it sounded like German, although the woman never mentioned that she could speak anything but English. The men didn't utter another word. *She's definitely in control.*

Rachel tried to get closer to the vent, but her aching legs fought her. She rested them, but not for long. She stretched again and paid close attention. The men were talking again and in English. For that, she was glad, but what she heard scared her more than anything she'd ever heard in her life. In those few short moments she listened to the two men talk about murder, espionage, and treason. One wanted someone protected; one wanted that same person dead. Phrases like, 'knows too much,' 'valuable asset', 'a threat to the organization,' and 'Samael's choice' were batted back and forth between the two. The two men spoke freely, not realizing someone outside of their circle was listening. The woman said nothing more. She may have even left the room. Rachel couldn't tell.

The meeting was short, but when it was over, Rachel knew more than she bargained for. Things like who had tried to lay blame on Joshua for a staged robbery at Aberman's house, and that he wasn't on furlough, but dead. He'd been murdered, his death made to look like a suicide. She heard things that confirmed why Trace had been killed. She heard threats and ill-fated promises. She heard anger and cussing.

She knew the answer to why she was in this situation and who put her there. She knew who was guilty of it all. But what she didn't know was how to take her name out of it. She couldn't record the conversation. There were no pictures. It would be her word against theirs if she made an accusation. She had no proof against them...but she would!

**

Before going back upstairs, there was one more room she had to visit, the Mail Room. A sign-in sheet lay on the counter. She perused the names and dates. The last time someone had signed in was the day of Aberman's house fire. Apparently, those who came down earlier didn't bother to follow protocol and sign the sheet, but that was in her favor. Someone had written a note on a different piece of paper and their message was pressed deep into the page. She tore page and crammed it into her pocket.

She found a couple of advertisements in her mailbox along with several event fliers, the events already come and gone. There were various lab update notifications, and a letter from the CDC. Pulling it all out, a plain white envelope fell to the floor; her name scribbled across the front.

"What is this?" she whispered.

She turned it in her hands a few times, but there was nothing else written on it. She slid it into her pocket too and threw everything else away. It was time to get back to her lab. If she was gone too long, people would talk.

Or talk more.

CHAPTER TWENTY

The envelope, the blank piece of paper with the embedded message, and the file folder lay crumpled on her desk. She opened the file drawer, crammed all of them into her purse, then sat back in her chair and looked around her small lab. It seemed like a long time ago that her life was so uneventful, so dull; no one here but her, these two desks, the microscopes, piles of Petri dishes, test tubes, eyedroppers, and Bunsen burners. How in heaven's name had she been pulled into the middle of murder, espionage, and super-soldiers?

"Ugh," she moaned. "Stay focused. All that matters right now is what you have in your pocket. It may hold the answer for so many people."

She pulled the small plastic dish out of the pocket of her lab coat and carefully pried the lid off. Looking at the contents, she smiled. "And presto," she whispered. "Here's some modern magic."

Swiping some of the growth from the dish onto a clean slide, she placed it under her microscope and focused on the cells. Cells that from the naked eye, looked like small pieces of cottage cheese, but to Rachel, could hold the answer to a medical mystery. "Lord, I hope this is what I think it is."

In the stillness of her small work area, she heard, or thought she heard someone say her name. "Yes," she answered out loud. When no one responded, she lifted her head from the microscope and looked around. Not seeing anyone, she lowered her head again, turned the knob on the scope and brought the smear into clear focus. Then, just as if someone were sitting beside her, she heard her name again.

"Rachel."

"What?"

No one answered.

The voices she'd heard through the air vent began to materialize in her head. Glancing over her shoulder, she said "Hello?" one more time. Still, there was no answer.

Her eyes went back to the microscope, stopping just long enough to take a few more notes, then, when she was satisfied, she sat back in her chair and smiled, quickly vanishing the paranoia that had crept in earlier. "This is it," she muttered.

After adding various liquids to the contents of the dish, she set it on a burner for a few minutes. All that was left to do was inject a sample into a mentally injured lab rat. Once injected, she would just have to monitor the cellular transformations in his brain and the time it took for him to wake from his deep sleep.

Her test should prove that not only would her patient 'wake up' in record time, but with little or no brain damage. The stem cells in the Petri dish had regenerated themselves. If they were able to do so in the dish, they should also be able to do so in the living, blood filled brain of the rat.

She was so excited she almost squealed. She had to tell someone, but who? "Carmen," she said softly. "I've got to tell Carmen."

Sliding her chair over to her computer, she quickly typed out a detailed report, adding equations and expected results of the experiment. Satisfied, she printed out two copies; addressing one to Carmen and the other to herself. She then filled out a work sheet for Doctor Aberman.

Adding Carmen's envelope to her bulging bag, her knuckles raked the envelope she'd stuffed into her purse earlier. She pulled it out and stared at her name; trying to recall the handwriting. Her curiosity got the better of her and she dumped the contents onto the desk.

A sticky note had Joshua's name scribbled across it. *Are these the files I had asked Joshua to copy for me?* Some things didn't make any sense at first glance, so she stuffed everything back into the envelope and slid it back into her purse. She'd look closer when she was at home later that night. Every little detail was vitally important, or he wouldn't have made sure she saw them. Nothing was to be taken for granted. Glancing at her watch, she muttered, "Six o'clock. Time to go!"

She walked briskly down the hall and slid her work sheet under Doctor Aberman's door. It happened so fast she almost didn't realize there was a thin line of light beneath it.

"This is wrong," she whispered. "This is all wrong. I've been here before. I've done this before. But when? What's going on?" She thought about going back to the lab, grabbing her coat, and running as fast as she could, but her heart wouldn't let her. She had to get to the bottom of this. And now was as good a time as any.

She walked up to the thick oak door and gave it a light tap. "Doctor Aberman, are you in there?" she asked quietly. No one answered. She tapped a knuckle against the door again, this time a little harder. There was still no response. She tried the handle, but the door was locked. Putting her ear against it, she held her breath. She heard what sounded like the shuffling of paper, but nothing else.

Pressed to the door, she called out loudly, "Doctor Aberman?" This time, she heard nothing. No shuffling noise, nothing. She waited a few long seconds, but when no one came to the door, she backed away slowly.

Before leaving, she glanced at the floor. What she saw, or didn't see, made her freeze in mid-step. The light was gone.

Someone had just turned it off.

The loud pounding in her ears made it hard to concentrate. She wiped her sweaty palms on her pants. She carefully placed her ear back against the cold wooden structure and said loudly, "Doctor Aberman, it's Rachel Wall. Is everything alright?" Nothing came from the dark office.

Something told her to get out, get out as fast as she could. She couldn't explain this to herself, let alone to anyone else. Someone could be robbing Doctor Aberman's lab again, but Sheriff Jones would think she was insane if he came over here and all of this was just a big nothing. Lights left on, the security system kicking on...As she turned to walk down the hallway, she glanced over her shoulder at the locked door one last time. As she feared, the light had been turned off. It was the same scenario.

But this time, Rachel ran back to her lab. Before grabbing her coat and purse, she quickly made copies of the files that Joshua had given her, shoved them into a clean envelope along with her copy of the experiment report and dropped it into her purse. She scribbled out a note to Director Osborn and put it in a stamped envelope. "A couple quick stops," she muttered, "the bank, the post office, and then home."

At the bank, she put Joshua's envelope in her safe deposit box. She'd leave it there until it was needed. The original information Josh had gathered for her remained in her purse. After leaving the bank, she ran next door to the post office where she mailed Director Osborne's note and Carmen's copy of the experiment report. Then dodging the rain, she slid behind the wheel of her car.

CHAPTER TWENTY-ONE

She'd often heard of the 'after life experience', when folks supposedly left their physical bodies and upon seeing a bright light, followed it into an indescribable place. She definitely saw something bright, but she wasn't sure if it led to somewhere wonderful or not. She heard her name, but when she tried to open her eyes, pain ripped through them; tearing at her temples. Light was blinding. She didn't remember reading about this in any of the 'after death' accounts.

Then she heard it again; her name. "Rachel."

It was Carmen. She'd recognize that voice anywhere.

Well, I must still be on planet Earth, unless Carmen had died and gone to Heaven too. She tried to speak, but words wouldn't form around her thick tongue. All she could muster was "Wamen." She heard Carmen yell something to someone, and then the recognizable sounds of crying.

"Wamen," she said again, trying to calm her friend. "Ib otay."

Carmen cried harder.

Eric's voice sounded in her ear. "Rachel, squeeze my hand if you can hear me."

She squeezed, although she wasn't sure if Eric felt it or not.

"Good girl," he whispered. "You're a genius!"

She wasn't sure what happened next, or when it happened. She just couldn't open her eyes. Her lids felt like they weighed tons and when she could crack them, spears of light pinned her pupils to the back of her skull. She couldn't handle that for even a few seconds.

The next several minutes, or hours, she didn't know which, were filled with different noises; subtle noises that usually went unnoticed, but for her were magnified and painful. Nurses scurrying in and out of the room, Carmen questioning them, Eric whispering in her ear, the sounds of IV poles being moved, the shuffling of feet, squeaky wheels from monitor carts, the beeps of various medical devises, and over it all, the sound of deep, heavy breathing. She was certain that was her.

Carmen leaned over the bed railing and whispered, "What do you want? What can I get you?"

Rachel ran her tongue across her lips, hoping to wet them enough to move them. She concentrated as hard as her sleepy brain would allow and muttered the words, "thung wasses."

"Thung wasses?" repeated Carmen.

"You want a pair of sunglasses?" Eric asked softly.

Rachel squeezed his finger.

Carmen giggled. "Of all the things in this world I could get you right now, you want a pair of sunglasses? You're such a fashion diva."

Rachel smiled, or thought she did, and nodded slightly. Mustering as much energy as possible, she managed to form the word, "th...th...thhheee."

Carmen looked quizzically at Eric.

Eric smiled. "She wants to see. She wants sunglasses to cut the glare when she tries to open her eyes."

Rachel nodded as enthusiastically as a post-coma patient could nod.

Carmen grabbed her purse. "They have some in the gift shop downstairs," she said excitedly. Leaning over the bed railings, she kissed Rachel's forehead. "Don't worry, girlfriend," she said softly. "I'll make sure they're stylin." She kissed Rachel again then all Rachel could make out were Carmen's footsteps quickly leaving the room.

Rachel heard male voices and strained to listen. Eric was close, maybe at the foot of the bed. She didn't know who he was talking to; the voice wasn't familiar at all.

"So, what was it?" Eric asked softly "What did she do?"

The doctor shifted his feet. "What she did was so simple, yet so complex," he said quietly. "We're not quite sure how to describe it, or how it works, but in clear-cut terms, she took a medication that is normally used for Parkinson patients, combined it with the ingredients in an over-the-counter-sleeping pill, known on the market as Dreamzzz, and incorporated stem cells that can regenerate without the influence of temperature. Once administered, it quickly brings the patient out of a comatose state. The stem cells rejuvenate the brain. For years, once brain damage was diagnosed, there was nothing we doctors could do. Brain cells don't regenerate." His eyes moved over to Rachel. "But her's did."

He subtly shook his head. "If Ms. O'Leary hadn't brought me Ms. Wall's report, along with her written permission to be used as the guinea pig, we may never have known to try this concoction. She may have lived out her life in a vegetative state."

Eric whistled. "Will there be permanent brain damage?"

"We're not sure at this point," admitted the doctor. "This is so new, so cutting edge, we're not sure what the outcome may be. All I know right now is that her remarkable and speedy recovery is one degree short of miraculous."

"What do you mean?" asked Eric.

"The ingredient Dreamzzz is most effective on people

whose brain doesn't produce enough melatonin," explained the doctor. "People use this particular drug to help them sleep as it activates receptors in the brain that enhance chemicals involved in inducing sleepiness. When brain damage occurs, these receptors change shape. It seems that this new shape is then distorted again by her drug and causes the nerve cells to resume normal activity. It reverses the distortion of the receptors. We're not quite sure how dopamine, the chemical needed to stave off Parkinson's, comes into play, but believe me, I won't be the only one probing into her discovery. It's absolutely phenomenal!"

Eric looked over at Rachel. "Yes, it is," he whispered. "And I don't think the doctors are the only people aware of that fact."

"Excuse me?" said the doctor.

"Oh, nothing," Eric said almost apologetically. "Just muttering to myself."

"Well, I've got to make my rounds, but I'll be back later to check on her. Will you be around?"

"If I'm not here, Carmen will be. We're all the family Rachel has, so please, let us know anything and everything."

"When I know, you'll know," the doctor said warmly.

Someone left the room. Eric leaned over the bed whispered into Rachel's ear. "I know who did this Rachel. You outsmarted them, and you'll soon be awake enough to report your findings, but for now, rest. I'll do the footwork. You rest."

Rachel's words wouldn't come. She had things to tell too, but she wasn't sure to whom. And telling wouldn't necessarily help her case. She could only report what she'd heard from an air vent in a small forgotten room, but she couldn't say who all the speakers were. One voice was familiar, but she couldn't place him. And what did she hear? All of it was such a blur. Certain elements of the past were now just empty spaces cluttering her brain with dark debris.

Apparently, Eric knew of something she couldn't put into its proper place or time.

Fast walking feet came into the room. Eric pushed her hair back with a gentle hand. Carmen slid a pair of sunglasses over her eyes. Without opening them, she could tell they would help, eventually, but right then, she couldn't. She didn't want to. Her brain beckoned her back into the abyss, back into nothingness, and her body complied.

CHAPTER TWENTY-TWO

A soft light came from somewhere behind her. That, and the green glow from the brain scanner provided the only light to see by, but for her, they were enough. The draperies were pulled tightly together, but she saw enough to know she was in the green room. This time, along with the television hanging from the ceiling, she made out a small sink with a mirror in the far corner, a wide door beside that, which she had no doubt led to a bathroom, and a small closet with side shelves. At the foot of her bed, was a dark figure, half-sitting, half-laying in what she remembered was an oversized recliner. From the soft snoring rising from the darkness, she knew it was Carmen. She wouldn't wake her. Not yet.

She felt silly when she realized she was still wearing the sunglasses Carmen bought for her earlier. That would explain somewhat why the room looked so dark. Tubes and monitor cords weighing heavy on her arm, she managed to take them off without poking herself in the eye. She glanced at her arms; taking notice of the dark bruises. An IV tube ran along the top of her right hand and pinched whenever she moved it.

Carmen stirred under the thin blanket; trying to readjust her round frame. Rachel whispered her name. Sitting up a little and pounding on her pillow, Carmen muttered, "Wha."

"Carmen," Rachel whispered again.

Mumbling something, Carmen yanked the blanket up to her shoulders, exposing her feet. She grabbed the edge and threw it towards her feet, but it didn't make it. She grumbled and sat up. Still fussing at the blanket, she pulled on it to cover her feet, but fell back onto the chair with an exasperated cry when the blanket fell from her shoulders.

"Ask for another blanket, Car."

Carmen lifted her head and looked around with sleepy eyes. "What?"

"Ask for another blanket," repeated Rachel.

Carmen jumped forward, but pushing the footstool down into the chair without pulling the blanket out of the way, she unwittingly pinned her feet down and couldn't move. "Oh, for Pete's sake," she growled.

Rachel tried not to laugh. It hurt too much.

Carmen finally wrestled away from the blanket and threw it to the floor. "You awake, Rach?" she said, half-walking, half-falling to the bed. Leaning over the railing, she cradled Rachel's hand in her own. Tears trickled down her face. "What some people do for attention," she whispered.

Rachel's throat felt like sandpaper. "That was quite a show you just put on," she said hoarsely. Both chuckled until Rachel grimaced.

"Broken ribs," Carmen said quietly.

"What happened Carmen?"

Carmen looked at her watch. "It's two o'clock in the morning, Rachel. I think you should probably try to go back to sleep. Want me to call the nurse so she can give you some more sleepy medicine?"

"No," Rachel said quietly "I want to know what happened."

Carmen's eyes searched her friends face. "Do you remember anything about the car accident, Rachel?"

Rachel shook her head slightly. "Not much. Everything

looked like it was in slow motion, but it happened so fast. Did some guy run the light or something?"

Carmen fiddled with a couple of Rachel's fingers. "I'm not sure how much I should tell you," she slowly replied.

"Please stop playing mom. Tell me everything, Car. No secrets, remember!"

Carmen sighed heavily.

"Tell me, Carmen," insisted Rachel.

"You were on your way home from work. It was raining. You stopped at the light, and when it turned green, you started to cross the intersection. That's when the guy coming from the opposite direction hit you head on."

Rachel's face went pale. "Is he ok?"

Carmen cleared her throat and looked deep into her friend's eyes. "No, Rachel," she said swallowing hard. "He died at the scene."

Carmen fell quiet, giving Rachel time to let what she was just told sink in. Something was stuck in Rachel's bruised brain, like a piece of broken film clacking over and over again.

"Who was he?" she finally asked.

Carmen hesitated. "You didn't know him, Rachel."

"I think I did," she whispered. "I think his name was Trace James Arthur. TJ for short."

Rachel felt Carmen's hand go limp, just a little. She knew she was right.

"How in the world did you know that?"

"Because in a way, he's been with me the whole time I've been in this hospital room, Carmen," replied Rachel, "except to me, he was Trace Ardor."

She looked up at Carmen and could see that she had completely confused her friend. "I'll have to explain it to you when I can think clearer, but not now. Just know that although you aren't sure what I'm talking about, I do. I know exactly what happened and why. I just can't explain it to you yet."

Carmen's eyes burst wide. "And you expect me to be able to sleep, eat, think, work; act normal with that explanation. I can't go on with my everyday life as if whatever you just said should be dismissed as a bunch of mumbo jumbo coming from someone with a cracked skull. I know you better than that, Rachel Wall. You don't talk mumbo jumbo, and you've never met TJ, not that I'm aware of anyway, so yes, I'm going to ask, what are you talking about?"

Rachel smiled weakly. "It'll all come to light soon," she whispered. "I promise. I've got questions too, but I can't think straight right now. Not enough to know what to ask and then to remember the answers. We'll get around to it all in a day or so."

Carmen shook her head. "There are so many questions your simple statement raises for me."

Rachel closed her eyes. "Would you hand me my purse, Carmen?"

Before Carmen could tell her that her purse and all its contents were destroyed in the accident, Rachel slipped into the darkness again.

Later, while Rachel nibbled on some toast and Carmen laid motionless in the recliner, a nurse came in to take Rachel's vitals. She was tall, but very square; a real no-nonsense kind of woman. "We're going to wheel you down to the MRI center later this morning" she said in a loud, husky voice.

Carmen stirred from her cocoon; raising her sleepy head. "MRI?" she muttered. "Why MRI?"

The nurse turned and eyed her. "And you are?" she said sharply.

"My sister," quipped Rachel.

The nurse's eyebrows went up.

Carmen took the opportunity to play with the confusion she could see on her face. "Same father, different mother," she teased.

Rachel laughed. "Really, I always thought it was the other way around."

Carmen wrestled herself away from the grip of the small blanket and managed to get her feet on the floor without falling over. "No way," she said with a straight face. "Your father was Samuel P. O'Leary, same as mine. It was our moms who were different."

"Then why is her last name Wall?" asked the nurse.

Carmen tilted her head. "Well, I don't know," she said slowly. "I guess I'm gonna have to ask dad about that!" The two girls burst out laughing. The nurse murmured something about disrespect and left.

"Oh, oh please," begged Rachel. "Don't make me laugh. It hurts." Between jagged breaths, she managed to say, "Who was that? Please tell me she isn't *my* nurse."

Carmen walked over to a small white board hanging by the door. "She's your day nurse. It says here her name is Sandy, but we call her Nurse Ratchet."

"Nurse Ratchet?"

"Oh, I forgot, you're just a geneticist, not a teacher like me," Carmen teased. "Nurse Ratchet was the name of the nurse in *One Flew over the Cuckoo's Nest*. She was a mean gargoyle too. Eric and I thought the name fit your nurse rather nicely."

Rachel giggled. "That's terrible."

"True," agreed Carmen, "but we've had to put up with her 'I'm large and in charge attitude' while you've been asleep. Believe me, that woman ain't no Mary Poppins."

Carmen took Rachel's hand. "You *are* my sister, you know."

Rachel smiled faintly. "Yes, I do," she whispered.

"Ech hem. Don't mean to interrupt this family reunion, but may I come in?"

Rachel looked past Carmen and broke into a big smile. "Please do," she said warmly.

Eric stepped into the room holding a big teddy bear in one hand and a dozen roses in the other. He bellied up to Rachel's bed, leaned over, and kissed her on the forehead.

"Are those for me?" she asked.

"Well," he said awkwardly. "The teddy bear is." He laid it beside Rachel's arm. "But the roses are for the love of my life." He handed them to Carmen and kissed her on the lips.

"Thank you, sweetie," she said softly. "I miss you."

He put his hand on the back of her neck and pulled her closer to him. "I miss you too, baby." He kissed her again, passionately.

Rachel hugged her bear and smiled. "Ok," she finally said. "I get it that you two probably haven't seen each other for a few days, but either deal with it or go get a room."

Carmen and Eric glanced at each other, their eyes sending a silent message. Rachel knew she had no part in that conversation. She'd written men off, but it was nice to see her friends so deeply in love.

Eric finally turned his attention to her and started asking the mundane questions like: When did you fully awaken? How much do you remember about the accident? How much do you remember about events prior to the accident? and so on until Carmen interrupted him and told him about TJ Arthur, whom Rachel called Trace, and that, for some reason, she thought he had been with her until the accident.

Eric grabbed a chair from a nearby office, slid it up close to Rachel's bed and started the inquisition again. "Tell me about this Trace," he said quietly.

Rachel explained how Carmen had called her a couple of

weeks ago to see if she was alright. There had been a bad accident in an intersection that Carmen knew Rachel went through every evening on her way home, but it must have happened shortly after she'd driven through it. Once Carmen calmed down, she reminded her of their yard sale date. The next morning, after going to several, Carmen found a Book of Spells, and how, on a whim, the two of them summoned a, well, a zom...Trace.

She went over the robbery at the lab, the fire at Aberman's home, the Halloween dance, going to the FBI detention center, all she could remember, the best she could, right down to the sound of her cracking skull.

"Incredible," was all Eric could say. "The mind is an incredible thing."

Rachel and Carmen didn't say a word, but stared at Eric, expecting him to go on with his explanation. He leaned his elbows on his knees and looked at Rachel through the bars of the bed. "Most of what you remember is true, Rachel," he began. "Other parts, well, a few parts were created by your mind while in coma."

He nervously rubbed his hands together. "See, Rach, the accident you remember didn't happen a couple weeks ago. It happened two days ago; this past Friday night when you were on your way home from work. You think there were two crashes, that one, and the one that landed you here right now, but there weren't two, there was only one."

Rachel's mouth fell open. "But, but..."

"Just hold those thoughts and hear me out, ok?" he asked.

"Ok," whispered Rachel.

"Some of the things your active brain relived while you were in your short coma did happen over the last several weeks, the accident; however, did not."

"Why would I do that?" asked Rachel. "Why would I relive things in my mind?"

"You were busy working on things, meeting people, living

life, Rachel. The brain took those memories and made you relive them while you were, let's just say, sleeping."

Rachel turned pale and started to shake. "Go on," she whispered.

"Some things were apparently a little jumbled up," continued Eric, "like your memory of TJ. You called him Trace...Ardor, I believe."

Rachel nodded slightly. "Yes, there was a Trace with me, or in my memories."

Eric smiled. "Well, I introduced you to TJ a few months ago. He'd been assigned to the lab to help sort some things out over there and you two hit it off. Your damaged brain apparently connected him with all of what you told me; however, although he, in a subtle way, let you know he was interested in you, you'd recently been hurt and told him to lighten up. I find it interesting that you gave him the name Trace Ardor though." Eric glanced at the floor and then back to Rachel. "Do you know what that name means, Rachel?"

She shook her head.

"Trace Ardor," repeated Eric. "Trace...means a small amount, or to discover. Ardor means love...so you took part of TJ's name, and his persona, mixed him with your feelings of being hurt, and named this persona who was with you, Trace Ardor." Eric took Rachel's hand. Everything is jumbled together right now, Rach, but his name, the name you gave him, is pretty clear."

Rachel looked up at him questioningly.

"Regardless of how hard you try to convince yourself that you don't like men, you still want to find or discover love, Rachel."

Rachel covered her face with her hands. "No," she moaned. "How am I supposed to know what is real and what isn't," she asked sullenly. "Every time I believe I've found someone real, something real, it turns out to be a lie. My life is one big lie."

Eric shook his head. "No, no it's not," he said enthusiastically. "Trace was real. He was very real." Eric's eyes drifted to the windows; losing himself in his own thoughts for a minute. He eventually cleared his throat and looked at Rachel again. "His name was Trace James Arthur, but we called him TJ. He was my partner, Rachel."

Deep lines dug across Rachel's brow. Nodding slowly, she said, "He did say he was FBI. And that he had a partner." Looking at Eric's face, her eyes widened. "Eric, yes, you *were* Trace's partner. I remember now. You introduced me to him when, when..." She grabbed her head and fell back on to the pillow. "Oh God, help me remember."

Carmen wiped the hair out of Rachel's face and caressed her cheek. "Take it easy, Rachel," she said softly. "It'll all come back to you in time."

Rachel looked back up at Eric. "Tell me what you can," she pleaded. "Don't let me try to figure this out all on my own."

Eric squeezed her hand. "You brought some things at the Lab to our attention several months back, Rachel. Some things going on at the lab raised red flags for you, and you asked to speak to me about them. I brought TJ in because we were investigating some of those, well, some very serious allegations. We were hoping what you were going to tell us would fill in some of the pieces we were missing."

He smiled at her. "And he told me once that you were one of the brightest, most interesting women he'd ever met, and if given the chance, he'd ask you out. I think you knew that and that's why he became Trace Ardor to you."

Rachel slid the sunglasses back over her eyes and stared at the ceiling. "I suppose," was her only reaction.

Eric stood to his feet and leaned against the rail. "Let's back up a little," he said. "Do you mind if we go back to the beginning?"

"Not at all," she said eagerly. "I'd like to have something, anything cleared up."

"Do you remember when I first introduced you to TJ? You called and asked to meet with me because you believed something was going on at the lab. Something to do with strange deliveries and such."

"I remember now," she whispered. "You, Carmen, and Trace, came over to my house to talk about the strange things I'd seen and heard at the lab. We ate dinner, pizza and beer, I think, while we talked about my suspicions."

Rachel's liquid eyes searched Eric's face.

"That's right, Rachel. And do you remember the phone call you got while we were there? Do you remember Aberman's office being robbed?"

That question startled Rachel. "Was that real?"

Eric nodded. "It was."

"Did I go to the lab, then to the police station?"

Smiling, Eric nodded again. "You did. Excellent job remembering all of that, Rach!"

She smiled feebly. "You, Carmen, and Trace went down to the lab with me, right?"

"Carmen and I did," agreed Eric. "However, TJ didn't. He said he had other things he had to take care of and he left. I think what he did was go see if anyone down at the dog food plant could've been connected to the robbery."

Rachel closed her eyes. "Ok, then what?"

Carmen laid a hand on Eric's arm. "I think we should let her rest," she said in a muffled voice. "This may be too much for her right now."

With one eye opened, Rachel looked at Eric, then Carmen, then back at Eric. "No way," she said weakly. "I couldn't rest now if my life depended on it. Go on Eric."

Carmen sighed and plopped back down into the recliner. Eric hesitated a second too long. Rachel pushed the button on her bed and came up to a sitting position. "TJ and I helped chaperon the Halloween party at the high school together didn't we, and then agents came and I was put in FBI detention, wasn't I? Because I brought my concerns to you, I was a suspect for the robbery and everything. That part is true too, isn't it?"

Eric slowly shook his head. "Yes, Rach, I'm afraid it is."

"I was in detention when I met, oh, what's his name...you know, Director..."

"Osborn," replied Eric. "Yes, you met Director Osborn while in detention."

"And then the accident happened, and I've been in this hospital for how long? Two, three weeks?"

Eric stole a glimpse at Carmen. She was stressing. Looking back at Rachel, he said, "No, not that long, Rachel. Like I said, you've only been in here two days. The car accident that killed TJ, and almost you, happened Friday night, today is Sunday."

Rachel held up a trembling hand. "Wait," she said wearily.

"One thing that wasn't real Rachel was Carmen's phone call to you, the one you remember her making because she wanted to make sure you were ok."

Rachel grabbed her head. "God, this headache is killing me."

Carmen stood up again. "You have a concussion, Rachel. That's why your head hurts so badly." She put her hand on Eric's shoulder. "Come on, Eric. It's time to go."

Rachel grabbed his hand and held on tight. "Don't you dare," she said as sternly as possible. "You got me this far; get me to the end."

Carmen's eyes looking pleadingly at Eric, but he had to turn away from her. Rachel could be persistent.

"You think you got safely home in the rainstorm. You think Carmen called to check on you and you think she told you about the accident, and you remember the two of you talking about going to yard sales the next morning?"

Rachel nodded again. "Yes."

"All of that never happened, Rachel. This is where your mind started to process things and because of your brain injuries, well, they got a little muddled. Instead of being at home safe and sound, you were here, fighting for your life. Those memories were your brain's way of helping you to calm down, I guess."

Rachel glanced at Carmen. "The yard sales? We didn't go?"

Carmen shook her head. "No," she said, fighting back the tears. "We were supposed to go, um, yesterday, but you never made it home Friday night, Rachel."

Eric continued, "The FBI investigation into the lab and dog food plant started a few months ago. Your accident, my partner's death, happened two days ago. Your brain thought you were living everything, but in reality, you were remembering it, or pieces of it. Some of it, maybe a part of it, a dream, but regardless..."

Rachel's eyes darted between her two friends. "I'm so sorry about TJ," she said sympathetically. "And thank you for attempting to explain all of this, but I must admit, I'm so confused."

Eric got up. "Don't worry, little angel," he whispered. "We'll get all of this straightened out soon. I'm afraid I've shared too much heavy stuff and your brain can't take it all in. Rest now. We'll talk again later."

"But, but you haven't told me where you are in the investigation, what you've discovered, all the..."

"No arguing, young lady."

Carmen stepped up and stroked Rachel's hair. "Eric's right," she said. "You'll understand all of this in due time. Right now, you just need to rest."

"I'm tired of resting," said Rachel. "How can I rest when I've so much to sort out, so much to determine what was real and what wasn't?"

"It'll all come back," said Eric. "Just let the brain heal and it'll tell you in its own time."

"I need my laptop, my notepad. Please, at least give me a piece of paper and a pen."

"I've got to go over to your house and feed Mikey," said Carmen. "I'll pick up a few things while I'm there. In the meantime, please rest, okay?"

Rachel nodded and closed her eyes. Her head was really pounding.

Carmen and Eric left, hand in hand, but not before Carmen promised she'd be back as soon as she took care of a few things. Eric promised he'd be back too, although he wasn't sure when.

When they were gone, Rachel felt something she'd not felt in a long time...loneliness. "There's no one," she whispered. "Not even a...a... trace." She was wiping away tears with the back of her bruised arm when Nurse Ratchet came in and shot something into her IV. "Sleep now," she said gruffly. "No more talking."

CHAPTER TWENTY-THREE

*W*hat *time is it? How long have I slept?* Her eyelids felt like someone had sewn twenty-pound weights to them. She couldn't see, but she knew someone was in the room with her.

"Hello?" The word didn't sound right to her. *Did anything even come out of my mouth?* She tried again, but all she heard was a soft, "haaaaaaa."

Why, she thought. *Why are they sedating me when I'm trying to wake up?*

If she forced her eyes open, they'd only crash back down before she could focus on her surroundings. She tried to speak, but nothing came out. *Be still, Rachel,* she told herself. *Stop panicking and use your other senses. Listen, smell, touch, taste. Don't just rely on sight.* Her body relaxed into the bed. Neurons took over. Information started coming into her sleepy head.

A man. I can smell body odor. Breathing. Breathes through his nose, heavily. Must be overweight, or older.

She heard the door of her room open. She counted five footsteps; then nothing. "May I help you, doctor?" Nurse Ratchet said loudly.

"Oh, I was, um, looking," he stammered softly. "I'm looking for Miss Wall's chart, but I can't seem to find it."

The nurse mumbled something about charts on computers then sighed, as if irritated. "If you'll come with me, I'll take you to the nurses' station. You can talk to Doctor Epperly. He's head doctor for Miss Wall."

"Certainly," said the man. "After you."

She knew the door to her room had been closed because the hallway noise vanished, but there was shuffling, and a muffled sound just beyond reach, so the nurse and the stranger were still in her room. *Did someone just try to scream?* Her eyes still wouldn't open.

Then she heard the indisputable sound of a gunshot. It was silenced, either by a silencer or a pillow, she couldn't tell, but someone had just been shot. She wanted to scream, to get someone's attention, but even though she opened her mouth, no sound came out.

The bars to her bed screeched slightly as they were lowered. His hot breath was in her face. "What are you trying to do?" he said with a chuckle. "Scream? No use, little girl. No use. The IV has been tainted with a paralyzing serum. Nothing will move. Soon, not even your eyes will roll behind those locked lids. When it's over, your lungs will stop, then your heart. The brain will be the last to die, but before it shuts down, you will remember. You will remember seeing me at the coffee shop and sitting in the lab parking lot on a motorcycle. You'll remember seeing my shadow cut across your yard, you'll remember the tattoo of the pentagram I have on my arm." He chuckled in her ear. His breath reeked of...the only thing Rachel could think of was something she'd smelled in the lab at times, decaying flesh, death.

She tried but couldn't move.

Forcing the word over her lips, she whispered, "Why?"

She heard the snap of rubber gloves. "Oh, not because of anything you've done personally," he sneered. "But because of your family history. Let's just say you're guilty by association. Tough isn't it. To be hated because of who you're related to."

He shuffled around to the other side of the bed. "But believe me my dearest, I'm being merciful. If I could, I'd rape you, batter you, crush your bones, and rip you from limb to limb, and as the final act, I'd rip your heart out and make you watch me eat it before you died."

"What did I do...to deserve such evilne..." the word caught in her throat. The Nephilim raced across Rachel's mind. "Evilness," she whispered.

"Nothing, my dearest," he growled. "You were just born into the wrong family. See, I couldn't kill a certain woman a very long time ago, so I decided to take my revenge out on her later. And that time is now." His breath was nauseating, but she couldn't turn her head from him.

His lips caressed her ear. "This is the last thing you will ever hear, Doctor Rachel Wall, daughter of Jael of Sargon," he whispered. "Mora; my name is Mora. When you stand before Samael, tell him I did this to you."

Her heart tore against her breast bone. Her lungs exploded in pain. "Ok," she whispered, gulping in air as she spoke. "With my last breath...I'll tell you...I'm ready to die...I can face God...I believe in him." She gulped in another lungful of air. "But you...you make sure...you look over your shoulder...every time you move...No matter where you go...When you walk to the kitchen...get in your car...go to the bathroom...You look over your shoulder...because someone is going to get you...whoever you are... Someone is going to find you...and then...it will be your turn."

The stranger laughed a horrific laugh. "Oh, my dearest, I've nothing to fear from your FBI friends. They're nothing compared to me. But I will say, it's so nice to know you believe in God. So many people do, yet how many can say they not only believe in him, but they've actually seen him. They've lived with him, walked beside him? Well, I have. I believe in him too, no one does more, but it is not enough to just believe in him." He chuckled again. "When all of this is over, my dear, you won't be standing before Jehovah God. You'll be standing before Samael. You've no idea what awaits you because of your attempt at belief," he hissed.

Rachel lay paralyzed, gasping for breath.

"Ah, you're struggling to breathe. Here," he said quietly. "Let me help you."

The pillow felt cool at first, flowing across her hot face like a chilled liquid. Since she had a tough time breathing, it didn't make a difference at first, but as he applied force the pillow quickly became hot and suffocating. Her lungs burned for air. The pain in her head felt as if it were ripping her brain to shreds, and she was alive to feel every tear.

A flash of light bolted across the darkness of her eyes, as if someone had just walked into the room and switched on the light. In the brightness she could just make out the form of a man standing at the foot of her bed. He was tall and stood very still. She thought it strange that she could see him with a pillow over her face, but there he was, as real as life. He was wearing a white robe, or something like it, and held a long sword in his right hand.

She couldn't see his face, the light was too bright, but she could see the sword and the large, blood-red stone that sparkled like fire from the tip of its pommel. Finally, he said in an audible, but tender voice, "No, I'm not here to take your soul, Rachel. I am here to fight for it. God wants you to know he has heard your prayer and has sent me here to protect you."

"Protect me?" she asked. "From whom?"

"From yourself," answered the man. "Elohim loves you, Rachel and is patiently waiting for you to believe in him."

"I do believe in him," she said rather perturbed.

"Yes, you believe in Elohim, but so does Samael, the one the wretched Mora serves. If anyone truly believes in Elohim, Rachel, it is The Fallen One. Just believing in Him isn't enough. What you were taught as a child was true. You often pray but cannot be heard because he is waiting for you to not only believe in him, but to accept him, Rachel."

"Who are you?"

"My name is Michael. I am Jehovah's archangel."

"Archangel?"

"Warrior."

"Why does God need a warrior?"

"He doesn't," answered the angel. "You do."

"Why do I?"

"Because Elohim has a plan for you, Rachel Wall, and if you let him, he will help you through this, but before you can learn to be the protector, you must be the protected?"

"Protector of whom? Protected from what?"

The questions fluttered in the air like two birds fighting against the wind. The warrior, and his beautiful light had disappeared.

Another man telling me not now, but hey, I'm here to protect you. Will there never be a hero? A knight, a white horse? She heard herself chuckle.

Floating in darkness, Rachel suddenly thought of her mother; how she prayed with her, sang with her, and talked to her of Elohim's love. Since childhood, Rachel was taught of the Holy Sacrifice, but until now, she had never really appreciated the depth of corruption that sacrifice had to destroy, nor the power the resurrection had to overcome. Until now, the unseen spiritual realm had never entered her mind, she'd never given it a second thought, but now, now she could see it as clearly, perhaps even more clearly than the physical world.

Floating in darkness, death wrapped its cold arms around her and pulled her further into the abyss. Disappearing into its folds, Rachel whispered, "Dear God, please forgive me, but I can't...not yet," and she released her last breath.

CHAPTER TWENTY-FOUR

S he stood at edge of a deep, dark chasm, trying to fathom its depth when suddenly she was distracted by a flickering light coming from the darkness on the other side. At times it looked like a camp fire, others like a glint from a candle, but it always remained on the other side of the gorge.

At one point, it waned; looking as if it was ready to go out, but it didn't. Instead it rose up and inhaled the oxygen around it. Renewed, it waved and banished the rushing darkness. Rachel reached out for it, but with every forward step she took, it retreated. Her scream echoed within the dark chamber, but it was the laughter that stung her. *No one can hear you, silly girl. You're dead, remember!*

Outside of Rachel's tunnel, a young woman quickly fastened a plastic bag onto an IV hook and inspected the drip chamber. She opened the roller clamp and watched as the cool liquid rushed down the tube and into Rachel's lifeless arm.

The second the medical juice touched Rachel's blood, it turned into a starving fiend; whipping through the small fleshy channels with relentless force. Hungry for more, it sped through her veins, gained strength in the large arteries then slammed into the tiny capillaries. Rachel's system sucked up the solution like hot desert sands devouring an icy rain. But she wasn't ready for it. Her body jerked in violent spasms.

The small flickering candle turned into a raging inferno. From somewhere in the darkness, someone yelled, "Down. Turn it down."

"Rachel! Wake up!"

Her eyelids fluttered. *Who on God's green earth would do that to me? Who would pull me from death's grasp just to shove me back into this world? The audacity!*

"Rachel, this is Doctor Epperly. Can you hear me? Squeeze my hand if you can hear me?"

And what's with the squeezing hands thing? Someone's got to come up with a better signal. Don't you know how much energy it takes to squeeze a hand? Geez! She squeezed, but it wasn't much.

"She's alive, but barely."

"Rachel, please don't leave me. Please."

Carmen?

"Is that a tear, doctor? Is she crying?" asked Carmen.

Someone wiped something across her face. It was damp and cold. She shuddered violently.

Another voice, "Go get a blanket from the heater."

"Rachel, I love you? Come back. I can't do this by myself. You're my only family. Rachel, please. Can you hear me?"

"Nurse," demanded the doctor, ".05 milligrams of Fentanyl, stat!"

Another cold rush crashed through her veins, but this time, she didn't convulse. Instead, it flooded her with calmness, a sort of peace. Her tense body relaxed into the bed and her mind started to clear.

In his rush to end her life, Mora had forgotten one simple detail...that little clip on her right index finger, the little instrument that measures oxygen intake. When she started to suffocate, her oxygen level went down so fast, that little device sent an emergency signal to the nurses' station. They rushed to her and saved her life. Mora had escaped, but help got to her in time.

Slowly, carefully, she opened an eye. Everything looked clear. Carefully, she opened the other and looked around the room. A nurse, not Nurse Ratchet, but a younger, thinner nurse was looking up at the IV bag hanging from the pole, flicking at it with her finger. Doctor Epperly was leaning over her, his stethoscope pressed against her chest. He hadn't seen her open her eyes.

From the other side of the bed, Carmen was looking into her face. "Rachel," she whispered, "can you see me?"

Rachel barely nodded.

Carmen's loud, quick yelp startled the Doctor. He came up so fast; he almost knocked heads with her. "Miss O'Leary, I'm going to have to ask you to sit down," he said sternly.

Carmen threw a hand over her mouth and pointed to Rachel. "She's alive," she whimpered. "You did it, she's alive." Carmen sat down and buried her face in her hands.

Doctor Epperly took one look at his patient and started to spout orders. A slew of nurses and techs ran in and out of the room. Something ripped close to her ear. Her arm tightened; tighter and tighter; holding...holding...and then a slow pshhhh. Oh, the sweet release from the blood pressure cuff.

A male voice rang out, "She's stable, doctor."

"Is the MRI room available?"

A female answered, "Yes, sir."

"Take her down then. Don't let anyone, but a life-or-death case bump her. I need to see her brain and I need to see it now."

A choir of voices said, "Yes, sir."

Two quick clunks and Rachel felt the gentle sway of her bed being rolled out into the hallway. Her eyelids relaxed.

There was nothing she could do, nothing she could say, so she just surrendered to the world of medicine to let it work its magic.

The bed came to a stop.

Ding.

She could hear the elevator doors slip open, but the bed didn't move.

A feeble voice of an old woman said, "Excuse me."

"No, it's ok, we'll wait. Come on out," said a female voice.

"Thank you." The old woman shuffled to the edge of the elevator doors but stopped. "Before I get off, is this ICU? My granddaughter is in ICU and I don't want to miss..."

"Yes, ma'am," answered a male voice. "This is ICU. The nurses' station is right there. They can help you find your granddaughter's room."

"Thank you, young man."

Rachel didn't bother opening her eyes; she just listened to the shuffling of old feet as the woman passed her bed. But it wasn't what Rachel heard that made her eyelids fly open, it was what she smelled. Something familiar; the scent of a certain cologne, one she hadn't smelled in a long time. She forced herself up onto her elbow and looked back into the hallway. The old woman had stopped, turned around to watch the two orderlies push Rachel into the elevator.

She wasn't a small, dainty woman, as her voice painted her to be, but she was broad and thick. Her shoulders were stooped, but even then, she was too tall. And though her face was shrouded by a wrinkled tulle veil that drooped languidly from a pillbox hat and sat awkwardly on a head full of thick grey hair, Rachel knew who *he* really was.

When she was in the basement of the lab listening to two men quarrel through the air vent, he was the one who said she had to die. It was his voice she couldn't place as he argued she was too naive to be let into their circle, that her assertiveness and determination could be their demise. If they waited too long, her research would help her connect the dots and either she'd have to become one of them or die. He was the one who voted for death.

And now since she knew 'who' he was, she understood all the 'why's.' Why TJ? Why Joshua? Why her? Why the Genesis Factor? It all came flooding back, just as cold and harsh as the IV medicine that had wreaked havoc in her veins.

The old woman raised a large hand and wiggled a couple of fingers at her just as the doors to the elevator closed.

Exhausted, Rachel fell back down onto the bed.

A young black man punched a button next to the door then looked down at her. "You ok, Miss Wall? You're mighty pale."

"I'm fine," she mumbled. "Just tired."

"Did you know her, that old woman?"

Rachel's eyes searched the handsome face for a second.

"No," she replied. "She just sounded like someone I knew from a long time ago."

"Well, the way you came up on your elbow, I thought she was *your* grandma."

The other orderly laughed. "You did surprise us by movin' as fast as you did with them broken ribs and all," she said.

"Surprised me too," whispered Rachel.

"Well, you just relax now. This MRI won't take long then we'll get you back up to your room. K?"

Rachel nodded and closed her eyes.

Relax. If you only knew. That old woman isn't a woman at all; she's a man and he wants me dead. I guess he came back to finish the job since his stinking minion Mora, if that's who he was, tried and failed.

Ding.

The bed rolled out of the elevator. A pleasant voice greeted the orderlies.

"Is this Doctor Epperly's patient?" she asked.

Rachel rolled her eyes open and searched the person standing beside the bed. *Another stranger. Can I trust her?*

"Yes," answered the young black man.

"Right this way."

She knew the MRI would hold no secrets. The doctors will marvel at the miracle of her experiment. Her brain was at full capacity. She had survived coma by her own research and discovery, and now a second attempt at her life, but alive she was, and very awake. Her brain was pumping out more information than it had ever done before. The situation that had puzzled her was almost over. She knew the important answers. She would get out of here, back to her own lab, and figure out the rest. She would close this mystery.

And she would talk...but to whom? Again, that question popped up. *Who can I trust? Is Eric really FBI? And Carmen? She always seems to be one step ahead of me. Even to put me in a 'protective circle'.* They'd promised there would be no secrets between them, but there were plenty, and it seemed Carmen had them all.

And then Rachel saw her...her hand on the bed rail, walking behind the female orderly as they wheeled her down the hall to the MRI room. *Special Agent Montgomery. Glad to see you're real.*

CHAPTER TWENTY-FIVE

Doctor Epperly's smile almost preceded him as he walked into Rachel's room. "You're a living miracle, young lady," he said, leaning on the bed rails. "Your brain is showing normal waves, your blood pressure is stable, your ticker is beating as it should. I'd say all in all, you're in fine shape considering..."

"I want to go home," Rachel said emphatically.

Doctor Epperly frowned and shook his head. "Uh, no, I can't release you for a couple more days. You still have cracked ribs, a severe concussion, and internal bruising. There are a few more tests I need to run and then..."

"I want to go home, today," interrupted Rachel. "You just said I'm fine. I feel fine. I've got work to do. As you know by having to remove Nurse Ratchet, um, I mean the nurse's body from my room; someone is trying to kill me. I'm a sitting target here and I need to go."

Doctor Epperly chewed on the inside of his cheek then said, "Actually, you're safer here than anywhere. FBI is stationed outside your door 24/7. Nothing is going to happen to you while you're here."

Rachel threw her head back and sighed heavily. "And nothing is going to get done while I'm here either."

"I'm sure there are other people out there who can do what

needs to be done, Miss Wall. Right now, you need to concentrate on getting better."

"No, Doctor. Right now, I've got to concentrate on getting to the bottom of a lot of things, and I can't do that lying here in this bed. I want to go home, so you either sign my release papers, or I'll walk out on my own volition. We can do this nicely, or we can cause a scene, your call."

The doctor swiped at his chin. "You drive a hard bargain, don't you?"

"Normally, no, but I'm learning."

"Ok, I'll let you go home, but only home. I'm putting you under house arrest for medical reasons. Work on your laptop, read, use the phone, but from home. And then you come see me day after tomorrow, so I can finish running some tests. Deal?"

"Deal!" Rachel said enthusiastically. She threw the covers off her legs and swung them to the side of the bed.

Epperly grabbed his patient's shoulders and stopped her cold. "Whoa there! You can't just jump up and run out of here. You're not ready for that just yet. Your brain's fine, your body is pretty banged up, so let's take baby steps first. And I mean literally."

Rachel sunk back down onto the bed.

"It's going to take me awhile to finish my rounds then get your release papers ready, so in the meantime, why don't I have a nurse come in and the two of you can take a stroll around the floor a couple times. Let's see how strong your legs are, after all, you've got to walk before you run."

Rachel's shoulders slumped. She hated to admit it, but she was already drained. The doctor was right. Leaving here, going home, and working on this situation was going to take all the energy she could muster so she had to pace herself and let her body heal, but still, she had no doubt she could do that better at home than in a small, stuffy hospital room. She needed to be in her own home, in her own clothes, and with her cat.

"Okay," she said quietly. "I'll walk while I wait."

"Good," replied the doctor. "It'll be a few hours, so don't overdo and make sure you rest a lot." He placed a hand on her arm; his face frozen in grim. "And Rachel." He paused before wiping a large hand across his face.

"What, doctor? What is it?"

"You've *got* to take it slow. I know you don't want to, but that is some concussion you have and we may need to run more tests, just to make sure you're really alright."

"What do you mean, to make sure?"

"We've never dealt with anything like this before, Rachel. You're a walking science experiment, excuse the pun. We just don't know if you coming out of coma so fast was detrimental on the brain or not. The last thing we want to deal with is a stroke."

"I see," muttered Rachel. She glanced out the window; her eyes squinting against the glare of the sun. "Thank you, doctor," she whispered. "I think I need to rest now. I'll walk later."

Doctor Epperly smiled again. "Good patient! Take your time. I'll be back in a few hours."

As the doctor was leaving, she heard him mumble something to someone just outside the door. A few seconds later, Carmen walked in. Rachel closed her eyes. She was so tired, but there was no way she was going to let anyone know how she really felt.

"How are you doing, Rach?" Carmen said delicately.

Rachel didn't open her eyes. "Fine," she answered. "The doctor's going to let me go home this afternoon."

Carmen dropped her bag into the chair. "No way! There is absolutely no way!"

Rachel sighed and squeezed her eyes. Pushing a button on

the remote, she pulled herself up into a sitting position. "Look Carmen, I just went around and round about this with Epperly. I can't, nor do I want to go around again with you. Bottom line, I'm going home. I've got work to do, and besides, I want to see Mikey."

"But Rachel, you..."

"No buts, Carmen! You're not going to win on this one. Support me or go home." Rachel knew the words bit hard, but she wasn't budging. Carmen was accustomed to having the upper hand, but not this time. Carmen fell into the recliner and pulled a book out of her bag. Rachel laid her head back and closed her eyes. Sleep came fast.

Squeaky sounds woke her up to a young woman pushing a cart up to the side of the bed. She took Rachel's vitals; recording each detail on the small computer. When she finished, she pushed the cart aside. "Doctor Epperly says you want to walk," she said smiling kindly.

Rachel rubbed her eyes. "I do."

"Are you ready to go now?"

"Sure."

Rachel saw Carmen frown, but didn't have to say anything as Carmen turned back to her book; her dark eyes lingering over the rim long enough to send an disapproving look.

The nurse didn't even look in Carmen's direction. "Let me take this cart back to the station and we'll be off," she said warmly to her patient.

Rachel slid out of bed and onto her feet. She was so ready to walk so she could get out of this place and on with her life, whatever that meant. Carmen cleared her throat but didn't look up.

A few minutes later, the nurse was unhooking the brain cap from the scanner and taking Rachel by the elbow. "Ready?" she asked.

Rachel gave a slight nod. "Ready as I'll ever be."

Grabbing the IV pole, the nurse rolled it over to her and said, "Well, let's go darlin'."

Rachel's steps were awkward; painful from the heels of her feet to her hips. Every bone, every muscle, everything hurt. But she wasn't about to let Carmen know that.

Nurse Janice held her up on the left, the rolling IV pole held her up on the right, as she crept down the hallway, stopping to catch her breath every few steps. Twice around the nurse's station and she was done in.

"You did great!" said Janice. "You'll be dancing in no time."

"Humph," replied Rachel. "I couldn't dance before the accident." Walking into the room, she glanced at the recliner. Only Carmen's book was in the seat.

"Well, now is as good a time as any to learn," said the nurse.

"Time," sighed Rachel "Not enough of it."

"How 'bout I take all these tubes out of you since we seem to be alone for a minute? Let's get this part over with," Janice said cheerfully.

Rachel gladly laid back onto the bed and let the nurse take care of her. When all the tubes and needles were gone, the nurse pushed a button and Rachel's bed rose to a sitting position.

"Would you like me to order something from the kitchen?" she asked while securing the brakes on the bed. "Doctor Epperly did say he wanted you to use the bathroom before you left the hospital. We need to make sure all the plumbing is working properly before we send you home."

Rachel put her head back against the pillow and closed her eyes. "Sounds great," she said quietly.

Carmen came in soon after the nurse left and sat in the conference chair Eric had rolled in the day before. "Can I get you anything?" she asked.

Lifting her head Rachel suddenly said, "While I have a little energy left, would you mind chatting with me?"

Carmen's eyes brightened. "Okay. As long as you don't try to pull me into something deep."

Rachel fluffed her pillow and pulled the blanket up. "Sorry," she said restlessly. "Got a little chilly all of a sudden."

"That's alright. Take your time."

Pushing a strand of hair out of her face, Rachel let her head fall back into her pillow. Carmen waited, watching her friend from the side of the bed. Finally, Rachel cleared her throat.

"I know you told me that we didn't go to the yard sales. I guess we were supposed to have gone on..., well, I don't know what day it is, but we didn't go, it was just something we'd talked about doing, and this may sound like a silly question, but is there really no book of spells? Did I imagine that?"

Carmen took a few seconds before answering. Taking a deep breath, she said, "No, there is no book of spells that I purchased at a yard sale. I think you might have confused that with something I do have. I have a Book of Shadows, but regardless, these books are like journals, Rachel. They're very private. It's a book where I write my most private thoughts, any spells that I may use, or craft on my own, oils and potion recipes, things that I consider important. It's not something I share with people very often."

"But..."

Carmen held up a finger, "But," she said with a smile, "I did share mine with you, or at least part of it with you, once. I found a great lavender oil recipe and wrote it down in my Book. One time, when we were talking about how you needed to take some time for yourself, to find time to relax, I told you about the recipe and let you copy it from my Book."

"So, you have a Book of Spells, or...Er...Shadows, whatever, and you showed it to me, and while in coma, if that's what you want to call it, I got that mixed up with our planned yard sale adventure?"

Carmen nodded. "That's what it sounds like to me, Rach."

Rachel glanced at the window. "Okay. Wow. I wonder how long it's going to take me to sort out the real from the unreal."

"I imagine it will take some time," Carmen said quietly. "You had a traumatic experience. Your brain has to sort it all out."

"Yeah, I guess," Rachel whispered.

"Anything else?"

Rachel snapped out of whatever she was thinking and nodded. "Yeah, I do have a couple more questions."

"Okay."

She played with the edge of the blanket. "Um, have you ever done a ritual for me?"

Carmen's brow furrowed. "What?"

"Let me rephrase that." She hesitated a second, then said, "Carmen, are you a practicing witch?"

Carmen chuckled until she realized Rachel wasn't smiling.

"I don't consider myself a witch," she said slowly. "That often has a negative connotation; I do however, consider myself a caster, or a gnostic; and I do practice the Wiccan religion."

"Ok, then I'll repeat my question. "Was there ever a time you and a couple of your Wiccan sisters sat me down in the middle of a circle and prayed for me, or cast a protective spell over me, or something like that?"

"Yes, Rachel. We did. Do you remember that night?"

"I do. It was so enlightening for me, in so many ways."

Carmen leaned over the bed; excitement bursting in her large brown eyes. "Oh, Rachel, do you remember that you...?"

Carmen's excitement agitated her. "I what?" she

interrupted.

Carmen backed away and fell into the chair. "Never mind," she said quietly. "Please, go on. How did the ritual enlighten you?"

"Well, I found it enlightening because I realized a couple of things. First, you really do love me, as a sister. You care enough to ask your gods to protect me. I found that very touching. It also instilled in me a desire to be closer to my God; to pray more, to be more focused on my spirituality."

"That's good, Rachel."

Rachel felt an uneasiness rise within her; a battle of sorts. How could she be such a hypocrite? She tried to force a smile, but it wouldn't come.

You're not a hypocrite, Rachel. You haven't told Carmen everything because you don't know everything, so stop being so hard on yourself. It's she who has some answering to do, not you. Now, get on with it!

This wasn't going to be easy no matter how she said it. She stiffened her back then said, "The second enlightenment was that, although we've promised time and time again not to keep secrets from each other, I believe you have kept several from me."

Carmen's mouth fell open. He eyes widened with surprise. "What are you talking about, Rach?"

The agitation rose its ugly head again, but this time, Rachel had a hard time keeping her voice even. "Come on Carmen," she blurted. "You've always thought me naive, even stupid, but I can see. I'm not blind. You never told me you were a practicing witch, or caster, or whatever you want to call it. You always made your beliefs sound so personal, but your part of a coven and you're practicing real magic, aren't you?"

Carmen looked stunned.

"That's a bit different than growing an herb garden and making your own soap. So, what else, Car? What else haven't you told me? Like, why you seem to know something is about to happen before it does? Why have you been one step ahead of, of, whatever?"

Carmen bit her lip. "I don't believe this?" she whispered. She stood up and grabbed her purse. "Maybe," she said, fighting back tears, "it's because I never considered religion a 'make or break' issue regarding our friendship. I wouldn't give a flying flip if you started to attend church somewhere, Rachel. In fact, I'd encourage it. To practice any religion is a personal choice, no matter what religion it is.

"And maybe I didn't tell you some private things because I thought we'd be best friends no matter what. And as far as knowing things before they happened, well, maybe it's not because I'm part of this plot to frame you, but because I'm married to and in love with an FBI agent, Rachel. Maybe it's because he talks to me, shares things with me, and even though I'm sworn to secrecy, knowing the things he shares with me, I do what I can to help you without scaring you to death."

The shock wave hit Rachel in the chest so hard, her vision blurred for a moment. Sitting as still as she could, she tried to take a breath, but her lungs wouldn't fill with air. Finally she was able to mutter, "Married?"

Carmen walked toward her friend. "Yes, Rachel. Eric and I are married. We have been for six months now."

"I, I didn't know."

Carmen snickered. "Yes, you did, Rachel Wall. We were married in my garden. It looked almost like it did when we performed the ritual. Lots of candles and the sweet scent of herbs and flowers."

"I don't remember..."

"And I suppose you don't remember who officiated the ceremony either?"

Rachel shook her head.

Carmen's face grew grim. She stared hard into Rachel's

eyes then very quietly said, "You did, Rachel."

Rachel stared at her in disbelief. "Don't do this to me, Carmen," she said angrily. "I don't have the authority to perform weddings. I'm not ordained. And even if I were, I wouldn't forget your wedding."

"I'm not doing anything to you, Rachel, except telling you what you need to hear. You performed the ceremony. No, you're not ordained, but in Virginia, you don't have to be if you only want to officiate one wedding."

"But I'm not Wiccan either. I..."

"Yes, you are," interrupted Carmen. "Or you were! In fact, the coven that I'm a member of, well, guess what Rachel, you're the reason I joined it. You were a practicing Wiccan when we met in college, Miss Wall; running as fast and as far away from your parents as you could get. And me, starving to do something on my own; without my parent's dictating my every move. We became friends and you drew me into your circle. You gave me a chance with Wicca and I jumped into it, but not necessarily into witchcraft. With that, I'm taking it slow, but now you want to get all self-righteous on me?"

Carmen lowered her head and inhaled deeply. "I haven't kept any secrets from you, Rachel," she said calmly. "You just don't remember things." She hesitated a second, then forcing a smile, said, "But you will."

Rachel stared at the ceiling. She didn't know what to say.

"I'm sorry if that isn't good enough now, Rachel. Somewhere down the line, you laid down some conditions, and apparently, I don't meet them anymore. While Wicca became the center of my beliefs, I've always known that it never really was for you. You escaped to Wicca after your parents died, to hide your pain in the power of magic. Trying to find peace, that for some reason, your God wouldn't give you. Knowing your faith truly was different than mine was never a deal breaker for me, but apparently, it is for you."

Carmen walked to the door. Before leaving, she turned and

looked back at her friend. "And as far as keeping secrets, why didn't you tell me you were working on this special experiment? Why couldn't you share that with me? Why did I have to find out because of some test they had to run as they were fighting to save your life?"

Her face drained of color, her brain drained of words, all Rachel could do was shake her head.

Carmen stepped back up to the side of the bed. "You're a great scientist, and we're proud of your work. Simon would have been so proud of you, too," she said softly. "He loved you, Rachel. He would've..."

Rachel snapped. "Shut up about Simon," she snarled. "I'm so tired of people talking about him like he was some wonderful guy. He was a liar and a thief. He left me. He asked me to marry him and then he left me."

Carmen's eyes filled with tears. "Rachel! Stop! Simon didn't leave you!"

"If you're going to drudge up my hurtful past, Carmen, maybe we don't have such a strong friendship after all. You know every man I've ever loved left me."

Carmen sighed heavily. "I'm going to chalk this up to memory loss because of the accident, Rachel, and forgive you up front, but hear me out about this. I don't know what kind of pain you've been carrying, apparently a lot of denial too, but Simon didn't leave you. You were the love of his life."

"Enough," Rachel said quietly.

Carmen stepped up, her eyes searching Rachel's face in subtle desperation. "He was killed, Rachel, in a plane crash. You two were married two years ago, in that little church in the valley, the one that rings the bells every Sunday morning. About six months into your marriage, he was called to New York for an emergency board meeting and the private plane he was on crashed in the Shenandoah Valley."

Carmen touched Rachel's hand. "I'm sorry you can't remember him. He loved you so much."

Rachel didn't blink; she just stared out the window, unsure if she'd heard what Carmen had said. *Widowed after six months? He really loved me?*

Carmen slid her fingers off of Rachel's hand so gently, Rachel didn't feel her move.

"I didn't know..." she whispered.

But when she turned, Carmen was gone.

CHAPTER TWENTY-SIX

A couple weeks passed before Doctor Epperly's invisible chains of house arrest were unlocked, rolled up, and taken away. He had done his tests, and Rachel was given the okay to work; albeit at a much slower pace and not so many hours.

She waited until Saturday to go to the lab. With no one there, she could work alone; unhampered by questions or silent stares. She flipped the light on and walked to her desk. Everything was in place, just as she'd left it.

She opened the drawer to put her purse away, when an envelope fell against her hand. At first, she didn't think anything of it, almost tossing it aside, but her name, scribbled across the front caught her attention. She pulled it out and dumped the contents onto her desk. Several pieces of papers landed in a pile in front of her. It surprised her to see one was a note from Joshua. It read:

Rachel,

I hope this helps.

Let me know if I can do anything else.

These people need to be stopped.

Joshua.

She laid his note aside and then picked up another piece,

studying it meticulously before moving on to the next. When she finished, she nervously wiped her fingers across her mouth. "This is incredible," she muffled. "He found it! He found it all."

She looked at the flier for the medical seminar Doctor Aberman was to attend again, concentrating on the date Josh had circled. Something nagged at her...It was something someone said. Thinking back, it dawned on her. It was Mrs. Aberman, at the High School Halloween party. She said Doctor Aberman had to leave the family for a few days to attend the seminar, disrupting their vacation.

The flier clearly showed the medical seminar was for a day, not several. Why did Aberman leave New England for several days? Why did he come back to Virginia? When they were in Sheriff Jones' patrol car, he said it was because Mrs. Aberman had fallen ill, but at the Halloween party, Edith said herself that was with her children and grandchildren in New England and that she was fit as a fiddle at the time.

"He lied," she muttered. "He lied!"

The next piece of information she looked at was a flight itinerary, signed by Doctor Aberman. She circled the date, time of departure, and destination, and the date and time of when he went back to New Hampshire. He came here for a reason and then the sheriff let him go so he could get to the airport and fly back to New England without Edith knowing it. Why?

She opened the folder marked 'Genesis Factor' and there, saw the sloppy signature on the delivery receipts for skeletal and frozen remains. According to the new structure put in place by the feds, no one at this lab had authority to do that anymore. Nothing was to raise a flag regarding cloning. But that didn't matter. She slid another receipt for "foreign DNA" to the front on the small pile. She couldn't make out the name on that one either, but she knew whose it was.

Then there was the bank statement from Union Bank of Switzerland. A large deposit had been made just a month ago into the account of a joint account for Aberman and Sanford. "My lord," she whispered.

There was documentation from various foreign countries. From what she could tell, they were bids for information on the science of cloning and regeneration. Some were offers of partnerships between a foreign company and one named, GenTrak, Inc. There were other offers from countries that the US considered enemies.

Stapled to the back of the bidding contracts was a list of the names of the officers of GenTrak, Inc. and their addresses. It was officially addressed as a Delaware Company, but Rachel was sure, a little more research would uncover that it was only formed in Delaware for tax purposes. GenTrak, Inc. was probably somewhere in Plum Creek, like in the back of an old dog food plant.

The last picture she held up was of the robot that delivered and retrieved microscope slides. It was similar to the one she'd taken with her cell phone just days before.

"So that's it," she whispered to herself. "You figured out how to create these super beings, sell them or the science to foreign governments. You get rich, they get control. Hmmm, but what good is it to be rich if you're not in control?"

"That's what I was wondering."

Rachel jumped; quickly turning to the voice that had come from behind her.

"Director Osborn. What are you doing here?"

"Sorry if I scared you, Miss Wall," he said, stepping over the threshold. "I guess I should've called first."

"No, it's fine. Please come in, and have a seat," she said, waving him into her lab.

"I didn't know if you'd remember me or not."

Rachel snickered. "You're not easily forgotten, Director."

He pulled a chair around and he slid it across from her desk. Transfixing his eyes on the pile of paper she had in front of her, curiosity etched in every line of his face. "To answer your question, I'm here because I'm doing the same thing you are, following a lead," he said smiling. "Big stuff going on here in little Plum Creek, huh?"

Rachel nodded. "Yeah, there is; however, if you're here to ask me more questions, I'm not really sure I can help you right now. I'm trying to put a lot of things together in my head. Some things are still so..."

"Unanswered?" he said, leaning back in the chair and crossing his arms across his chest.

It took some effort to push her defenses down. She forced a half smile and said, "To say the least."

"Well, I'm not really here to ask questions, but maybe help answer some for you. Do you mind?"

Rachel raised her eyes and looked at the Director over the rim of her glasses. "Why would you want to do that? Not too long ago, you pulled me in for questioning. Didn't want to hear anything I had to say about being framed. So why are you interested in helping me now?"

"Maybe I have additional information," he said calmly. "Maybe, we can help each other."

"What? What are you talking about?"

The Director sat up. "You know, I can help you get the bad guy, and you help get me a few of those millions in that Swiss Bank Account."

Rachel stared back at him for a second and then broke out into laughter. "You had me going there for a minute," she said chuckling. "Now, really, what brought you here this morning?"

"Hmmm, I see I didn't ask very clearly. Let me try again. How about, if I give you some information on who is behind all of this and how he wants you to become a part of his plan, you get me some of that money hidden in that UBS bank account. Is that clearer?"

Red streaks flared up the sides of Rachel's neck. Her eyes darkened for a second, then glazed into subtle calmness. "No, it isn't," she said angrily. "I don't know what you're talking about. It's ludicrous to believe that I'd have access to this account, or that I could even get access to this account. You're still barking up the wrong tree, Mr. Osborn. I tried to tell you that before. Looks like you're still not listening. I mean really, if I had access to $56 million do you think I'd be working in Peanut, Virginia living in a one-bedroom house with no one but a cat?"

Osborn sighed heavily. "Rachel, my dear, you're right. I'm sorry if I came in like a bull in a china shop. I work long, painful hours too, and well, I want to get to the bottom of this. I wasn't trying to bribe you, but, well, I thought it was worth a try to see if I could get you so riled that maybe you'd slip up and take an offer."

"A bribe? An offer?"

"Whatever. I didn't think you'd accept it. I was right about you, and I'm glad I was, but I had to try. I had to make sure."

Rachel rolled her eyes and folded her arms across her chest. "Nice," she grumbled.

"Look Rachel, we both want to get through this and on with our lives, so let me start over, okay?"

Rachel wasn't about to take any more chances. She pulled a tape recorder out of her top drawer and slapped it on the desk. She poked the "ON" button with a stiff finger and began to speak.

"Saturday, December 17, 2015. Plum Creek Laboratory. This is Doctor Rachel Nicole Wall and I am talking with Director Zachary Osborn of the FBI. Considering all that has happened in the last several weeks, Director Osborn and I were just discussing putting all the pieces of this puzzle together. For that reason, I've pulled out this recorder and will record everything that is said, in lieu of any witnesses to this conversation. Does this meet your approval Mr. Osborn? Because if you refuse to allow me to tape this conversation, it's over, here and now."

"Oh, no, I agree completely," said the Director. "In fact, I'll make sure I speak loud and clear so there's no question regarding my statements."

The smirk on Rachel's face slowly disappeared. She'd thought he'd shy away from having a recorded conversation, but he didn't. She pulled herself together and sat up. "Well then, let's get started. Please continue with your explanation of the events in question."

"Gladly," he said, "but do you mind if we start from the beginning or at least the beginning when I was brought into the situation?"

"Not at all, Director, please go ahead."

"Well, the night I'll start with is the night Doctor Aberman's office was broken into; do you remember that night, Rachel?"

"Yes."

"When you, the Doctor, and the Sheriff sat in the Sheriff's patrol car, the Sheriff mentioned you were the prime suspect in the robbery; do you remember what you said?"

"Yes. I said I believed I was being framed. I've said that all along and I still believe that."

"Well, I believe you too, Rachel. Come to find out, you are being framed. I know that for a fact now."

Rachel's shoulders fell. "Really?" she said somberly. "And would you happen to know by whom?"

"I believe I do, yes."

"Who?"

"We'll get to that in a bit."

"Okay. Go on."

"Thank you. As noted by the federal prosecutor, all the evidence against you was circumstantial. Starting with your fingerprints. Of course, your fingerprints would be all over Doctor Aberman's office. As you said that night, everyone is in and out of his office. And then you being at the Lab alone. Nothing new there, you're often the last one to leave the building; in fact, look at you now, sitting her on a Saturday morning. All of this plus your story that you heard someone in his office, but you weren't in his office, and so forth. Remember?"

"Yes."

"Good. So, so far, we're on the same page?"

"Yep."

"Okay. Then we had to ask ourselves who would have access to Aberman's office, and why would they want to rob it? What information would he have that someone would risk being caught in a government facility stealing government documents? What would they gain by doing that?"

"Money," whispered Rachel.

Osborn slapped the desk with his hand. It startled Rachel and she flinched. "Spot on, detective," he said jovially. "Spot on. Money! So that would answer the 'why', but not the 'who.'"

"So, you suspect someone?"

Osborn nodded. "Indeed, we do. We spent a lot of time searching, investigating, and digging deep into who would have access to Aberman's office? Getting past the security alarm, having a key, knowing when he'd be out of town?"

Rachel bit the inside of her cheek and thought for a while. Osborn sat and watched as the questions permeated her brain. "You remember." It was more of a statement than a question.

She slowly raised her eyes to meet his. "I do," she said breathlessly. "I remember. But why would he?"

"Because he could," replied the Director. "See, all he had to do was make sure your fingerprints were noticed. Of course, his would be there, it was his office. He staged a robbery and tried to make it look like you did it."

She looked at the envelope on her desk. "So, all of this is proof that he wasn't in New England at the time of the robbery, but was here, right here in his own office?"

"Yes," said Osborn. "Seems Doctor Aberman, a man who both the FBI and the local police trusted, is indeed a very bad man."

"But,"

"No, please, let me finish. See, I know he's a bad guy, because he and I worked together. I knew he was delving into cloning again, mainly stem cell cloning, but I've learned his goal was to eventually clone humans. His research often took him outside of disease control, but he swore he'd not cross the line into human cloning. Well, ok, blood cloning, but that was it, so I, in turn promised I'd turn a blind eye, if nothing illegal was being done.

"Stem cell research isn't illegal and honestly, that's what I thought he was doing. But since this lab is federally funded and we are both federal employees, I had to make sure everything remained copasetic, albeit, pushing the envelope sometimes. So, I would cover his back, he'd cover mine, only one day, he decided to step outside our agreed parameters, making it difficult for me to protect him under the shield."

Rachel swallowed hard. "I was given a directive to work on blood cloning, Director. In fact, I've been working on that project for months, along with my own. Was Doctor Aberman working on the same thing?"

The Director shifted in his chair. "The project we're concerned about is called The Genesis Factor." He watched the lines deepen across her forehead as her head tilted slightly and her eyes skated across the surface of her desk.

"You know about the Genesis Factor, Rachel." Again, more of a statement than a question.

She glanced up at the Director. "Yes," she muttered.

"Then why do you look so confused?"

"I'm, I'm not sure how I found out about it."

"You overheard a conversation, Rachel, between Doctor Aberman and a couple other people. You heard that someone at the Lab was processing and experimenting with foreign DNA. You may not have been privy to the desired result, but you knew that someone was doing something illegal, so you started to investigate. You started collecting data, and if you couldn't get it, you asked someone to help you."

"Joshua?"

Osborn nodded. "And he paid dearly for it."

"My lord. I never would've gotten him involved if I'd have known how dangerous it was."

"Well, you got too close, Rachel. They found out, somehow, what you were doing, but instead of killing you then, a plan was devised to use you as a scapegoat. After all, as mentioned, your fingerprints would already be in the Doctor's office. You were here alone, often into the night. You had access to almost everything in this building. You could be as guilty as the next guy. And being a junior scientist, you would make an easy sacrifice. Not having done anything to become world renown; not discovering any major medical breakthroughs; your name not plastered in the medical journals, they could simply say you did it for fame and fortune. You did it for the recognition and the money."

Rachel defenses softened, but not too much. "What changed your mind about me?"

The Director pointed to the pile of papers on her desk. "The documents that lay before you, especially the picture of the screen on the big computer downstairs, the one that manages microscope slides. That picture solidified our suspicions that Aberman was in his office, pulling slides and working here when he should've been in New England. He could've said he came back here to Plum Creek to, well, I don't know, let the dog out, but that picture tells us exactly where he was and what he was doing. See, you didn't leave a paper trail revealing your personal illegal ambitions, but you furnished proof of who was."

Rachel frowned. "How did you see these documents before now?"

"You don't remember sending me a note just before your accident?"

"No, I'm sorry I...," Rachel hesitated. "Wait a minute," she whispered. Looking up at the Director wide-eyed, she said, "I do. I do remember."

Osborn smiled. "Clever clue, too. Let me see, I believe it said, 'Fall on your knees before the Egyptian god. It is then he will deliver the key of proof." He chuckled. "Then you wrote, 'You know what I'm talking about Director. You know everything!'"

Rachel smiled. "Well, apparently, you did know. After all, the only way you could've known about the papers I have here is to find the key to my safe deposit box."

Osborn shifted in his chair and coughed. "Well, I actually had no idea what you were talking about. It wasn't until I showed the note to your friend, Carmen. She knew exactly where you were directing me. With her help, I found the key to your safe deposit box, and in the box, proof of Aberman's illegal pursuits."

"Carmen would know," said Rachel, slightly smiling. "She's into Egyptian gods and the like."

"Quite the historian," agreed Osborn. "I never in a million years would've guessed you were referring to your cat until she explained that centuries ago, they were worshipped in Egypt. Clever idea, taping the key inside his collar. I literally had to get on my knees too, he scrambled under your bed and wouldn't come out, even for Carmen."

Rachel laughed. "Ah, my sweet Mikey. Hence why that was a part of the clue, Director. I knew he'd do that."

Osborn cocked his head. "So, you must've known that your

life was in danger."

Rachel closed her eyes and sat quiet. Finally, she looked over at the Director. "I did," she confessed. "I heard them say so myself, during the same conversation which you just referred to."

"Do you know who 'they' are?"

Rachel shook her head. I recognized Doctor Aberman's voice, but not the other two, until recently."

"Where were you?"

"Downstairs, in the basement."

The Director looked interested.

"In that one small room," continued Rachel, "you can hear voices and conversations. I heard someone talking and listened as long as I could."

"Would you mind showing me that room later?"

"Not at all."

"Before we do that, I'd like to get back to the case at hand. Once I found out that Doctor Aberman was selling organs, performing all kinds of experiments with stem cells, and not doing what this lab is being federally funded to do, I had to step in. It was then I learned of the Genesis Factor; how he was trying to advance some species called the Rephaim, also known as the Avatar.

"From what I understand, all of them are giants, if not in stature, then definitely in personality, charisma, and character. They're strong, intelligent beings. If he created an army of them, he'd be rich. If he could sell the secrets to the highest bidder, he'd be rich. Either way, he'd be rich. But none of this came easily mind you, he had to have help, so the doctor worked with a couple other accomplices. They had to work long, hard hours on the project."

The palm of Rachel's hands began to sweat. "Who were his accomplices?" she asked.

Osborn rested his elbows on his knees and rubbed his hands together. She took that as a sign that something interesting, yet disturbing was forthcoming.

"Well," he hesitated, "I have to swear you to secrecy."

"Ok," agreed Rachel.

"I'm serious, Rachel."

"So am I."

Osborn hesitated just slightly. "One accomplice was someone who went off the radar about a year ago. Made a big public announcement that he was retiring and moving with his wife to Maui. I believe he sat right over there, at that desk."

Rachel sat straight up in her chair. "Doctor Burwell?"

Osborn nodded. "Yes. Doctor Vincent Burwell. They didn't move to Maui. No, he stayed much closer, so he could secretly 'help' with Aberman's financial endeavors."

Rachel stared at the empty desk for quite a while. She was searching for something, a memory...

"He was a nice guy, to be sure, but there are a lot of 'nice' guys out there, Rachel. In fact, he isn't just a crook. He's a ..."

"Murderer!" she said rather loudly.

Osborn nodded again. "Yes, sad but true. We traced the gun that Joshua supposedly used to kill himself back to Burwell. Although he tried to create a suicide scene, Burwell forgot one tiny, but important detail."

"And that would be..."

"A fingerprint. We found his in Joshua's apartment. Granted, it was a partial print, but we were able to match it."

"Good lord," Rachel said quietly. "And to think I sat beside him in this very room for so long."

"And that is probably why you were targeted as the patsy."

"And Joshua. He was innocent in all of this. Why did they

have to kill him?"

"He saw too much, Rachel."

Again, she looked down at the envelope on her desk. "He saw too much," she said quietly. "He was killed because of these."

"In his position, be it ever so humble, he saw receipts, cataloged things coming and leaving the building, that sort of thing." The Director shuffled through the papers until he found what he was looking for. It was the receipt with the signature that Rachel couldn't decipher.

"See that signature there? That's Joshua's. He didn't know what he was signing for, but they knew he would eventually start to figure out what was going on, and because of it, he could become a risk to the operation." Osborn picked up the sticky note from Joshua. "And apparently, by what he wrote here, they were right. He did."

"And his girlfriend?"

"We talked to her, several times; as well as his parents and other friends. We're convinced that Joshua wasn't initially tied to anything illegal. He may have been used at first, or told he'd be promoted, whatever they thought they could get away with, but he was a smart kid."

"I'm glad to hear that, but so sorry he died for nothing; just because one day, he might remember seeing something."

Osborn cocked his head and looked at her with one eye. "Same for you too, Rachel. Even though you were used as their patsy, you were eventually considered a risk too, and had to die."

"But how did they know I was going to be at the intersection the same time TJ Arthur was. He was targeted, I just happened to be at the wrong place at the wrong time."

"Yeah, or they were just real lucky; but, as you said, it was Special Agent Arthur they were after, and sadly succeeded in killing that night. Anyone else who might be hurt was just considered collateral damage. But there was a time they did try to kill you. Being in the hospital just made it easier for them to find you. Remember?"

Rachel closed her eyes. "The doctor in the hospital? He said his name was Mora."

"We still have no idea who that Mora fella is, but we do know he was no doctor. He impersonated one, so he could get to you without anyone suspecting anything. Burwell swears he doesn't know who this Mora guy is either, but we're looking into several scenarios."

The Director rested his finger on his chin. "Burwell was right behind him though. Frankly, just minutes behind him. We caught him as you were being wheeled to the MRI room."

"Yes," Rachel said excitedly. "The old woman on the elevator. I knew it was Burwell."

The Director raised an eyebrow. "You recognized him in that get up?"

Rachel chuckled. "Not by sight, but by smell. Burwell always wore a unique cologne. I recognized the scent when he walked past me before I was wheeled onto the elevator."

"Good job, Doctor."

Rachel blushed. "Thank you, but you said you arrested him when I was being taken into the MRI room. That must've been why I saw Agent Montgomery. I wondered how she ended up beside me so quickly."

The Director nodded. "She stayed with you to make sure you were safe while a few others took Burwell down."

Rachel rested her elbows on the desk and rubbed her hands across her face.

"You were drug into this as a patsy, Rachel. You were given what seemed to be an innocent project, to simply help the blood banks by cloning blood to keep them stocked for emergency purposes. You were to be portrayed as a bright, assertive young woman who discovers new medicines, new DNA and then sells these discoveries to our enemies, making millions. Then you were to be tried and convicted of murder and treason. But then you started investigating, and yes, you started to learn things."

"How easy I made it for them," she said solemnly.

"Fortunate for you, we now know all of that isn't true, but you did put yourself in a dangerous situation. Once the prosecutor realized what was going on, my team was instructed to protect you."

"So that's why my doctor said the FBI was outside of my door 24/7, although Mora was able to get in for some reason."

He slipped in when Agent Montgomery went down to the cafeteria to get a bite to eat. She was only gone a few minutes, but that's all it takes. She's been tailing you for a long time. If you ever saw a shadow in the night, heard an unusual sound that stopped you, yet no one was there, well, that was Special Agent Montgomery. She's been your guardian angel, if you will."

Rachel's face turned ashen.

The Director pulled himself erect and leaned forward. "What's wrong," he asked quietly? "What do you remember?"

"That Mora man, he said the same thing to me before he started to smother me. That whenever I saw a shadow, heard a strange noise, it was him. It almost sounds like he was following Agent Montgomery who was following me."

The Director scratched his head, slowly eased back down into his chair, and mumbled something. Looking out the window he muttered, "We'll have to investigate that."

"Well, I'm just glad that animal didn't think about the little oxygen reader that was stuck on my index finger. With Montgomery gone, that's what actually saved my life."

Osborn turned his eyes back to her and nodded slowly.

Rachel bit her bottom lip and looked over at the Director. "You did say accomplices, as in plural, didn't you? Is there someone else involved in all of this, besides this Mora guy, who no one seems to know anything about?"

Osborn pulled at the corner of his mustache. "There is one other person Rachel, but I'm not sure if I should disclose this to you just yet."

Rachel could feel the heat rising in her neck. She really did want to control her anger, but sometimes...

"I deserve to know," she managed to say without scowling. "I think I've earned it."

Osborn wove his fingers together and laid them across his stomach. He twiddled his thumbs for a minute while Rachel watched. She was really trying to keep it together.

"Ok," he finally said. "I guess you have. The other soldier, so to speak, was Jones. Sheriff Elijah Jones."

Rachel was speechless. Her anger suddenly dissolved into shock.

"He hid things, Rachel. He knew what was going on, but he played into Aberman's hands. He was ready to arrest you just to throw off the investigation. He was the one who squealed and informed Burwell of who our undercover operative was. It was because of him, Burwell was able to kill Agent Arthur, and inadvertently, injure you in the process. He isn't just guilty by association; he's as guilty as if *he* were selling secrets to the Russians."

Rachel massaged her temples. "Is there no one we can trust anymore, Director?"

"I don't know, Rachel. In my world, there aren't many."

She lifted her head and inhaled deeply. "I'm so glad you found the truth, Director Osborn. We may not be able to stop the advancement of the Nephilim, but you caught a few of those who are trying to, so we may have slowed the process down. At least this part is over."

Osborn sat back in his chair. "There's more to this," he said softly.

Rachel looked at him inquisitively. "More?"

"I've found out through various channels that Aberman wasn't the ring leader in all of this. He apparently took orders from someone higher up. Right now, I don't know much about who that might be. I'm still working on that piece, but I do know one thing; this person is referred to as The Coordinator. He is the one giving the orders."

"And since you've no idea who he is, he isn't in jail with the other three," she said nervously.

"No. And I've no idea where to start looking."

Rachel tried to keep calm. "When you start to dig, aren't you afraid of the Coordinator's retaliation?"

"I suppose I should be, but I decided a long time ago that I wasn't going to spend my life being afraid of what is going on in the dark places of this world. No, I decided I was going to be smack dab in the middle of whatever bad stuff is being planned. I'm not going to let innocent people be put in danger."

"I guess I got mixed up in this just by the nature that I work here, so, I am one of the innocents you're protecting. This may sound contrite but thank you."

The Director paused. "Aberman and his cohorts have been arrested Rachel. They're being held at a secret location. It's because of you that we've been able to figure out as much as we have. You investigated like a solid FBI agent and then had the forethought to let me know where I could find the evidence if anything happened to you. You knew you were in danger, but you kept on. You're the brave one, Rachel."

The Director stood up and rapped his knuckles on her desk. "I do want to thank you for, well, for everything. I'd like to see you again, if you don't mind, to, um, to talk more about this."

For some reason, Osborn didn't look as intimidating anymore. In fact, the light pink that radiated from his face made him look quite 'normal'. Rachel, looking up at him, smiled, but said nothing.

He cleared his throat, "Well, I have to get going, I've got work to do. Someone out there is calling themselves The Coordinator and planning to initiate major chaos on a planet I call home. I'm going to go find out who that person is, and hopefully, rid my state and this lab of anything to do with the Genesis Factor."

"Maybe you should start with the Swiss Bank Account," Rachel said, holding up the statement. The account is Aberman's, no doubt, but the money had to come from somewhere."

Osborn tapped his chin again. "Not bad," he said, looking at her with new found admiration.

"Before you leave, Director, I just remembered something else."

"What is it?" he asked, trying not to sound too eager.

"Before the accident, when I went downstairs to the basement and found the room with the air vent in it, although I can't remember all the details regarding the conversation I overheard, I do remember one thing."

"And what might that be, Miss Wall."

"The voices I remember hearing most were men's voices, but then there was one that sounded very female. Not exactly feminine, but definitely female. I couldn't make out what she was saying, she spoke in what sounded like a German, or Swiss accent, something like that, but when she spoke, the men didn't, they listened. It was like she was in charge or had some kind of authority. When the men started to argue, there was nothing said in a female voice again, so I assume, whoever it was had left the room."

"Your point?"

"This may be a long shot, but maybe, Director Osborn, just maybe the person you call the Coordinator isn't a man. Perhaps the Coordinator is a woman."

Director Osborn raised his brows. "Hmm. Who knows, Rachel, as I further my investigation, I may call on you to assist me, if you would be willing to do so. You've proven to be a strong asset to the FBI. In fact, I'd like to talk to you further about a position here in Plum Creek that I've asked DC to fund. They've agreed, and I'm looking to hire. Do you think you'd be interested?"

"I...I..."

The Director smiled. "Don't forget, Miss Wall. I already know your answer. I know everything. Just call me when you find your tongue."

He made it to the doorway before she said, "Zachary."

He turned around slowly, trying to hide the smile that was creeping up around the corners of his mouth. "Yes, Rachel."

"I'm free tomorrow evening, if you'd like to have dinner and talk more about your proposition. Say six o'clock, my house."

He looked at the floor, rapping a knuckle on the door frame for some time. Rachel finally said, "Well, if you're too busy, I understand. Perhaps we can,"

"Six o'clock, Rachel. I'll pick you up. There's an excellent restaurant in Roanoke I'd like to take you to. The food is great and not too spicy."

"Sounds perfect."

She turned the recorder off and sat there, in her chair, completely speechless as she watched the tall, middle aged man walk out of her lab. "He's filled in so many pieces for me," she whispered, "but he still doesn't know everything."

CHAPTER TWENTY-SEVEN

The papers on her desk stared up at her; she stared back without touching them again for several minutes. It had been quite the journey; quite the challenge at times, but...

The corners of her mouth turned upward, just a little at first, then slowly, the smile got broader until finally she couldn't contain the laughter that bubbled up from way down deep. She threw her head back and laughed until tears streamed down her face.

She'd done it!

Everything, every little thing, had fallen into place. She had to be so careful at it all. Every word, every gesture, every question, every answer, especially after the accident, but she did it. She framed him, and the FBI was no wiser for it.

Wow! I should get an Oscar!

Aberman was an oaf. A right wing nutjob. He constantly downgraded her performance and achievements; always thinking her less intelligent than her peers. *Well, I showed you who was the less intelligent one, didn't I?* She sat back in her chair and closed her eyes. She was going to take a few minutes and allow herself the joy of watching it all unfold frame by frame in her mind.

The ransacking of Aberman's office. Of course, that was

his doing. He knew what she was doing. He knew who she was working with; he found that out on his 'vacation'. Her directive to work on blood cloning didn't come from him. It came from his wife; the ruler of all things in Plum Creek. "Bet that was a rude awakening, Doctor A," she said smiling.

After learning the truth who was leading the Genesis project in little Plum Creek, Aberman flew back here to the laboratory earlier than scheduled, leaving his wife in New England, to retrieve his cloning files from years ago and destroy them. After all, he didn't want *his* name attached to anything illegal, or immoral. But while searching, he thought he might as well make it look like a robbery, and who better to pin a 'robbery' on than her. It would be so easy to do, her being here by herself so often. He had to make her look bad because just claiming she was a 'mad scientist' wouldn't fly, would it?

"I bet he almost wet himself when I knocked on his office door," she whispered. He didn't realize by trying to frame her, he gave her the window she was looking for...a way to get him. She'd gone into his office earlier and pulled out the hard drive from his computer, both to protect herself and incriminate him. She didn't care about the paper files, but the hard drive was priceless.

So, when he ransacked his own office, he unknowingly helped her. After all, once he discovered the hard drive was missing from his computer, he couldn't tell the FBI there were two separate robberies. How would he have known, unless he was part of the second robbery? "Thank you for deciding to frame me, big buffoon."

And Trace. Eric thinking she came up with that name because she needed the love of a man in her life. Possibly, but a zombie? No, her Trace wasn't real. He wasn't anything more than a sounding board; someone she'd invented in her bruised brain to help her through all of this. Why, he'd even said himself that he was just a shadow and, oh how did he put it, he was a shadow of conscience.

Yes, he was. He was a shadow of her conscience. He was

the inner turmoil she faced; he exposed the possibilities, the scenarios needed to help her come out of this mess unscathed, famous, and rich. He was the process she used to thoroughly think things out, so she should continue to prove her innocence. Trace was the devil's advocate. He helped her see from the other perspective when she couldn't see it alone. Like when she sabotaged her own experiment. She did it, so she could report it to the police and hopefully strengthen her case that she too was a victim, not the thief, but Trace had a different take on it and talked her out of it, or rather, she talked herself out of it. Trace Ardor was just a means to an end.

But TJ Arthur? He was a different matter. He was the real Trace. Trace James Arthur; FBI Agent, not Trace Ardor, made up zombie man.

She and TJ struck it up nice and cordially at first. Nothing serious. A couple beers, a few movies, but then he got too close; too close to breaking down the wall around her heart and too close to finding out about the purpose behind her blood cloning project. He was almost there, finding out the truth about who was working on the Genesis Factor at the lab. She knew he suspected Aberman at first, but finding his file at the police station was a stroke of luck. It confirmed just how close he got to learning the truth.

It was an old newspaper clipping about the purchase of an estate by the world-renowned archeologist, Dr. Thomas D. Arthur, TJ's great-great grandfather. She never dug deep enough in her research to find out information on the past owners of the Aberman's house, but of course, a break-in at the old house would have grabbed TJ's attention. It was that incident when he had turned from watching Doctor Aberman to watching her, and that cost him. She had no choice; she had to report him to Mrs. Aberman.

One phone call to the Coordinator was all it took. She didn't know he'd be killed, but she'd been ordered to report anyone who proved to be a risk to what she first thought was innocent research. Problem was she was almost killed too.

But that was sheer coincidence, wasn't it? The Coordinator didn't know she'd be at the same intersection at the same time TJ was driving home. Or did she? Had Mrs. Aberman, or the Coordinator as she preferred to be called, double-crossed her? Rachel slid that question to the back of her brain to be addressed later.

As for the intrusion at Aberman's home; before leaving for Boston, Mrs. Aberman had asked Rachel to watch over the house while they were gone, so one chilly afternoon, she paid the old house a visit. The upstairs was the usual; antiques and shaded lamps, but hidden in the basement, she found what she believed the Aberman's didn't even realize existed...a hidden room, actually, a hidden laboratory. Everything in the room was covered with a thick layer of dust, it hadn't been used in years, and over in the corner were three large wooden boxes, each containing skeletal remains; giant skeletal remains.

Of course, she couldn't get the boxes out of the house by herself, and this wasn't something she could ask Eric or Carmen to help her with, so she paid a couple goons to snatch the three boxes out of the house and get them over to her rooms in the basement of the Laboratory. It was unfortunate that just as the hired hands brought the second box up from the basement, Joshua showed up. It seemed Doctor Aberman had asked him to keep an eye on things too. His good intentions had dire consequences.

"Josh," she whispered. "I don't think you linked me to that robbery, or what was in those boxes, but it wouldn't have taken you long. Like the Director said, you were seeing too much and when I asked a simple task of you, unfortunately, you started connecting the dots. I'm sorry."

Joshua was young. He had a bright future ahead of him, and he was quite innocent in all of this, until he saw what he was copying for her and no doubt, related that information to the boxes of bones. If he'd have only kept his suspicions to himself, but no, he had to write that little note. She'd seen the imprint made on the top sheet of a tablet when she'd slipped into the mail room to look around. That's why she put what looked like a blank piece of paper into her purse with everything else. It was evidence.

The moment he wrote that note, he'd become a liability and as much as she hated to, she sent his name to the Coordinator. It was necessary. Eliminate the risk!

Then there was Burwell; joined at Aberman's hip. He must've jumped for joy when she was almost killed in the accident, but when he found out she wasn't, he decided to do the job himself, or have Mora do it. Mora had to be an accomplice of his. And the stinking animal almost succeeded too, if it weren't for that small oxygen reader. "So much for being so smart Burwell," she muttered.

And let's not forget good ol' Sheriff Jones. He was the legal instrument Aberman used to frame her. He was so determined to find her guilty of something that he and Aberman put the FBI on her tail so he could protect the good doctor, and hopefully, be rewarded handsomely for it. After all, Aberman was a rich man, in his own right. But nothing compared to what he could've been if he'd have taken lead on the Genesis Factor.

No, he decided to be the good guy. He made it his mission to make sure the negative reports and public outcry never wrapped themselves around Plum Creek Laboratory again, but cutting-edge cloning, billion-dollar deals, and history in the making was still taking place right under his feet...literally.

Downstairs in Cold Storage, when she erased some of the data on the fat man's monitor, namely the date and time when she retrieved a few slides; and in the cryonics room, the place everyone thought had been shut down and locked up tight, had a back room with an old sequencing machine, the Genesis 2000, and an old desk where she tested her own blood; she took the so called foreign DNA and started to, oh, how did Trace put it, reestablish the Nephilim. She wasn't sure about that, all the Coordinator had asked her to do was clone blood, under the guise of fulfilling orders for local blood banks, but she was sure about one thing. What she was being paid to do was lucrative. That told her it had to be more important than that, so why not find out what was really going on.

Fortunately for Carmen, Eric only knew what Rachel had given him. She fed him enough information to keep him off her scent. Hidden in plain sight. The culprit he was looking for was right in front of him, but he didn't suspect her of a thing. If he did, she would've had to report him too.

She liked Eric, but he was a man; a successful man, and she hadn't yet concluded if she could trust him or not. He didn't understand what it was like to be constantly compared to his peers, looked over, cheated out of opportunity, and lied about. He wouldn't understand what drove her, so it was best, for his sake that he never knew the truth. Same with Carmen.

"I know we've promised to never keep secrets from each other, Car, but some things are better left unsaid. I want to keep you safe, so let's keep it that way, okay," Rachel said softly.

And then there was Osborn. The thought of him made her smile. Despite the fact that Osborn was a man, she needed him. Whether he knew it or not, he was her protector, her guide, her confidant, and her shield. He would never know the truth. The file he carried into the 'living room' at the FBI headquarters in Roanoke was full of everything she was guilty of, but to the FBI and the prosecutor, it would all be circumstantial. She made sure of that!

Yes, she wanted fame, fortune, notoriety, and she did what she did to get it. The discovery of her coma formula would get her name in all the medical journals; she'd tour the country lecturing doctors on her discovery. Who knows, she might even make a buck or two as a speaker. But it was her other 'special project' that would change the world.

She picked up the statement for the Swiss bank account. Looking at the balance, she smiled. Osborn really did have her scared a little while ago when he tried to get her to admit to having access to this account. It took a second for her to get her thoughts together, so she could react correctly because she did in fact have all the pertinent information needed to get to that money. After all, per the contract she and Edith Aberman agreed on, it was part hers. In fact, it was all hers now. Sanford, the second name on the account was her paternal grandmother's maiden name, and sometimes, her alias, but he'd never know that.

She didn't expect what happened next. She didn't expect the air to be sucked out of her lungs with such force she almost vomited right there. But Osborn did know, didn't he? He knew everything about her, he just couldn't do anything because the facts were circumstantial and the prosecutor already denied charges. "He's blaming Aberman for me," she whispered. "He's leaving things up to me. Turn myself in, or continue to play the game...for the rest of my life."

She didn't expect the tears or the terrific sense of guilt to hit her chest so hard she couldn't swallow. What had she done, turning something so simple into something so sinister? This wasn't a game. People were dead. Innocent people. People who had lives of their own and were now gone, their deaths leaving trails of devastation for others to pick their way through and walk alone in all because she had a bruised ego and wanted to 'show' Doctor Aberman. It had all started out to simply protect herself from someone who wouldn't blink to ruin her, but then her relationship with Edith Aberman took things further...too far. Her anger with Doctor Aberman cost more than what she gained. What was she supposed to do with that?

CHAPTER TWENTY-EIGHT

Across town, Edith Aberman picked up the phone and made an overseas call to Geneva, Switzerland. After several rings, a man with a heavy German accent picked up on the other end.

"Good day Kommandeur von Guten," she said cheerily.

"Yes, I will be attending. No, the doctor will not be accompanying me. He is being detained.

Yes, he was sloppy. He knew of the plan, they all did. I made sure of it, but he decided to take matters into his hands and he failed. That was a grave mistake.

No, he won't talk. He won't make it through the night. I've already made the necessary arrangements. The same is true for Jones and Burwell.

Yes, it is a shame, but I will not let their stupidity ruin the plan.

Yes, I know that Burwell almost...yes, he knows she's involved in the Genesis Factor. I assure you, his decision to kill her was his own. He will pay with his life.

Yes, I know about the loss of the baby after her husband's death, but her husband Simon was a protector, he wasn't one of us, so how could...

My apologies Kommandeur. I will not question the plan

again.

The other one?

No sir. I will not allow something like this to happen again. In the future, there will not be any men to stand in my way.

No, Kommandeur. My apologies again, I have no hatred toward men. Please don't take my comment personally.

My family? No, they've no idea. They're completely innocent in all this Kommandeur.

No, the laboratory at Plum Creek is no longer useful to us. I must move the project elsewhere. Probably somewhere in remote New England. If I immerse myself into my family, no one will be the wiser as to why I am really in that part of the country.

Yes, I will be moving after the funerals. It is only fitting that I attend. I will dab my eyes and play the part of a grieving wife.

Yes, sir. I look forward to seeing you and the other Coordinators in the spring as well. Auf Wiedersehen, Kommandeur von Guten."

CHAPTER TWENTY-NINE

A couple days later, <u>The Plum Creek Gazette</u> ran an article about the deaths of Doctor Bruce Aberman of Plum Creek Laboratory, Sheriff Elijah Jones of the Plum Creek Police Department, and Doctor Vincent Burwell, retired scientist of the Plum Creek Laboratory. Details revealed how the three men had died the evening before in a fiery car accident. According to the Gazette, *Sheriff Jones was escorting the two scientists to a medical seminar in Washington, DC where secret technology that will benefit genetic research would be revealed.* Rachel knew that wasn't true. A secret technology was going to be revealed, but not until spring, in Geneva, Switzerland, and definitely not in Washington, DC.

The last paragraph of the article reported: *Mrs. Aberman, 69 years old, of Plum Creek, Virginia, died of an apparent heart attack upon hearing the news of her husband's death. She was alone at the Aberman's home in Plum Creek when his death was reported on the evening news.* It has also been reported that *Mrs. Aberman had a strange mark etched into her forehead, like that of a pentagram, but the local mortician reported it was allegedly caused by hitting her head upon falling and not the result of sinister forces. The FBI will be investigating their deaths.*

Rachel sat in her overstuffed chair and read the article again. She had masterminded a plot to turn the guilt of the laboratory's crimes toward Doctor Aberman and the two others, but for what? Money in an off-shore account she admits she'll never be able to touch? Fame? Only if her picture in the FBI files means she's now on their list of 'persons of interest'. Not quite the type of fame she wanted.

Did she really want to be like Edith Aberman? This woman was ruthless; involved in something so dark, the average person wouldn't believe it to be true, and when her husband failed her expectations, she had him killed! The mortician may claim sinister forces weren't to blame, but Rachel wasn't so sure.

So, who killed Edith, and why carve a pentagram into her forehead? Had she been in the same organization as Mora? He bore a pentagram on his upper arm. If so, Mora wanted her dead...and so did Burwell. Did Edith?

Outside, snow was silently falling; collecting in the corners of the picture window of her house. For a moment, it was a beautiful distraction; it looked so beautiful, so picturesque, even enchanting. The subtle ugliness left in the wake of fall's preceding winds and rain was gone.

But not really gone, was it? Just covered. As beautiful as everything looked, for the first time, she understood the deception of it all. Snow was the great equalizer, but only for a while. When it was gone, the ugliness that had been hiding underneath would reappear.

The same was true of her ambition to rise on the success of the Genesis Factor. Wealth and fame looked wonderful, but what good is having all the riches in the world if how it was attained unleashed an evilness so vile, only God could resist it? The truth of the Genesis Factor was as deceiving as a blanket of snow; beauty on the surface but hiding death underneath.

From across the valley the sounds of bells floated on the chilly air. *Silent Night.* Rachel snickered. *Knowing how things happened and what it all meant, how could he come here as a baby and sleep in heavenly peace?*

"What have I done?" she moaned. The article brought the heavy feeling of guilt back and the reality of her own wickedness enveloped her. People were gone, and she was the reason. There was only one place she could go, one person she could talk to. She didn't know if anyone would be at the small valley church to help her figure things out, but she had to go.

"I don't know what I can do to make up for this," she muttered, pulling on her boots. "I don't know how to redeem myself, but I need to talk to God. He'll tell me how I can make things right, and I will, or I'll die trying."

She wiped the tears from her cheeks with the back of her hand as she slid the other down the sleeve of her coat. "I'm sorry Doctor. I'm sorry TJ and, and Josh. Somehow, I'll get to the truth of what's going on. Somehow, I'll uncover the ugliness that lies underneath all of this, and then maybe...when I have your forgiveness, I'll be able to forgive myself."

CHAPTER THIRTY

Rachel's breath came in gasps; her heart beating ferociously against her chest. She couldn't believe she was standing there, just outside the gate of the small church. The scene before her was serene. The snow encrusted yard, glittering with millions of diamond-like crystals held her in an enchanting grip while the scent of the surrounding pines; their welcoming arms drooping under the weight of their heavy white coats, rushed her senses. Carmen came up beside her and slid her hand under Rachel's elbow. "I'm not sure I should be here," she whispered. "This is so personal for you. I don't want my presence here to make you sad."

"If you're referring to my wedding, and if this is where Simon and I were married," she said staring at the front of the church, "then there can't be any sad memories here, Car. Although I can't remember that day, the memories would be very happy ones. And I'm glad you came with me. You didn't have to."

A cold breeze fluttered the scarf around Carmen's neck. "You're my best friend, Rachel," she said, shivering slightly. "I mean, of course I'd come here with you. The cake I was putting in the oven when you tracked snow through my living room can wait."

Rachel closed her eyes and laughed.

"Would you like to go in?" asked Carmen, staving off a few

giggles. "Maybe that would help you remember some things." Rachel raised her chin and eyed the door of the church. Swallowing hard, she nodded.

The old iron gate creaked under Carmen's gentle push. Rachel stepped into the church yard, her eyes darting up the sidewalk to the church door. She thought it strange that although the sidewalk had been shoveled, there were no footprints in the snow.

At the door, she turned and looked back at Carmen who was still standing at the gate. "Are you coming in?" she asked.

"No," answered Carmen, shoving her hands deep into her coat pockets. "I'm not sure how I'd be...Well, no, you need to do this part alone, but I'll be right here if you need me."

Rachel turned back to the worn wooden door. Standing on her tiptoes, she cupped her hands around her eyes and peeked through the little window. The church was dark, but she made out two columns of wooden pews; counting six rows before the front of the sanctuary disappeared into shadows. She tried the round, handle, and to her surprise, it turned in her hand.

The door squeaked loudly as she carefully pushed it open and stuck her head inside. The floor was wood, the walls were beige; in need of paint, the pews were high-backed; their blue cushions faded and worn. It smelled like old hymnals. It was an old church, but she recognized it.

She walked slowly down the aisle, very aware of the squeaking floorboards under her feet. The memory of flowers and ribbons draping the ends of the pews, smiling faces, a man wearing a white robe with a gold satin sash falling from his shoulders standing in front of brass candelabras, and, and Simon, her Simon, standing beside him looking so handsome in his black tuxedo rushed her brain. The church was empty and dark now, but she knew Carmen had told her the truth. She remembered. This was where she and Simon had been married.

Before sliding into a pew, she stopped and looked around.

A large, plain podium stood in the middle of a tiny dais. On the wall to the left of the podium hung an attendance chart, the number 75 blaring in white numbers. Under the chart was a single door. To the right of the podium hung a picture of a flying dove with an olive branch hanging from its beak.

Two brass candlesticks sat on a dark cabinet behind the podium, but it was what was painted on the wall above the cabinet that caught Rachel's eye. A verse:

"For although there may be so-called gods in heaven or on earth—as indeed there are many "gods" and many "lords"—yet for us there is one God, the Father, from whom are all things and for whom we exist... I Corinthians 8:5"

"Strange," whispered Rachel, sitting down but not taking her eyes off the verse. "Why not John 3:16? Everyone knows John 3:16."

Just then, the door under the attendance chart swung open and an older man, bundled in a thick red coat, wellingtons, mittens, a scarf, and a stocking cap stepped into the sanctuary. His face was covered with a white beard and if Rachel didn't remember she was sitting in a church, she'd have thought Santa just stepped in from putting up the reindeer.

He stomped the snow off his boots and took a step; stopping short when he saw her sitting there. His eyes, round with surprise, sat atop round, rosy cheeks. Rachel couldn't help but smile.

Quickly removing his cap, he held it close to his chest and took a deep breath. "Good heavens, child," he panted. "You just took my breath away."

Standing to her feet, Rachel stepped out into the aisle. "I'm sorry. I didn't mean to startle you. I wouldn't have come in if I'd have known..."

The older man tossed his hat onto the front pew. His coat, scarf and mittens soon followed. He limped up the one step dais, past the podium, and to the dark cabinet that rested against the far wall and under the curious verse.

"Not come in?" he mumbled. "Of course, you should've come in." He moaned a little as he bent to rummage through whatever was in the cabinet. "These doors are always open to whoever wants to come in."

He turned to her and gestured toward the pew. "And please, sit back down." Reaching over, he hit a switch, bathing the sanctuary with light.

Rachel slowly sat back down and watched the old man as he pushed candles into the two candle sticks and lit them. When he'd finished, he hobbled back down to the front pew and sat down, turning so he could see her.

"Bout time too, don't you think?"

Rachel's eyebrows furrowed. "For what?"

"That you showed up here."

"I...well, I..."

"It's alright, Rachel," the man said softly. "I was going to stay here as long as I needed to. I knew you'd show up one day."

Rachel jumped up and grabbed her purse.

"Wait a minute," said the old man. "Please stay."

"Did Osborn put you up to this?" Rachel said angrily. "I don't know how he could've known I was coming here, it was sort of spontaneous, but did he..."

The old man shook his head. "No," he answered quietly. "Zachary Osborn didn't put me up to this. I'm here because you needed someone to be here for you, so I'm here."

Rachel could feel the blood draining from her face. "Who are you?"

The old man's eyes looked kind. "Sit Rachel," he said motioning to the pew. "Sit, and let's talk."

Rachel slowly took her seat.

"So, as for who I am, do you want my full name or the short version," he asked grinning.

"Let's start with your full name," Rachel answered sharply. "After all, you know mine, so it's only fair I know yours."

"Ok," agreed the old man. "But I'm warning ya. My ma loved the Good Book and…"

"Your name," sighed Rachel.

The old man cleared his throat. "Well, it's Jethro Ezekiel Samson…"

Rachel's eyes grew wide. "You weren't kidding, were you?" "Nope," the old man chuckled. "But instead of trying to remember all that, why don't you just call me Jess."

"Jess," whispered Rachel. "I like the sound of that." Her voice faded, her eyes stared into nothing for a few long seconds. Finally, she looked at the old man. "I thought I remembered my father mentioning your name once, but that couldn't be could it?"

"Well, I imagine it could have happened. I know a lot of people…"

"But this was right after the car accident, before he fell into a coma. He kept mumbling something like 'I hear you, Jess. I'm ready, Jess'. The nurses thought he was rambling because of his injuries, but…"

"Your father was a good friend of mine, Rachel. As was your mother."

Rachel's heart climbed into her throat. Reaching for her purse, she tried to stand up, but couldn't. Her knees felt like jelly. She grabbed the back of the front pew to steady herself. "How do you know me?" she asked nervously. "We've never met."

"I knew you as a child, Rachel. And I'll never harm you. You're safe here, so please, let's talk. After all, you're here because you're seeking something, aren't you?"

Rachel kept a white-knuckle grip on the pew in front of

her. "Yes," she whispered. "I am."

"Then perhaps I can help you find it."

Rachel sighed heavily and relaxed back into her seat. "I don't even know what I'm looking for though," she muttered, staring at the verse on the wall. Jess turned and looked up at the verse too.

"Perhaps you do," he said quietly. "Perhaps that verse is telling you what you need to know."

Rachel read it again. "It strikes me as a strange verse to have in a church sanctuary. I think one like John 3:16 would be more appropriate."

"Perhaps," said Jess. "Perhaps those who need to see John 3:16 see John 3:16. Perhaps, like your friend outside, some will see Matthew 11:28, 'Come unto me all ye that are heavy laden, and I will give you rest.'"

"You met Carmen?"

"I did. And she's quite a good friend to have, but she's searching for something too, Rachel."

"She is my best friend," said Rachel. Her chin fell to her chest. "I know she's looking for something to believe in too, Jess. I'm afraid I've not been much help to her in that area. I do hope she finds whatever it is she's looking for someday."

A few quiet seconds passed between them. Finally, Rachel lifted her face to Jess' kind eyes. "If she were in here right now, she'd see something different up there? The verse changes, depending on what the seeker needs?"

Jess looked back at Rachel. "Could be."

"Then what do I need from this one," she muttered. "What do I need to learn from..." She quietly read the verse to herself, her eyes skipping across the words until in the still, quiet moment, they widened with recognition. "Many gods, lords," she whispered, "but only God, the Father *for* whom we exist..."

Jess smiled. "Many, but only One," he said softly. "And we

all exist *for* the Father *through* his son."

Rachel lowered her head. Her eyes blindly skimming the floor. "The Genesis Factor," she said softly. "It's the Genesis Factor."

"Genesis Factor? The making of the modern Nephilim?" asked Jess.

Rachel's head jerked up; her eyes boring into the old man's face. "How do you know about the Genesis Factor?"

"I don't know much about this Factor stuff, but I do know about the Nephilim. That was a dark, dark time for mankind, but despite their attempts to destroy everything, their deception is part of the greatest love story ever told."

"Love story? How could they be part of a love story?"

Jess shifted his weight. "Because, although their evilness changed mankind so drastically it left God no choice but to destroy the world, he showed mercy by setting Noah apart, and from Noah, came the human lineage of Christ. It's through his son, God bestowed his love to us and once again, we can have that perfect, sinless life that the Nephilim tried so hard to take away."

"I've never thought of it that way; Nephilim as part of God's love story. And now...will God still love us if the Nephilim are resurrected?"

"Oh, come now child. You know the Fallen One has been trying to overthrow God's plan for mankind since the beginning. You learned the story of Adam and Eve a long time ago. And Noah and the Ark. All through the ages there's been attempts to stop the birth of Christ. So much so, that because of the crucifixion, the Fallen One was sure he'd finally won the war he started eons ago, until three days later. And now for this age, this Genesis Factor? Well, trying to bring back the Nephilim is just another way to destroy God's plan, but rest assured, it too will fail."

"I thought I was only supposed to clone blood, not bring back evil giants so some whacked out terrorist can take over the world. I didn't know that labs around the world were going to..."

Jess patted Rachel's hand. "It's ok, child," he whispered. "God has all of this under control."

"But I, I need to make things right. I need to..."

"Right now," interrupted Jess. "Today, the only thing you need to do is come to terms with what God's love story means to you personally, Rachel. You can't control what the Fallen One has planned, but you can control what happens in your own heart."

A tear slid down Rachel's face as she fought back the panic. "I don't understand."

"Ah, but I think you do," assured Jess. "Just as the verse up there says. "It is for God you exist. He has a large plan for the world, but he has individual plans for all of us. Learning of, and accepting his individual plan for you is the first thing you need to do if you wish to make a difference in this world."

"But I can't," she cried.

"Why?"

"Because I've done too many terrible things, I've caused people to die, I've cared only about myself. I've helped to advance evil, I'm...

"The very reason the Christ child was born, why he died, and rose again," said Jess. "You my child, and all like you, are the very reason he came to us."

Rachel inhaled deeply then slowly let the air out of her lungs. "But how will he ever forgive me?"

"How can he not forgive you? If he can't, then the battle between good and evil has been in vain."

Rachel brushed her hands across her face.

"It's still as simple as it was when you were a child, Rachel," Jess said warmly. "The verses and stories you were taught still have the same truth. God loves you. Go back to what you know, Rachel. Remember what you learned when you were younger. You are being offered a gift."

She couldn't ignore the tugging at her heart. Jess was right. Her parents had taught her the stories; Adam and Eve, Noah and the Ark, the Crucifixion, and the Resurrection. It all came flooding back. She buried her hands in her face and cried. "Oh, dear Lord," she pleaded, "Please forgive me. Forgive me of all that I've done wrong."

When Rachel opened her eyes, she knew something was different; something had changed. The guilt was gone. And in its place an inner peace like none she'd ever felt before. She wiped her eyes with her fingers until Jess handed her a tissue. "Thank you, Jess," she whispered. "For this," tipping the tissue, "and for taking the time to talk to me, to help me understand." Jess smiled brightly and tipped his head to her.

She closed her eyes and ran the tissue across her cheeks before blowing her nose. When she finished and opened her eyes, the tiny sanctuary was just as she'd found it; empty and lit only by the waning light coming through the stained-glass windows. She sniffled, her eyes darting around the room. Jess was gone.

After stuffing the tissue into her coat pocket, she turned to gather her purse, and to her surprise, beside it was a small Bible. She picked it up and flipped it to the front page.

To my friend Rachel,

This is God's BIG plan for you. Read it, learn it, and trust it always. It will never steer you wrong.

With love,

Jethro Ezekiel Samson Uriah Samuels

She couldn't help but smile. "Thank you again, Jess," she said softly. Standing up, she glanced at the verse on the wall.

"For God so loved the world that he gave his only begotten

son that whosoever believeth in him will not perish but have everlasting life. John 3:16"

***

Carmen was quiet on the drive home; chewing on the inside of her lip, a tell-tale sign that she was in deep thought. Rachel wanted to talk about her conversation with Jess, but knew it wasn't the right time. She had questions, Carmen had questions, and they'd get to them, but not now. Now was time for both of them to be still, to reflect on where their separate conversations with the strange man at the church might lead them.

Rachel wasn't sure where Carmen's thoughts were, but her's were on the next person she had to talk to; someone who probably wouldn't understand anything beyond if he considered her guilty or not guilty, and if that was the case, Zachary Osborn would find her guilty.

CHAPTER THIRTY-ONE

The roads from Plum Creek to Roanoke were clear, the snow pushed up into small mounds on either side of the highway, lending the drive to be uneventful except for the waves of anxiety that rolled over Rachel as she approached the parking garage just under the FBI offices. The worst one hit her as she pulled the key from the ignition. Wide, wild eyes searched her reflection in the review mirror. Her fingers, twisted around the steering wheel, squeezed until her knuckles burned.

More than ever now, she had to set things right, as much as she could. She was no longer proud of what she'd done. People had been killed and she was partly to blame. It was a burden she had to confess; to God first, and then to Director Osborn. God, she knew, had forgiven her. Director Osborn might be a different matter.

"Come on Rachel," she whispered over the lump in her throat. "Confessing to the Regional Director of the FBI shouldn't be harder than confessing to God. Granted, Osborn can have you in jail before the afternoon is over, but it's time to fess up, because no matter what, Osborn may be your jury today, but God is your judge."

Since their first meeting after she'd been released from FBI custody, she and the director had seen each other periodically; learning each other's personality, and frankly, getting comfortable around each other, and even though he hadn't fully gained her trust, she knew this was one time she had to tell him everything. What he decided to do with her after that was yet to be seen.

After a few minutes of small talk in his office, Osborn took her the Blue Castle in downtown Roanoke for lunch. While eating their sandwiches and soup, their conversation was warm and friendly, but when it was time to consider dessert, the murmured voices of the other patrons faded, the room seemed to get much smaller; things got serious. Rachel tried to start with the typical, "It all started out very innocently," but after a few seconds, she knew that wasn't true. It started out with an agenda, a not so innocent one to break through Aberman's grip. She started over.

"I'm going to tell you all I can remember, Zachary," she said wearily, "but you must let me finish without interrupting me because if I stop, I may never finish."

Osborn sat his coffee cup down and rested his elbows on the table. "Go on," he said, quietly. "I'm listening."

There in the small diner she told the Director everything. Everything about how her parents died and how she was determined to find a quick cure for those who suffered from coma after major accidents; how Edith Aberman had asked her to take on the blood cloning project, something she thought at first to be elementary and time consuming, but later learned it was part of a secret agenda. It was then her greed stepped in and she knew if both experiments proved to be a break-through, she'd have proven her worth to the medical world.

"I know all of this, Rachel," Osborn interrupted. "I know..."

"Zachary, please," warned Rachel.

The Director fell back into his chair and sipped his coffee.

"But what you might not have known was, although I didn't pull the trigger, it was because of me that Agent Arthur and the lab technician Joshua Connor were killed."

The Director sat up. "And how is that?"

"I was instructed to call a person I only knew as the Coordinator if anyone started to get too close to my research. I didn't know they'd be killed. I was told they'd be briefed and sworn to secrecy, but, as you know, that was a lie."

A young man walked up to the table with a coffee pot and refilled Osborn's cup. Ripping open a package of raw sugar, Osborn said, "And Edith Aberman was the Coordinator?"

Rachel nodded. "Yes," she said quietly. "I didn't learn until a few days ago, from an article in the newspaper, just how ruthless she really was; having her own husband and his colleagues killed for not, well, I'm not fully sure why, but the point is, she was working for someone far more sinister than I realized at the time."

Osborn finished stirring his coffee. Sitting the spoon on the saucer, he said, "I think I know the rest, Rachel."

"You do?"

Osborn stared into his cup, watching the black liquid swirl slowly. "Yes," he finally said. "I've read the complete file on the Genesis Factor."

When he looked up at her, she thought she could see a darkness brewing behind his brown eyes.

"And?"

"And there is a slew of charges I could recommend to the District Attorney."

Rachel's breath caught in her throat, but she managed to swallow. "Like what?"

"Oh, like obstruction of justice, treason, conspiracy, espionage..."

Rachel closed her eyes. "Ok," she whispered. "I get the picture."

Osborn leaned in toward her. "No Rachel, I don't think you do."

Her eyes opened wide and she stared into a face that was stern, unfriendly, and serious.

"You're in a heap of serious trouble Doctor Wall," he continued. "You could be spending the rest of your life out in Colorado, a resident of the high security federal prison with neighbors like the uni-bomber."

Rachel looked up at the ceiling and silently started to count to ten. It was an old trick she learned to keep the tears from welling up in her eyes.

"Buuuttttt...."

"But what?" she moaned.

"There is a way out, if you're interested." He picked up his coffee and took a long draw while Rachel stared at him like he was crazy.

"How?" she asked impatiently.

"What I'm going to propose is very dangerous."

Rachel snickered. "Dangerous, really? I think I've already done that Director."

Osborn looked at her over the rim of his cup; his eyes searching her face. "Ok," he said, placing his cup on the saucer. "Do you remember a few weeks ago, while sitting in your lab, I mentioned I had a proposal for you, that the government has agreed to fund a new operation and I wanted to talk to you about it?"

"Yes," answered Rachel. "I've often wondered why you hadn't brought it up since, thought maybe you'd changed your mind."

Osborn shook his head. "No, I haven't changed my mind. I've been waiting for this moment, when you'd come to me and confess."

"Well, I guess your patience paid off," she said humbly. "Here I am."

Osborn's eyes searched her face. Her lips were trembling

ever so slightly. Her eyes would find his, then dart to her lap. She looked scared, but more important, she was sincere. Osborn waved at the waiter. "Let's have some strawberry pie first," he said with a smile. "Then we'll talk business."

***

Not a crumb left, Osborn finally laid his fork across his plate and looked over at Rachel. She'd been trying to wait patiently, but was finding her patience growing thinner by the second.

"Can we talk now, Director," she said gravely.

Osborn dabbed his mouth with his napkin before draping it over the fork and plate. Smacking his lips, he said, "Man, that was good". Holding up a finger, he called for the waiter. "More coffee, please." He glanced at Rachel. "Anything else for you, my lady?"

She clenched her teeth and took in a deep breath, drawing upon her larynx to produce as pleasant a voice as possible. "No," she said, throwing him a weak smile. "No thank you. I'm fine."

The Director waited until his coffee cup had been filled and he'd added the perfect amount of sugar and cream before looking at Rachel again. Stirring, he said, "Ok, Miss Wall. "This is my proposal," he finally said.

"I'll wipe your slate clean, but only if you agree to be the bait, bait I need to catch the big fish. I'll dangle you from a big hook and you'll continue to play the game until we get to the bottom of this. You'll continue to gain the favor of this, um, Leader or whoever it is that Edith Aberman reported to and climb whatever ladder there is to climb until we can figure out who is behind this so-called world take-over."

Rachel sat quietly, her hands folded in her lap; her eyes staring at her plate. The greed and corruption she would have to portray would be a rouse this time, but, as bad as she knew it could become, she also knew she could play the part well enough to gain the attention of whoever was behind the Genesis Factor.

That would be the easy part. The hard part was their contract had to be kept solely between the two of them, not to be shared with anyone, not even Carmen.

Her stone-cold eyes found Osborn's and she nodded. "I'm game," she said. "Just tell me what you want me to do."

Osborn smiled. "Then consider yourself clean," he said quietly. "We'll start with a few weeks of FBI training under the guise of your new position as the Director of the Virginia Crime Lab. Nothing too harsh or physically demanding, but enough to teach you how to gather data, and then we'll concentrate on that Genealogy Conference you're going to in the spring."

Rachel's face turned white. "What do you know about that conference that I don't know?"

"It's where your journey down this path will actually start, Rachel. And it won't be as it seems."

"But Carmen is going too. How dangerous will this be?"

Osborn picked up his cup and held it to his lips. "Carmen will be well protected," he said, looking at her intently. "There will be several of our people there in the shadows and they'll all know what they're supposed to do."

Rachel sighed heavily. "Ok, that's good to know, but now, please tell me what I'm supposed to do."

Your duties to the crime lab will be as such: Minor cases, cases I've personally approved, will be sent your way. I don't want you bogged down with serial murders, bombings, and the like. There are other labs that will handle those cases. What I want you to handle are forensics for cases such as break-ins, car thefts, stuff like that, and in actuality, you won't be working those cases, but merely overseeing them. You'll have staff to do the grunt work."

Rachel looked appalled. "Then why bother?" she snapped.

"Why go to all the trouble of renovating the lab, changing my title, and..."

"Because those cases will just be covers, Doctor," interrupted the Director. "I want you to help me find out who's behind this cloning, world dominance thing. Your energy needs to be concentrated on that, not distracted by whatever cases I throw your way."

Rachel slumped back into her seat. "So, you want me at your beckon call to do whatever you tell me to do, regardless that my life's ambition is to have a microscope glued to my face?"

"Oh, believe me, Rachel, there will plenty of science for you in this investigation. Let's not forget about foreign DNA, weird specimens, and..."

"All right," she nodded wearily. "I understand. I'll have a small team here to take on these minor cases, and I'll be traveling, digging, becoming a part of a sinister organization to spy on them, and whatever else I need to do to find out who's creating this nightmare."

Osborn's cup clinked against the saucer. He nodded.

"This could be much bigger than either one of us imagines."

His grey eyes locked with Rachel's. He nodded again.

Fumbling with the napkin on her lap, she looked down at her fingers and swallowed hard. "I just wanted to be accepted as a Tier I scientist, Zachary. Appreciated for my skills and..."

"And you are," he said softly. "I know you never anticipated your life taking such a serious turn, especially one that leads you outside of the lab, your comfort zone, but here we are Rachel. Now you put your education, skills, knowledge, everything towards helping me catch the bad guys." He hesitated and searched her face before she lowered her eyes to her lap. "Either way, taking on this investigation or going to prison, you'll be leaving the serene world you once knew behind. Your own choices have dictated these changes."

"I know," she whispered. She kept her head bowed, still fumbling with her napkin, for several long seconds. When she looked up, her eyes met the Director's, burning with a fire he'd never seen before.

He was right. She was in. Ready to change the world...again.

"Now," she said firmly, "before I sign on the dotted line, let's talk about what the FBI will give me? After all, I started out making sure I protected myself, I'm not going to stop now."

The corners of Osborn's mouth turned upward, but the smile didn't reach his eyes. They were cold as steel; sharp like broken glass.

CHAPTER THIRTY-TWO

Several weeks later, Rachel was standing in the space that had once been her small lab watching contractors reconstruct it to FBI specifications. It was to be the new FBI Crime Lab and she was its Director. Director Osborn had given her an offer she couldn't refuse, literally.

Carmen stepped up beside her. "This is so exciting," she yelled over the noise of the table saw. "Whoda thunk it? Our little Rachel Wall, Special Agent and Director Extraordinaire."

Rachel laughed. "I'm not an agent, Car. I'm just the Director of a small crime lab."

"Oh *just*," said Carmen, rolling her eyes.

Rachel put her arm around her friend's shoulders and led her out into the hallway. "Thank you for staying with me, Carmen," she said in her ear. "I couldn't have done it without you."

Carmen looked up at her and smiled. "Got that right," she said with a wink. She looked down at the small bump protruding from her belly. "Besides, you've got a nephew, or niece, coming and it is your responsibility to make sure she, or he, will be spoiled rotten."

Rachel reached over and gently rubbed Carmen's belly. "And I will," she said softly.

Carmen removed Rachel's hand and giggled. "I'm not a genie, Rach. You don't have to rub the jewel."

"I know," she replied. "I just feel like I've missed so much. I mean, I can't even remember your wedding, so I definitely want to remember everything about this special time in your life."

Carmen patted her hand. "Me too. And I'm sure once the two of you meet, play together, become best friends, the world will never be the same. It will be a time everyone will remember!"

"Are you happy I officially stepped away from the coven?" Rachel asked quietly.

Carmen hesitated a moment. "I understand why you did it, Rachel, but I still think you could've worshipped in the way you want, the god you want, and still have been our Priestess. But on the other hand, I'm honored that the coven chose me to assist Kaida. Since she's agreed to be my crone, I'll learn so much about the craft."

"Kaida was ok with everything, too. That in itself was awesome," said Rachel.

"I know," Carmen said thoughtfully. "One isn't usually allowed to leave a coven so easily."

Rachel didn't respond, but she thought of the conversation she had with Kaida to convince her that it would be in everyone's best interest if she were allowed to just walk away. It opened a door for Carmen, to which Rachel had mixed feelings.

"I do want you to be careful, though, Carmen," Rachel said gravely. "We started out practicing Wicca to dabble in a little magic and grow some herbs, not to become full-fledged witches."

Carmen chuckled. "I'll be fine Rachel. I'm not going to go and get all voodoo on you."

Rachel smiled weakly. "I hope not. Kaida is a strong influence."

Carmen touched Rachel's arm. "I'll be fine, Rachel. Besides, I've been thinking about some things since our visit to the church a month or so ago. That old man, Jess, he said some things that I just haven't been able to let go of, and well, he made a lot of sense."

Rachel half-smiled and gave a slight nod. "Ok," she sighed. "Let's talk about that real soon. And speaking of our visit to the church, I do want to thank you for understanding my need to find my roots. I don't know where it will lead me, but I do want to learn about certain things. Perhaps I'll even start attending services at the little church in the valley."

"Of course," said Carmen, slipping her arm into Rachel's. "You need to grow in whatever it was your parents taught you when you were a little girl. And once you know, perhaps you'd like to share what you've discovered with me. I'd like to know too."

Rachel turned to her friend. "I'd like that Carmen," she said softly. "I'd like that very much!"

"See," said Carmen. "I'm not a full-fledged witch. I'm open minded, I'm cool. Just don't mess with my herb garden."

Behind them, someone cleared his throat. Turning around, they were both surprised to see a handsome man standing inside the front doors of the lab.

"Do you know him?" Carmen whispered.

Rachel shook her head. Carmen looked up at her and smiled.

Rachel ignored her and walked over to the stranger, carefully stepping over wood scraps, tools, and long orange extension cords. "Hi," she yelled. "Can I help you?"

"Hope so," he yelled back. He signaled for them to follow him further down the hallway away from the noise.

Once out of range of the hammers and table saws, he said, "Sorry. I didn't want to have to keep yelling."

Carmen's eyes twinkled. "No problem," she said merrily.

Rachel threw her a look that said, *"Be quiet you!"*

"So, how can I help you?" Rachel asked.

"I'm looking for Director Rachel Wall."

Carmen looked at Rachel. "Wow," she said almost laughing. "First time I've heard it said out loud by someone other than me. It sounds so official."

Rachel took Carmen by the elbow. "Excuse me one second," she said to the stranger, leading her friend back into the construction site. "I need you to supervise in here," she said loudly. "Do NOT go back out into the hall unless I signal you to do so. Got that?"

Carmen pushed her bottom lip out. "Party pooper."

"Yes," yelled Rachel. "That's me. Director Party Pooper. Now stay here."

She left her friend in the noisy room, but not without noticing Carmen was still wearing the poochy lip. She couldn't help but chuckle.

Stepping back over boards and sheet rock, she asked again, "Now, how can I help you?"

"Are you Director Wall?" he asked.

"Yes, I am."

"I just wanted to stop by and introduce myself. I've recently been appointed here as the new lead Scientist for Plum Creek Laboratory."

"Well, congratulations," said Rachel, extending her hand.

"Thanks," he replied, shaking her hand.

His shirtsleeves were rolled up to his elbows and she couldn't help but notice the tattoo on his left forearm. It was a sword, a long sword, and on the pommel of the hilt was a blood red circle, like the color of a ruby stone.

"I'm new here to Plum Creek," he was saying, "and was wondering if you'd be willing to give me a tour of the town, and maybe give me the low down on who's who."

Rachel tore her eyes away from his arm and looked into his face. He stopped talking and smiled again. He had a beautiful smile. And the most penetrating blue eyes she'd ever seen.

"Well," he said, pulling her back into the conversation. "I mean, if you're too busy with the construction and everything, I understand."

Rachel felt the warmth creep into her cheeks. "Uh, no," she said slightly embarrassed. "I was just intrigued by your tattoo. It's different, isn't it?"

The stranger's smile disappeared, a look of subtle surprise shadowing his handsome face. "So, you see it? I mean, you know what it is?"

"Well, of course I see it," Rachel said, a bit confused. "And it's a sword of some kind, right?"

The man's eyes lit up and he smiled. He turned his arm and displayed the ink. "It is," he said proudly. "Only a few of us wear it.

"Who?" asked Rachel. "A band of fraternity brothers?"

"No, more sinister than that," he said teasingly. "Actually, I am a member of an Order. The Order of St. Michael's Sword. Ever hear of it?"

Rachel shook her head. "No," she said chuckling softly. "Is it local or national?"

"Global, actually. You can search it on the internet if you'd like to. ..."

Rachel's eyes sparkled. "How does one join this global Order?"

The question took the stranger by surprise. "Well, um, um,"

Rachel didn't budge. She really wanted to know.

"You don't," he finally said. "The Order isn't something

you join. You're chosen and then invited. By personal invitation only. One has to..."

"Have we met before?" she interrupted.

He shot her a quizzical look. "Uh, I don't know. Before landing this job, I traveled a lot, so maybe. I lived in Denver before moving here. Did you ever live in Denver?"

"No," she said half laughing. "You just remind me of someone."

"I hope he was nice."

Rachel almost said something like 'he was a zombie', but she stopped herself. Instead, she leaned toward him and squinted at his name badge. "I'm sorry, I didn't get your name."

It's right there. "Knight. Michael S. Knight."

"Knight," she repeated. "Mind if I ask what the S stands for?"

The man shifted his weight from one foot to the other. "I can tell you, but then I'd have to..."

"Kill me?"

"Heck no," he said smiling. "That would be a waste. What I was going to say was then I'd have to take you out to dinner."

Rachel smiled. "Well, we'll see about that."

"Sterling," he replied. "My middle name is Sterling."

Rachel threw her hand up to her throat and fought back the laugh. "I'm sorry," she said earnestly. "I mean no disrespect, but your name is Michael Sterling Knight?"

She couldn't help but giggle. The stranger smirked and shoved his hands into his pockets. "Yes, that would be my name. Michael Sterling Knight. My father had a weird sense of humor. Everyone usually reacts the same way you just did, that's why I don't use my middle name. My friends call me Mike."

"Ok," said Rachel. "Nice to meet you Sterling."

"Ah, you're not yet a friend."

"Well, no, not yet. Maybe soon, but regardless, I rather like the name Sterling."

"Ok, so I see how this is going to go."

"Unless you really don't want me to call you that. I mean, I just met you. I don't want to offend you."

Knight shrugged his shoulders. "I won't take offense under one condition. After all, it is my name. But in order to make sure I'm not offended, after touring the metropolis of Plum Creek, you must have dinner with me."

Rachel smiled. "I'd love to, but would you mind if we made it a foursome. I've a couple of friends I'd like you to meet."

Sterling's eyes twinkled. "Great. The more the merrier. Just tell me when and where?"

"How about I talk with my friends and get back to you, now that I know where you work."

He snickered. "Ok, sounds like a plan. Right now, I'm going to go check out a house, but I'll be back here in the morning. Will you be here?"

"Bright and early," replied Rachel.

They walked back to the front doors and as he pushed them open, he said, "Ok, see you then."

"Ok."

She watched him step off the curb and walk across the parking lot, his blue jacket slung over his right shoulder. "Wow," she whispered.

Carmen quietly stepped up beside her. "No kidding," she said. "Nice car too."

"You're never going to believe this Carmen," Rachel muttered, not taking her eyes off of the car.

"What?"

"His name is Michael Sterling Knight and he drives a white mustang."

Carmen laughed. "No way!" she exclaimed.

"Yep," said Rachel. "I swear I didn't make that up. He said his friends call him Mike, but his name really is Michael Sterling Knight."

"A Knight with a white horse," Carmen said quietly. "I think God has answered your prayers. This guy has to be heaven sent."

Rachel watched as the white mustang left the parking lot. "I can't help but wonder how true that statement really is," she whispered. "I wonder why now, why a man named Michael, who bears the sword of the Archangel."

Carmen looked up at Rachel and smiled. "Girl, it must be a miracle because my magic isn't that strong."

The two women stood at the lab doors and watched the car until it disappeared behind the trees. "Miracles and magic," whispered Rachel.

Carmen slowly nodded her head. "No kidding."

The cell phone in Rachel's pocket vibrated. She looked at the number and almost sent it to voice mail, but for some reason, she stepped away from Carmen, from the noisy construction work, and hit the green button.

"Hello. Yes, this is Director Wall," she said quietly. "I'm sorry who? Antonia Schmitt?

How can I help you, Miss Schmitt?

Yes, I'll be at the GenTrak seminar next month.

Yes, I'm excited to see the new technology that will be presented.

My DNA?

Well, I guess so. I don't see how it would hurt if I participated in your experiment. I am, after all, a scientist." Rachel giggled.

After a long pause, the furrow in Rachel's forehead deepened. "Well, no, not really. I've just started a new job and I don't think I'll have the time to stay...

What?

Yes, I remember Edith Aberman."

The voice on the other end of the phone went into a lengthy explanation about the Coordinators, which immediately grabbed Rachel's attention, as well it seemed, Carmen's. Rachel could see her inching her way closer to her from the corner of her eye, so every time Carmen took a step to get into hearing range, Rachel would turn and take a step away from her.

"Well, that makes sense," continued Rachel.

"Yes, it was difficult, but I made it look like I was the one being framed, not them...and although they did their best to make the FBI think I was guilty, I kept hammering my facts to the Director.

"Yes, Edith was an asset. She helped me tremendously."

She was lying now, she knew that, but she had no choice. This was the call she'd been waiting for, the introduction to the game she had to play. She was after all, the bait.

"Yes, it's a shame her husband had to get in the way. Even sadder she died as well."

Finally, she said, "Yes, Miss Schmitt, I understand now. And the Council has requested that I interview when I'm in Geneva for the seminar? I don't know what I could've done to deserve that opportunity, but please express my gratitude to the Commander and the Council.

"Director Osborn? No, he doesn't suspect a thing. He thinks he's clever, but, well, you know, it is the FBI.

Yes, being here will help me manage everything regarding the DNA transfers as well as what will be given to the FBI and what will be withheld.

Yes, please do. I'll keep an eye out for the information.

Thank you, Miss Schmitt.

Good-Bye."

Carmen watched Rachel as she walked back up the hall toward her. "Who was that?" she asked.

"Just a business call," Rachel answered. "I guess I'll be getting a lot of those now that I'm overseeing the crime lab."

"Really? I heard you say the name Edith Aberman. I didn't know she had anything to do with a crime lab."

"Oh, she didn't directly. She was just involved in Aberman's research, or some of it, and the caller just wanted to know if I was aware of the part she played and then gave her condolences for Edith's passing."

"Seems kind of weird to call and send condolences now. The Aberman's have been gone for several months."

Rachel slid her arm through Carmen's and guided her towards the lab. She really didn't want to lie to Carmen, but right then, she had no choice. *But I can tell her the truth later, when all of this made more sense,* she thought. As they walked, she resolved that eventually, she'll come clean and explain everything to her, but right now, she had to keep all of this to herself.

"Yes, it does seem weird, to us anyway, but Miss Schmitt may not have known about Aberman and me working together. After all, I'm going to be talking to a lot of people who aren't aware of my former role at Plum Creek but are calling now because of my role with the FBI." She shrugged her shoulders and said lightly, "Who knows."

Carmen stopped, letting Rachel take a few steps ahead of her. "Are you sure?" she asked cautiously. "You're not keeping anything from me, are you?"

Rachel turned around and looked at her friend. "Absolutely not," she said with a wily smile. "No secrets, remember? Now come on, let's see what they're doing to my new digs. And then we have a conference to get ready for. It's only six weeks away, you know. My, my, the research we must do."

Carmen stood there and watched her friend practically bounce back into the construction zone. "I remember our promise to each other, Rachel," she whispered, "but do you?"

***

A couple days later, Sterling slid a chair around to the other side of Rachel's desk and passed a bag of chips, a roast beef sandwich, and a Diet Coke over to her.

She looked up from her writing, surprised to see him and lunch. 'What's this," she asked smiling broadly.

"Lunch," he said smiling back. "My way of thanking you for having dinner with me the other night, showing me the sights of Plum Creek, and introducing me to your friends." He took a big bite out of his sandwich. "Der great by da way."

Laughing, Rachel opened the bag of chips and unwrapped her sandwich. "Yes, they are. They enjoyed meeting you too."

Sterling stopped his sandwich just inches from his mouth. Looking at her from over the top of the bun, he said, "I find it interesting that Carmen is Wiccan. I've never met a real witch before, or at least I don't think I have."

Rachel swallowed and grabbed her drink. "She's not really a witch, or she doesn't consider herself to be a witch as we think of them. She worships in the Wiccan religion but prefers to be called a caster. Not a witch."

"Not quite sure what the difference would be," said Sterling, "but I'll learn more, I'm sure."

"Why?" asked Rachel. "Have you made it your personal mission to learn as much as you can about Wicca and witches?"

"I wouldn't call it a personal mission, but since I hope to become friends with them too, I'd like to know more about them...or her, I should say. Learning people is a hobby of mine."

Looking up at the ceiling, Rachel chewed on a chip. Her eyes fell down and met his. "And what is there to learn of you, Mr. Knight. We'd like to know more about you too."

"Really," he said with a half chuckle. "What would you like to know?"

Rachel looked at his face then down to his arm. "For starters, I'd like to know what that tattoo really means and who gave it to you?"

"Is that all?" he said before taking another bite of his sandwich.

"No," answered Rachel. "I'd also like to know how you came to Plum Creek."

"I told you why I'm..."

Rachel shook her head. "No, Sterling. The truth. If we're going to become friends and trust each other, I need to hear about The Order of Saint Michael's Sword and what brought you to Plum Creek. And I need to hear it from you."

"Why is that so important to you, Rachel? The Order is a group of people who strive to do our best to take care of certain things. That's all. And, like you, I'm a geneticist, I was hired to be the lead scientist here, just as Doctor Aberman was before."

Rachel laid the bag of chips on her desk and carefully wiped her hands on her napkin. "The reason Carmen and I are such good friends is because we don't keep secrets from each other. We tell each other the truth, regardless of how it might hurt. I believe if you share this secret of yours with me, we can possibly form the same type of friendship. If not, it will just merely be a pass in the hallway and a 'how are you today' kind of thing. Your choice, Sterling."

Sterling brushed his hands together then sat back in his chair. "You drive a hard bargain, Miss Wall."

Rachel chuckled. "So, I've been told."

"The Order is a group of Christians who have been asked to dedicate their lives to fighting against dark forces. We believe there is a battle, a spiritual battle, that is constantly going on around us. Angels versus demons, all for the souls of men. It is our duty to fight in the physical realm, alongside of God's warriors who fight in the spiritual realm, to overcome Satan and bring as many to Christ as possible."

Rachel was so engrossed in what Sterling had just said she didn't notice she'd knocked her chips onto the floor with her elbow.

"Can you see this spiritual battle?" she asked with interest.

Sterling hesitated and then said, "Sometimes. Some of us have seen our spiritual counterparts, while others haven't."

"Why? What allows some to see it and others not to."

"We're not sure," Sterling said quietly. "We think it may depend on the mission they've been given."

Rachel nodded and looked down at her desk. "I understand," she whispered.

Sterling leaned closer. "Why, Rachel," he said, his voice low and careful. "Have you seen one of God's warriors?"

Rachel looked into Sterling's face. "Yes," she muttered. "I have. A few times."

Sterling folded his arms across his chest. "I thought so," he said somberly.

"Why?" she asked curiously. "Why of all things, would you think I've seen a warrior?"

Sterling hesitated then held out his arm. "Because you saw this, Rachel."

"Yeah, so. It isn't a small tattoo."

"Not everyone can see it, Rachel."

Rachel's felt the blood drain from her face. "What does

that mean, Sterling?"

Sterling relaxed. Taking Rachel's hands in his he leaned across the desk and looked into her brown eyes. "I don't know. That will be up to God, or Elohim as we call him, to decide. But whether you're chosen to be a warrior or not, but because you're able to see this, you are a protector."

"What the difference between a protector and a warrior?"

"Protectors are witnesses. They're the sentinels who stand guard, the person who projects Elohim in their everyday life. A warrior is an infiltrator, he or she goes into the thick of world affairs to fight to change the course of evilness. We fight, and fight some more, knowing we'll never eradicate evil, but give our lives to keep it at bay.

So, all believers are protectors, but some are chosen to be warriors?" she asked cautiously.

"Yes," replied Sterling.

Rachel slowly slid her hands out of his grasp. "I wouldn't even know where to begin as a protector," she said quietly.

"I do," Sterling said carefully.

Rachel's eyes locked with his.

"Carmen," they said in unison.

CHAPTER THIRTY-THREE

The next six weeks went by so fast. She had stayed busy overseeing the construction of the crime lab, rather enjoying her new role in it as well as taking Sterling's words to heart and spending a lot of time studying The Word, the official book of The Order. She still wasn't sure what a protector was, but she wanted to learn, and by doing so, she spent time trying to figure out a way to tell Carmen what was going on. But that conversation would have to come later. Right then, she was in Geneva, Switzerland, standing in an enormous building which was part home, part office, called The Chalet, sipping on the best mimosa she'd ever had and wondering when Carmen would arrive.

The only thing about the place that resembled a chalet was its location. High up in the Swiss Alps, the mansion sat precariously on a rugged precipice, hidden in plain sight by surrounding rock formations, great spruce pines, and the magnificent colors of spring foliage that blanketed the mountains like a giant quilt. Below, the Rhine River wound around the loped bases and through the deep cut valleys. Snowcapped peaks stood rigid and firm; encircling the chalet like sentinels protecting a fortress. And a fortress it was. The only way to get to it was by helicopter.

Rachel turned from the breath-taking mountain views and studied the cathedral-like room where she stood; completely awestruck. She wasn't sure if she was in a library, a study, or an office, but whatever it was, she was taken in by the beauty of it. The stag heads, the marble floors, the gold leaf trimmings, the velvets and embroideries, the gargantuan stone fireplace, and the opulent leather furniture that filled it perfectly.

"All of this because of a 'Find out who you are' campaign?" she whispered. "I don't think so."

Behind her the sound of helicopter blades cut through the thin mountain air; pulling her back to the large windows. Her eyes followed the chopper until it flew out of sight to land on the helipad somewhere above her. "Hmm. Wonder if it's more distant relatives or a group of Coordinators? Either or, I can't wait to meet them."

"Doctor Wall?"

Turning too quickly, orange juice spilled over the rim of her glass. She immediately licked the liquid from her finger. "I'm sorry," she said apologetically. "I'm so uncouth."

The young lady smiled. "I don't blame you," she said. "Helga makes the best mimosas in all of Switzerland. Would you care for another?"

"Oh no," chuckled Rachel. "This one is quite enough. In fact, I'm feeling a bit lightheaded right now." She glanced curiously at the glass then back at the young woman. "Would I be wrong to assume this drink was spiked with something besides champagne?"

"Now Doctor," the aide scolded playfully. "Why would we do something like that?"

Taking the glass from Rachel's hand, she sat it on a small table then walked over to the lone suitcase standing by the antique desk. "I believe it's called jet lag, Miss, and probably a bit of altitude sickness. You've traveled a long way, an exciting adventure no doubt, but I'm sure you're exhausted. So please, let me show you to your room where you can rest before lunch." Grabbing the handle of Rachel's suitcase, she motioned to the archway. "If you'll follow me."

Rachel picked up her laptop case and purse and followed the young woman out of the library. A quick nap and a chance to freshen up would be nice.

As the two walked down a corridor, Rachel stopped along the way to admire several pieces of artwork that hung on the wall or stood on marble columns. "This place is amazing," she said, taking a few brisk walks to catch up to the young woman. "I've got to walk the whole mansion while I'm here. It's, it's...like a museum, but better."

The young woman laughed. "It is rather nice, isn't it?"

"Nice, doesn't even begin to describe this place."

The aide came to an abrupt stop. Rachel caught herself before running into her. "Whoa!" she screeched, "What? What's wrong?"

"Oh, nothing Miss. We're just going up."

"Up?" Rachel's eyes followed the brass doors up to the antique floor indicator that looked down on them with high polished brass numbers.

"An elevator," whispered Rachel. "We even have an elevator."

"There is a large semi-circular staircase in the lobby," replied her hostess, "but since we're going to the third floor, I thought taking the elevator would be more suitable."

"Third floor?" marveled Rachel. "This place has a third floor?"

The young woman chuckled. "It does, and you're the first guest to see it."

A velvety "ding" sounded just as the light behind the number one on the dial lit up. A smooth shhhhh and the doors opened. Stepping into the elevator, the young woman pulled Rachel's suitcase close to her and said, "My name is Lydia, Miss Wall. I've been assigned to you."

"Assigned to me?"

Lydia smiled a pleasant smile. "Oh yes, Miss. Each guest has a staff person assigned to them. We are to personalize your visit to the best of our ability. Anything you need or desire, we are to see you get it." She pulled a round silver device, about the size of a half dollar out of her apron pocket and handed it to Rachel. Rachel eyed it curiously.

"It's a curtron," explained Lydia. "We, the staff, call it a bell. Please keep it with you at all times. It's how you "call" me if you need anything, night or day. All you have to do is push the green button and I'll be there."

Rachel flipped the curtron in the palm of her hand. "And the red button?"

The number three above the doors lit up and the bell dinged again. The doors slid open and Rachel followed Lydia over the threshold into a magnificent foyer. Stepping to her right, she looked over the ornate banister into the mansion's atrium below.

Lydia went to her left and started down the hall. There are four suites and four apartments on this floor of the wing, Miss," she was saying. "The suites are for our guests; the apartments are for staff. My apartment is right next door to your suite."

"Only four?" asked Rachel walking slightly behind her.

"Yes, Miss, only four."

"But the hall is so long."

Lydia smiled. "That's because the suites are so big."

The third mahogany door on the left swung open under Lydia's touch. Stepping aside, she let Rachel enter first. Walking into the suite, Rachel gasped. "Oh, my. All of this surely isn't just for me?"

Lydia rolled the suitcase into the master bedroom leaving Rachel alone to roam the rooms. "Yes, Miss, it is," she called over her shoulder.

"And the views..." Rachel stood enchanted by the beauty of

the mountains looming over them.

Lydia stepped up beside her. "Beautiful, aren't they?"

"Divine," whispered Rachel.

"If you don't mind, I'd like to show you some details of the suite before I leave."

Reluctantly, Rachel turned from the picture window. "Not at all," she answered.

"Well, to start, when you want to pull the shades or curtains, there is a panel over here."

Following Lydia around the suite, Rachel learned that there were several panels, all with a button for everything; a button to start the stereo, a button to turn on the fireplace, a button to dim the lights, a button to raise televisions, there was even a button to start the coffee pot.

Lydia handed Rachel the key to her suite. "If everything meets your approval, Miss, I'll leave you to settle in and get some rest. Lunch is at 12:15 sharp in the main dining room. Everyone will have a chance to meet and greet there. The Kommandeur does not tolerate tardiness, so please be ready."

"Oh, don't worry," snickered Rachel. "I'm sure I'll be famished by then."

Lydia nodded at a Queen Anne desk sitting beside a large window. "There's a folder over there, on the desk, Miss. Inside you'll find the names and a brief biography of those who will be staying in the other three suites on this floor as well as the contact information for their personal aides, in case they can be of assistance to you. And there is also a map of the house, as well as the secured yards around it."

Rachel nodded.

"And it also has the names and short biographies of the twelve Coordinators that will be joining you and our other guests this afternoon for lunch. They're all very eager to meet you. I thought it would help if you had a little history on each member."

"Thank you, Lydia. You've done a wonderful job."

"You're welcome, Miss. I'll leave you…"

"Before you go, please tell me what the red button on this, um, bell is for?"

"Emergencies, Miss. Heaven forbid you should ever need to use it but should anything happen and you need more than just my assistance, just press the red button. That alerts our security staff and they'll be able to locate you by the bell's internal GPS system."

"Good to know, but unnecessary, I'm sure."

Lydia nodded. "Just don't go outside beyond the designated yards. Some guests have tried to hike, or explore, and ended up using the red button. If they'd only enjoyed the scenery and wild life from the gorgeous yards, there would've been no need for all the fuss."

Rachel smiled. "Have no fear about me," she quipped. "The closest thing I get to hiking is walking through the mall."

Lydia laughed. "Good," she chuckled. "I'll not worry about you, then."

Rachel stepped toward the bedroom. "I'll see you in a few hours," she said over her shoulder. "Right now, I'm going to check out the back of my eyelids."

"Perfect," said the young woman. "I'll be by in a couple hours to gather you up."

Rachel remembered thinking that was an unusual phrase, "to gather you up," but that thought didn't cloud her brain for long. She strolled over to the desk and flipped open the folder. Scanning the names of the other three guests who'd be sharing the suites around her, she smiled. "Carmen," she whispered. "Maybe now that we're away from the hustle and bustle of Plum Creek, we can talk. We really do need to talk!"

CHAPTER THIRTY-FOUR

The various shades of green, blue, and brown of the surrounding mountains sparkled in the afternoon sun and while she'd seen these mountains from the library and her suite, Rachel had never seen anything so spectacular as the views from the dining room. The room was as opulent as the rest of the mansion with its fine oriental rugs, wood paneled walls from which more breathtaking paintings hung in no certain pattern, and crystal chandeliers that cast soft light across the room. A very large table, hand carved from the trees of the Black Forest in Germany, dominated the room; but its masculinity was delicately balanced by the feminine touch of white alabaster china trimmed in gold and hand polished silverware.

Elegant candelabras had been placed every three feet down the middle of the table, their flames as beautiful as the one in the large stone fireplace that graced the north wall, but it was the west wall that held the most beautiful artwork. It was a plate glass wall which allowed the guests to look out onto the rolling river far below and the sun-kissed jewels of the Swiss Alps no matter where they were sitting or standing.

Rachel and Carmen stood at the glass wall, enjoying the view and talking in low whispers until someone tapped a crystal wine glass with a fork. The 'ting, ting, ting' reverberated through the room.

"Excuse me please. May I have everyone's attention?"

Reluctantly, they turned to face the room and the other guests, their eyes seeking out the owner of the feminine voice that had interrupted their solitude.

A beautiful young woman, who had stepped up behind the head chair of the table, beckoned everyone to gather around. "Ladies and gentlemen," she said in broken English, "My name is Antonia Schmitt. I am ze personal assistant to your host, Kommandeur von Guten.

A polite applause fluttered across the room.

"We are so glad to have you here with us at ze Chalet. We hope you have found your suites satisfactory, ya?" The long curls of her blonde hair bounced with the enthusiastic nod of her head.

Some in the crowd, including Carmen, answered her with a resounding, "Ya!" Others cheered, "Here, Here," and the rest, like Rachel, held up their glasses and nodded.

"And I trust you all have met your personal valet. It is his or her duty to ensure your stay with us is the ultimate experience, but please, we hope you will make yourselves at home as vell."

Again, cheers filled the room.

"Then without further ado, please allow me to introduce your host for the next couple of days, Kommandeur Henreich von Guten."

This time, everyone found a place to sit their glasses and gave the trim, attractive middle-aged man a round of hearty applause. *So, this is the famous von Guten*, thought Rachel as she followed along and clapped with mock excitement. *You don't look so threatening.*

Von Guten bowed his head a couple of times then waved for everyone to take their seats. Rachel eventually found her name card on the north end of the table close to the large fireplace. Carmen sat across from her, but the table was so wide, she could've easily been clear across the room.

Rachel casually scanned the name cards of the two men

who would be seated on either side of her. To her left 'Mr. Lei Feng, Beijing, China' and to her right 'Mr. Dakarai Gamba, Zimbabwe'. *This must be what it's like sitting on a United Nations Council. How in the world are we going to understand each other?*

But she soon found that language wasn't a barrier. The two guests beside her spoke English, albeit broken, but understandable. Conversations were pleasant and the meal of roasted duck, red potatoes, and asparagus spears was incredibly delicious. During her conversations with Misters Feng and Gamba, Rachel learned that Feng was a professor at the University of Beijing and Gamba owned a safari resort.

With a little more digging, she also learned that Mr. Feng didn't just teach, nor was Mr. Gamba just an inn keeper. Both held PhDs and were experts in their fields; Mr. Feng in Plant Physiology and Mr. Gamba in Animal Science. It didn't take long for Rachel to make the connection between the three of them and the Genesis Factor. All of sudden, she wasn't hungry anymore. Setting her napkin on her plate, she sat back in her chair and sipped on her water.

The water felt cool as it rushed down her throat. She'd never tasted anything so crisp and refreshing, yet in the water's perfect cleanliness, there was a slight bitter aftertaste. Almost as if a piece of lemon rind lay at the bottom of her glass. Yet, looking, she saw nothing but clear, clean water. Carefully, she set the glass down and folded her hands in her lap. She was sure it was just jet lag as Lydia had suggested, but she had to be careful. These people knew of her, but she knew nothing of them except what she could find on the web. Feeling the small curtron in her pocket, she felt better, a little anyway.

She listened to the bell-like tinkle of silverware against the expensive china. Voices murmured in undistinguishable languages, and once in a while, laugher floated up from the table on melodic wings only to land in some mysterious place on the dark beams above their heads. Glancing around the large table she watched each person for a few seconds. She didn't let her eyes linger on them too long. People can sense when someone is staring at them and she didn't want to set off mental alarms. She had to blend in, not make herself stand out. Watching everyone in the beautiful surroundings, Rachel relaxed.

Those seated closest to the Kommandeur seemed to be most familiar to him. There were twelve of them, four women and two men seated to his left, and six men seated to his right. She had no doubt they were the Coordinators. *His chosen twelve.* She half chuckled at the thought.

They've gained his trust and understand the mission. It's those folks I need to watch closely.

Next to the last Coordinator on von Guten's left sat a woman whose face Rachel couldn't quite see, but whose mannerisms seemed awfully familiar. She tried to get a look at the woman's face, but because she was so engrossed in conversation with the young man beside her, the woman didn't find the need or desire to turn and look fully in Rachel's direction.

Who do I know with long blonde hair, black rimmed glasses, and dresses so lavishly, thought Rachel? *Anyone from the lab? No, not dressed in a cashmere sweater, not to mention the bling, but who do I know that would be here, participating in some genealogy club in the Swiss Alps?* Rachel watched the woman a few seconds longer, but still couldn't see her face. *Well, no one I know, but boy, she sure does remind me of someone.* Rachel made a mental note to make the woman's acquaintance sometime during her visit at The Chalet.

After the dessert plates were cleared and the guests were sipping coffee, von Guten laid his napkin on his plate and pushed himself away from the table. A hush quickly fell over the group as he walked to a podium that a staff member had discretely rolled in during the meal. Watching him, Rachel couldn't help notice how he carried himself with such a distinct air of confidence.

"Good afternoon my friends," he said jovially. "It is so nice to have you in my home. I hope you have all found it to your satisfaction." The group clapped politely again and von Guten smiled broadly, his round cheeks turning crimson red. "Sehr gut," he chuckled. "Sehr gut."

"I know some of you have questions about our mission here at Ze Chalet and I want you to know that before this evening is over, each of you will have no doubt as to why you are here. And we will answer that question, and many more in just a moment. But before I introduce our speaker for the afternoon, I would like to introduce someone who recently surprised the medical world by creating an antidote, if you will, for coma."

Rachel felt her stomach flip. Blood rushed to her face.

"I'm sure you've read about her, and despite her humbleness and desire to remain out of the spotlight, she is here with us and it would be against all that is ethical not to introduce her. Ladies and Gentlemen, Doctor Rachel Wall."

Everyone turned their heads, searching the room for the special guest until Rachel stood to her feet. The applause was deafening, and no one was clapping with more fervor than Carmen. Rachel quickly threw a hand up to silence the applause, thanked the Kommandeur for his kind words then sat back down, as fast as she could without seeming rude.

"Thank you, Doctor. And now, to our speaker. I have asked Doctor Martha Stone, Chair of the Department of Molecular Biology and Genetic Research and CEO of our Corporate Sponsor, GenTrak to speak to us this afternoon. Doctor Stone teaches at some little college in the United States." Von Guten's eyes went to the ceiling and he placed his finger on the side of his face. "I think it is called Harvard University." The room exploded with laughter, von Guten's being the loudest.

"Please Doctor, come to the podium and enlighten us about the science behind our mission here...because," he turned back to the table of guests and said, "after her presentation, some of you will participate in a cutting-edge experiment, a journey of sorts, which no one else in the world has experienced."

Carmen looked over at Rachel with wide, excited eyes. "That'd be us," she said over the murmurs that were floating around the room.

Von Guten patted down the air. "But have no fear," he continued. "There is no harm in what we will do here. It is pure science. Believe me, you will be thrilled at what you will discover. Now, Doctor Stone, I turn it over to you."

To Rachel's surprise, the blonde-haired woman stood and walked to the podium. At last, Rachel would be able to see her face.

"Good afternoon," the doctor said in a very pleasant voice. "As the good Kommandeur said, my name is Doctor Martha Stone and I've been invited here to take each of you on a futuristic journey, if you will."

Several guests squirmed in their chairs, but Rachel was so captivated by the woman, she found herself sitting on the edge of her seat. Then it hit her. There was another time, several years ago, when she'd sat on the edge of a different seat, a fold down seat in a room at Harvard, so she could catch every word that was said, and ironically, it was this very woman who had been standing at that podium too. Doctor Martha Stone had once been Doctor Martha Long. She'd apparently married since Rachel was her student.

"I'm not going to get into things like proteins, RNA, and deep genetics this afternoon, but I'd like to talk to you about a specific segment of what we geneticists call genetic memory." A deep hush fell over the room, so deep in fact; Rachel thought she heard the breeze caress the window from outside.

The doctor subtlety straightened the glasses on her nose. "In 2001, when the human genome was sequenced, scientists found that only about 3% of human DNA actually consisted of coding genes. That means that 97% of our DNA is non-coding DNA, or what scientists often referred to as junk DNA. For many years, junk DNA was considered just that, junk. This DNA was thought to be void of anything...until recently."

Doctor Stone stopped talking and glanced around the room, waiting a few seconds before continuing. "Recently our labs have found that junk DNA shouldn't be written off so quickly. It has been discovered that these non-coding strands are actually small storage rooms wherein lies what we now call genetic memory."

Everyone around the table turned and looked at those sitting around them. "Genetic memory?" whispered Professor Feng.

"This *is* cutting edge," one woman muttered.

"Very cutting edge," agreed Rachel.

Carmen raised her hand and the group fell silent to hear the question. She glanced at Rachel before she stood to her feet. "I'm sorry, Doctor Stone, please excuse my ignorance. I'm just a lowly World History teacher at a small high school who thought getting her students excited about their genealogy would make them take their lessons more seriously, because, oh you, know, after learning about their ancestry they'd somehow feel connected to something besides their phones and iPods." A chuckle rose up from the table.

"So, I came to this seminar, hoping to glean something that I could take back to them, but I didn't expect to hear this. Are you saying that the genes within our DNA can remember? They have a memory?"

The Doctor nodded. "Yes, I am."

Carmen sat down slowly as murmurs floated around the room.

"I know," said Doctor Stone looking at the bewildered faces. "This all must sound so very strange, but believe me, it is true. I mean, let's think about this logically if not scientifically. All of my genes; whether coding or non-coding, were passed to me from my father and mother so wouldn't logic stand to prove since genes are passed down from parent to child, I would have also inherited some of my ancestor's genes as they were passed down to their children, and their children's children, and so forth?"

The room grew gravely silent.

"Mind boggling isn't it?" said the Doctor.

No one said a word. A few heads nodded, but no one uttered a word.

The doctor shifted her weight from one foot to the other and pushed her glasses back up her nose. "We know many diseases are hereditary, so why not genetic memories?"

"I'm sorry, doctor, but all of this sounds a bit preposterous," said one man, who Rachel thought for sure was a Coordinator.

A few voices rose among the group, but the doctor raised her hand and they quieted down. "I know it does, but consider the belief in reincarnation, or the sense of having lived a different life in a different time. While religions teach that souls of past lives leave their host body and are reincarnated into a new body, giving the host a sense of having lived before, but scientists have proven that isn't the case at all. These 'memories' experienced by the host are genetic memories placed in their DNA by those family members who lived before them. People *do* remember living a different life in a different time, but those feelings, or memories, are actually experiences that had been lived by an ancestor and brought up to the surface by the non-coding DNA within them.

"Let's say for instance you have a deep fear of being mauled by a bear. So much so, you don't venture out onto hiking trails or mountain paths, but in reality, you've never even seen a bear, except maybe at the zoo or on television, yet, deep down, you fear bears more than anything else on earth. You break out into a sweat every time you think of, or perhaps see a bear. Why do you think that is?"

The man shrugged his shoulders.

"Perhaps you have this fear because, at some time, an ancestor was attacked by a bear. Maybe it happened a hundred years ago, five hundred years ago, or even thousands of years ago. Our DNA is shaped not only by our environment and our experiences, but by our ancestors, so your fear of bears; not having a personal reason to fear them, was passed down to you from someone else's fear; someone who had a very traumatic and maybe even fatal experience with a bear."

A few people shook their heads in disbelief.

"It's true," said Rachel, a little louder than what she intended. Her comment drew Doctor Stone's attention. "Yes," she said. "Please Doctor Wall, stand and explain."

Rachel blushed. Not because she had been called on, but because she'd drawn attention to herself. She hesitated until the small voice in her head said, *Isn't this what you wanted? Fame?*

"Please," encouraged the speaker. "I'd appreciate the moral support."

Rachel cleared her throat and stood up. "I certainly didn't mean to interrupt you, Doctor Stone," she said timidly. "But I've heard of this genetic memory, as far as fear or paranoia being passed down to us from our ancestors."

"Go on," said the doctor.

"A few years ago, Brian Decker, a postdoctoral fellow at Eton University had reported that an experiment he'd conducted on rats proved that their pups could inherit specific smell memories from their father, even when the pups had never experienced that smell before, and even when they'd never met their father. What's more, *the pup's* children are born with the same specific memory."

Doctor Gamba, who was sitting beside her, looked up and said, "So what you're saying is that I could have certain fears because my ancestors experienced something and therefore, warped my genes because of it?"

A chuckle rose from a few guests, but neither Rachel nor Doctor Stone laughed.

Rachel looked down at her colleague and nodded. "In a nutshell, yes," she said seriously.

Doctor Stone smiled her approval as Rachel sat down.

"So, what we've discovered," she added, "is that an experience of a parent, even before conception, can and does influence both the structure and function of the nervous system. And not only of the parent, but of the nervous systems of subsequent generations that came before."

"But what does that have to do with us here?" asked Doctor Gamba.

"Well, you were all invited here because, as you know, we were able to trace your DNA. Many of you were traced back hundreds of years, but some of you, thousands of years, and we'd like to take you on that futuristic journey, as mentioned by the Kommandeur."

"Don't you mean a journey into the past," quipped one man.

Doctor Stone smiled. "Indeed," she said. "Futuristic only because in order to take you into your past, we have to use the cutting-edge technology of today. Technology so advanced; only a few people in the world know of its existence and now, most of them are in this room."

"How far back will it, Er, will we remember," asked an elderly woman. She looked around the table. "I'm almost eighty years old. I could be here for months just getting through my own memories."

The room exploded with laughter.

"As I said a moment ago, some of you may only go back a hundred years, others, maybe a thousand years. We don't know. Those of you who participate in this journey are the first to explore those uncharted waters."

"But won't you need months to sequence our DNA?" asked Doctor Feng.

"We already have," answered Doctor Stone. "And each of your DNA has been uploaded into the Coronus Sequencer we'll use to, well, shall we say, walk you through your journey."

Doctor Feng's face turned red. "But how did you retrieve our DNA without our knowledge," he scowled.

"I assure you, we did nothing illegal, doctor," said Doctor Stone. "We give out our DNA every day, in so many ways. A used glass, a cigarette butt, a brush or comb, a fingerprint. Collecting DNA isn't hard to do, but in your cases, we simply requested it from various government agencies around the globe. Yet, although we have your DNA, what we will need from you today is your permission. We will not take you on your journey if you do not wish to go."

Doctor Feng looked around for support, but he didn't get any.

"As the Kommandeur also mentioned, there is no physical threat to you during this experiment. My assistants will place a simple black mask over your eyes, similar to what many women wear at bedtime; you'll recline in a very comfortable chair and relax. It's that simple. I promise you, you will leave here just as healthy and intact as you arrived, albeit, a little more aware of who you are and where you came from, so to speak."

The room was so quiet the only noise to be heard was the sound of their own breath as it exited their lungs.

"Are there any more questions," asked Doctor Stone.

Carmen raised her hand.

The doctor peered over her glasses at her. "Yes," she said.

Chuckling, Carmen stood up again and asked, "When do we start?"

CHAPTER THIRTY-FIVE

A few guests milled around, talking in low voices; waiting to be escorted to wherever they had to go to be hooked up to take their 'journey'. Carmen came around to Rachel's side of the table and sat down in Dr. Feng's empty chair. Her eyes darted around the room. "When do you think it'll be our turn," she asked quietly. "How long do you think we'll have to wait?"

Rachel shrugged her shoulders. "I don't have the slightest idea. If there was an official agenda, I never saw it."

Carmen fidgeted in her chair. "Well, I feel like a kid at Christmas. This is going to be so cool. When we're done, if I can, I'd like to talk to Doctor Stone to see if grant money is available to get whatever gadget they're using over to Plum Creek. It would change how kids look at world history forever."

Not thinking, Rachel laughed.

Carmen didn't.

When Rachel saw the look in those black Spanish-Irish eyes she stopped laughing so fast it was like someone hit an 'off' switch. Her eyebrows rose slightly. "You're kidding, right?"

Carmen didn't answer; but her glare didn't change.

"This is just a prototype, Carmen. When and if these, um,

machines, servers, or whatever they are, are ready to be purchased, I doubt seriously if McArthur High School in Plum Creek, Virginia will be anywhere near the top of the manufacturer's contact list."

Carmen scowled. "Hey. You don't know that. My idea about connecting genealogy with a World History class could catch on. I mean, that's basically what this experiment does, right? Connects genealogy with world history?"

Rachel thought about that for a second. "I guess you could..."

"Miss O'Leary?" Antonia Schmitt, the Kommandeur's secretary had come into the dining room and was standing right behind them, but neither Rachel nor Carmen had noticed. "I'm sorry for interrupting, but..."

Carmen turned in her chair and looked up at her. Realizing who she was, she jumped up and eagerly said, "It's Mrs. Rodriguez now, but I'll answer to anything if it's my turn."

Miss Schmitt smiled casually, but was visibly uneasy. "My apologies, Mrs. Rodriguez, but I have to inform you that you won't be able to participate in the experiment as we'd initially planned."

Carmen's smile disappeared. Her bright eyes melted into dark pools. "No," she protested. "I came all the way from Virginia to..."

"You're pregnant," interrupted Antonia.

"The Kommandeur does not want to take the risk of subjecting you to unknown memories when that of another human being resides in your body. The experiment has not yet been expanded to include pregnant women and we do not wish for you to be the first to see if the process will or will not cause harm to an unborn child or its mother."

Carmen plopped down into the chair; her face blank of any expression. Rachel took her hand. "She's right, Car," she said softly. "You wouldn't want to hurt the baby, or yourself, would you?"

Carmen grimaced and bobbed her head slowly. "No, of course not," she muttered. "But man!"

Miss Schmitt delicately touched Carmen's shoulder. "The Kommandeur sincerely regrets this decision and would like to meet with you while Doctor Wall is on her journey. Would that be alright with you?"

Carmen glanced over her shoulder up at the woman and smiled. "Of course," she said quietly. "I guess."

"Zer gut," Antonia smiled back. "Now, Doctor Wall, if you will follow me."

Rachel squeezed Carmen's hand and leaned in closer to her friend. Pushing past the disappointment she saw written all over her friend's face, she looked into her sad eyes and said, "I'll tell you ev...er...y...thing, Car. Everything! I promise."

Carmen half-smiled and nodded. "Everything!" she reiterated. "Not one thing left out."

"Deal!" agreed Rachel.

Carmen stood up, lifted her chin, and stepped around the chair. "I'll wait for you in my room," she said definitively. "Don't keep me waiting, 'cause if you do, I might have to..."

Rachel looked up at her from her chair and chuckled. "Or you might have to what?"

Carmen shifted her feet and cast her eyes to the floor. "Well, you know," she said looking sheepishly at Rachel. "I might have to...to take a nap or find some movie on TV or something, and then I won't want to be interrupted to hear of your exciting experience." Carmen smiled her big smile. "Just remember, you promised to tell me everything."

"Yes, I did, and I will."

Carmen walked to the doorway alone while Rachel and Miss Schmitt walked a few steps behind her; Antonia quietly giving instructions. When they reached the great arch, Rachel watched Carmen walk across the atrium toward the elevators. Her head was bowed and her shoulders slumped. To see her happy friend so down broke Rachel's heart. If she could change places with her, she'd do it in a heartbeat, but there was the baby to consider now. Miss Schmitt touched Rachel's elbow and motioned her to follow.

The doors of the elevator opened to a dimly lit corridor that lacked all the luster of the floors above; very reminiscent of the basement at the Laboratory. Rachel stepped behind the secretary and glanced at the doors as they walked down the hall.

Laughter escaped from under one door on her left, while someone yelped a door down. "These are the rooms that have been reserved for our DNA experiments," said Miss Schmitt. "This one here," she pointed to the third one on the right, "has been set up for you."

She opened the door and Rachel walked into a windowless, grey room. A stainless-steel sink in the near corner gave the room a cold, sterile feeling. White cabinets and a black recliner were the only other things in the room; those and a blue towel on the steel cart beside the recliner.

Just beyond the cart, on the far wall, was a tall, narrow machine. The entire face of it was covered with blinking green lights and an assortment of switches. *Coronus Sequencer* was etched across the top in large, gold letters.

"Please make yourself comfortable," said Miss Schmitt, extending her hand out toward the recliner. "Anne, your clinic technician, will be here shortly to set things up for your journey."

Rachel looked at the pretty young woman and smiled as best she could without forcing it. As a geneticist she should be beside herself with excitement. This experiment was something only a handful of people would experience before revealing its existence to the world, and she was one of them. This was a historical as well as scientific breakthrough, but for some reason, she couldn't shake the uncertainty of it all.

As long as she was hooked up to that blinking, tweaking piece of machinery, her life would be left in the hands of people she didn't know, let alone, trust. But, not only was she a geneticist, she was contracted with the FBI, so she sat down on the recliner and took a couple deep breaths.

When Antonia was satisfied her guest was resting comfortably, she left Rachel alone, but it wasn't long before a bubbly, twenty-something year old threw the door open and bounced up to the chair,

"Good afternoon, Doctor Wall," she said cheerfully. "My name is Anne Thoren. I'll be the one seeing you off on your journey today."

"Nice to meet you," Rachel said a nervously.

"Now, once you've reclined back as far as you'd like, I'll help you get your mask on." She lifted the towel from table and picked up a thick, black mask.

"It doesn't look anything like what many women wear at bedtime," muttered Rachel.

"I'm sorry, what was that?" asked Anne.

Rachel blushed. "Nothing," she said quietly.

A few minutes later, Rachel ran her fingertips across the bulky mask that covered her eyes. She didn't like having it over her face. It reminded her too much of another memory when something was placed over her face; a very bad memory.

"Are you comfortable Doctor Wall," asked the young assistant. "I won't go on until you say so."

"I'm fine," Rachel said firmly. "Just a little claustrophobic."

"Most people are, but once we get started, you'll do fine, I'm sure."

Rachel took a deep breath and let her head relax into the cushiony headrest of the chair. "I'm ok, Anne" she said again. "Ready when you are."

"Ok. I just have to attach the wires from the mask to the sequencer. Then you'll be off on your journey."

A couple minutes later, Anne tapped Rachel's shoulder. "Ok, Doctor," she whispered. "You're set to go."

Rachel swallowed hard. White knuckled fists opened and she spread her fingers over the leather arm rests. "Ok," she murmured. "Let's do this."

A switch was flipped and immediately the room was filled with the soft hum of electronics. Nothing hurt. In a sense, she felt like she was floating, except for her arms and legs. They felt heavy. Unable to move, she started to hyperventilate. This was too reminiscent of what had happened in the hospital.

"It's ok," Anne whispered in her ear. "The machine is just doing a body scan."

Rachel tried to speak, but nothing came out of her open mouth, if her mouth was in fact open. All she could see was black. She could hear, so she listened, then, just as if she was watching a movie on a small black screen, scenes started to flash against the inside of the dark mask.

Rachel watched a younger Rachel sitting in classes at college, then, very fluently, she was in high school. If she thought her lips could move, she would have cringed when she watched herself walk across the stage in her cap and gown. Then there was a little girl watching cartoons with her mama and daddy, flowing over to a toddler in a frilly pink dress, white lace-trimmed socks, and white high-top baby shoes taking her first steps. She watched as her mother said, "Come here sweetheart. Walk to mama."

Rachel couldn't feel the tears that had welled up in the corners of her eyes, but her heart told her they were there.

A pregnant woman; her mother, much younger than Rachel, waved at her like someone would do in an old-fashioned home movie then in the blink of an eye, it was July 5, 1975 and a handsome young couple was standing in front of an altar exchanging vows. Rachel remembered seeing pictures of her parents wedding, but this was better. She felt like she was there.

Time continued to peel backward like pages of a book flipping in a strong wind. Her mother's mother, her great grandmother...

A Union soldier jumping into a ravine just as a cannonball exploded next to him; his pant leg ripped open, exposing a gash so big, Rachel could see the thigh bone; a British naval officer standing at the wheel of his ship, the large sails pulling against its thick masts as the sea pounded its bow mercilessly.

Back, back the Coronus machine pulled her into the depths of her past.

In a blood-soaked pasture in medieval England, she witnessed a knight in full templar regalia unsheathe his sword and behead his foe with one blow; the victim's blood splattering across the red cross on the warrior's white tunic.

Waves of time crashed against the small dark screen; antiquity, giants, a flood, a small ancient village; and a garden, a large, beautiful garden. Rachel had never felt such peace as she was standing in that...perfect garden.

Eden?

Then abruptly, everything stopped; leaving her standing in the whitest light. She couldn't move. She couldn't see anything around her until the light subsided.

Being just an observer and unable to speak or reach out to feel any of the beauty around her, she was amazed that it felt as though she was actually a part of all that was taking place around her. It was the most beautiful place, even more beautiful than the garden, yet there, in the dawning of time, Rachel watched wide-eyed and afraid; more afraid than she'd ever been in her life.

Donna R. Westover

CHAPTER THIRTY-SIX

In front of her was, what at first glance looked like a man, tall and muscular, but he wasn't a man at all, he was an angel, given away by his white robe, long sword, brass breast plate, and great, bird-like wings that arched from his back. He took a step toward her. She took a step back.

"Do not be afraid, Rachel," he said.

"That's easier said than done," she muttered.

The aura around the angel dimmed and he stepped toward her again. "No one will see or hear you. You are safe."

"But you see me," she said quietly.

"Only because I have been asked to step beyond the veil."

"Who are you?" Rachel blurted out nervously.

"My name is Uriel. I am one of Elohim's archangels."

"Are you going to guide me on this so-called journey?"

"No," answered the angel. "I am merely here to deliver a message to you."

"A message?"

The angel nodded. "What you're going to observe are but mere memories; Rachel, albeit, they are memories of real events of which every human has embedded in their very souls.

"Are you a memory too?"

"No," answered Uriel. "I am real; however, from this point on, what you see, the events, and the humans in them, will be the memories that had been hidden deep within your DNA, and through these memories you will not only hear the speaker's words when they speak, but you will hear their thoughts as well, and sometimes, feel their pain."

Rachel looked up into his golden eyes. "Where am I?" she asked." "Why was I brought here?"

Uriel's eyes searched hers. "To learn the truth, Rachel."

With that, he extended his arm and moved aside to reveal a throne room like none she could ever have imagined. Walls of opal; a vast marble floor, and on a dais stood a throne, made of purest gold, glistened with rubies, emeralds, diamonds, and sapphires.

Two angels, dressed like Uriel stood on either side of the throne. On the floor in front of the dais stood another angel, tall and muscular, but very unlike the three in white. If Uriel was holy, the one standing in front of the dais was pure evil.

A short leather tunic stopped at the top of his dark legs; his feet were shod in leather sandals, the straps wrapped around his muscular legs up to his knees. A golden serpent, its onyx eyes glistening in the brightness, wrapped taut around his right bicep.

His arms rigid at his side; his hands balled into tight fists; he raised his bald head and squared his broad shoulders; unfolding his massive black wings to their full extent. Steel eyes darted back and forth between the two nemeses who were watching him from their posts above him. "Michael! Do you dare risk taking me?" he growled. "Raphael! I know you want to and I am ready to fight."

Michael, his hand tightly gripping the pommel of his sword, stood to the right of the throne, and Raphael, his dark, piercing eyes never leaving the dark one, stood to the left of it. They said nothing to him. A sneer swept across the dark one's face when they made no move toward him, choosing instead to watch him.

"Pity," he sighed. "I take it you've been given a command and we will never fight in this room again."

He brought his wings in and folded them against his back. Standing at ease, he broke away from their glaring eyes and glanced around the room. "Perhaps that is best," he said quietly. "The coup failed here once and Elohim makes sure I'll never forget."

His eyes darted to the golden doors, but the two warriors were watching his every move. "No," he whispered. "Their swords are sheathed, but they are at the ready nonetheless."

Without warning, the golden doors opened and an indescribable light filled the room. Rachel's hands flew to her eyes, but through her fingers she watched Michael and Raphael take a knee. Bowing their heads, the sound of their fists hitting their gold breast plates resounded throughout the throne room.

Rachel could only believe that it was Elohim who had just entered and sat down on the throne. Studying the rebellious angel for several moments before speaking, he watched the angel for several long minutes. Finally, his booming voice echoed against the walls.

"Lucifer."

The dark angel's knees bent under the sound of the strong voice and he reluctantly fell to the white marble floor. More out of apprehension than respect, he unfolded his wings and drew them up over his head. "My Lord," he hissed.

"I know what you are planning."

"Of course, you do," he muttered sarcastically. "Why would this time be any different?"

The cold steel of Michael's sword broke through his thick feathered barrier and pressed against his throat. "Reverence, Lucifer," he whispered.

Only when Lucifer bowed his head did Michael retreat into the light.

Elohim stepped down from the dais and slowly walked around the dark seraph. Lucifer could feel the heat coming from The Most High's radiance.

"The punishment for this will be more than your servants realize," Elohim said heavily.

Even in the shelter of his wings, he had to shield his eyes from the Elohim's glory. "They're loyal to me regardless of the cost," the dark angel grumbled.

The Most High continued his measured cadence around his rebellious son; the swishing of his purple robe filling Lucifer's ears.

"Are they?" he asked. "If they knew the truth, would they remain loyal?"

The dark angel shook his head. "I don't understand. When have I ever lied to them?"

The swishing sound of the royal robe stopped. "Do not talk to me like I'm a fool," Elohim warned. "I am not one of your subjects."

A bead of sweat slid down the dark face, stalled on his jaw, then splattered onto the floor beneath his feet. He slowly raised a hand and wiped his brow.

"You think you slipped into the garden unseen, don't you? You believe because you deceived Eve, and then Adam, you succeeded in abolishing me from the throne you so coveted? You really believe because you deceived them, you've become a god?"

"I...I have never thought that."

"Oh, do not lie to me, great deceiver! You believe I failed. That mankind no longer desires to reside with me and now you can do as you wish. That's why you believe you can get away with this chaotic plan."

Lucifer swallowed hard. "Do you forget you created us

with a free will too? If my followers don't want to go, they don't have to. The decision will be theirs, just as it was when...when...I chose to leave this place."

The Most-High paused for just a moment. "They will go because of what they will believe to be a victory for you in this so-called war between us. They will go because you are a formable persuader, but if they do this Lucifer, they must be ready to accept their eternal fate."

Lucifer snickered. "And what might that be? Banished to live among the stars in the expanse of the great Universe?"

Elohim hovered over the dark angel. "Hear me, son of perdition," he said gravely. "All who cross over the heavenly threshold to take on human form will be doomed to remain in human form, bearing the same mortal sorrows and burdens as those whose lives they destroy. They will suffer unfathomable mental and physical pain as they are perpetually devoured by their sinful lust, and then, upon their earthly deaths, when they once again become spiritual beings, they will be chained to the sides of the Pit. Never again will they be glorious celestial beings, Lucifer."

Lucifer bit his bottom lip. "The Pit? Why the Pit?"

"Where they will never be free, never be celestial again, forever burning, but never dying, Lucifer."

"But..."

The Most High climbed the stairs of the dais and sat on the throne. "Tell them, Lucifer. Tell them what their reward will be for breaking the Holy Code. Tell them that once they step through the veil, they will never be allowed to step back. Tell them of the chains, of the flames, of their forever punishment. Tell them of the Pit, Lucifer and after you've told them all I've said, measure their loyalty to you then."

The dark angel said nothing.

"Perhaps," continued Elohim, "once they know the depths of your deception, they'll remain as loyal to you as you were to me."

CHAPTER THIRTY-SEVEN

Fiery daggers of pain ran through Rachel's body; stealing her breath and tearing at her flesh. Doubling over, she held her stomach; hoping to subdue the torment of the invisible grip that squeezed her insides.

The marble floor began to spin. Dizzy, she fell to her knees. Pulled into blackness by an invisible vortex, the throne room disappeared. Moments past before she understood what was happening. Her genetic memory had reversed itself. She was no longer being taken into her past; her coding was moving her forward, returning her to the future.

Seconds later, the spinning stopped. Subtle light replaced the darkness and shivers overcame the pain. Sitting on a large rock; she waited until the uneasiness subsided. Once she felt confident enough to lift her head, she found herself in what looked like a small, but beautiful courtyard behind an adobe bungalow. The remnants of a setting sun glinted over the west side of a stone wall that surrounded the private estate.

Carefully, she stood on her feet. Satisfied the dizziness was gone, she made her way over to the wall, climbed up onto a boulder, and peered over the ledge. From a quaint, but primeval village scattered across rocky hills, the smoke from a hundred adobe chimneys swirled into the evening air.

A sobering thought pulled at her mind as she observed the

quiet setting. Something the angel Uriel alluded to. He said she was being shown the truth. Apparently, this village had something to do with what she witnessed in the throne room.

It was then she realized she wasn't just a participant in an experiment of genetic memory; but she was being shown a genetic message. Like a handwritten note, rolled up tightly and slipped into a bottle before being thrown into the sea, she was seeing the unraveling of an ancient note that had been rolled up tightly and slipped into eons of genetic coding. The places where she would stop on her journey were specific and pre-planned. But what was the message...and why was she chosen to receive it?

Palm and olive trees swayed in the evening breeze. It was so beautiful here. Gazing up at the indigo sky, a few stars twinkled above her. Her face felt the sun's last caresses of warmth as the slowly bid the small village adieu.

Rachel stepped off the boulder and looked around. Although lovely, something in this place, not just the courtyard, but the whole place felt wrong. The feeling of peace didn't embrace her as it did when she stood in the larger garden earlier. Here, the air felt tense, almost saturated with a sense of dread. Why?

A flicker of light waved from a window in the house. If something was wrong here, maybe those inside could help her understand what. She quietly walked up to the door, unhooked the latch, and slipped inside.

The room, dimly lit by the red glow of embers that had spilled across the mouth of an adobe oven, looked to be an ancient kitchen. Wood shelves lined the wall across from the door, each one holding clay urns, bowls, and cups. Bouquets of dried spices hung from the beams above her head, and next to the door, two water urns sat against the wall; one half full, the other empty. The air was filled with the smells of wood, rosemary, and freshly baked bread.

Two female voices floated from a room beyond the kitchen. Following them; she found two women, both younger than her, standing in a small front room. They were dressed in ancient halugs, but spoke a language she could understand.

Rachel learned the two young women were sisters, the oldest around twenty from what she could guess. Her name was Jael. The youngest of the two was Lilith, about sixteen, beautiful, and apparently, rebellious.

The room was plain, but cozy. To Rachel's left, were a few cushions scattered on the floor in front of a semi-circular fireplace. A rocking chair, made of cut limbs, stood in the far corner, and something that resembled a daybed was just below her left elbow. To her right, a brass oil lamp that Rachel first mistook as an old genie lamp, sat in a recessed nook built into the adobe wall. Across from her was the front door, wood, thick, and sturdy, and to the left of it, a small window where the two sisters stood, and argued.

With no fear of being discovered, Rachel sat down on the arm of the daybed and listened. No one would see her or feel any disturbance by her presence. This was, after all, just a memory.

CHAPTER THIRTY-EIGHT

"**L**una is beautiful tonight, isn't she," Jael said softly.

"It's just a light, sister," Lilith said smugly. "A big, yellow ball of light that hangs in the night sky. What's so beautiful about that?"

They watched the sun slide behind the hills as Luna, a pale watery moon, paraded through the stars. Luna's evenings use to bestow comfort and a sense of security; invoking family gatherings in flower scented courtyards, laughter around adobe hearths, and passionate kisses beneath the quivering branches of nearby olive trees. But no matter how brightly lit the golden paths were now or how glorious the river glistened by Luna's light, Jael couldn't help but feel a deep sense of dread. Luna's serene twilights were gone.

"So sad," whispered Jael, looking past her sister at the rising moon.

Lilith glanced over her shoulder. "What?" she asked impatiently.

Jael shook her head. "Nothing. I'm just talking to myself."

Grabbing a silk coverlet, she folded it and laid it across the daybed, hoping Lilith would get the message, but her sister's eyes never left the window. She grabbed another blanket and did the same thing, but the younger woman didn't budge.

Sighing, Jael gave in. "Please step away from the window, Lilith," she said gravely. "And pull the shutters in as you do."

With her arms crossed against her chest and her jaw set, the young woman stood rigid. "You're not my mother," she said coldly. "I will do as I please."

"Do we have to do this every night?" muttered Jael. Gently pushing her sister aside, she reached for the wooden planks, but stopped, drawn to look outside before blocking out the smile on Luna's face.

Seduced by the silence of the evening, Jael's eyes darted up and down the street that once defined her village. Sargon had once been a place where oil lamps burned brightly from friendly windows; welcoming the passersby to come in and partake of food and drink. It was where songs of praise floated out of open homes and onto the street. But now the windows were dark; their oil lamps sitting tarnished and cold on dust covered sills. Songs of joy had been replaced by whispered prayers as people hid behind bolted doors and walked through their rooms in silence. This once happy street was now an alley of nothingness. No light; no laughter; no one.

Jael lowered her eyes, closed the shutters, and turned to her sister.

"No, I'm not your mother," she said calmly, "and Jehovah be praised she's not here to see you now. You've changed so much."

Lilith pressed past her. "You know nothing about me." Grabbing the wooden latch, she twisted it with an air of defiance, but before she could push the shutters open, Jael grabbed her arm and pulled her away from the window.

"Stop acting like a child."

Sparks of rage erupted in Lilith's eyes. Jerking her arm from her sister's grip, she clenched her teeth and hissed, "Let go of me, witch."

"Lilith?" Standing face to face, Jael bit her bottom lip,

desperately searching Lilith's face.

Where are you? she asked silently.

Lilith, stone-faced, stared into her sister's eyes offering nothing except a cold, hollow gaze. Jael's heart sank. All she wanted was the peace that once filled this home, but it, along with everything cheerful, was gone.

"Lilith, you've no idea what's going on," she said sadly. "It isn't safe out there. To gaze out at this time of the evening only invites trouble."

The corners of Lilith's mouth slowly curled upward. Her brown eyes took on a smoky glaze; brooding with a mature seductiveness. "Well, as I see it," she purred, "trouble is awfully handsome. Have you seen some of those men? They're absolutely gorgeous. So muscular, eyes that gleam, and their smile. If nothing else steals your heart, their smile certainly can."

Her raven eyes peered at Jael from beneath a lock of hair. "I swear, they're straight from Eden," she said breathlessly. Stepping up to the window, she peeked between the locked shutters. "And I'd love to see what's under those..."

"Lilith!"

The younger woman pushed away from the window and giggled. "Oh, Jael, you're such a bore. Haven't you ever wondered what it's like to be with a man? And I don't mean the little excuses of men we have here in this hole we call a village. I mean one of them; a real man."

Jael shook her head vigorously. "No," she said adamantly. "Heaven forbid I am ever alone with one of them."

Her heart pounded in her ears as a desperate sense of fear gripped her. "Nor you, Lilith," she said anxiously. "Don't ever put yourself in a situation where you find yourself alone with one of them either. Look at me, Lilith, and promise."

The younger woman ignored her sister's sullenness. "One in particular has caught my eye," she replied defiantly. Turning back to the window, she pushed her face closer to the threadlike crack. "Or I've caught his."

Jael's eyes widened with fear. Her heart raced as she waited for the screams of that awful night to fade from her memory. "Their beauty is only skin deep," she finally answered. "They're dangerous men, sister, and you must stay away from them. Their presence here isn't one of peace."

"Oh, what a poor, old woman you are," Lilith scoffed. "Even though you're engaged, you'll die before you'll let Asa caress you, kiss you; touch you in places that Jehovah created for him to touch."

Jael rounded on her sister. "That's enough! You speak like a harlot. I will not have the house of our forefathers, the house of Adam soiled by your insolence."

Lilith backed away from the window and walked across the small room toward the hallway that led to the sleeping rooms, playfully pulling her halug up with every step. Once under the archway; the folds of her skirt gripped firmly in her olive-skinned fists, she spun around and faced her sister.

Jael's face flushed pale. Lilith's deep, throaty laugh echoed off the adobe walls. "What, sister," she said in a velvet voice. "Does how we're made embarrass you?"

Heat pulsated from Jael's neck. She pointed trembling fingers toward the hallway. "Get out. Get out of my sight," she yelled over broken sobs. Lilith dropped her skirt and ran down the hall, every dark corner of the small clay house filled with her laughter.

Confused and angry, Jael ran past Rachel and into the cooking room; grabbed the empty water urn and stormed out the front door. Rachel jumped up from the arm of the daybed and followed her.

"I have to do something," mumbled the young woman. Anger told her to go to the Village Elders and report her sister's blasphemous remarks and sinful behavior, but to do so would bring down their wrath. Lilith would be stripped of her halug and flogged in the village square until she begged for her life. She couldn't do that to her. Lilith was all the family she had left.

But she had to do more than just cry.

Run, she thought. *Run far away*. Wiping her wet cheeks with the back of her free hand, she glanced at the horizon. "I will," she mumbled, "but not tonight. Tonight, I can only run as far as the well."

The urn beat against her hip as rage energized every quick and deliberate step. "How can I be a mother to my sister when I have no mother of my own?" she argued. *Lilith and I are alone now. Our parents are forever gone because of their ignorance of how to properly care for horses.* "We didn't need horses," she whispered angrily. *Yes, our world is different now, but why so vastly different? What has changed my sister so subtly, yet so drastically?*

"Dear God in Heaven, what am I to do?" she groaned. "Please help me help her."

As she prayed, her pace slowed and her anger subsided. Lilith was sixteen. Young, beautiful, and so very naive, yet, according to their laws, she was past the permissible age to take a man as her husband and old enough to understand the ways of men.

"But she knows nothing about the ways of these men," Jael said with quiet animosity. They were definitely handsome, but that was the end of their attractiveness. Underneath their tanned skin and masculine seductiveness, they were dark, evil men.

More stars sparkled in the distant twilight. With night approaching, she settled in her heart that it was time she told Lilith of the night she witnessed what these men would do to a woman. What they would do without any provocation.

The memory haunted her. Having witnessed such evilness seemed to have torn a hole into her soul. It even robbed her of her love for Asa. He was nothing like these men, she knew that, but he was a man, and because of these strangers, she grew to trust none of them. *Who are they, these men that come into the lives of peaceful people and steal their joy?*

"You don't trust men either," whispered Rachel, "and you passed that on to me."

Reaching the well, Jael was relieved to see several women still there, gathered in a small group and gossiping about the events that had unfolded throughout the day.

The bucket disappeared into the inky black liquid as she listened to Tai, the wife of an Elder, tell of a caravan of traders who had stopped at the well earlier that day to water their camels.

She was telling how the nomads told the Village Elders about similar men who had appeared in their villages and shortly after their arrival, sinister, evil things started to happen. No one spoke anymore. Fear gripped every home. If they hadn't convinced the soldier's Captain that they had to trade goods and spices in order for the people of the village to survive, these few wouldn't have escaped with their lives.

The women's talk turned to whispers and Jael turned away from them. She'd heard enough. Glancing at the setting sun, she tried to hurry. There was little time to get home.

She quickly pulled the bucket up and poured the freezing water into the urn until it flowed over the terracotta rim. Sitting the bucket down, she blew on her frozen hands a few times, hoping it wouldn't take long before her fingers stung with life.

Tai came up beside her. "Hurry, Jael," she warned. "Several are out and about. We must leave...now!"

Rachel suddenly became alert; her eyes darting around the crowd and up the street. Knowing Jael couldn't hear her, Rachel glanced around nervously and asked, "Who? Who's out and about?"

Jael lifted the jug to her shoulder and tried to steady it, but it was too full. An onslaught of cold splashed down from the urn and across her shoulders. Icy fingers ran down the front of her halug, hungrily looking for dry cloth. She looked at the dark stain spreading across her chest and shivered.

Steadying the urn, she turned slowly away from the well, but her elbow hit something hard; something where nothing should have been. Rachel let out a soft scream, but only she heard it. There was no way she could warn Jael of the man standing behind her.

The urn tipped again, sending more water down the front of Jael's dress. A shudder rolled through her whole body, and although the evening was warm, it brought her no relief. Carefully, she turned to see what had stopped her so suddenly.

It surprised her to see her reflection staring at her from the silver breastplate of a soldier, but the surprise only last for a few seconds before it changed into sheer terror. She could no longer feel her arms. Everything was numb; everything except the aching in her lungs. Her eyes slowly traveled up to the soldier's face, and although handsome, his dark eyes burned through her. She clenched her jaw firmly to control the cold fear that convulsed through her, but it was no use. Panic came in waves, pushing harder and harder against her air starved lungs.

Moonlight danced in his eyes as he watched her struggle with her fear.

Even though she was soaking wet, her throat was dry. She tried to roll her tongue for moisture, but it stuck to the roof of her mouth. When she swallowed, nothing moved except her uncontrollable teeth. Her arms ached and her fingers stung with cold, but she held tightly onto the urn as if it was a shield that would protect her from whatever he was thinking. She glanced around the well. All the other women were gone. Tai's warning blared in her ears.

Beads of sweat trickled down the side of her face and dripped onto her aching shoulders, yet she wasn't warm. She was trembling; from the freezing water or the deep fear, she wasn't sure, but she prayed her legs would continue to hold her. The soldier took a step back from her; his eyes rolling across her body until his gaze finally rested on the firm mounds that had revealed themselves under her wet halug. The tip of his moist tongue slid across his lips. Jael carefully let go of the urn with one hand and covered herself with her arm.

"Don't cover yourself, woman," he commanded. "I want to see you."

"Puh, please sir" she stuttered. "It's ge, getting late and, and, I pray you let me pa, pass to get home."

"Ah," sneered the burly man. "You're afraid of the night."

Jael boldly looked up into his face. "No," she replied. "I, I am not afraid of the night, but, but rather the beasts that roam in its shadows."

His laughter shattered the darkness. Stepping up to her, he pulled her arm away from her wet dress, slid his arm around her waist, and pulled her to him. The urn ground into her shoulder; water gushed down over both of them. The Captain chuckled, his rotten breath hitting her face.

"Dear God," she said softly.

"Yes?" he murmured in her ear.

"I, I..."

"Shh..." His large hand slowly slid up to the wet stain on her chest and he caressed her with a thick, calloused finger.

Her arm started down again. "Sir, please," she started, but he whispered a warning. "Ah, ah, ah. Keep it up there and don't move."

Rachel stood horrified at what was happening right in front of her. Why did she have to see this? What good would all of this do her when this genetic memory is over?

Jael hesitated, but knew to resist this soldier meant death, or worse. His hand felt warm as it pressed against her and although she wanted to be brave, tears mingled with her sweat. He smiled, basking in the terror he saw on her face.

Slowly, he moved his other hand up and repeated the torment.

She closed her eyes to hide the hatred that was churning up from deep within her. If he saw it, she had no doubt he'd kill her, right there next to the well. She stood frozen as he ran his hands over her body and as much as she wanted to run, she knew better than to object in any way. She'd seen all of this happen before. No matter how hard she tried to forget it, the memory of that dreadful night filled her brain. And now, it was a memory on fire.

Rachel closed her eyes and watched Jael's memory unfold. Uriel told her this would happen, but she was amazed how real it felt; how much it felt like it was her own.

CHAPTER THIRTY-NINE

T he horrible night of Jael's memory started out as a warm, beautiful evening. Brilliant stars peered at the village from the dark dome above it. Jael was in the courtyard behind her small house; her haven, the place she would go to enjoy the evenings when left in quiet solitude. Lying in the grass, she breathed in the aroma of firewood that wafted from nearby chimneys and watched the thin, finger-like wisps of smoke dance in the darkness before fading into the night.

As her relationship with Asa grew, she'd often lie there and think about how it was going to be to care for him, to make love to him as his wife, and eventually give birth to his children. He was so manly, yet gentle, and so sweet. He cherished her and she loved him more than she ever thought possible. But on that fateful night, the serenity of her peaceful haven and the beauty of her secret feelings were broken by terrifying screams.

She thought nothing about her own safety before running to help whoever it was that needed it, but once at the scene, she realized there was nothing she could do to ward off the danger before her. *Soldiers!*

She barely escaped the brutality of these men, only saving herself by quickly crouching behind the remnants of a crumbling wall. From behind the ruins, she watched a soldier torment his victim just as she was being tormented now. But that woman made one terrible mistake. She wrestled against her captor. That was just what he wanted her to do.

Aroused by her rejection, one of the soldiers signaled for his cohorts to restrain her then watch as she writhed against their grip. Her screams, though stifled against the huge man's chest, started a sexual fever among the men and, to Jael's horror, called more soldiers. Repulsed, yet frozen with fear, Jael couldn't pull her eyes away. It felt as if her head was being held by an invisible hand, forcing her to watch the evilness that was unfolding.

The attacker's howls, grunts, and laughter drowned out his victim's cries until finally; when she lay naked and lifeless in the middle of the dirt road; only an occasional cackle or snort rose from the gang.

From her hiding place, Jael couldn't tell if the woman was dead or alive, but with all her heart, she hoped she was dead.

"Be merciful, Lord Jehovah," she begged.

After what seemed like hours, the men began to leave; some alone, some in small groups, but eventually they all disappeared into the shadows, leaving their victim in her shame. Jael waited a few minutes and listened. The night grew quiet again. So quiet that when the footstep ground into the gravel just beyond the lifeless woman, she heard it and froze. A dark figure stepped out of the shadows and knelt beside the body, placing something that looked more like a claw than a hand on the woman's stomach. Standing up, he looked at the darkness from where he'd come and nodded.

The shadowy recesses erupted with a terrifying noise; filling the night air with howls like those of mad dogs. Emerging from their hiding places, the creatures circled their prey, their cries rising to a wicked crescendo. Cursing the name of Jehovah, their sinister ritual turned into a horrendous tribute to someone they called Samael.

Eventually the soldiers left the circle once again and slipped back into the darkness leaving only one to stand over the woman. He muttered something about success and then he too, walked away.

Jael waited several minutes longer then stood up. On aching and trembling legs, she staggered to the woman's side. Slowly kneeling, she grimaced with every crack of her knees until they rested on the dirt road.

The stench of sweet, sticky blood and acrid urine hit Jael in the face. She gagged and turned her head, but the smell was so strong, her stomach heaved and she vomited into a pool of blood. Covering her nose with the back of one hand, she placed the other under the woman's nose. Soft puffs of air brushed her fingertips. Amazingly, the woman was still alive.

Quickly glancing around, Jael saw several pieces of the woman's shredded simlah scattered around them. Ignoring the pain, she pressed her knees into the dirt and reached for the pieces closest to them. When she'd gathered enough, she covered the most intimate parts of the poor creature. It wasn't until she pushed a wad of blood matted hair from the battered face that she realized the victim wasn't a woman of her age, but a younger woman; a girl not much older than Lilith.

"My lord," she whispered.

Thin white lines buried deep inside swollen mounds of blackened flesh were all that stared up at her. The once delicate mouth hung open like a gaping wound; the lower jaw falling loosely off to the side. When Jael moved the bone ever so slightly, a couple of teeth, floating in blood, slid from the corner of the young woman's mouth. Fighting back her own tears, Jael softly caressed the shattered jaw. "What has become of us," she moaned.

The girl groaned and rolled her head away from Jael's touch. "It's ok," whispered Jael. "I'm not going to hurt you, but I do have to get you out of here." She looked up at the moon and whispered, "Dear Jehovah, please give me strength," then scrambling to her feet, she pulled the battered woman-child up from the dirt.

Rachel instinctively lunged forward to help, but stopped short; realizing regardless of what she tried to do, she could do nothing.

The half-naked body fell heavily against Jael's chest stealing what little energy she had left, but Jael wouldn't let go. She had asked Jehovah to give her strength and now she had no choice but to believe he would. With her arms wrapped tightly around the girl, she glanced up and down the dark street.

The windows of nearby houses were tightly shuttered, their doors barred and bolted. Mottled voices drifted out from behind them, but Jael dared not stop and ask for help. Surely those behind the barred doors had heard the attack, but chose not to get involved. It wasn't her place to involve them now.

"By your strength alone," she prayed, and then inhaling deeply, she threw the girl's right arm around her shoulder, grabbed her tightly around her small waist, and started down the road toward the house of the village mid-wife.

The young woman left a small pool of blood in the wake of every step. Her weight pressed against Jael's numb arms, but they kept on, one small step at a time. Hours later, they stood in front of a thick Cyprus door.

The small house was as dark as the sky above them. Jael hadn't thought of the time, or perhaps the old woman might not be home, but they'd come too far to turn back. She pulled the young victim closer to her with one hand and pounded on the door with the other.

Several poundings later, the door slowly creaked open against its leather hinges. A small, opaque face with steely black eyes peered up at them from the darkness inside. Between gasps of breath, and several attempts to rearrange the dead weight that pressed against her own small frame, Jael explained what had happened. It didn't take much for the old woman to be convinced of the crime, not with the victim standing right in front her, but it did take a while for her to trust that the costs of her services would be paid in full. It wasn't until Jael had been reduced to begging that they were allowed to enter the house.

The front room of the tiny adobe was murky, lit only by a light that came from somewhere on the other side of the wall. Large pillows and several blankets were strewn around the room, herbs hung from hooks on the walls, and a large woven rug covered the dirt floor. Oil musk, mingled with the aromas of the hanging herbs, hung thick in the air. A thin layer of smoke wafted throughout the rooms. Jael thought she smelled a slight scent of oak and bread.

Jael carefully laid the young woman on the nearest sofa and the mid-wife covered her with one of the blankets. Turning to each other, they haggled in quiet tones until Jael was satisfied that the girl would be cared for to her expectations.

When the heavy door closed behind her, Jael turned and faced the black, menacing streets of the sleeping village. She hadn't thought about the walk home.

Creeping along in the shadows, she listened and watched for any sign of a soldier. Luna was high in the sky above her; but a few clouds shielded the moon's light from exposing hideaways and crevasses. She kept walking, ever watching and listening until finally, she was standing in front of her own fireplace.

It was then the blood stains on her halug and the acrid smell of urine on her fingers told her what she had witnessed had really happened. Crumbling to her knees, she buried her face in her shaking hands and cried until she had no more tears. Exhausted, she rested her head in the crook of her elbow and there, in front of her fire, she begged Jehovah once again to be merciful. "Take her life," she whispered.

"There will be nothing for her to live for now. She'll have to stand before the Village Elders and relive the whole crime, not to convict the soldiers, but to be deemed unclean. She'll be damned to live the life of an outcast, either in solitude or as a harlot. Time will determine that fate. Please Jehovah. Take her life now. She did nothing wrong. But she will live as if she did unless you grant her mercy."

The fire crackled and enveloped Jael in its warmth. Real tears ran down Rachel's face while sat on the daybed and watched this brave young woman fall asleep. Neither moved until Jael stirred to the crowing of a rooster.

Lilith boiled some water and set out a clean halug for her sister, but didn't ask about the blood on her dress or the putrid smell that filled the house. For that, Jael was grateful. She'd explain later, when she could talk about it without falling apart.

Later that morning at the mid-wife's cottage, Jael learned Jehovah did not grant the young woman the mercy for which she had prayed. The girl had lived through the night. Jael sat on the side of the sofa and dabbed the bruised and battered face with a cold cloth. Looking into the blank eyes that stared up at her, she cried. "Poor girl."

Before leaving the house, Jael counted out more silver coins than she and the old woman had negotiated, but only because she knew there would be more to this young woman's healing than what was apparent the night before. The old woman smiled and watched with wide bright eyes as the coins fell from Jael's small leather purse into the palm of her hand.

Walking home, Jael admitted to herself that it seemed strange that while paying for the young woman's help, she also prayed for her death, but before reaching her adobe, she came to terms with the fact that the choice between the two outcomes was not her's to make. It was Jehovah's. It was only her responsibility to care.

She never learned the girl's name, or where she lived, but a couple months later while filling urns at the well, she learned that the girl had survived the ordeal, but not without being with child. At that same time, she also learned that a few weeks earlier the Captain of the mysterious warriors had announced by decree that anyone who attempted to clean an unwanted child from a woman's womb would be slaughtered openly in the village square.

Now months later the people had become captives in their own village. Men who believed in Jehovah strangely disappeared. Young women were used as sex slaves. To leave would be to die in the surrounding desert. To revolt would be to die by one of their incredible swords.

And now, with the sun sleeping behind the hills, Jael stood completely alone with their malevolent leader.

CHAPTER FORTY

The Captain leaned in and pushed himself against her. His stench choked her and she turned her face from him. "Please sir," she whispered.

He laid his wet tongue against the crook of her neck and slid it up to her jaw. His putrid, breath nauseated her. It smelled like...death. Yes, his breath smelled like the bodies of her trampled parents before the priest applied the spices and incense. Bewildered, she looked at him from the corner of her eye. *A rotting corpse* was all she could think of.

"Prefer a more private setting?" he whispered in her ear.

"I'd prefer to go home...alone," she said quivering.

He took a step back and stared into her trembling face. His grimace softened. Caressing her cheek with the back of his hand, another smile shaped his perfect lips.

"Yes," he said tenderly, his calloused fingertips brushing beads of sweat from her forehead. "I believe I will escort you home."

Jael swallowed hard. *Perhaps his heart has softened and once there, he'll leave. Dear God in Heaven, please.*

The man took the urn from Jael's shoulder with ease and extended a large hand outward. "After you, my lady," he said, almost respectfully.

Jael lowered her aching arms and looked down at her numb feet. They wouldn't move. She was so scared, she couldn't move. The Captain sighed heavily and placed a large hand on her shoulder. Spinning her around, he shoved her forward. "Get going," he growled. She stumbled, but caught herself before falling into the dirt.

Making sure he didn't notice, she swiped at a falling tear.

Prepare yourself Jael, for surely this will not be the last tear you shed tonight.

The two of them walked in silence until they reached the door of her small house. Before reaching for the latch, she turned and looked up into his face. Her eyes asked him not to follow, his face told her he would.

She reached for the latch, but hesitated. If he were allowed inside...if Lilith was still awake... The man's hot breath slid down the back of her neck and smelling it, she again felt the presence of death. *I can't do this. I can't let him in. It would be best if I screamed and died here than to let him into my home...*But before she could do anything, the Captain swore, and kicked the door in.

The door exploded.

Jael yelped. Stepping back into him, she peered down at the thick military boot that had destroyed her door then back into his face. Everything about him told her not to hesitate again.

Jael tried to sound a warning to her sister as she stepped over the threshold. "I live here alone," she said loudly. "There's no one here but me."

Her eyes darted frantically around the room until they met those of her terrified sister peering at her from behind the chair. Jael tried to motion for her to run, but it was no use. The Captain saw her too and ordered her to come out and stand in front of him.

Lilith came out from hiding. Her eyes darted from Jael to the Captain then back to her sister. "Jael?" she said quietly.

"Jael, so that's your name. I thought you said you lived here alone," he said into her ear. "In all your righteousness, you find an excuse to lie. My, how Jehovah must be pleased."

His large fingers dug into her shoulder.

He looked over Jael's shoulder at her younger sister. "My name is Mora. I am High Captain of the motley crew that has taken your village." His eyes wandered hungrily across her body. "And you are?"

Jael watched in horror as Lilith's face softened. The terror that had filled her dark eyes was fading; turning into curious wonder. Jael shook her head hysterically. "No," she yelled, but Lilith had already been caught in the spell of the Captain's compelling smile.

"I'll ask again. What's your name?"

Lilith's shoulders relaxed. The reflection of the warm fire danced merrily in her brown eyes. "Lilith," she replied softly.

"Lilith," he repeated. "Like Lily, pure and white?"

Lilith blushed, or pretended to. Jael wasn't sure.

"Yes," she said smoothly, casting her eyes down to the floor like a shy spinster. But when she brought them back up, they met his with a noticeable intenseness. Even Jael saw the "come and get me" look her sister was throwing at the handsome soldier.

"But not as lily white or as pure as you think," she purred.

"Lilith," cried Jael. "Please, you've no idea..."

The younger woman walked over to her sister and, pulling Jael's chin up with her fingertips, looked into her eyes. "What?" she pouted mockingly. "Are you jealous? Did you think you could bring this big, strong man home and keep him to yourself?"

Jael's eyes widened. She shook her head vigorously. "No," she whispered.

But before she could say another word, anger raced red up

Lilith's neck and poured across her cheeks. She pulled her hand back and slapped her sister's face so hard Jael's head jerked to the side, rocking her on her heels.

Blood trickled from the corner of Jael's mouth and tears down her cheeks. Feeling her knees buckling beneath her, she prepared to fall, but before she could, the Captain grabbed her by the arms and kept her upright.

Lilith stepped up close to Jael's face again and bared her teeth. "After the little sermon you gave me earlier, after you called me a harlot, you go out and find one of these gorgeous creatures for yourself," she spat. "You lying piece of cow..."

The Captain bellowed loudly as Lilith's hand came down across her sister's face again.

"Lilith, please, it isn't like that," Jael groaned.

Lilith ignored her and stepped around to the large man. Gently taking one of his hands, she sensuously ran her slender fingers around and between his, then, looking up into his beautiful eyes, she gently kissed his fingertips. "Do you want this?" she whispered.

Fear gripped Jael's heart as she watched the merriment disappear from the Captain's dark eyes, witnessing instead the birth of unadulterated lust. His eyes, turning from a deep brown to crimson and criminal, exploded with a hunger like nothing she'd ever seen before. There was nothing about them that resembled the human man that had once stood before her.

Lilith saw it too, but before she could back away, the Captain shoved Jael to the ground, grabbed Lilith by the hair and pulled her to him. Knitting his thick fingers into her long black hair, he lifted her slender body off the floor. She couldn't turn her head without his grip ripping her scalp from her skull, but her eyes searched frantically around the room for her sister. She would never see her sister's face again.

"Don't scream," cried Jael, "Don't scream Lilith." But as

the Captain carried her to the back rooms, Lilith's screams echoed off the adobe walls, and Jael knew others would come.

Lying on the floor, she understood all too well what was going to happen, but she couldn't move. Her lungs burned for air. Her eyes blurred. Nothing in the room looked familiar anymore. In the distance, she heard the pounding of heavy boots against the dirt road. The more Lilith screamed, the louder the pounding.

Rachel ran to the door and peered outside. She could hear the rumbling of boots against the dirt road getting closer. Turning to Jael, her face etched in fear, she screamed, "Run, Jael, run." But her voice died the minute it left her lips.

But Jael heard them coming too. "Run or stay here and die," she said aloud.

The sound of her own voice awakened her, giving her the strength to crawl through the cooking room and out the back door into the courtyard. She kept crawling. *Get as far back as you can. Move Jael!*

As a group of soldiers burst through what remained of the front door, she pulled herself behind a large boulder. But even there, the noise reached her. The cursing of the soldiers and Lilith's screams cut through her defenses and filled her brain.

The oil lamp hit the floor; its flame and that in the fireplace extinguished. The house went dark, but the noises still came. Strange grunts, howls, and screeches, raged above Lilith's muted screams. Jael closed her eyes and begged God again for mercy.

The assault seemed to go on forever, and although Lilith's screams eventually stopped, the crazed orgy did not. Jael quietly made her way closer to the back door, hiding behind trees and large stones until she was close enough to see inside her house. What she saw made her stomach lurch. She caught the bile with her own hand just before it spilled over her lips, but her stomach lurched again. She had to stay quiet. Burying her face in her halug, she vomited into its folds until her stomach was empty. When she had finished, she wiped her halug in the grass and slid the back of her hand across her mouth.

The soldiers had drug Lilith's naked body into the front room. Some hovered over her as if they were waiting, hoping she would wake up and scream one more time.

The vision of the lifeless body of her sister struck her hard, but it was the grotesque forms of the soldiers that shocked her. They no longer resembled handsome, strong men, but instead, had turned into horrific creatures. Bright red eyes burned from faces that were ugly masses of deformed flesh. Spittle dripped from yellow fangs that hung from malformed mouths. They no longer stood tall and straight but were bent and crooked as if burdened by the black wings that arched out from their hunched backs.

One creature lifted a long spindly finger and poked Lilith with a sharp, milky fingernail.

"Is she dead?" asked another.

"No," said one who sounded like the Captain. "Near death, but she'll live." That one placed a large, crooked claw on Lilith's stomach. "And she'll deliver," he said coldly. The others grunted in response.

"But from now on," he growled, "no more orgies. We can take any woman we want, but let's not take one at the same time. Humans are weak and for risk of losing the offspring, we need to be more careful."

Some of the monsters protested, but the Captain threw up his claw. "This isn't just about our own desires my fellow warriors," he barked, "but the end result must be first and foremost to create offspring. If Samael is to be victorious with his own version of creation, we must produce children!"

Rachel fell against a tree. "These are the fallen," she cried. "And, and the children..."

The demon tossed Lilith's head aside. "As much as we

despise these useless organisms, we need them, for the time being anyway. The women must carry our offspring. We must be careful not to destroy the vessel. No more than two of you in an attack from now on. Understood?" The grunts and moans of the soldiers eased. Most nodded in agreement.

The house fell silent. Rachel stood behind Jael and both watched in horror as the soldier's black wings morphed once again into broad shoulders; hunched backs straightened; short, thick legs lengthened to form tall, muscular pillars; and ugly grotesque flesh turned into handsome faces. Quietly, the soldiers laced their loin aprons, strapped on their leather corselets, and buckled their boots, kicking Lilith to the side as if she were a piece of trash lying in the street while they shifted around the room. In time, each beast turned back into the armor-clad soldier that had burst into Jael's home hours earlier.

Finally, the Captain broke the silence. "And one other thing," he said sternly. "The older sister, Jael, if you see her, do not approach her. Do not touch her. As a matter of fact, don't even look at her." While the men protested his order, Jael stepped back into the shadows and sighed deeply with relief.

But then the Captain raised a hand and quieted his men. Staring out the back door, he searched the courtyard and although Rachel knew he was searching for Jael and couldn't see her, she felt his eyes cut to her very soul. This was Mora, the same who tried to kill her in the hospital. He told her then of Jael, although she had no idea what he meant at the time. And now his demonic eyes bore into both of them.

"I tell you this," he said callously, "because she's mine. She is the one I chose."

His men cheered loudly as they fell out onto the dark street. Jael's breath caught in her throat. Lifting her eyes, she saw him standing in the doorway, his glistening eyes cutting across the courtyard.

"I know you're near, Jael," he snarled. "I can smell your

fear. Do not think this is over. As I said before, you're mine."

She closed her eyes to block out his image. She had seen him as he really was and she hated him. "Asa," she whispered. "Please forgive me."

Just then a cold breeze pushed against her and held her frozen in its chilling grip. Through the swirling leaves a strange voice, a hissing voice, whispered in her ear telling her that Asa couldn't hear her. He would never hear her again.

A few streets away, Asa had been found lying on the cold dirt floor of the house he'd been preparing for his bride. His open eyes stared blindly upward into nothingness; his hands lay lifeless at his side and under his head lay a large, crimson pool. The blood that had poured from his throat had already jelled around him.

CHAPTER FORTY-ONE

Lilith squeezed her eyes against the coldness she felt pressing on her forehead. Jael noticed and smiled weakly. *It has been three days since... No,* she corrected herself. *You won't think of the evilness, but of Jehovah's goodness. Lilith has been with you for three days.* She pushed the evil memory from her mind, determined to be grateful for her sister's life. "Fight, Lilith," she whispered. "Don't let them win."

The bruised eyelids fluttered until Lilith could hold them open for just a second. Looking up with blind eyes, she pushed a whisper from her bruised throat. "Let me die. I don't want to live, not with this," she said coarsely. Closing her eyes, she ran her broken fingers across her stomach.

"Shhh," comforted Jael, wiping a bead of sweat from Lilith's face. "Jehovah will help us, Lilith. All of us. Even your child. Don't worry."

Lilith snickered. "Jehovah? What Jehovah? How could a loving God allow this?"

"Lilith, please don't..."

Her face contorted in pain, but she forced out the words. "Is he not the creator of all things?" she interrupted. "Did he not create those horrid animals that do unspeakable things to innocent people?" The lids of her eyes moved again, but they failed to open.

"Don't talk to me of Jehovah," she said weakly. "He did not protect me. He allowed this to happen." She turned her head to the wall. Inhaling deeply, she finished her thought. "And he will not protect you," she sighed. "Don't think you're better than the rest of us, Jael. You're not. There will be no Jehovah to protect you either."

Jael set the cloth in a bowl and stood up. "Rest Lilith," she said. "I'll be back in a while to feed you." Lilith moaned, but said nothing else.

Jael went to her courtyard. Clouds hung grey and heavy above her. Looking up at them, she sighed. "I know. My heart feels the same." Sitting on a large stone, her face fell into her hands. "Oh, dear God," she moaned. "Please, don't forsake us. Please, show me that Lilith is wrong. That you do care and you will protect us. Please God, have mercy."

"Jael!"

Jael's head flew up from her hands. That voice had been emblazoned in her brain, but she hoped with all hope that she'd never hear it again. But there he was, standing in the back doorway of her house facing her. Her body shook with unspeakable terror and his laughter filled the house.

She stood up and nervously wiped her shaking hands on her apron. *Lilith*, she thought. *I must get to Lilith.*

"Your sister is fine," he said snickering. "Besides, it's you I wish to, um, see."

Jael's mouth fell open. "How did you know what I was..."

Mora's mouth curled at one corner. "I know," he interrupted. "I can read your thoughts, Jael. I have so many mystical powers, so many wonderful things that, well," he half-chuckled, "will be passed on to my offspring as well."

The Captain stepped off of the threshold and into the courtyard. "This is nice," he said coyly, looking around. "I've never been back here." He nodded his head and looked at her. "Yes, this will work for our visit."

She quickly glanced around. There was nowhere to run.

She couldn't get past him and the surrounding wall was too high to jump. She was trapped in a place she loved, but now, if she survived, it too would become part of an ugly memory.

He walked toward her; she stepped back, but knowing there was nowhere to run, she hid her face in her hands. *If I am to die here, I will die with honor. I will not scream. He may take me, but he will be the only monster that steals my innocence.*

Expecting to be grabbed and thrown to the ground, she waited, but instead of hearing his breath close to her, she heard something else. Something that made her blood run cold. It was the swift sound of a sword being pulled from its sheath. *Is he going to just kill me instead?* She slowly pulled her hands from her face and opened her eyes, expecting to meet her death as he brought the weapon down upon her head.

But there was no sword hovering above her head. There was no evil smile teasing her fear. In fact, the Captain was nowhere to be seen. She'd heard him coming toward her, but she'd not heard him leave. Where was he then? Behind her? She quickly spun around to meet him, but there was no one there. Turning around again, she was met with a light so bright she had to throw a hand up to her eyes to shield them.

"Who's there?" she called as she stepped forward.

No one answered.

Taking another step, the light dimmed just enough for her to make out the figure of a man, dressed in white and shimmering as bright as the morning star. The light gradually softened until she could see him without shielding her eyes. He was tall and muscular. One arm hung at his side, but the other held an unsheathed sword. It was made of shiny silver; its ruby pommel glowed like fire.

"Who are you?" she asked calmly, slowly approaching him.

"Michael," whispered Rachel. "In my hospital room...on the right side of the throne."

"Stand where you are, Jael," he ordered. "Come no closer."

Jael obeyed. If he wanted to kill her, he could do so from where they both stood.

"Do not be afraid. I will not harm you."

"But how do you know..."

"I am Michael the Archangel. I am Jehovah's warrior. He has sent me here because he has heard your pleas."

Jael's heart beat in her ears. "Jehovah sent you?"

"Yes, Jael. You have found favor with God. You and your line are to be protected by my sword."

"But my sister, Lilith. I'm afraid you've come too late. The warriors, she's been..."

"God has granted her the mercy for which you've prayed, Jael, but Lilith will account for herself," warned the angel. "It is you and your lineage that I am to protect."

Jael fell to her knees. "Dear God in Heaven," she whispered. "How am I to understand all of this? Thank you for showing mercy to Lilith. She is but a child and I am so insignificant to have found favor with you. I do not understand your graciousness."

"God has heard you and you have been chosen." The angel stepped closer to her. "You will marry soon, and in that marriage, you will bear a son. He too will find favor with the Lord and God will use him and his lineage to start new generations."

"But my fiancé is dead," she said softly. "I have no one to marry."

"God will provide, Jael."

She looked up at the angel, her eyes searching his for meaning. She tried to speak, but she couldn't find the words to convey the depth of her confusion or the sincerity of her gratitude.

"I hear your heart, Jael, and I will carry your message to

the Lord. But he asks that you believe," he said with conviction. "God will lead if you believe."

Jael lowered her head. "I may falter," she said quietly, "but I will always believe."

"Then you have nothing to fear."

"But the soldiers, the Captain," she said, lifting her head.

"The soldiers have been given what they desired most, to live as humans, except upon their death," replied the angel. "At that time, God will fulfill a promise he made to their leader a long time ago. As for the Captain, he is gone from this land, Jael. He cannot hurt you."

Jael closed her eyes. "And the children that will be born from the soldiers' seed; are they gone as well?" The angel fell silent for a moment, but then softly answered, "No. They and their children after them will remain until the final day. But do not fear. Follow the Lord, Jael. And he will overcome."

"I will follow," but her commitment seemed to float away on empty air. The angel was gone. She knelt alone in the courtyard.

Jael gathered her skirt and ran into the house. "Lilith," she cried breathlessly. Her heart raced with a joy she had never felt. "God has heard, Lilith. He has heard our prayers."

A soft ray of light fell through the window and spilled across Lilith's face. Jael bent low, hoping to see her sister's eyes, but instead, saw where the torment of the fever had etched itself in what was once a young, beautiful face. Jael grabbed the wet cloth from the bowl and dabbed it across her sister's brow.

"God has heard us, Lilith," she said joyfully. "He has shown his mercy, and..."

Lilith didn't move. Jael stopped talking and looked into the ashen face. "Sister?" she whispered. Still, Lilith didn't move.

Jael lowered herself down onto the floor. Burying her face in the crook of her elbow, she wept for her sister. God truly had shown mercy. Lilith, and the half human, half demon child in her, were dead.

***

Although Rachel's journey had lasted only minutes, in the memory, years passed. She witnessed the creation of a new race by the raping of human women by demonic creatures, soon to become known as the Nephilim. They were giants that roamed the earth, destroying all that was good and beautiful. They were master craftsmen and taught mankind how to make and wield weaponry; mix herbs into magical potions; cannibalize other humans, but in the darkness that ravaged the earth, the message Michael had given to Jael was fulfilled. Jehovah brought Jael a man of faith to marry. His name was Lamech.

After being blessed with three daughters, they had a son whom they knew from the moment he was born had been chosen by God. Not because he looked different than the three children born before him or sounded differently when he cried, but because of how comforted their hearts felt when they looked at him.

Lamech took the crying newborn from the mid-wife, held him above his head, and prayed, "Baruch ata Adonay Elohanu Melech Haolam, haTov v'haMeiteev." [Blessed are You G-d, L-rd of the Universe, who is good and brings us comfort.] Lamech then kissed his son's forehead and held him in his large arms. "He's beautiful, Jael. He looks so much like you."

Jael giggled. "I think you've said that about all of our children, dear husband. One of them surely has to look like their father."

"You're right, wife. Our daughters are beautiful like their

mother, but this strong specimen of a son looks exactly like me. I just didn't want to hurt your feelings."

Jael stretched out her arms, "Now that we have that settled, hand me our bundle of joy so he can eat."

Lamech reluctantly handed the baby to his mother, but not before kissing his son's cheek and whispering, "Thank you, Jehovah for this son. He is yours to be used as you will. His mother and I don't know your plan for him, but we are grateful to be a part."

Jael took the baby and laid him against her breast. His cheek felt soft and warm against her. Carefully, she turned his little head until his lips found her sweet milk. Listening to the suckling noise of her feeding baby, she closed her eyes and rested her head against the stone wall behind her head. "Jehovah has brought me such peace, such comfort," she said softly. "I don't know why he chose us, but right now, my heart couldn't be more grateful."

The cavern grew quiet except for the tinkling noises made by the young mid-wife as she cleaned her birthing tools. The couple's three girls were just outside the mouth of the cave playing in the sun under the watchful eye of their nurse.

Jael could hear her husband's rhythmic breathing, but he said nothing. Her newborn son tugged hungrily at her breast. In the silence, she had never known such peace.

The chair creaked as Lamech leaned over and laid a large hand on his son's head. "God has spoken to me. He has told me what to name our son."

Jael didn't open her eyes, but she whispered, "Noah. His name will be Noah; one who brings comfort."

Lamech smiled at his sleepy wife. "Yes. Our son's name will be Noah."

***

Rachel stepped into the mouth of the cave and looked at the valley below. On the horizon, black wisps of smoke rose up from the ground marking where the small village of Sargon once stood. Up and down the hillsides, smoke rose toward Heaven. The march of evilness was leaving its mark across the land and those who managed to stay alive were hidden in the caves and crevasses of the surrounding mountains.

In the few short minutes Rachel was allowed to see the rampage of the Nephilim, she saw the ramifications of the Dark Angel's decision to break the Holy Code. Before her journey ended, she fully understood why God had decided to cleanse the earth under the waters of a great flood.

It was a vision that would haunt her for the rest of her life.

CHAPTER FORTY-TWO

The screen across Rachel's eyes went dark. She lay motionless in the recliner; completely stunned by what she'd seen. Her mind reeled as she tried to reason and think logically, but she couldn't concentrate on anything except that her genetic memory had taken her all the way back to an era shortly after creation when demons mated with human women and gave birth to the Nephilim. *What does all of this mean? It isn't real, is it? I've had the Genesis Factor on my mind so long; is this what my mind produced as a genetic memory?*

But then she thought about the blood she had tried to clone; that only positive types could be cloned, but not negative types. Negative types were minus the rhesus antigen. *The rhesus antigen, from the rhesus monkey... Is the antigen a genetic memory in people with positive blood types? And what about human DNA being changed because of Nephilim sperm? Their genetic memory combining with human genetics, and then actually changing human DNA strands. That was science; undeniable science.*

"My lord," she whispered. "If that truly is the case, there's no need for cloning Nephilim DNA. No need to sell body parts on the black market from the dog food plant, no need for cryogenics in the basement of the lab..." Suddenly she felt monstrous, dirty. "Because, because, they're already here. All of us...we are Rephaim."

The voice beside her was familiar. "Make no mistake, Rachel Wall, your research was correct. It is all about the blood."

Even with the mask on, Rachel could see the Archangel standing beside her. "Michael," she whispered. "I saw you at the hospital, when I was dying, and...God's throne room, in Jael's courtyard, and now here."

"Yes, I am the same."

"Are you here to help me understand all of this?"

"You already know the answer, Rachel," the angel said firmly. "You just haven't considered the powerful significance of it."

"Powerful significance? So, what you're telling me is that those of us with the Rhesus antigen are Rephaim. We're related to them, they're our ancestors..."

"Think more powerful than that, Doctor Wall."

Rachel searched every crevasse of her brain, but couldn't find an answer.

Michael stepped up within arm's reach; his piercing eyes searching her face. "The powerful significance is in the blood, Doctor Wall. Mankind will not understand it fully until they are before The Way himself, but to help you prepare for the plan Elohim has for you, understand this...it took a race of half-demon and half-human beings to cause Elohim to destroy mankind, but only one man who was all God and all human to redeem them.

"Satan set out to destroy the temporary, physical part of man, but God provided a way to redeem the everlasting, spiritual part of man. It does not matter what type of blood flows through human veins, Rachel. It does not matter if one's blood does or does not contain the antigen, it only matters whose blood covers the individual's heart. Consider that *perfect* blood. Study *that* blood, Doctor Wall; because that is the *only* blood that matters. It is the only blood that saves humankind from Samael, and the only blood that will protect you in the battles that lie ahead."

"Battles?"

"You were protected, Rachel. A battle was fought for your soul, and you were protected from it. Now that you're a follower of The Way, it is your duty to be a protector."

"Protector? Protector of whom? And how?"

"Your friend. She is with child."

"Carmen? Yes, she's pregnant."

"Samael has plans for Carmen and her child, but so does Elohim."

Rachel gasped. "What are you talking about? What's going to happen to Carmen and her baby?"

"Her child could be the last, Rachel Wall. A message has come from our Captain that she has been deemed to be the last."

Rachel's brow furrowed deeply. "The last baby?"

Michael slowly shook his head. "No Rachel. She is to be the last heart. The last to be redeemed, but Satan will fight to keep that from happening. If she is to be the last, he wants her to be his last."

"And it's going to be up to me to protect her from the devil so she can grow up to accept The Way and then..."

"Yes," Michael answered. "You and a few others."

Rachel's head fell back onto the pillow. "I can't do that," she moaned. "I don't know how to fight the devil."

Michael unsheathed his sword and touched Rachel's forearm with the blade. It burned like sandpaper scrubbing a wound, but only for a second. When the pain stopped, Michael sheathed his weapon and Rachel raised her arm to see what looked to be the tattoo of a sword, just like the one Michael carried at his side.

"Simon," she whispered. "And Sterling? They're

protectors?"

"Yes," Michael said gravely. "Some die while protecting others, Rachel. Simon gave his all for you." Tears formed in Rachel's eyes, but she was at a loss for words until she remembered Carmen and her circle of protection. "Some even use other means too, don't they?"

"Those seek to protect, but are doing so with false hope."

"In other words, Carmen means well, but her prayers are useless?"

"She seeks protection from the very one that wishes to destroy."

Rachel groaned with a broken heart. "How do I protect them, Michael?"

"Study The Word and learn to use your sword," Michael said with authority. "Elohim will teach you how to wield it and when to use it. Pull from all you were taught as a child. Believe when all seems lost. Fight as if the souls of Carmen and her child depend on it...because they do. Remember Doctor Wall, there is power in the blood, and his is the most powerful of all. Believe."

Rachel sighed. "I am the daughter of Jael. How can I not believe?"

Michael smiled.

"The daughter of Jael," whispered Rachel. "Where have I heard that before? I was called that before, but by whom?"

Someone pushed the door open and walked across the room toward her. The light dimmed and the room fell silent until the wheels of the cart with the blue towel squeaked as it was pushed closer to the recliner. "Be still, Doctor Wall," said Anne. "I need to disconnect the wires and then..."

Rachel relaxed at the sound of the technician's voice. She was so glad this "journey" was over; there was so much to think about and consider, but her thoughts were suddenly interrupted by something that smelled revolting.

"Anne?"

The mask was removed from her face and she immediately threw her hand up to her nose. "What is that?"

She opened her eyes slowly.

Paralysis grabbed her.

The scream never left her throat.

"Yes, Doctor Wall, human DNA *is* Nephilim DNA," he said, with a menacing smile. "Except those with negative blood; the pure bloodline. We couldn't degrade everything."

Rachel stared into his dark, sinister eyes. She'd never seen his face, but she knew that voice. It was the voice she heard when she was in the hospital; before he placed the pillow over her face, and it was the same voice she heard when her journey took her into Jael's world.

The fingers of her left hand trembled against her lips. The fingers of her right hand groped the pocket of her sweater for the curtron.

The beast leaned in closer to her face. He smelled like rancid death.

"My name is Mora, Doctor Wall. Perhaps you 'remember' me."

CHAPTER FORTY-THREE

W ithout making a sound, two masculine figures apparated into the room; their right hands firmly on the pommel of their swords and their hard, blue eyes boring into the back of Mora's head. But instead of directly subduing the perpetrator, they immediately stepped back into a dark corner of the grey, sterile room, quietly wondering if Rachel would be able to ward off the demon by herself. She had what she needed to do so, they just weren't sure if she'd come to understand that yet.

Mora's eyes widened. Without turning from his captive, he sniffed the air. "Did you feel that?" he muttered.

Rachel's pulsed quickened. Were there more of his kind in the room?

"They're here," he growled. "I felt a slight shift in the cosmos when they appeared, but I can smell them; their purity; and it nauseates me."

Panicked, Rachel asked, "Who's here?"

Throwing himself around to face the wall, Mora roared, "Guardians. They're here for me, but they won't take me without a fight."

Rachel's heart beat hard against her chest as her shaking fingertips fumbled inside of the pocket of her sweater, searching for the small curtron. A fingernail caught something round, but her spirit sank when she didn't feel the two small buttons on its face. It was only an old breath mint.

Where is it? I know I dropped it right in...here, here it is! Her fingertips finally slid across the face of the quarter-size electronic 'bell', feeling the two small buttons on its face.

But which one is the red button and which is the green? I can't tell. This is an emergency; I need to press the red button! But how was she to know she was pressing the right button without bringing the little bell up to her eyes? To do so would reveal the only means of communication she had. If he saw it, the monster would surely destroy it before she could save herself.

From the corner of her eye she could see the young clinic tech lying on the hard-concrete floor. Her blank eyes stared upward, unmoving and lifeless. Her long hair fanned out around her head like the rays of a blond sun. Rachel knew right then, she had no choice. She wasn't the only one who needed help. Swallowing the uncertainty, she squeezed a button, any button. Either one would bring someone.

Mora flashed a wicked smile. The stench of his breath hit her square in the face and she flinched. Not giving the two warriors behind him a second thought, he quickly raised his hand to cover her mouth. More from reflex than a prepared defense, she lifted her arm and blocked him. His gnarled fingers grazed her forearm and he touched the mark left by Michael's sword. Screaming in agony, he jumped up, his hand turning into a black, burnt claw. "What have you done? What...?"

His high-pitched, horrendous screams swirled around the dimly lit room. Mora's eyes flew from Rachel's startled face to his blistering fingers.

"What kind of magic is this?" he growled, holding his hand close to his chest. Before she could answer, the demon stumbled back into the dark corner. Rachel turned her arm so she could see the mark for herself. It looked like a sword, glowing white hot, except for the tip of the pommel that burned ruby red.

"The tattoo on Simon's chest, just above his heart, and the tattoo Sterling has on his right forearm; they were the same, the same as this." She dabbed the blade of the tattoo with a fingertip. It didn't burn. Rubbing the mark gently with her hand, she whispered, "Why? Why did it burn him, but not me?"

Mora screamed again and Rachel's head flew upward. Mora was kneeling before the Dark Angel.

"I gave no permission to take on human form," sneered the Dark One. "Your rebellion against me will cost you dearly, Mora."

The Dark Angel lifted his eyes toward the corner of the room and nodded his head. Before leaving, he turned to Rachel; only emitting a low, guttural growl.

Rachel's large round eyes met Mora's red, demonic orbs. He groaned then doubled over and fell to the floor with a heavy thud. She wasn't sure, but just before Mora vanished, she thought she saw the glint of silver blades.

Shaking uncontrollably, she pulled herself upright and swung her feet off the recliner, making sure not to step on Anne's hair. It was easy to fall to her knees; she doubted if her legs would've held her up long enough to reach the door anyway. Placing her fingers on the side of Anne's long slender neck, she felt for a pulse. After moving her fingertips under Anne's jaw, she finally found one. It was faint, but it was there.

Suddenly the door was thrown back and Lydia burst into the room. "Doctor Wall. Are you alright?"

Someone behind Lydia flipped on the lights. Rachel threw her hand up and covered her eyes.

"My god, Doctor Wall," screeched Lydia as she fell to her knees beside Rachel. "What happened here?"

A man and a woman pushed past the two women and started emergency procedures on Anne. Another team rolled in a gurney and started an IV drip. Lydia helped Rachel up. Throwing an arm around her shoulders, they walked toward the door. "What happened?" she asked again.

Rachel hesitated. "I don't know. I'd finished my journey and she came in, telling me to stay still so she could undo the connections and then, then she went silent. I pulled the mask off and found her there, lying on the floor."

Rachel looked over her shoulder at the people working on Anne. "They sure showed up fast," she said.

"You called for them," replied Lydia. "You pushed the red button."

Rachel half-smiled. "I was hoping that was the one I squeezed, but I wasn't sure. I, I couldn't see the curtron."

A few silent seconds passed. "Is she going to be ok?"

"I don't know, Doctor Wall. We can only hope so, but she's in the best care now."

Lydia turned somber, keeping her arm around Rachel's shoulder all the way up the hall until they stopped at the elevator. She pushed the 'UP' arrow then stepped back. "I'm sorry, Doctor Wall," she said with an air of defeat.

Rachel looked stunned. "Sorry? Sorry for what, Lydia? You've done nothing wrong."

Lydia didn't look up into Rachel's face, but kept her head down as she stepped onto the elevator. "Yes, yes, I did," she whispered, turning around and facing the large brass doors. Her fingers brushed against the brass knob. "I wasn't assigned to you just to make sure you enjoyed your time here at The Chalet, but, well, you are my sole responsibility...and I failed."

The elevator jerked upward and Rachel turned to Lydia. "Failed? Good grief, Lydia, failed at what? Anne fell. I don't know why, but you couldn't have done..."

Lydia looked full into Rachel's face. Her eyes were cold and hard. A muscle in her jaw twitched as she rolled up the sleeve of her sweater. "You don't understand," she said firmly. "I'm not talking about Anne. It's my responsibility to protect *you*, Doctor Wall."

Lydia turned her arm toward Rachel so she could get the full effect of what she was trying to say. Lydia's sword tattoo was just a little smaller than the one etched into her own arm.

Their eyes met and Rachel understood without saying a word. "You know what happened in there, don't you?" she finally said, almost choking on her words. "You know about my genetic journey."

Lydia nodded and pulled the sleeve back down to cover the mark that had been scored into her arm by an unblemished blade.

"Who," asked Rachel? "Who assigned you to protect me? How do you know what took place in my journey, and, and how do you know who was with me in that room back there? How do you know him?"

Lydia gently touched Rachel's arm. "It's ok, Doctor Wall. We'll talk, but not now. After your interview."

Rachel shook her head. "My interview? What interview? I don't understand."

"You don't remember now, because of the shock you just experienced," whispered Lydia. "But wait a minute and you will."

The elevator stopped and a soft 'ding' confirmed they were on the third floor.

"What interview, Lydia?" persisted Rachel.

Again, Lydia touched Rachel's arm; giving a slight nod toward the brass doors. Rachel fell silent and watched the doors slide open, a subtle swishing noise filling the small cube as they separated.

Lydia was right. She suddenly remembered the interview, but more importantly, she understood that Lydia's touch had been a warning. Somehow the young woman knew that when the large doors opened, Kommandeur von Guten would be standing there, just on the other side, ready to gather Rachel up as soon as she stepped from the elevator into the beautifully adorned hallway.

CHAPTER FORTY-FOUR

He stood tall and handsome in his pin-striped suit. His grey eyes, twinkled with amusement. "Ah, Doctor." His thick German accent bounced off the pristine walls. "You've finished our little experiment."

"I did, Commander," Rachel answered with a weak smile.

"And did you find it pleasant?" he asked.

"Some of it," Rachel answered truthfully. "Other parts, not so much, but I guess we all have those parts in our past, don't we?"

She noticed a shadow slide across his dark eyes before relaxing and softening again. "Indeed, we do, I suppose, but I hope you found your journey, if nothing else, enlightening."

Remembering the horrific scenes of her ancestor's torment bestowed upon them by the lust of the demon that just fled from the room below, Rachel chuckled lightly. "Enlightening, yes; that's a good word for it."

The Kommandeur stuck out a hand and stopped the elevator doors from closing. For a second Rachel thought he was going to tell her to get back on, but to her relief, he stepped into the lift himself.

"Well, if you'll excuse me, I'm going down to see how our other guests are doing. I look forward to our interview in an hour, Doctor Wall. I hope you are ready."

All Rachel could do was nod.

Von Guten turned to the valet. "Lydia."

The valet's eyes bounced upward to meet his gaze; unable to hide the surprise that he knew her name.

Von Guten chuckled. "Please bring Doctor Wall to my office in thirty minutes. I'd like a few minutes with her before I present her to the other Coordinators. Will you do that?"

"Yes, Kommandeur," she said. "Thirty minutes."

They waited until the brass doors closed before turning and walking to Rachel's room. "Only twenty-five minutes to get ready," Lydia said quietly. "That doesn't give you much time. Are you alright?"

Rachel nodded nervously. "I'll be ready," she said, swallowing hard.

At her suite door, she stopped and glanced down the hall toward Carmen's room. Her best friend, a person who trusted and loved her, was waiting to hear about her wonderful journey into the past, but how would she ever be able to tell her of what she saw? They promised there'd never be any secrets between them, but Carmen wouldn't understand anything about the Genesis Factor, about Mora, let alone about the sabotaging of human DNA by creatures known as Nephilim.

As if reading her mind, Lydia gently nudged her. "Hurry. I'll go to Mrs. Rodriguez and explain that you'll see her later, after the interview."

Rachel looked down into the kind face of the brave young woman beside her. "Thank you, Lydia," she whispered. "For everything."

Lydia smiled, opened the door, and stepped aside to let Rachel through. "I'll be back in twenty-five minutes."

Rachel peeled off her clothes and jumped into the shower. She needed the hot water to pound across her shoulders, to clear her mind, and steady her nerves. Fifteen minutes later, she was dressed to impress in a dark blue suit with matching purse and pumps. Her heart wasn't in this interview, but she had no choice. It was her mission to infiltrate the Coordinators to understand who Edith Aberman reported to, and the only way to do that was to become a Coordinator and find out who actually led this organization. Von Guten was the Kommandeur, but he took his orders from someone, and she had to find that person.

"If that doesn't sound completely insane," muttered Rachel. "But it's true. And I've got to undo the damage I've done by finding out who's on top and stop him, or her."

Twenty-five minutes later Lydia tapped on the door and Rachel stepped out into the hall; greeted by the valet's nervous smile. "He doesn't usually ask for a personal audience before an interview," she said, turning and leading Rachel toward the elevator. "He usually greets the candidate in the conference room and makes a quick intro to the rest of the Council. This is highly unusual."

"No worries," Rachel said with false confidence.

Lydia stopped in the middle of the hallway and dug through the pocket of her sweater. "And I have this for you," she said cautiously. "I don't know who delivered it or when it came, but Helga, a girl on the house staff, brought it to me a few minutes ago, just before I came up here to get you."

Rachel glanced at the handwriting on the front of the white envelope. The name S. Knight beamed up at her. A smile pulled at the corners of her mouth. "Excellent," she said. "I was hoping to hear from him."

"Who?" asked Lydia.

Rachel's brow furrowed slightly.

"I'm sorry, Doctor Wall. I don't want to come across as a nosey busy-body, but as I said, it's my job to protect you and..."

"It's ok, Lydia. This is from the new Director of the lab I use to work for. He took Doctor Aberman's place. I'm sure it's just a "how ya' doing?" letter.

Rachel ripped open the envelope and quickly read Sterling's message. He was in the grand atrium of The Chalet. He was there. Rachel didn't know why or how, but he was there. The thought made her feel better; perhaps safer. She may have even felt her heart trying to skip a beat.

Lydia watched Rachel smile as she folded the letter. Her shoulders relaxed and the muscles in her face loosened. "I'm glad you're smiling," she said quietly.

Rachel tucked the envelope into her purse; followed Lydia into the elevator, and watched her hit the '1' button. Down they went to the first floor where Lydia led her to a beautiful corner office. The front office, Antonia's office, had a masculine flair, reflecting the wealth of the man beyond the inner door, but regardless of all the leather and oriental rugs, it was a welcoming room.

The Kommandeur was sitting behind his large desk when Antonia opened the door to announce Rachel, but it wasn't the Kommandeur that demanded Rachel's attention, it was the large glass wall that framed a stunning afternoon view of the beautiful Alps surrounding The Chalet. But the awe of the beauty didn't last long as von Guten extended an arm toward a leather wing-back chair across from his desk. Rachel sat down rigid on the edge of the chair, her knuckles turning white as she unwittingly squeezed her small blue clutch.

"Our time is brief, Doctor Wall," he said. "So let me get straight to the point."

"Yes, please," replied Rachel.

"Your journey, the genetic journey you just experienced, it was alarming, yes?"

Rachel could feel the blood draining from her face. "Yes, it was, very, but how would you know that?"

Von Guten rubbed his chin and sighed. "This is my home, Doctor," he said, bringing his eyes up to meet hers. "There is nothing that takes place in my home that I do not know about."

Rachel closed her eyes. "The server," she whispered. "The wires from the mask, or whatever it's called, were connected to the server."

Opening her eyes, she met a face showing no emotion and eyes as hard as steel. "Yes," he said quietly. "I saw everything."

"Then you know about this demon called Mora? You know about the Nephilim, and, and..."

Nodding slowly, he said, "Yes. And the Genesis Factor." He chuckled lightly. "In fact, I knew you were an ancestor to this Jael of Sargon months ago...and I let Mora know I found you."

"You? You set him on me, to kill me?"

"I did, but that was before I realized the part you had in the Genesis Factor. As you know, that is what Edith Aberman was working on before she met her fate."

Rachel felt nauseated. "Why did you have *her* killed?"

Von Guten sighed heavily; weaving his long fingers together and placing them gently on the desk in front of him. "She gave me no choice," he said frankly. "She failed to control her team, she allowed too many people to become involved, the FBI was getting too close." He nonchalantly waved a hand, "so many reasons."

"And now you want me to take her place?"

The man nodded. "I do."

"And after seeing my so-called journey, knowing how I believe, why would you trust me?"

"I do not have to trust you, Doctor, I only have to control you. I know you won't take anything for granted, and you've seen the consequences for those who I can no longer control. Those consequences that pertain to the success of this mission as well as those that pertain to its failure. Understanding is knowledge and you are a very intelligent woman. I don't believe you will fail us."

Rachel didn't say anything. She just nodded.

"And besides," he added, "you now work for the FBI and can steer them away from the project; give the Director false leads, etcetera."

"And what if I'm caught doing that?"

Von Guten smacked his lips. "Well, then you failed both the FBI and me," he said matter-of-factly. "So, it will be your responsibility to make sure you don't fail either of us."

Rachel's stomach flipped; she could barely breathe as she began to understand the direness of the situation. Even Osborn didn't foresee this.

"You'll have one mission and one mission only," the Kommandeur continued. "Your job will be to protect your friend, Mrs. Carmen Rodriguez. and, more specifically, the child that grows within her."

"You want me to protect Carmen and her baby?"

"Yes, I do. That child has been chosen by, well, let's just say that we have plans for the little one. It is an heir, shall we say, and it is your job to make sure that nothing happens to Mrs. Rodriguez while she carries the child to term."

The bile rose within up Rachel's throat as the complete picture came into focus. She was going to be made to play one against the other. She would have to deceive Zachary, making him think what she was reporting to him was true, while doing the same with von Guten. She would be living the biggest lie ever conceived. The deception, the degree of contention she'd have to live with, work in, would be more than she could bear.

"And if I refuse?"

Von Guten scowled, his face turned grim. "Doctor Wall, let me make myself clear. You don't have a choice in the matter. I'm not asking you to be a Coordinator, I'm telling you. See, if you do not accept this position then you will be marked as a person who 'knew too much' and, oh, how do you American's put it, as a loose cannon. We can't have loose cannons going around blowing things up, can we? Loose cannons are too dangerous and risky. We can't have that. Do you understand what I'm telling you?"

Rachel squared her shoulders and stared into von Guten's eyes. "Yes," she said firmly. "Accepting this position is the only way I'll be allowed to leave The Chalet alive."

"Yes, Doctor Wall," he answered. "That is correct. But the same goes for the rest of your life. As I said before, I do not have to trust you. But you will obey my every command. I cannot have it any other way."

Rachel couldn't help but wish she'd had chosen prison when Osborn presented her with choices a few months ago. Too late to think about that now. "Does Carmen know all of this? Is she aware that..."

"Yes. We spoke while you were on your genetic journey."

Rachel's blood turned to ice. *Carmen. Alone with him?* She felt the anger pulse in her chest. *She'd better be okay, mister!* She cleared her throat and steadied her nerves.

"And once the child is born?" she asked calmly.

"You will be notified of those plans when the appropriate time comes."

Something von Guten just said bothered Rachel, but she couldn't put her finger on it until several quiet seconds passed. Finally, his words came back to her.

"May I ask one more question, Kommandeur?"

Von Guten smiled. "Of course, anything," he said a bit too warmly. "You may ask anything you'd like. I may not answer, but you may ask."

"Thank you."

He nodded courteously.

"You just mentioned that Carmen's baby has been

chosen."

"Yes."

"Chosen for what...and by whom?"

The Kommandeur tugged at his jacket sleeve and glanced at his watch. Pushing away from his desk, he nodded toward the door. "You may or may not learn that in due time, Miss Wall. As things stand right now, your sole duty is to protect that child from all outside forces, especially those that are associated with The Light."

He glanced at his watch. "It is time to meet the other Coordinators, Doctor. Are you ready?" Rachel nodded at him, her eyes wide.

The décor' of the great conference room mimicked that of the beautiful dining room across the hall from it, but unlike the luncheon, there were only twelve people around a smaller table; the infamous Coordinators. For reasons she couldn't quite grasp, while the chandeliers above her sparkled by the flames of the fire in the large stone fireplace and every face wore a smile, she felt as if she'd just walked right into the middle of a lion's den.

And the lions were hungry.

CHAPTER FORTY-FIVE

When Kommandeur von Guten walked into the room, what sounded like the buzzing of a hundred bees suddenly stopped; immediately replaced by the scuffing of chairs pushing against the slate floor. Some people got to their feet a little slower than others, but when all the chairs fell silent, everyone was standing in a casual at-ease position. Awaiting permission to sit back down, their ears may have been tuned to hear what their Leader had to say, but their eyes were on Rachel.

"Sit, please," said von Guten, patting down the air around him. "Thank you, thank you."

He stood at the head of the table and motioned for Rachel to sit in the chair to his right. It wasn't until she'd taken her seat, he pulled out his own chair and sat down.

The whispers, coughing, and chortling eventually died down and Rachel glanced around the table; greeting each face with a warm smile. Every member was dressed in business attire according to their host country. Some wore turbans, others sashes, but all were dressed very colorful and lively.

They're not monsters, she thought, *just ordinary people*. But then her thoughts flashed to Edith Aberman. She too came across as a warm, inviting person. Well organized and well liked, but in the end, she had ordered the murder of three men, one of whom was her own husband. Rachel looked into the eyes of each face again. Their smiles were warm, but seemed to stop in the middle of their faces. None touched their eyes.

"Ladies and Gentlemen, please allow me to introduce Doctor Rachel Wall," said the Kommandeur. "She has come here all the way from a small town by the name of Plum Creek, in a state by the name of Virginia. Anyone ever hear of this place?"

The group chuckled lightly.

"Ya, you have heard of it," snickered von Guten.

"Doctor Wall has come to accept the position of Coordinator vacated by the late Edith Aberman..."

A murmur rippled across the table, bouncing from person to person like a small pin ball. "Yes, you heard me correctly," he said, shaking his head while his eyes grazed his audience. "There will be no formal interview; your presence is merely a means to introduce you to our newest member."

Rachel's eyes flickered around the table. Practiced smiles seemed to melt. Life showed itself behind those stony eyes. No one looked upset, put out, like they were disappointed not to have the opportunity to ask her questions. It became apparent, and rather quickly, that there were never formal interviews. None of them had been interviewed. Every one of them had been chosen, and then appointed.

No questions asked. Just promise your soul, take the orders, and the money, and run with it. Von Guten's comment wasn't to inform them, but to inform her. She'd already been told she had no choice, but to accept this position or die. Why would he allow any of the other members a voice in the matter?

The lions relaxed.

"Does anyone have any questions of me regarding my decision?" he asked. Of course, no one raised their hand or uttered a word. They wouldn't dare. He'd made up his mind and asking this question was a formality. Every one of them had been through the process.

"Zer Gut, then let us get down to business."

As if on cue, his secretary Antonia stepped into the room, quietly closed the door behind her, and slipped into a chair at the far end of the table. Laying an electronic tablet on the table, she acted like she hadn't noticed the men running their eyes over her body and the women swallowing down bitter lumps of jealousy. She didn't look up, but her cheeks turned a pale shade of pink before she started tapping lightly on the small keyboard.

"Before I open the floor for discussion regarding your specific missions, I would like each of you to introduce yourself to Doctor Wall. Please tell her where you live and your main focus of responsibility within this organization." He looked at the black woman to his left. "Lesedi, please begin."

Lesedi turned her dark eyes to Rachel. She was a beautiful woman. Her skin was the color of caramel, her black hair, what Rachel could see of it, was tucked up under a colorful turban that matched her kanga.

"Hello, Doctor Wall," she said softly. "My name is Lesedi Sefu. She chuckled then said, my first name means Woman of Light and my surname, Lion." She looked over at Rachel as if expecting a response.

"It's a lovely name," Rachel replied.

Lesedi slightly bowed her head, "Thank you. Think on it though."

Rachel thought the suggestion was a bit strange, but she clung on to every word. She'd have given her right arm for the chance to write all of this down, but she wasn't given that opportunity, so she'd have to rely on her memory, as shaky as it was.

"I live in Zimbabwe, Africa in a small village named Victoria Falls," Lesedi continued with a smile. "Yes, the town is the gateway to the breathtaking falls of the same name. My main responsibility within The Light Bearers, of which this group is a smaller part, is to influence the Zimbabwe government to follow the Kommandeur's lead. Often men and women are voted into, or appointed into, office and are rather conservative in their way of thinking. It is my duty to help them understand our agenda and move them toward submitting to a one-world government."

Rachel sat back in her chair, feeling as if she'd just been punched in the stomach. This woman was serious, even about her name. She was soft spoken and beautiful, but dangerous.

Lesedi turned and looked at the man to her left. "Your turn, Andre'," she said chuckling.

Andre' Roux looked to be about forty-five years old, slightly graying at the temples, short, and round. He was from Bourges, France, but worked in Paris as an administrator in the French government, specifically to influence the country's socialist president.

To his left sat a beautiful middle-aged woman whom Rachel thought could give Antonia a run for her money, but sure she was too confident, and busy, to give something so trivial a second thought.

She too smiled at Rachel, her high cheekbones rosy and cheery.

It's hard to believe these people are evil. But then, she reminded herself, *looks can be deceiving.*

"Welcome, Doctor Wall," she said warmly. "My name is Tindra Ahlburg. I am from Stockholm, Sweden and am the editor-in-chief of a socialist media known as the Ashtomblast." Her eyes sparkled and she giggled. "Perhaps you've heard of it?"

Rachel reluctantly shook her head.

"No?" Ms. Ahlburg said mockingly. Looking around the table, she chuckled. "I guess I need to work harder."

One by one, everyone introduced themselves to Rachel. Twelve people from various parts of the world; twelve people who spoke different languages, twelve people who lived different lives, but had one common mission, to bring all the governments of the world together to not just form an allegiance, but to form one government. And all of them would use the means of the Genesis Factor to make that happen.

Von Guten smiled and looked over at Rachel. "And when all is said and done," he said smugly, "I will be the Kommandeur of it all. That is until the Dark Heir becomes of age and takes the reins of leadership."

Rachel forced a brave smile on the outside, but inside her head she screamed, *this is ludicrous. Carmen's baby the Dark Heir? Me helping formulate a one-world government. This can't be happening. How in the world did I get here?*

"And now," von Guten said, interrupting her thoughts, "let's not delay the filling of the thirteenth seat any longer. Doctor Wall?"

"Yes."

"Do you wish to become a member of this elite group? Devoting the remainder of your life to the illumination of the human race; promising your devotion to the advancement, even upon death, to the agenda of its all-powerful leader?"

Rachel swallowed hard. *What I wouldn't give to be back in little old Plum Creek right now.* The little lab she called her haven; the little house she called home; and the little white church standing among the beautiful oak trees flashed across her mind. A deep sense of loss filled her heart.

"It's not lost."

The voice came like a wisp of jasmine on a summer breeze. From somewhere deep inside her, she heard it again. "I am The Way and I'm here to help you through this, Rachel. My Word is your sword. Just tell me you trust me and I will give you the strength to fight like a warrior."

"Miss Wall?" asked the Kommandeur. "Do you accept?"

Rachel's eyes bore into von Guten's stern glare. Several seconds passed before she thought *This is for you, Elohim.* Taking a breath, she firmly said, "I do."

Von Guten clapped his hands. "Very good," he said triumphantly. "All in favor of Doctor Wall becoming a Coordinator, filling the late Edith Aberman's position, raise your hand."

No one hesitated. No one argued. No questions were thrown around the room in a last-ditch effort to 'make sure' she was the right person for the job. No one crossed the Kommandeur.

Twelve hands went up and instantly Rachel became a Coordinator; a link in the backbone of the world's most secret and powerful organization. The very organization that planned on using the DNA of Rephaim to rule the world.

To those around the table, she became one of them.

To God, she became a warrior.

EPILOGUE

The two angels appeared out of nowhere, a few feet apart, in the middle of the dimly lit basement of The Chalet. For a moment, they stood quite still, swords at the ready, then, realizing the corridor was empty, they stowed their weapons and started walking toward the stairs that led to The Chalet's central atrium.

At the heavy wooden door leading into the lobby, they hesitated for the span of one breath before Uriel turned the handle. The atrium was large, lit only by one stunning chandelier, and decorated with magnificent paintings of mountain settings. Lights from the chandelier glinted in a huge stained glassed window on the far wall giving the atrium the feel of a gothic cathedral. The sound of cascading water could be heard coming from just beyond the radiant colors of glass.

Uriel unfolded his great, feathered wings, ready to soar upward to the third floor when Raphael placed a hand on his arm and stopped him. He cautiously raised a finger to the dark corner left of the large window.

A creature, darker than the place where it had been hiding, slowly crawled down the wall. It's blood-red eyes glistened in the light from the sparkling chandelier. Spittle dripped from yellow fangs, noiselessly pooling on the marble floor below him. Its slimy leathery skin reeked of the stench of a dead animal.

"Leave," it hissed. "This place is not for you."

"We're here for one purpose only," answered Uriel. "Let them go, and we will leave."

The demon's eyes flared. "Leave now," it growled. "Or meet your fate." The sound of talons raking across stone echoed through the atrium as more demons emerged from the dark corners.

Raphael drew his sword and spun around to face the enemies behind them. "Only until we have the two women," he said. His words reverberated off the walls.

Uriel stepped forward, his eyes never leaving the malevolent creature above him. "You are Balthasar," he said boldly. "I've been told of your evilness."

The demon snickered and slid further down the wall. "Then you know to leave while you can."

From the corner of his eye, Uriel saw more dark shadows sliding down the walls. "When we have the two women, we will go," he said firmly. "Draw your soldiers back, or you will meet your own fate."

Balthasar laughed. His eyes darted around the room. "Two against two hundred," he hissed. "And how do you suppose I will meet my fate this evening?"

Uriel stepped back, his shoulder brushing against his comrade's as he pulled his sword from its sheath. The blade sliced through air with a loud shhh.

"That's right," sneered the demon. "Retreat, you coward."

The demons jumped from the walls, rising like a black cloud above the two angels. Fiendish curses and cries of war filled the atrium above the thunderous noise of their membranous wings.

Uriel and Raphael braced their feet firmly on the floor and raised their swords above their heads, the tips pointing toward heaven.

The silver blades began to hum, subtly at first, then so

powerfully, the stone walls shuddered from their vibration. The demons screamed obscenities. Some fell from the black cloud as red beams burst from the ruby hilts of the swords and cut through the room.

The angels, holding tightly to their weapons, closed their eyes and shouted, "For the saints of God and King Iesous." Immediately, white light, fiercer than the strongest lightning, flooded the room. In its center, the angels glowed as if bathed in sunlight.

What was once order quickly turned to chaos. The bold threats of the demons turned to screams. Blinded, their talons dug aimlessly into the walls, as they groped for the shelter of darkness, but darkness had been obliviated. Many of the creatures exploded into black smoke, dissipating into the white light, while those closest to the walls escaped, flying through the stone and disappearing into the twilight.

Once the room was empty, the angels lowered their swords and the light subsided. "There are more," whispered Uriel. "This isn't over."

Raphael sheathed his sword. "No, it isn't," he agreed. "But it is for now."

Uriel's sword was still reverberating with power as he pushed it into its scabbard. "We must complete our mission and leave this evil place."

Their large, feathered wings lifted them upward just as a slimy, obscure beast slid through the stone wall and nestled itself back into the shadow of the corner. Balthasar had been wounded in the blast of light, but he had survived.

While fighting for his life at the foot of the garden fountain, he'd sent his watchers to tell others of the intrusion in The Chalet. Licking his wounds, he smiled. More demons would come to defend this fortress. He'd be prepared this time, and before they could escape, Balthasar swore the two angels would die.

"For we wrestle not against flesh and blood, but against principalities, against powers, against the rulers of the darkness of this world, against spiritual wickedness in high places."

Ephesians 6:12 (KJV)

COMING SOON:

The
Genesis Factor:
Contention

OTHER BOOKS

By Donna R. Westover

The Mysterious Ways series:

White as Snow: a Christmas Novel

Rock of Refuge: a Frontier Novel

In Green Pastures: a Frontier Novel

The Crimson River: a Frontier Novel

ACKNOWLEDGMENTS

There is no purpose for an author if there are no readers. While writing, editing, and re-writing more, there have been a few who stepped up to the plate and volunteered to read and critique the manuscript at various stages of its evolution. I wish to thank the following people for their gift of time: Char Wixson, who's been with me since my very first book; Steven Blevins, Ruth Bott, Kathi Carr, Don Cook, Suzanne Everett, Cathy Gott, Michealle Hobler, Roxanne Marzka, and James Penfold, who read, and re-read to bring to light those things I overlooked, and Charlie Wolcott, a fabulous editor.

I wish to thank Cristina Velasquez for her moral support and attending events, even after putting in a full day of overtime.

To Julie Scholfield for taking lunch and break times to answer my many questions as well as offer tips through her knowledge and experience of being an indie author.

And my husband, Don Shaw, whose critique of the manuscript, encouragement to keep writing, help at events, and assistance in the development of North Star Publishing have been priceless. His love for me and my endeavor was my guiding light when writing this book became very dark.

Most importantly, I wish to thank the Lord, who, when I felt like giving up; when the battle became too hard to fight; when I couldn't see the light at the end of the tunnel, never let go of my hand, gave me the will to write, and lit my way until the story was done.

ABOUT THE AUTHOR

Donna R. Westover lives in Eaton, Colorado with her husband, Don Shaw. She is the author of the best-selling series, *Mysterious Ways* and is working on a new series, the *Genesis Factor*, of which *The Genesis Factor: Deception* is the first book of that series.